VAMPTASY PUBLISHING
PRESENTS

ANOTHER
BEAUTIFUL
NIGHTMARE

WOMEN OF HORROR

CONTENTS

MERCURY FALLING

(A Paranormal Detectives Series Story)

BY LILY LUCHESI

PID Headquarters
Chicago, Illinois
November 2016

OR THE FIRST TIME IN over a century, the offices of the Paranormal Investigative Division of the FBI weren't focused on catching rogue creatures. Every single person's attention was focused on the footage being projected onto the wall from the local sports' report. It was the World Series, and their local team was about to break records. All they needed was one more out.

It was the bottom of the ninth, there was a man on first base and another on second base, and the other team had two outs. The closer for their team had pitched three balls, and no strikes. It looked as though their team was going to lose with one swing of the bat.

"I don't think I can take the stress," Danny Mancini said to no one in particular.

Angelica Mancini, nee Cross, was biting at her black painted nails. She'd been there the last time this team had won the World Series ... a century ago. And she'd waited that century for them to win another one. Now because of a shitty closer, they were going to lose it all. She wished she wasn't a full-blooded vampire and could drink liquor, because damn she needed it!

"I'm going to vomit," she said, though vampires weren't usually capable of vomiting. "Or have a heart attack. Or a combination of the two. ... What the *fuck* are you waiting for? Throw the damn ball!"

The pitcher listened and threw a slider. Dead center in the middle of home plate. The batter swung ... connected ... and the ball went flying into right field.

Everyone gasped as the ball bounced once, the guy playing right was too slow to catch it. Their only chance at getting the out they needed and winning the Series lay in tagging the runner between first and second before the runner at second made it to home plate.

"They'll never do it," whined one agent. "They need The Flash or something."

The guy out in right field threw the ball to the second baseman. It was a terrible throw, and would be considered an error in any normal game. This wasn't a normal game or situation, however. The second baseman, a young-looking man hailing from an island in the Atlantic who was closer to right field than he was to second base, leapt in the air, caught the high-flying ball, and dashed to second base before the baserunner. His foot on the bag, he got the out at second base, thus winning the game, and the Series.

The room was silent for one moment, and then erupted in raucous cheers, mimicking those on the TV now.

"Fuck yeah, Hermes!" a few people shouted, using the nickname for the second baseman. They called him that because Hermes, or Mercury, was the god of many things, including athletes and speed.

People were hugging. Grown, burly werewolves were in tears. It was a beautiful moment.

Angelica shook her head and laughed. "Oh, Hermy, you slick bastard." She raised her glass of blood and downed it like a shot, toasting her friend's athletic accomplishment.

***

"Are you sure you won't come with me?" Danny asked Angelica the day after the World Series win.

"Danny, I'd stick out like a sore thumb on a farm in Wisconsin," she replied. "Besides, how would you explain my eating and sleeping habits to your cousins? Go, have fun. Rub the Series win in their faces for me. I'll hold down the fort here," she said. Truthfully, a long weekend with Danny's cousins who owned a farm sounded like torture. Most of his family was deceased, and these were the only relatives he had left, so he tried to maintain a good connection with them.

"Are you at least going to miss me?" Danny asked with a goofy grin.

She threw the pen she was holding at him. "No. While you're gone I'm inviting half of the Knotfest lineup over to have an orgy. ... Don't talk like an asshole, Danny!" She stood up and kissed him. "Of course I'll miss you. But I'll console myself with the fact that I won't wake up smelling cow shit every day."

Danny left not long after, and Angelica sat at her desk in their room. With her recent promotion to vampire Empress, she was taking a break from running the PID for a while to focus on her new duties. However, the paranormal community didn't give a damn about her plans.

Her cell phone chimed with a text from Harriet Galbraith, the current PID director. "*911*" was all it read. Sighing, Angelica got up and grabbed her jacket. It looked like a sabbatical was going to be next to impossible.

Once she got to the offices, she went to Harriet and asked, "What part of 'leave of absence' didn't compute in your brain?"

Harriet, a witch and former Coven Mistress, chuckled. "I think you're going to want to see this." She turned her computer screen to show Angelica the magical activity shocking all over Chicagoland.

"Fuck, who's doing this?" Angelica asked. "I've never seen anything like it."

"Hecate," Harriet replied, her eyes wide behind her glasses. "The goddess of witchcraft."

Angelica's mouth dropped. Hecate was never seen amongst humans. She hid away in the Underworld, the magical realm other gods and goddesses usually inhabited, letting her children -- witches and wizards -- handle magic. Angelica had met her once, at a celebration in Ireland in the early twentieth century. She was rude, abrupt, but not a threat to humans ever since Wicca became more acceptable and Christians left them alone.

"There's only one person who made her show up like this," Harriet said.

Angelica ran a hand through her long black locks. "Hermes. All right, I'll pay him a visit and tell him to have his girlfriend calm her tits."

Harriet gaped at her. "Are you absolutely mad? You're going to tell *Hecate* to *calm her tits*?"

Angelica smirked at her obvious distress. "I know Hecate is like, the underling of Gaia, or something. Which I guess makes her like your Christ. Maybe if Jesus came back down and started blowing up our censors, I'd be a little freaked out, too. But Hecate is just another paranormal creature having a hissy fit to me, and I'm going to treat her accordingly."

She turned on her heel and headed for Hermes. Because Hermes wasn't just the nickname of the famous baseball player -- and now MVP and Gold Glove prospect -- he *was* Hermes, the Greek god of speed, thieves, and tricksters.

Angelica had first met him when she was nineteen and still a half vampire, when her parents were alive, when her father was still human, and when life was a lot simpler.

He'd come to London, purporting to be a visitor from Spain. His dark curls were coiffed, his equally dark and sparkling eyes hinted at mischief, and his smile was unrivaled. Angelica wasn't sure if she wanted to slap him or kiss him. He was a smart, sassy, and extremely sexy visitor. For an immortal paranormal god, he was kind. Angelica liked him, one of the few people she ever actually liked, and protected him as much as she could when his fellow minor deities got sick of his shit every few decades.

Hermes and Hecate had had a thing, once upon a time. But like most gods from way back then, there was enough drama between them to earn them a reality show on cable TV. Angelica wasn't positive, but Hecate's hissy fit had to be because of the World Series.

Hermes shouldn't have shown off like that, sure, but no one thought he was an immortal. There was no reason for her to be behaving this way. It just made things difficult for Angelica and the Covens.

Hermes lived in a nice apartment complex not far from Danny and Angelica's home. Angelica didn't know why he liked to live as a human, but he always did, and she let him, keeping an eye to make sure he and the humans around him were safe. He was a good guy, but his mischievous nature could mean trouble, even if he didn't cause said trouble on purpose.

Angelica walked up to his apartment door and knocked once, twice, three times, becoming impatient quickly. "Hermy, you open the door this instant!"

The door was wrenched open, and it looked as though she'd woken him mid-hangover. His curls were askew, eyes half-closed, and he still smelled of alcohol. It figured. The team had probably partied late into the previous night. But he was a deity, he'd be fine in a few minutes now that he'd woken.

"Um, Angie? What's the matter?"

Angelica pushed past him and into the apartment. "*This* is the matter! Please don't tell me that the Underworld didn't know that you were moonlighting as a baseball player."

"Okay ... I won't tell you that," he said sheepishly. "What's that?"

She held out her phone, which showed the intense magical activity surrounding Wrigleyville. "This is what your girlfriend is up to right now. No one's seen her, but electronics have been affected. Including traffic signals, satellite broadcasts, and electronic safes. Now you are going to call her up here and work this shit out before Chicago is fucked because you were bored and decided to join the ML-friggin'-B!"

Hermes leaned against the wall, arms crossed. "What's her problem? I didn't do anything wrong."

"Evidently you did, or I'd be at home, taking a long, hot bath and watching *Supernatural* like every other twenty-something."

"You're two hundred years old!" Hermes said, laughing.

"That's a minor detail. The thing you need to focus on is going to talk to *her*." She jabbed her long, black-painted nail at the phone's screen, as if Hecate was trapped in there.

"All right, don't get your panties in a twist," he said. He rolled up the sleeve of his thermal sweater and Angelica saw his tattoo. Two guardian serpents wound their way around Caduceus, Hermes' staff -- or wand, if you prefer. It was how he protected the staff and had it with him at all times in case of trouble.

This was trouble.

Hermes cast the incantation to make his staff visible and in a flash of light he was holding it. "Hecate," he called, voice deepening and eyes darkening. "Hecate, I know you hear me! Come to me now!"

Angelica's mouth dropped and she wanted to slap his handsome face until it resembled a tomato. "Don't call her *here*!" If Hecate got angry enough, she could destroy the entire city with her magic, if not the state.

Hermes was the Father of Magicians, and Hecate the Mother of Witches. While Hecate was known for her physical virginity and chastity, she still allowed herself to be courted by Hermes due to the many things they had in common. While Hermy was virtually ignored by magicians, Hecate was worshipped by witches, and she was filled with pride and pure attitude because of it. Angelica hadn't seen her since that one day over a century ago and didn't want to, especially not when the goddess was in such a hissy fit.

She didn't even know how to kill her if it came down to that. She'd figured that Hermes would listen to her and go meet Hecate in the Underworld to work their problems out. Had she thought he'd be reckless enough to call her here, she'd have been better prepared.

With her vampiric hearing, her ears began to tingle as, one by one, all the dogs in the neighborhood began baying at once. She glanced out the window to see it wasn't yet a full moon, so there was no reason but one for the baying canines. Hecate was coming.

Resisting the urge to cover her ears from the incessant howling, Angelica backed away towards the threshold that connected the kitchen to the living room. She had no idea how the goddess appeared, but just in case it was in a bolt of lightning or something equally damaging, she wanted to be out of the way.

Slowly, she watched the air in front of Hermes begin to shimmer. As if a hologram was slowly being projected, a doorway appeared, sparkling and shimmering with the edges ringed by flames.

Runes of some sort appeared on the door and then it opened, revealing a deep, velvety blackness that was so intense, Angelica found it difficult to look directly at it.

Oh my God, she thought, amazed. *I'm seeing the actual Underworld.*

A form appeared, lighter than the blackness, and stepped through the portal. In a flash of flame, the portal was gone, leaving behind one of its inhabitants.

Tall, almost as tall as Hermes, who stood at six-one, full of classic curves and draped in midnight blue and silver robes, was Hecate, the Goddess of the Underworld. Her black hair was as dark as ink, ending in long curls past her bottom, shining like starlight. Her aquiline nose was upturned in a haughty display, as were her full lips quirked as if to say, "I know I'm hot shit". She turned, and ever so slightly, Angelica saw the images of her other two faces, the ones she kept hidden lest they were needed: the Crone and the Maiden. The face she usually presented to the world was the Mother.

"What are you doing, Hecate?" Hermes asked.

"Oh?" Even her voice was beauty personified, but Angelica could hear the other two voices, barely suppressed. "Not even a 'hello'?"

Hermes sighed. "Hello. Now can we dispense with pleasantries? I was having a perfectly good time and you suddenly started blowing up magical sensors for whatever reason and you gotta stop. It's making stoplights and shit not work. Humans could get hurt."

She clucked her tongue. "What do I care about a few pesky mortals?"

"You should care that you're close to killing them for nothing," Hermes said. "Isn't that your rule? And ye harm none, do what ye will?"

She flapped a negligent hand. "That's Gaia's rule, not mine. And you got most of America calling you by your rightful name, you impudent little plebeian. I have every right to be livid with you."

"No, you don't. I have them thinking I'm one talented as fuck mortal, and isn't that the point? Keep letting everyone think we're myths?" Hermes asked. "I don't want to deal with this right now, *carissimus*. I have done nothing to incur your wrath this time."

Hecate glared at him, and Angelica thought that even she'd be a little worried at being on the receiving end of that stare.

"You have pushed the boundaries of what you are and are not allowed to do too far," she said. "By rights, I should have killed you two centuries ago when you decided to live as a mortal in England. Sentimentality got the best of me, but I shall not let that happen again. I suppose she's still protecting you, the vamplet."

"If you paid attention to anything besides me, you'd know that Angelica is a full vampire now, and an Empress. She's got better things to do than babysit me," Hermes said.

Hecate cocked her head and asked, "Then why do I smell blood?"

Fuck, I forgot someone said she had the form of a dog or some such shit, Angelica thought. *Of course she can smell me.*

Angelica walked back into the living room, letting herself be seen. "Clever of you, Hecate. Now why don't you go home? I am handling this. We don't need you."

Hecate narrowed her golden eyes and took two menacing steps

forward, almost like she was gliding. Her robes moved with her, as did her curls.

Angelica didn't move back, despite being a little worried. She had no idea what Hecate's powers were and didn't want to find out the hard way.

"This is not your business, vampire," Hecate hissed. Again, Angelica heard the two voices of her other faces barely concealed below the surface.

"This is my city. It is my business. But you're getting angry over nothing. Hermes isn't in trouble, and hasn't risked the discovery of your precious Underworld," Angelica said. "So why don't you go home? Because the longer you linger here, threatening someone who is innocent, I will have to take action."

Hecate threw her head back and laughed. "*Take action?* Oh how quaint. I would love to see you try and defeat me."

Angelica stood her ground. It wouldn't do for her to be seen to bow to the Underworld. The vampires would never respect her then. "I don't *try*. I succeed in everything I do. I'd say ask my old adversaries, but they're all dead."

Hecate's smile faltered a little. "I am a true immortal. You cannot kill a Titan."

"Can't I?" Angelica asked, pushing back the worry in her heart that she couldn't kill Hecate. And if she incurred her wrath once, it would last for an eternity. Because Angelica might be immortal, but she was still able to be killed with one well-placed blow to the neck.

Hecate smirked. "You dare to challenge me still? I will not make it easy for you. You are protecting a god who is in the wrong. He must die, and so must anyone who tries to shield him from his punishment. So it was written, so mote it be."

Angelica rolled her eyes. "Spare me the rhetoric. Are you going to fight me, or stand here talking?"

"I don't need to kill you myself." She raised her hands and began to chant. "Guardians of the astral world, I call you to my side. Reveal my spirit animal, my protector and guide. Heed my summons! Hear my cry! Show me the path! Time for communion is nigh! Show me the power, beauty, and grace. In the radiant eyes of my guardian's face."

The howling began again, and thunder crashed somewhere in the distance as the portal into the Underworld flickered in the center of the room again.

As soon as the doorway appeared, Hermes leapt into action. He brandished his staff and launched himself forward at Hecate. He swung his staff and lightning flickered at its tip. It hit the goddess and knocked her back into the Underworld with a shout.

However, she was gone, but what she summoned wasn't. Standing in the middle of the apartment were two animals. One resembled a ferret, only larger, and the other was a dog the size of a Great Dane. It was black, with white markings that resembled a skeleton all over its fur. Its eyes glowed red, and saliva dripped from its snarling mouth.

"Hermes, you've really fucking stepped in it now," Angelica said. She didn't know how to kill these things, but silver was always a good bet as she drew her gun from its holster on her hip. She fired the gun but the shot went wide as the little ferret-thing leapt faster than any animal should have been able to and embedded its needle-sharp fangs into her forearm. It tore through the fabric of her coat's sleeve and she yelped.

She shook her arm sharply and tried to dislodge it, but the little bastard held fast. She whipped her arm toward the wall, slamming the ferret's body against it once, then twice. Something snapped and it let her go with a screech of pain.

Her arm throbbed and blood leaked, but only for a moment as her vampiric blood healed her wounds. She hoped that the thing wasn't venomous, or if it was that her blood would take care of that, too. She had never been poisoned before, unless you counted garlic and holy water.

Steadying her hand, she fired two silver bullets into the writhing creature and it finally seemed to die, glassy eyes staring fixedly at the ceiling. Across the apartment, Hermes held his staff before him, trying to keep that monstrous dog at bay.

"Um, wanna aim that gun this way, *amor*?" he called, not even blinking as he stared the dog down.

As if his voice unlocked something, the dog snarled and dashed forward. Hermes held his staff before him, and the dog gnawed on it, spittle flying as it tried to chew it.

The thing looked pretty flimsy to Angelica, but it must have been sturdier than she thought as it held.

"*Exorizo!*" Hermes cast. The head of the staff glowed a bright, royal blue and knocked the dog away.

While it bought him a moment of reprieve, it didn't do much damage. In fact, the spell only seemed to make the dog angrier and want a new target: Angelica.

"Fuck, Hermy, think before you act!" she cried, shooting twice at the dog. One bullet missed, and the other caught its leathery ear.

"You sound like my coach," he complained.

The dog whinnied in pain as its ear leaked thick blood, almost as black as its fur. It reared back and leapt toward Angelica, and she did something that was at once clever and dangerous.

She slid so she was on the floor, her gun discarded. There was always a knife or two in her pockets for emergencies like this, and she grabbed one in each hand, flipping them open and shoving the blade straight up as the dog barely missed her.

The pure silver slid smoothly into its stomach and Angelica let the dog's own momentum be its downfall. The blades sliced into its flesh in two straight lines, as if she was going to perform surgery on it.

Thick, rank-smelling black blood oozed out on top of Angelica, splattering her face, soaking her hands and arms, and turning her clothes into something that resembled a sewer rat.

The dog fell over as it landed, her blades still embedded in its flesh. It whimpered and howled at once, and then the evil red light in its eyes died as its guts spilled out all over Hermes' kitchen floor.

Hermes stood there, mouth open and eyes wide. "Holy shit!"

Gingerly, so she didn't slip in any more Hellhound blood, Angelica stood up and shook herself off. She smelled like ichor: vile and muddy, almost like compost or infected pus.

"Disgusting," she muttered. "What the Hell were you thinking?

Challenging Hecate in the middle of the city? Your neighbors must have called the police, and I'll have to glamour them, because there's no way to cover this up." She gestured at the black ichor and general carnage in the apartment.

"I didn't think she'd do that," Hermes protested. "I thought she'd listen to me."

"Oh, because you're so damn charming?" Angelica commented. "You're not able to get out of everything with a smile and apology, Hermy. *Now* how angry do you think she's going to be? We just killed her familiars!" She paused, taking a deep breath. It wasn't something to take lightly, murdering the familiars of the Mother of Witches. While few magicians nowadays had animal companions, it was once a sacred practice. Killing a familiar used to have grave punishments, and she was sure that Hecate would be more than happy to tear Angelica's skin off and hex her silly.

"Why are you worried? I thought Dark magic didn't hurt you," Hermes said.

"But that's not Dark magic," Angelica replied. "Hecate's magic is pure, and that's where she can get me." She walked up to him and said, "You, my dear deity, are going to help me finish this once and for all. Or Hecate will seem like Little Bo fucking Peep compared to me."

***

"Here." She threw a keycard on the table in front of Hermes. She'd taken them both back to the PID and left him in a conference room while she went to shower and change her clothes.

"What is this?" he asked.

"A key to get in and out. Until we handle Hecate, you'll be staying on our residential floor," she explained. "This place is warded, so Hecate can't get in."

"Oh. Thanks. And for what it's worth: I'm sorry. I really am. But I never meant any harm, not by joining the team or trying to talk to Hecate on the mortal plane."

"The road to Hell is paved with good intentions. It's my favorite saying and it still rings true," she said. "I wasn't angry with you, but rather with your inability to consider the long term when you make decisions. So from here on out, you sit there and look pretty while I make the decisions."

He leaned back and smirked, running a hand through his black curls. "You think I'm pretty?"

"Shut up." She slid into the seat across from him. "We need to plan. They say you can't kill a god, but I disagree. Everyone has at least one weakness. No one is truly immortal. So what's hers?"

Hermes paused, eyes wide. "You can't know that everyone has a weakness."

"Yes, I *can* know that. I may not have proof, but that doesn't mean it isn't true," she replied. "So tell me hers before I stab it out of you."

"Y'know, I liked you better when you were a naive Victorian girl," he commented. "We do all have one weakness. I don't know how you figured that out, but it's true."

Angelica smirked. "And for your information, I was already a hunter by the time we met, lest you forget my holding a blade to your throat when I figured out you weren't human."

He rubbed his throat reflexively. "How could I forget it? Well, Hecate's weakness is inside of her. She presents the face of the Mother to the world, and uses the Maiden and the Crone when she needs to.

"For the Crone, it's to invade dreams and frighten people. For the Maiden, it's to coerce people into doing things in her name. Lately, the Maiden has had little use, much to her chagrin. That was her favorite persona. No one wants to do things in the name of anything except chaos and greed."

Angelica was inclined to agree.

"She hates the Crone. Wanna know why?"

"If it's relevant," she said.

"The Crone is ugly. I mean, she'll give you nightmares for the rest of your life kinda ugly. Where do you think the legend that witches looked like old women with crooked teeth, big noses, and moles all over started? With the Crone," Hermes explained. "And you've seen Hecate's Mother face, her true face."

"She's hot," Angelica relented.

Hermes arched an eyebrow. "Right. So anyway, Hecate hates that face. And there's one other thing Hecate hates: mirrors. Similar to vampires, when she looks in one, she sees her true soul, not her face. And her soul is as ugly as the Crone. That's where that persona came from."

"So mirrors weaken her?" Angelica asked.

"Sort of." Hermes sighed. "It's hard to explain, since it's just part of her legend, albeit a little known part. It's not like anyone's seen it happen. Legend says if you catch her between mirrors in the Crone form, she's trapped. Forever. Eternity. No getting out."

Now we're getting somewhere, Angelica thought. "Excellent. We just happen to have some mirrors here from the Victorian era. Pure silver. Do you think she'd come if you summoned her again?"

Hermes shrugged. "We can only try, right? If not, there are summoning rituals I can perform."

"Let's be prepared." Angelica took out her phone and called Harriet. "Can you escort my friend through the Coven's floor so he can get what he needs to perform a summoning ritual? And tell the Coven to lower the wards on the roof only."

"Hello, Harriet. How are you?" the witch teased. "Sure, I can do that."

"Excellent." Angelica went to hang up when she remembered a talk Danny had had with her about her conduct with the employees ... even the one who was, technically, above her in the ranks. "Thank you."

"Well, the world is ending, isn't it?" Harriet said with a small laugh before she disconnected the call on her end.

"You can go to level thirteen. That's where we keep the local branch of the Coven. I'll meet you on the roof," she told Hermes.

"What are you going to do?" he asked.

"Get the mirrors and make sure I have better weapons in case she sends any more Hellhounds after us," she replied.

"Good thinking."

Angelica went to the level where agents could sleep in apartments if they needed a quick nap or were staying there on liason from another PID office. Or, like Hermes, needed a place to hide out.

The building was modern in most standards: a hundred stories high and made of steel and glass, equipped with the best tech available. But Angelica had grown up in Victorian England, and she had a soft spot for classic comfort. So she had done the interior design on the living areas with plush carpeting over marble tile, feather beds, velvet curtains, old fashioned vanities, and mirrors bought at antique dealers in England. It made her feel more at home during the odd times she had to remain sequestered there, instead of at her home with Danny in Wrigleyville.

She grabbed two of the heavy silver mirrors from the walls, carrying them with ease. She went to the top floor, where her office was, along with the head of security and the director's office.

Most weapons were kept on the ground floor, in the armory, but she liked to keep a personal arsenal in her office, including her favorite silver falchion. It was blessed with holy water and carved with ancient runes, to be certain to kill almost anything she came across.

After refreshing her silver bullets, she went to the roof to wait for Hermes, who shouldn't take much longer now.

The night was clear and the stars were shining, which was good. Hecate only showed her face at night.

At last, the trickster showed up, carrying a small brown sack. "I'll try summoning her my way first, but I have everything I need for a manual ritual." He laid the bag down and brought forth his staff again in a flash of light.

He tried calling Hecate, and nothing happened. No dogs bayed, no lights flickered nearby. Nothing. Not even a ripple in the air.

"Well, we knew she'd probably not want to just show up the next time you called. What do you need to set up the ritual?" Angelica asked, going inside the small bag.

"Start getting things out, I'll set the fire," Hermes said.

"You'll what?" Angelica cried.

"Hecate doesn't have a rune or sigil: you summon her by fire," he explained. "My magic can contain it, don't worry. It won't harm the building."

Angelica watched him as he drew an invisible circle with his staff, wide enough so that the entrance to the Underworld would fit inside of it. He stood before it and said, "*Pyrkagiá* érchontai."

Fire appeared inside the circle, sudden and intense. Angelica worried what anyone looking from one of the other high rises would think.

"You're supposed to summon her at a crossroads, but it's not the only place she'll come," he told her. "Help me place the items around the fire."

Angelica took out an old silver key, dried lavender, a bottle of pure, raw honey, and ... then she dropped her hand from the bag. "*Garlic*? Do you want me dead?"

"Sorry, Hecate likes it," Hermes said sheepishly, reaching for the herb himself. He placed the garlic furthest away from Angelica, and she put the lavender down, and then opened the bottle of honey before she put that down as well. She handed Hermes the key.

"Now the incantation. *Hecate, mighty Goddess of crossroads, darkness, death, wisdom, and the moon, please come to me. Please Hecate, protect me and help me when I am in danger. Treat me as one of your own and give me all that is needed. Hecate, surround me in your darkness so that I can bring forth my light.*"

Angelica stuck out her tongue and made a light retching noise. What nonsense. Hecate was power-drunk and the bringer of death. And they definitely didn't need her version of help. She knew that the witch had to come when summoned directly, but still ... the incantation was a bit much, in her opinion.

It took a moment before the wind picked up, swirling in the center of the flames. But this time there were no dogs baying, no lightning striking. Whatever was coming, it most likely wasn't Hecate.

She had one hand on the butt of her gun in its holster as the portal to the Underworld appeared. From within, there came an ear-piercing shriek that sounded like a cross between a seagull and a banshee. With her enhanced hearing, Angelica worried that she might be struck deaf by the sound.

"What the Hell was that?" she asked Hermes.

"I think it might have been--" Hermes was cut short as a flurry of winged creatures began to spill out of the portal and onto the roof.

Angelica blinked a few times at what she was seeing. About the size of cocker spaniels, these creatures looked like birds, with beige feathers and large wings, but had the heads of women with tight black curls, like those worn by ancient Grecians, atop their heads. Their eyes were birdlike, and their mouths sported tiny fangs, like geese. She could swear that the things had feathered boobs.

"Harpies!" Hermes cried.

"Oh come on!" Angelica said, ducking as one of the creatures flew at her head. Talons caught in her thick black hair and she grabbed a blade, slicing straight upward. The blade bit flesh and the harpy screeched, though it flew off Angelica's head. "How do we kill these things?"

"Heart," Hermes replied, trying to dodge a couple of them. "Stab, shoot, whatever. Doesn't matter, as long as you use silver. Just don't look them in the eyes. They're distant relatives of Medusa."

Angelica sliced the throat of one and it fell down, dead. "Great. Next you'll be telling me that you've got a Basilisk down there in the Underworld. It'll be a regular old Chamber of Secrets."

"A what?" He batted away one of the harpies.

Angelica rolled her eyes and turned so she and Hermes were back to back, to fend off more of the winged women. Her sword bit flesh and severed wings. It was beginning to look like a chicken slaughterhouse on the rooftop.

"I thought Hecate had to come when she was summoned?" she asked.

"She made the rules, she can break them," he replied.

Another loud screech sounded and more harpies came from the portal, which was still open. Two of them dove toward Angelica. One tangled in her long hair, and the other dug its talons into her shoulder.

Pain burst from her flesh as blood began to soak down her arm. The harpy screeched in triumph. Angelica dropped her sword and grabbed her gun with her unharmed hand. "Hermy, if you want to keep your limbs intact, duck!" She fired off two silver bullets into the harpy on her shoulder and it fell away, dead. The talons dragged a little as the heavy corpse fell, peeling back more of Angelica's flesh. And she had no human blood in her system to help her heal.

The harpy in her hair screeched at her and tried to pull her toward the portal, into the Underworld. With effort, she bent down and retrieved her sword once more. She grimaced as she stabbed blindly upward. The sword bit flesh, but it was not a fatal blow. She tried again, harder. It was like trying to stab a piece of meat in a thick stew with a plastic fork.

Finally she hit it where it hurt, and dark ichor dripped into her hair, over her head as this harpy fell away to join its dead brethren. Some of it dripped into her open wounds and began to burn.

"Oh fuck that hurts," she gasped. "Hermes, close the gateway! *Now!*"

A harpy knocked into her from behind, sending her sprawling on the floor. As she turned over, it flew atop her and she closed her eyes, not desiring to be turned to stone any time soon.

Claws ripped into her stomach, tearing cloth and flesh with wet ripping sounds. Her scream couldn't be contained, but she didn't let the pain stop her. She shot blindly, and even without seeing killed the creature.

Dreading opening her eyes, she peeked at her flesh. It was a bloody, mangled mess, but it didn't seem like the harpy had hit any vital organs. From her spot on the floor, she shot the remaining three harpies dead.

Hermes was chanting in Greek behind her, and there was a cold wind as the portal finally closed.

Angelica groaned and leaned her head down against the metal and concrete that made up the roof.

"Holy... Are you okay?" Hermes asked, kneeling down by her.

"I need blood. Now," she said.

Hermes simply nodded and rolled up his sleeve. He put his wrist near her mouth and Angelica could hear the blood moving in his veins. The blood of other immortals was extremely beneficial to vampires.

Her fangs had already been elongated because of her bloodlust in the fight, and she bit into his flesh without preamble. Hot, thick blood spurted into her mouth and she swallowed quickly, feeling her wounds begin to heal and her strength return.

Once she had drunk her fill, she groaned and sat up, willing her head to stop spinning from the sudden influx of fresh blood. "Oh boy do you owe me, buddy," she said. "Big time."

***

It was too close to sunrise to try anything else. They would need to wait till the sun had set once more to make another attempt. But if Hecate wouldn't come when they summoned her, how were they going to get her to look in the mirrors? They were a bit too heavy and conspicuous to carry around everywhere.

To distract herself a little, she text Danny, asking how everything was going with his relatives.

"I milked a goat today," he text back. "Please send me some sound clips of the city, or smog in a bottle. I think I'm dying here."

"Pics or it didn't happen," Angelica text back.

When he sent back a slightly blurry photo of a smiling brown and white goat with the caption, "Tomorrow they want to show me how to make the cheese," she fell back onto the cushions of her coffin in a fit of laughter.

"Bring some home. I haven't had good goat cheese since I visited France in 1845," she replied. If there still is a Chicago to come home to and Hecate hasn't been blown off the face of the Earth.

Angelica hated being unable to kill an enemy immediately. Or imprison them. Or take their powers away. It all depended on the enemy. But she was known for her efficiency. One goddess shouldn't throw her off her game so easily. She'd already faced down some of the most vicious paranormal criminals on Earth and defeated them. She wouldn't let this one bitch waste any more of her time.

Once the sun set, she hopped out of her coffin to make more plans. It really was too bad she couldn't just cut her head off like every other adversary.

Hermes stayed overnight at the PID as they had planned, and he met her in the sitting room of his temporary apartment.

"I made a decision," he said. He looked grim, his jaw was set and there was no sparkle in his dark eyes.

"Why does something tell me I'm not going to like it?" Angelica asked as she sipped a mug of microwaved blood.

He stood up and said, "I have to humble myself at her feet. It will placate her and then she won't destroy Chicago looking for me."

Angelica slammed her mug on the coffee table. "You mean give up? No. I refuse to allow you to do that. I'd rather see you torn to tiny pieces than see you give up."

"Death is not preferable to surrender!" he protested.

"Death is always better than giving up and slinking away in defeat with your tail between your legs!" she countered. "I was once pinned to the ground, nearly decapitated by my own sword, and still I chose death rather than surrender. Now get up and help me kill this bitch, and stop talking like an idiot."

Hermes crossed his arms and said, "Well, maybe I'm not as brave as you are, Angelica."

"It's not about bravery, it's about honor and loyalty. We were given our freedom, our existences. To surrender to an oppressor is to lose all honor." With that, she turned on her heel and exited the room, too angry with him to keep up the conversation.

How childish; how weak. How cowardly, she thought. *Fine. Let him give up. Hecate threatened my city, and even if she agrees to stop, I still have to kill her. Any paranormal entity who treats humans as inferior creatures is on my shit list. And that list doesn't come with an eraser.*

When she got halfway to her office, she heard a strange noise coming from inside a bathroom. It sounded like someone was stuck in water. *Did someone get their fucking head stuck in a toilet?*

She pushed the door open and called, "Hello? Anyone there?" More splashing. "Are you okay?" *If it's a water nymph playing again, I'll throw it right back into Lake Michigan.*

Nothing.

"I'm going to regret this," she muttered to herself as she drew her gun. She couldn't smell any humans in the room, or any other typical creatures. However, the sewer stench wafting up was rancid. There was no reason for it, unless there was a backflow problem. If something was overflowing, it would explain the noise, too.

She checked each of the stalls, and all were empty, save for a pair of false eyelashes someone had dropped. None of the toilets were overflowing, either.

As she turned to the sinks, she jumped a little. She had lived as a half vampire for so long, it was still a bit shocking to see nothing in the row of mirrors, despite standing in front of them.

The noise came again, and she walked toward the sinks. Inside one, blackish, fetid water was bubbling up, as if something down in the pipes was pushing it upwards. It smelled like the ichor that was inside all of the Underworld's creatures.

"This is not good," she said, backing away. The sound intensified, and she turned toward the toilet stalls again. Now the water in the bowls was black and bubbling, too. She peered closer to see if there was anything else there, but the stench was so severe, she backed away.

And just in time, as the toilet bowl nearly exploded in her face. A spray of ichor/water hit the ceiling, the floor, and the stall walls. One by one, each toilet began to spew it, and they started to shake. Something else popped up out of the bowl then, within the water. The basins shattered, sending shards of porcelain in every direction.

Angelica couldn't quite see what was coming out of one of the pipes, except it was wriggling and an off white mixed with beige color. It began in one toilet, and seemed to interconnect to each of them, right until the head of it popped up out of the one that has just exploded in front of her face. It launched directly at her, and she felt a stabbing pain in her neck.

She moved sharply, hoping to yank it out, but she bumped into a rather large piece or porcelain and she went sprawling on the cold, hard tiles. Her head smacked against the floor and her vision blurred as the pain radiated down her neck.

"Fuck this shit," she said. She reached up and felt the scaly, wriggly end of the creature and pulled hard, praying the wounds would heal. She threw the creature across the room, and saw that it was a … snake. A long, wriggling snake with horns. Horns that were now covered in her blood.

She still had her gun in her hand and she aimed and fired multiple times. The snake twisted and writhed with every bullet that embedded itself in its skin before it lay still, soaked in ichor. The toilets stopped bubbling as its tail end ceased its movement in death.

"Angelica?" Hermes called. He ran into the bathroom and looked around, wide-eyed.

"What is that thing?" she asked him.

"A cerastes," he replied. "Did it bite you or hit you with its horns?"

"Horns," she said, slowly getting into a sitting position. "Why?"

"Because the fangs contain venom that would kill anyone, even you, instantly."

Angelica leaned her head back against the wall. "You know, I didn't *actually* mean for a poisonous mythological snake to come out of the pipes when I said this was turning into the Chamber of Secrets."

She felt her neck, relieved to feel that the wounds were nonexistent. Only sticky blood remained. "Hermy? Get Harriet. If Hecate won't come for us, perhaps she'll come for one of her witches. Because I am beyond done with all of this."

***

"What? No! That's against everything I stand for!" Harriet said, arms crossed.

"Let me explain this again: Hecate just sent a poisonous Hell-snake into our pipes to poison me. She sent out half-woman, half-chicken creatures yesterday. Earlier that same day, it was a Hellhound and demonic ferret. Now, I am not your superior on paper any longer, but you can bet your magical ass that I will strip you of your title if you insist on breaking our own laws and not helping me apprehend a paranormal criminal!" Angelica snapped.

It wasn't clear who was more unnerved by her attitude, Harriet or Hermes. Harriet's sea green eyes were as large as saucers.

"You don't understand--"

"I certainly do understand," Angelica interrupted. "I killed my own father because he was a criminal. Loyalty cannot be given blindly; it must be earned. And Hecate is not someone who has earned or deserves any loyalty. Not anymore. She's gone off the deep end and must be stopped. Or magicians all over the world will get an even worse reputation than human fiction already gave them. You led the UK Coven for over a century, do you really want that to happen?"

Harriet mussed up her brown hair. "Damn it, of course I don't! But this is... You know, before I started working here, this would have been unthinkable."

"I love the Covens, but you're all far too insular with an 'us versus them' mentality when it comes to the PID," Angelica commented. "No species is perfect, but right now I need you. Please, believe me when I say that Hecate has to be stopped."

"If it makes you feel better," Hermes said, "we're not killing her."

The witch looked between the god and the Empress, uncertainty written on her face.

"Have I ever steered you wrong before?" Angelica asked, forcing herself to sound a bit gentler.

Harriet shook her head. "All right. I'll do it. But if it bungles everything up..."

"It won't," Angelica promised. "As long as she lives, all magicians will be fine. And no one will ever know what happened here."

Harriet nodded. "I will prepare the summoning ritual. But ... people have to summon her frequently. How can I be certain that she will appear and not just write me off?"

"She knows who summons her, and she'll see you were a former Coven Mistress," Hermes explained. "Trust me, she'll be flattered you need her help and show up immediately."

Harriet began to prepare the ritual, and Angelica began hanging up mirrors all over the room. Multiple on every wall, so there was no way she could possibly miss her own reflection. There were dozens of Hermes and Harriets reflected back, but no Angelica.

"Damn, that's creepy," Hermes said, glancing at the mirrors. "How do you put on makeup?"

"Magic," she said sarcastically. She took out her blade and made sure it was sharp enough in case they needed more than the mirrors to trap the witch. Likewise, Hermes called out Caduceus.

Angelica stood in one corner, and Hermes stood in another, to trap Hecate and make her unable to escape.

Soon, Harriet was prepared and she began to chant.

> Hecate, Wayfarer, Path Finder
> Mistress of the Thresholds we all must cross
> Goddess of the Triple Crossroads where destiny meets choice
> Keeper of wisdom, teacher of the wise
> Destroyer of illusion and Guardian of the Gates
> Hail, Owl-eye Goddess of Magick and the roads of Mystery!
> I, your Priestess, ask for your aid!

They all waited with baited breath. The temperature in the room dropped, and the candles in the summoning circle began to glow brightly, their flames stretching high toward the ceiling. The smoke began to swirl, despite the lack of wind in the room. It centered itself in the circle, growing and twisting like a tornado until it was about the length of a person.

It began to coil and tighten, slowly turning into a solid form, that of the Mother. Hecate looked down at Harriet, who was knelt before the circle, and she smiled a little. It wasn't a nice smile; it reminded Angelica of how she would smile at prey.

Harriet was looking up at her with a nearly blank expression. Shock and awe had rendered her nearly helpless in the face of the goddess.

"You have called me here, my child?" she asked, her voice crystal clear.

"No," Angelica said, stepping forward from her shadowy corner. "*I* did. Take a look around, Hecate. I brought you a few presents."

Her golden eyes flared at Angelica, and then she turned and saw her reflection. One by one, in each mirror, her beautiful face began to shift and change. To morph into her true visage, the face of her soul.

She shrieked as she closed her eyes tightly. *"Nox!"* she cast, and all the light in the room seemed to vanish.

"Harriet, Hermes, do something about this!" Angelica ordered. She could usually see in perfect darkness, but her vampiric eyes couldn't see through the spell. She had never been sightless before. Fear pricked at her mind and she pushed it out. The last thing she needed was to be off her game, which was what Hecate wanted.

Trying to remain still, she listened for movement to see where Hecate was and possibly attack her. Movement hit her ears, thick fabric rustling, and she turned toward it.

Knives were a useful, often underutilized tool in a vampire's life. Angelica always kept at least three about her person at all times. Quickly, she drew one and tossed it expertly through the darkness. There was a thick sound, like the blade had penetrated living flesh, and Hecate roared in pain.

"Lux!" Harriet cast. Slowly, the darkness began to abate, giving way to a bright, warm light.

Hecate had been stabbed in the right eye. Blood rained down her face, black like ink, standing out against her dark skin. She didn't appear to be hindered, however, but she was still fighting to stay out of the light … and out of view of the mirrors.

"You dare turn against me, witch?" she yelled, the two voices of the Crone and Maiden mixing in, making her sound nearly demonic. "Volant!"

Harriet went flying into the far wall, cracking the back of her head on one of the mirrors. The spider cracks in the vintage glass were spotted with blood, but Angelica knew she would live, as long as Hecate didn't cast anything else at her.

"Hermes!" she cried.

The god of speed lived up to his name as he ran so fast across the room it appeared that he had teleported and stuck the staff into Hecate's back. *"Astrapi!"* he cast, and lightning emerged from the wand's tip. It engulfed her, and she arched her head back and screamed as her body trembled uncontrollably.

Hermes wrenched his wand from her body, and the lightning disappeared. Still, Hecate twitched, now upright only by sheer willpower.

Angelica didn't allow her to get her bearings. She leapt forward and drew her sword. She stabbed Hecate through the stomach, splattering her blue robes with black blood. Hecate gasped and ichor flew from her mouth, hitting Angelica in the chest.

She kept up her momentum and shoved Hecate against the wall, pinning her there with her sword like a bug on a stick.

"Volant!" Hermes cast, his wand moving about the room to pass over every mirror. They circled Hecate, enclosing her so that all she could see was herself, the vile image of the Crone.

"No!" she cried, still coughing up ichor. "No, damn you! I will not be defeated by a lesser god and a vampire who thinks she *is* a god!"

"Then you should have listened to me and backed off. Because no one is safe from my blade. Not even the gods themselves," Angelica declared.

Hecate said something in a language Angelica didn't understand, and then began to cry and shriek at what she was forced to look at.

"No no no!" she screamed. There was a flash of blue light, so blinding that Angelica had to cover her eyes.

When it faded, Angelica was able to see again. It was eerily silent in the room. Then there was a pounding, like someone knocking on glass.

"Let me out! Damn you, *let me out!*" Hecate screamed. She cast a few spells, but they must not have worked, because she nearly howled.

"Should we go look?" Hermes asked.

Angelica nodded. "Hell yeah. This I have to see."

He lowered his wand and the mirrors slowly laid down on the floor. Inside one was Hecate as the Crone. Her true face. Her final face. She pounded against the glass and shouted threats, but Angelica just laughed.

"Is a witch in the glass like a genie in a bottle?" she asked. She tapped the glass with the tip of her boot. "Get comfortable, because you'll be spending eternity in here."

She flipped the mirror facedown to muffle the witch's shouts and turned to Hermes.

"I don't know how to thank you, Angelica," he said as he put Caduceus away.

"Stay out of trouble," she replied.

He grimaced. "Maybe I can get you season tickets to the games next year? Or buy you a unicorn? Those are much more likely."

Angelica threw her head back and laughed as she pulled her friend into a tight hug. "You're a menace, Hermy, but I couldn't adore you more."

***

Danny returned home the next night, and Angelica was sitting on the sofa, sipping a mug of blood and reading a book.

"Hey, here's my handsome farmer," she said. She put the book and mug on the coffee table and pulled him in for a kiss. "I missed you."

"I missed you, too," he said, his arms wrapped tightly around her. "I will never, ever go away without you again. Between being lonely and my psycho cousins, I wanted to tear my hair out."

She really had missed him, she realized as she kissed him again, deeper this time. "Good. Now you can be back to normal ... or whatever passed for normal in our lives."

"Speaking of hair ... is your hair a bit shorter?" he asked.

She had forgotten that a few inches had been cut off by the harpies. She nodded.

He smirked. "How about you? How was your weekend? Anything fun happen while I was away, besides the haircut?"

She chuckled, recalling the past two nights. "Oh. No, nothing much." For more books about the adventures of Angelica and Danny, check out the award-winning Paranormal Detectives Series, available on Kindle Unlimited!

ABOUT THE AUTHOR

Lily Luchesi is the *USA Today* bestselling and award-winning author of the Paranormal Detectives Series, published by Vamptasy Publishing, as well as various short stories in the horror, paranormal, and erotica genres.

Her first young adult novel, *The Coven Princess*, hit #1 on the Amazon hot new releases chart and remained in the top twenty for two weeks.

She is also the editor and curator of the bestselling *Damsels of Distress* anthology, which focuses on strong female characters in horror and paranormal fiction.

Lily is an active and out member of the LGBT+ community, a self-professed nerd, music-lover, and a little obsessed with vampires and comic books. When not writing or reading, she can be found drinking copious amounts of coffee, getting tattooed, going to concerts, or watching too much of the CW.

She was born and raised in Chicago, but now resides in Los Angeles. You can find her on Facebook, Twitter, Instagram, Goodreads, and Pinterest. You can also keep up with Lily via her newsletter ... and receive a free e-book as well!

A BLOODY BEGINNING

LAURENCIA HOFFMAN

1936. THE SMELL OF COPPER lingered in the air. It wasn't the kind of scent that remained present after Silas had fed – the aroma was too strong. It was pleasant to her nostrils but it sent a pang of worry through her chest. Picking up the skirt of her dress, she followed that scent, and it led her down the staircase, through the hallway, and into what they called "the dungeon".

"Darling, are you–"

Before she could finish her question, Melina tripped on something. When she looked down, she saw that it was a body. Furrowing her brow, she let go of her skirt as her gaze focused on the floor. There was more than she had expected.

So many bodies were strewn about that she couldn't see the stone floor between them and the pools of blood. This wasn't an unfamiliar sight, but a confusing one.

"My God. What did you do?"

Silas was wiping the crimson liquid from his hands onto what might have been a white cloth at one time, though now it was entirely soaked in blood.

"I couldn't leave them alive," he said in a low voice.

Melina glanced at him, taking a step back as she felt the blood traveling down the floor and seeping into her skirt. The act itself was not shocking – they had indulged in slaughter regularly, but never of their own house staff. "Were they spreading rumors? Gossiping with the people in town?"

Shaking his head, Silas tossed the bloody cloth onto one of the bodies. "Not that I'm aware of."

"Then why did you do this?" Taking the candlestick that was on the floor – the only source of light in the room, she moved forward, even though she didn't need it to see in the dark "Silas, you murdered our entire staff. If you think I'm going to clean this mess, you're gravely mistaken."

Her lover said nothing as he exited the room. Heaving a sigh, she followed him. "Do you have any idea how much skill it takes to walk up the stairs holding up this dress *and* this damn candle?"

"You should have left it with the bodies. We don't need light to see in the dark, Melina."

"Don't speak to me as if I don't know our abilities as vampires." As she trudged up the stairs behind him, she contemplated leaving the candle where it was, but since the staff were all deceased, she knew that she would have to be the one to fetch it later. "If you would allow me to modernize the house, we wouldn't even need candles."

"I hate electricity, Melina. You know that."

"Did you also know that we're likely the only house in town who doesn't have it? I thought we were supposed to be avoiding unwanted attention, but something like that will draw it right to us."

He didn't seem to care about her opinion as they stepped onto the main floor. She set down the candlestick on a nearby table and folded her arms across her chest.

"We are the only people in this city with a sizable property and a house that resembles a castle. Don't you think we look conspicuous as it is?"

He did not answer.

The house was so quiet. And she hated silence. It had a strange effect on her, reminding her of all the times she'd felt lost and alone in her life.

Silas sometimes had to leave for reasons he wouldn't say. She assumed that it was his way of protecting her. As strong and independent as Melina was, she knew that there were things that she needed protecting from, even if she didn't know what those things were.

When Silas was gone, the staff had kept her company. She didn't consider them friends, but the house had always been active. There had been voices, the shuffling of shoes, and even music. Now that they were all dead, Melina wondered what noise would grace her ears to pass the time.

"What a waste of perfectly good food," she mumbled. "You could have at least let me help you."

Slowly, Silas turned to face her. His expression had softened. "Melina..."

She had not seen that look very often. If her heart had been beating, it would have been racing. "What is it?"

He took a step closer to her. "Do you know how much I love you?"

"You only tell me every day."

"Do you know how sorry I am for everything I did to you?"

It was not unusual for him to bring up their past. It had been the worst time in both their lives. And though nothing had been left unsaid between them, they did reflect on how awful their relationship had been, and how relieved they were that it had changed.

But Melina had thought that they had finally agreed to leave all of that behind for the sake of moving forward. All that mattered now was that they were happy together.

"I thought we'd moved on from all of that. Why are we dwelling on it?"

Silas placed his hand against her cheek. "Because when you look back on our time together, I don't want you to remember me for who I was then, but who I am now."

Melina's gazed searched his. They had discussed this before. Something was different this time. "You were a different person when we met. I've forgiven you."

He shook his head. "I never deserved to be forgiven."

"Well then, I understand and accept you. I don't know what happened to you, but whatever it was, it twisted you into the monster you became." He had never told her about his past. For the most part, all she knew about him was what she'd learned by his behavior over the years. Silas had always been secretive and it was just something she had learned to live with. "Although you are still a monster in some sense, I am happy that you've softened toward me."

"I wish I could have told you everything," he said, his voice breaking. "What happened to me, what made me who I was, and who I am…"

It was as if he was reading her mind. Being so honest was rare for Silas. While she knew the way he felt about her, they preferred not to relive the beginning of their relationship over and over again. All it did was bring them both pain. So for him to speak of it now, without any warning, made her think that something was terribly wrong. And yet, she didn't want to believe it.

"You can. That's the beauty of being a vampire, my darling."

He lowered his gaze. "It's too late."

"Silas, enough of this." She took his hand in hers. "You're scaring me."

"I know. And I'm sorry." Silas pulled her into a tight embrace. "But they're here."

She furrowed her brow. "Who?"

There was a loud noise. It sounded like someone was attempting to break down the door. Their house was sturdier than most, and built in ways that most homes today would not be built. Everything had been made to Silas's specifications – mostly for protection. To her knowledge, no one had ever tried to invade their home before. But the banging was shaking the walls. Whoever was outside sounded determined.

Melina hurried over to the windows, closing the curtains as if that would shield them from the danger somehow.

"If you sensed they were coming, you should have told me. We could have run."

"This was inevitable, Melina."

Silas crossed his arms behind his back. His demeanor was as calm and collected as she had ever seen it, and that bothered her.

"You have no idea how long we've been running," he continued. "And from how many others."

She threw her hands in the air. "Because you never tell me!"

It sounded as though the intruders had broken through the basement entry. These people, whoever they were, had intimate knowledge of their home. They knew how to come inside through the secret entrance. How was that possible?

As their footsteps could be heard coming ever closer, Melina saw an instant change in Silas' stance. His features had fallen, no longer composed. Whatever brave front he had been projecting was failing and all she saw was a defeated vampire. For the first time in decades, she was frightened.

Her first instinct was to act, but they were outnumbered. It would be unwise to do anything rash.

"I wanted to protect you," he whispered.

The footsteps ceased and Melina turned to see several men in black cloaks. She couldn't make out their faces no matter how hard she tried.

"You seem to be doing a poor job of it, Silas," one of them said.

When he pulled back his hood, Melina's eyes widened. She knew this man.

"Arthur?" her voice came in a whisper. She couldn't make sense of the sight before her. "You're human. How are you alive? And so..."

Melina tried to think of the correct word as her gaze scanned over his figure. He hadn't aged at all since the last time they had seen each other.

"Youthful?" he offered. "Well, my dear, after you slaughtered my family, I vowed to hunt you and your maker to the ends of the earth." With a sly smile, he waved his hand in the air. "So here I am."

Furrowing her brow, she shook her head slowly. "But how?"

Crossing his hands behind his back, Arthur took a step forward. "There are forces in this world far beyond your understanding. I was just as ignorant as you are until the Devil paid me a visit." He glanced briefly to Silas before returning his attention to Melina. "I sold him my soul so that I could find you and kill you, but not before I killed your family." His voice deepened when he spoke next, "It's only fair since you killed mine."

Melina's mouth was agape. The man, or whatever he was, had clearly lost his mind. While she didn't know everything, making deals with the Devil was not something she believed to be possible. "You've gone mad."

"Have I?" He took another step closer to her and she stepped back. "Vampires and werewolves exist, but you don't think that other creatures might? Vampires, werewolves, demons, angels, the Devil...even Heaven and Hell. And I'm going to send you both to the latter."

She had not seen this man in decades. In her mind, he had been long dead. She could not form words that accurately described how this felt.

There was a discussion among the men behind Arthur, and though she should have tried to eavesdrop, all she could do was stare at Silas. He hadn't said a word. He'd said that he had sensed this was coming, but had he known about Arthur all along, or had he simply been speaking from instinct?

They didn't stand there for very long in silence, but it seemed like a lifetime. And in that time, her anger was building. Arthur was harboring hatred toward her, and rightly so, but she couldn't stand that he was acting as though he was blameless. "Hate me all you want, but admit your hand in what I've become! You were my husband and you abandoned me, leaving me no choice but to turn to the vampire who had terrorized us."

"You had a choice, Melina," Arthur spoke in a bitter tone before pointing at Silas. "You didn't have to be with *him*."

He would never understand what she had been through. All she could do was shake her head. "And where would I have gone? What could I have done? I was alone and I was weak." This time, she took the step forward. "But I'm not so defenseless now."

"Oh," he raised his hand, a gesture to the others, "But I think you are."

The men swarmed Silas, likely deeming him as the greater threat. Four of them were able to subdue him using silver chains. Melina gasped when she saw blood trickling down her lover's neck. When they had first arrived, she must have known what their intentions were, but it was only in this moment that she realized them.

"No, don't!"

She reached out, and even though she hadn't meant it in a threatening manner, two men tackled her and wrapped her wrists in silver. Now she and Silas were both bound. If they tried hard enough, they might be able to break free and overpower these people, but did they want to risk losing their limbs? It would only hinder their escape.

"Let her go," Silas spoke in a pleading tone. "She is only what I've made her."

"I deserve more credit than that, Silas," she hissed.

Arthur stood in front of her, paying little attention to the vampire at the other end of the room. He stared down at her with fury in his gaze. "Do you know how long I've waited for this moment? Years. Decades. Silas is right, you know. I'm not the only one out for your blood. That is how I know that this was destiny. I–" he gestured to the others in the room, "–we, found you first."

Melina was shaking with anger. The chain was burning her skin, making an unpleasant sizzling sound. The pain brought tears to her eyes, though she tried to appear stronger than she felt for Silas' sake. "It was wrong to murder your family. We should have only killed you. I'm sorry for that mistake."

"So am I. Because I gladly would have sacrificed my life for the lives of my wife and children." His voice broke in the last sentence. Raising his hand and closing his eyes, he appeared to regain his composure before speaking again. "I wonder, would you do the same, Melina? Vile creature that you are. Would you die to save the people you love?"

She furrowed her brow. Vile though she may be, why did he not think that she would sacrifice herself? "Yes."

"Well, you won't get that chance today. Gentleman," Arthur turned back toward Silas and the others, "Gag him. I don't want him to have any chance to say his farewell." He turned back to her, his chin lifted and nostrils flared. "You took that from me too, Melina. I was forced to watch my family die. Now you will be forced to do the same."

She stared at him, blinking rapidly in disbelief. This was real. This was happening. In all the ways that she had imagined their deaths, Arthur returning from dead and exacting vengeance for their past deeds had not been one of them.

Melina's gaze attempted to locate Silas', but her view of him was obstructed by the men who were tightening his chains. She could hear him hissing, smell the burning of his flesh, and see the blood dripping onto the floor.

"Arthur, don't do this!" she begged. "It won't bring your family back!"

"No," he drawled. "But it will give them justice."

"And what about *my* justice? Did I deserve what happened to me?" Blood oozed down her wrists as she struggled against her restraints. "You asked me for mercy that night, but where was mine? I was never protected from the evils of this world."

All she could think to do now was bargain with him albeit she had nothing to offer. Melina was used to people asking for mercy from her though she had never been afforded the luxury. She had endured a relentlessly violent and cruel world and lost herself to it – until one day, she had decided that enough was enough.

Through all the heartache, the fear, and the trauma, Melina had turned her back on everything she had once known, refusing to acknowledge the helpless and feeble woman she had once been. The world had done nothing but take from her and now it was going to take again.

She had not begged anyone, for anything, in a very long time. But for Silas, she would. For all the past they had put behind them, for all the metaphorical demons they had vanquished, for all the love they shared and the life they had built, she would.

With tears filling her eyes, she tried once more to see Silas' figure, but she could not. "Spare him. Spare *us*. There will be no retaliation for this, I swear to you."

Arthur raised his brow, his hand gesturing around the room. "This isn't just about my revenge. It's for every person in this room. You've wronged every one of them in some way either directly or indirectly. Your actions have consequences." His eyes narrowed, his soulless gaze fixated on her. "Bring in the executioner."

She scoffed. "You can't even kill us yourself?"

"Only one of you will die tonight. And the final blow was promised to someone else."

What did he mean by that? Melina was aware that she and Silas had made their fair share of people unhappy, but usually, they killed them before they ever became an issue. So who was the mysterious person who had been promised the fatal strike of her mate?

Perhaps it had something to do with all those times when Silas had left her to her own devices, never revealing what his important business was. Perhaps they had more living enemies than she realized.

A figure moved behind her, and when it came into view, she saw another man in a hood. At least, she assumed it was a man. The scent was masculine. For a moment, she could have sworn that she could recognize his smell, but the thought was fleeting – she was snapped back to the situation at hand as Arthur spoke again.

"Let this be a lesson to you," he hissed. "Perhaps you will be more careful of the people you cross."

Though she had heard every word, her mind had difficulty processing it. The room was a blur and she blinked several times to try and clear her vision, but she was aware that there was nothing physically wrong with her.

"Let me go," she spoke in a whisper. And then she repeated the words as the mysterious man drew closer to her lover, the phrase becoming louder each time she said it until she was screaming.

With the man in front of Silas, her view of him was fully blocked. All she heard was the sound of a sword slipping from its sheath and Silas uttering the words, *"you"*.

Then there was the whooshing sound of a blade moving through the air. And a thud.

"No," she gasped in disbelief, even as Silas' head rolled into view.

While the others laughed, she stared at her deceased companion, his eyes glazed over and mouth wide open. There was no dignity in this and no honor. They didn't even have the decency to let her say goodbye.

Sobs racked her body. As she was released, she fell onto her hands and knees.

"Let me go to him," she cried. "I have to be with him."

"Leave her be," Arthur said in a dull tone. "She's no threat to any of us, not without him."

The men stepped aside and Melina crawled to Silas' body. Lifting her head briefly, she searched for the one who had killed him. But she couldn't place him.

With shaking hands, she gently gripped Silas' head and placed it on top of his neck. The hooded men laughed again. This was entertainment for them.

Melina had not been a victim in years. She had gotten used to being the one who enjoyed the pain of others, who laughed at another's expense. While she could have taken this moment to reflect on all the suffering she and her lover had caused, she couldn't bring herself to give a damn.

She had always understood the implications of her actions, but she had expected to pay for them with her own life, not with Silas'. And while he had been no saint, he shouldn't have died because of her. He deserved better.

"It should have been me," she said through her tears.

Arthur stepped up behind her. "Someday it will be, Melina."

Gritting her teeth, she carefully placed her hands in her lap. She didn't want them to see her as a threat. "And why not today?"

"Because it's better to make you suffer."

Her nostrils flared as she lifted her gaze to meet his. "Be careful, Arthur. You're beginning to sound like a monster yourself."

"Don't compare me to you." He waved his hand toward Silas' body. "Or to him. We are nothing alike."

"Did you not stalk your prey? Did you not take pleasure in our pain and suffering?" Melina rose to her feet and turned out her palms so that he could see the blood on them. "Is this not what you wanted?"

When he didn't speak, it sent anger surging through her body. She slapped him across the face, leaving her lover's blood on his cheek. "Once again, you have left me with nothing!"

Arthur gripped her wrists, his jaw clenched as he stared at her. "The last time we met, you murdered my wife and children and left me with my life. I am returning that *kindness*."

"I don't care what sort of deal he made," one of the others whispered. "We can't leave her alive."

"What difference does it make to you?" a third man chortled. "She is only a woman, after all."

Melina's hands balled into fists. *Only a woman.* Arthur must have noticed the change in her demeanor – he let go of her wrists and turned to the others.

"You fools. Never underestimate an immortal, no matter their sex."

The anger had started as a spark, turned into a flame, and was now spreading like wildfire. She was so enraged that her hands were shaking and her eyes had shifted to a deep shade of red.

Without warning, her hands cupped the back of Arthur's head and twisted it at an unnatural angle until she heard the *crack* of breaking bone.

It sent the others into immediate action. They charged at her and she was delighted to find that their strength did not match her own – they were human.

They attempted to subdue her with chains, but she wouldn't allow them to hold her back now. Seeking out the man who had insulted her, she grabbed his throat and pulled him close so that their faces were mere inches apart.

"I may be a woman, but I am also a vampire. And you are only a man."

With a satisfied grin, her hand squeezed his throat, crushing his windpipe in an instant. The man's eyes were bulging out of their sockets when she tossed him to the floor.

The others were in a frenzy, some trying to flee. It appeared that it was every man for himself now, and divided, they would be easier to pick off.

Two of the men threw a silver chain at her – Melina dodged it, though as the chain was pulled back, it made contact with her cheek, leaving a bloody mark.

Hissing, she bared her fangs and lunged at the man. Even though it burned her hands to the point of nearly severing them, she wrapped the silver around his neck and tugged on the ends until it sliced through the man's flesh, decapitating him.

Melina flung the chain to the far end of the room, and before she could catch up with the men running for safety, there was a painful burning in her back. She shrieked and then reached for the object sticking out of her skin, piercing her lung.

The silver of the blade again burned her flesh, but she was far too determined to care – they would heal. The man's hands wrapped around her throat, and she laughed; clearly, he had forgotten that she didn't need to breathe. She took the knife and cut his neck open from one end to the other. His blood spurted onto her face and she opened her mouth to taste it. The flavor was disappointing, so she kicked his useless corpse to the floor.

Her next opponent preferred to use his fists, throwing them against her body while she repeatedly blocked them. Did these humans truly think that they could move faster than her?

Raising one of her arms to block his punch, her other hand plunged through his chest and ripped out his still-beating heart. She had never seen the color drain from a person's face so quickly. His body crumpled while she delighted in the blood of his warm organ.

Crimson liquid dripped from her mouth and fangs as she tossed aside the heart, her gaze moving between the last two men at her disposal.

"What's the matter?" she questioned with a grin. "Not so mighty without your leader?"

Before they could even respond, she was standing in front of them. She took hold of one arm from each man and ripped them out of their sockets, the crunching and popping noises making her smirk. Their screams were like music to her ears, a revenge well done.

They were still alive and she had no intention of keeping it that way. The first man staggered away while Melina had a hold of the second one. The look on his face was familiar. She had worn it before several times. It was one of terror and defeat, one that held the knowledge that death was imminent. It was the expression she imagined that she'd worn when Silas had turned her, and just moments ago when he had been killed.

"Don't fret," she said in a mocking tone. "You're about to meet your maker."

Pinning the man to the floor, Melina dug her fingers into his abdomen amid the horrifying squeals coming from his mouth. It almost didn't sound human. He must have been in excruciating pain. Good. Her only regret was that she couldn't prolong it.

When his eyes glazed over and his body was still, she left him to follow the sound of breathing. Someone was still alive. Stepping over the bodies, she stopped where Arthur had fallen. It was not hatred that swelled in her eyes, but tears of sadness.

They had loved each other once. He was a painful reminder of everything that had gone wrong in her human life, of everything she had once had and lost.

"I wish it could have been different. This is not what I imagined for us, Arthur."

"Nor I," he croaked.

She could have sworn that there was a tear in his eye.

"For the love we once shared, I will do you the mercy of putting you out of your misery."

Melina's gaze wandered the floor, searching for the weapon that had killed Silas again, but it was nowhere in sight. There were no swords, only knives and silver chains. It made her wonder which man the sword belonged to and where it had disappeared to.

Putting the mystery out of her mind, she decided that the most fitting way to end her former husband's life was to drain it.

She knelt beside him, her fangs then sinking into his neck. Melina only ceased when his blood stopped flowing.

Vampires could not overeat – they were made for this, for torture and carnage. But no matter how satisfying it was, her mate was still dead. No amount of bloodshed would bring him back.

The finality of the silence settled in her chest as tears streamed down her cheeks.

She sat near Silas' body, gaze set on his face as her mind wandered.

"What will become of me now?" she whispered. "You made me everything that I am. Without you, I am lost."

If he were alive, he would speak words of encouragement. He would assure her that she was strong and capable, that she didn't need him to be those things. But without him to say the words, she wouldn't believe them. It wasn't the same.

The only person left in the world was her fledgling and he was not a shoulder she could cry on. That was mostly her fault, she had not allowed him to be a part of her life with Silas. Though now she wondered that if he had been there with them, would he have been murdered by the hooded men as well?

Blood soaked the hem of her dress and her hands were drenched in the same liquid. Melina stared at her palms even though the tears blurred her vision to such an extent that she couldn't see.

With no one to turn to, and nowhere to go, she already felt the sanity she had clung to all these years slipping away.

Memories of her time spent with Silas flashed before her eyes, good ones and bad. For so long, he had been her lover, her most trusted friend, and her faithful companion. Not even Arthur had shown her as much devotion as Silas had.

Life had taken away anyone she had ever loved. The bond between a sire and their fledgling was more powerful than anything known to man, so to be without hers was devastating.

Melina's thoughts raced, thinking of what she could have done differently. If Silas had trusted her more, would this have happened? Why had he seemed so defeated in the end? Why had one man been promised the kill, and why had it seemed as though Silas had recognized his killer?

There were so many questions swirling in her mind and she was certain that they would never be answered.

She let out a blood-curdling scream, loud enough to wake anyone nearby. If anyone came to investigate, she would deal with them. The only thing that mattered was her grief.

She could either allow this to be her end or her beginning. Even with despair clouding her judgment, Melina knew which option sounded more appealing.

Somehow, someway, she would start anew. It may not look like the future that she and Silas had planned, but the least she could do for him was live.

It was what he would have wanted.

It wasn't long before she heard footsteps coming to the front entrance. For a moment, she feared that Arthur had prepared reinforcements.

Melina got to her feet, her dress, hands, and mouth still wet with blood. Opening the door, she was relieved to see a young man with a lantern, looking as though he'd come straight from his bed.

"Pardon me, madam, I heard–" the man stopped speaking but his mouth remained open as he witnessed the state of her.

"You shouldn't have come here," she spoke with a graveled tone.

The man, too stunned to say a word, dropped his lantern.

Grabbing him by the scruff of his neck, Melina pulled him inside and closed the door.

Just like all the other men who had entered her home on this night, he would not get out alive.

ABOUT THE AUTHOR

Laurencia Hoffman is the author of several novels and novellas and co-author of The Wages of Sin series. She specializes in horror but loves to dabble in other genres including fantasy and romance.

When she's not writing, she also enjoys making her own line of natural products, satisfying her sweet tooth, and watching films.

To see more from Laurencia Hoffman, follow her on the following sites:

Amazon

https://www.amazon.com/default/e/B009AXY1G2

Facebook

https://www.facebook.com/authorlaurenciahoffman

Twitter

https://twitter.com/iwritestories7

Instagram

https://www.instagram.com/laurenciahoffman

A MOTHER'S INSTINCT

BY JAIDIS SHAW

S HE DIDN'T MEAN TO KILL her father. That's what I kept telling myself as people lined up, one by one, to give me their condolences. It wasn't her fault. I knew that with every piece of my shattered heart. Her father and I knew that there was a chance that Grace would inherit the family gene; that every full moon would call to her and bring upon the change. Every time the moon grew full in the night sky I would wander into the darkness and plead to the moon. With each tear that fell down my cheek, I would beg the moon not to take my child. The gene had remained dormant in my family for three generations. I had never witnessed the transformation personally, but my grandmother had passed down stories of what she saw when her own mother changed. She viewed it as a blessing. I saw it as nothing more than a curse. How could a child, my child, survive in today's society when something so dark and animalistic lived within her? It was hard enough to be a human child these days; Grace certainly didn't need this burden too.

"I'm so sorry for your loss."

"Charles was such a charming man and devoted father."

"If there's anything you need, please let us know."

The sympathy rolled from each tongue that passed. I knew that friends and family were sincere, but this was a burden that I would have to carry to my own grave. There was no way that I could tell them the truth. They would never understand anyway. It was my single goal now to protect Grace. I vowed to do everything I could to protect her the day she was born, and now that meant teaching her how to control the beast within. However hard that may be. I didn't know where to start, but I did remember the stories that my grandmother had taught me before she succumbed to cancer. We would be strong, and we would make it through this together just like a family should. Well, Grace and I would. Charles was laying in the coffin behind us, cold and lifeless. We wouldn't forget him though, and just like everyone else, Grace would never know the real way he died.

A fresh tear escaped and rolled down my cheek. I looked down at the small child resting her head on my shoulder. Barely a toddler and already she had more power than most people could dream of. I should have known that something was wrong when she stopped eating most of her food. She had grown pale in the last few weeks, but I had just assumed she was fighting off a bug of some sort. The night her father died had changed that. She had gotten her fill, and now her cheeks held a rosy glow. She was a beautiful child, and although I hated to admit it, her beast within was just as lovely. I would have to rework her diet to ensure she was getting the added protein she needed. Grandmother had always insisted that the heart and liver were the most filling but that any organ would do. Even straight blood would work in a pinch. I did remember that animal blood, and organs would not suffice. She was very adamant about that. Something about the enzymes or something being different: I couldn't remember. It didn't really matter now anyway. There was no way

I could change what fate had in store for my little girl. The only light at the end of the tunnel for me were ramblings that my grandmother had whispered on her deathbed; that our family could control our inner self and suppress the demon. She had asked why anyone would want to quiet that power, to shut it away and allow it to never see the glow of the moon before exhaling her last breath.

The last person approached me, and I nodded my head in acknowledgment. I didn't even hear the words that came out of their mouth, nor did I care. I had more important things to worry about. I would mourn Charles always, but I knew that he would want me to focus on Grace.

"Here, let me take Grace." My mother reached out for my daughter. I let her take her from my grasp as my arms had grown heavy and I didn't have the energy to argue. I followed them to the front row, and we sat, the minister taking his position behind the podium. The sun sat high in the sky, the rays doing their best to provide warmth. I sat in a daze, trying to listen to the minister as he dragged on about Charles being in a better place and how he would forever live in our hearts. A hand tapped on my shoulder gently.

"It's time to go." My mother's voice pulled me back to reality. I glanced and saw retreating backs as the people who came to witness the funeral slowly sauntered away from the gravesite and back to their regular lives.

"Give us a minute please, Mom. I want to say my final goodbyes." I nodded to the gravediggers, and they began prepping Charles' coffin to be lowered into the ground. They went about their job so briskly, taking no regard for the man within the coffin. I guess they didn't mean anything by it. They were doing their job after all. To them, this was just a paycheck, something they did every day to pay the bills. I couldn't fault them for that. They tossed the wreath of flowers that adorned the top of the casket to the ground nearby and began hooking the coffin up to a wench. The loud clang the machine gave when they turned it on made me jump. The casket slowly disappeared, and my heart shattered all over again. This was it. The last time we would be physically near Charles.

I straightened my black dress and held my chin up high. Grasping

Grace's tiny hand in mine, I walked toward the hole. I'm not sure why I was prolonging my agony, but I knew that it was the right thing to do. The dirt shifted between my fingers as I grasped a small handful, its earthy scent filling my nose. Scattering the soil over the coffin, I exhaled the breath that I hadn't realized I had been holding. I glanced at Grace as she walked over to the dirt pile. With two hands she grabbed fistfuls of soil and flung it toward the hole, twirling and giggling as the particles fell everywhere. A small part of me wanted to be angry, to tell her that it wasn't respectful to the dead, but the other part knew that she was just a child. She was so young that she wouldn't even remember her father and what a loving man he was. Or how he used his body to shield mine as he clung to Grace while her beast ripped itself from her. Charles protected me, and I would honor him by protecting Grace. Picking her up and putting her on my hip, I walked toward my mother who was waiting patiently ahead. I could do this. I would do anything to protect my daughter and prevent her beast from taking over again.

***

"I've got another one for ya." The cute redhead hefted a cooler up on the counter.

"What was wrong this time?" I stood up from my desk and cracked the lid open. Another heart. This month was working out very well for Grace. This was the fourth heart that we had received that was unable to be used. Four people who had been registered as an organ donor and yet nobody was within the four-hour drive to receive the heart. I knew that there was a family out there mourning the loss of a loved one, but to me the heart represented food. A stranger died and wanted their heart to help someone else live, and that is exactly what it was going to do, just in a less conventional way.

"The closest recipient is over seven hours away. There's no way it would still be viable. Anyway, I'm off for the night. You working tomorrow?" The nurse glanced at a cell phone that she had pulled from her pocket. "You got the papers ready; I have to go."

I scooted the clipboard closer to her, and she quickly signed off on the organ delivery.

"You know it. It seems like I never get a day off," I replied. "Are you working too?"

"Nah, girl, I have the day off. Troy is taking me to get matching tattoos." She giggled and ran her hand through her ponytail.

"Don't you think it is a little, uh, soon for that? It's only been like three weeks."

"Oh no, he's definitely the one. I just know it." She retreated through the lab doors before I could say another word and I just shook my head in disbelief. Who was I to get between her and Mr. Right Now?

The air in the laboratory was stale and dry. Every other day that I was on the schedule to work I found myself in this little space filling out papers and making phone calls for the organs that came in that could be used to give patients extra life. The days that I didn't spend in the lab I was drawing blood for testing. I enjoyed my job as a nurse and it provided me with opportunities that I normally wouldn't have access to. Like organ donations. I reached for the filing cabinet and pulled out the remaining paperwork that was required to document that the heart I'd just been given needed to be put in the medical waste depository. Filling out the paperwork was the easy part. Smuggling the heart home was a completely different story. Just like an organ needing to be fresh for a transplant, it was the same for getting it home in time to process for Grace. The longer the organ sat on the ice, the more the tissue broke down, and it would lose its beneficial properties. Not to mention that it would take me some time to make the commute back home. I grabbed my lunch cooler from my locker and threw the remnants of my ham and cheese sandwich in the trash. Glancing out the tiny glass door window to ensure the hallway was clear, I opened the cooler and swiftly transferred the heart and ice into my cooler. I zipped up the bag and was shutting the other box when the door swung open.

"Oh good, it is still here."

Startled I just stared at Dean, the head of the surgery department. "What's here?" I asked confused.

"That's the heart that just came in for the medical waste bin, right?" He reached for the cooler and slid the lid back. "Wait. Where is it?" His questioning eyes burned into mine before slyly eyeing my lunch pail.

"I'm not sure what you mean." Casually I slid my pail over on the counter and reached for the paperwork. I glanced at the sheets of paper and acted as confused as I could. My gut told me that this wasn't going to end well. Dean had questioned me once before when a liver went missing. I did the best I could then to convince him that I had already put it in the bin, but I don't think he believed me.

"Lillian, where's the heart that was just brought in. I see that it was signed in."

I didn't know what to say, and so I didn't say anything at all. What was I supposed to say? That I had been stealing organs for the last few months to feed my child, so she wouldn't change and rip out my throat? I don't think he would understand, and I couldn't let her secret get out anyway.

"Let me see your lunch pail, please."

"Excuse me?"

"Please just let me see in it. This cooler is empty, and there have been a few reports that the paperwork for organs coming in and going out haven't been matching up. You have been the only one in the office on those dates. I want to give you the benefit of the doubt because I know you recently lost your husband, so I know things must be hard, but something just isn't adding up."

We stood in awkward silence, and my brain raced to try and find a solution that would get me out of this mess. I was out of solutions.

Dean reached over the counter and grabbed my lunch bag. I grabbed the strap and tried to hug it to my side. "You don't have the right to search my belongings." My voice cracked, and even I knew that it sounded like a guilty sentence.

"Lillian."

That one word was all it took. I knew that there was no use in fighting or trying to hide my actions. He unzipped the bag, and he sighed when he saw the heart inside.

"Why? Why are you taking this heart? Did you take the other organs too?" I could see the various emotions passing over his face. "I just don't understand."

"What's going to happen now." I straightened my posture and tried to act as if I wasn't shaking from head to toe.

"But why?" He asked again.

"I can't tell you that. I know what I did was wrong, but I can't change that now. Are you going to call the police?"

"Well, I certainly can't let you stay working here. I don't want to call the police either. You've been through so much, and Grace needs her mother. I just don't know what to do." His voice trailed off, and he ran a hand through his disheveled hair. He paced the cold tile floor for what seemed like an eternity. My heart thudded in my chest, each beat becoming more intense than the last.

"Dean?" I questioned. "I can just take my things and go. If I quit, then you don't have to take any action, and you can even tell everyone that you tried convincing me to stay. You'll get to look like the good guy that you are and in return, you won't send me to jail. Then we both win." The words sounded lame, even to me, but it was all I had.

Dean paused and looked at me before letting out a sigh. "Fine. It's only because of Grace, do you understand me? If she still had a father to take care of her, you'd already be in handcuffs. I don't know why you would take organs and frankly, I don't care anymore. I just want to wipe this night from existence. You have five minutes to be off the property." He rushed toward the door but turned on his heel quickly and made his way back. He yanked my lunch pail off the counter. "This stays here." With that, he was off, and I released the breath I hadn't realized I had been holding. What was I going to do now? Maybe I could find another job at a hospital? I doubt that would be possible as it wasn't likely that Dean would write a glowing recommendation for me. Fear for the future rushed through me as I collected my stuff and pushed through the door. I just needed to get home. I'd figure things out later.

***

The rain pelted on my thin coat as I walked down the sidewalk. It rarely rained this time of year in Juniper Grove, but since this night had already gone to shit, it didn't surprise me that it was getting worse. I held my head down and pushed forward, knowing that the porch light at the end of the street would offer me protection. It was my sanctuary; my everything. A clap of thunder boomed overhead, and I jumped. Pulling my coat closer around me I quickened my pace. I'd be home before I knew it. The light drew closer, and I raced onto the porch thankful to finally be out of the rain. I opened my purse and rifled through the contents to find my keys. Where were they? I knelt to the wooden floor and sat the large bag down, taking out my wallet in hopes they were just underneath. I was so focused on finding my keys that I hadn't heard the footsteps thudding up behind me. A fist slammed into my face, and I fell against the front door. Before I could scream a tall figure stood over me, grasping at my coat and pulling me up from the ground.

"Inside, now." The man shoved me against the door again.

My voice cracked. "It's locked."

"So, unlock it," he growled into my ear.

"I forgot my keys. It was partly the truth, but I also wasn't letting this man into my house. My mother and Grace were inside, and they had to stay safe. "You can take my wallet. There's not much in there, but it's yours. Just take it and go."

"Get the spare. Everyone has a spare house key. Hurry up, let's go." He shoved my head against the door again, and pain exploded from my forehead.

Just then the lock to the door opened, and my worst fear was coming to life.

"Lillian, is that you?" My mother asked as she widened the door and took in the scene before her.

"Lock the door!" I screamed at her and grappled for the handle, hoping that I could shut it in time. It didn't work. The man shoved me through the doorway and pushed the door closed with his foot. My eyes frantically searched the room for the only thing that mattered to me. Grace. She stood mere feet away watching the scene unfold before her, a grape juice box in her hand. My mother ran to Grace and shoved her behind her legs, shielding her little body with her own.

The man glanced around the house, doing a quick check of his surroundings. "Is anyone else home?"

"No," I whispered.

"There better not be." Before I could reply, the man backhanded my face, and I collapsed to the ground. I raised a shaking hand to my cheek and gingerly touched my cheek. The sting radiating through my face was intense, and I knew that it was already bruising. I pulled my hand away, and blood dripped from my fingers.

"Mama hurt?" Grace asked as she peeked out from behind my mother's legs.

"I'm fine, baby." I did my best to reassure her, and my brain raced for a way to end this before it got out of hand.

"He hurt you." Grace's tiny voice was steady and held a tone that I hadn't heard her use before. Her nose twitched in the air, and her eyes flicked between the stranger and me.

"Mommy is okay. Go to your room and play, sweetheart."

"She's not going anywhere." The stranger pulled a roll of duct tape from his pocket. "I'm going to have my fun with you, and then I'll move on to them." He forced my hands behind my back and had already started to tape them together before I realized what was happening.

"No, please don't do this. Take whatever you want, just leave us alone," I pleaded.

"Oh, I'm going to take what I want. Everything I want," he whispered in my ear, his hot breath sent chills over my body. He shoved me to the ground and walked toward my mother.

"Your turn. Do what you're told, and I'll promise not to make the little girl suffer."

My mother turned around and placed her hands behind her back without hesitation. I couldn't believe that she would just give into the man's demands, but as I watched Grace, I didn't see any other option. It's not like I had done any different. I could be fighting back, but instead, I just sat in a heap on the floor. Tears rushed down my face and splattered to the floor, stained crimson with blood.

"Don't cry, mama." Grace's voice pulled me back to reality. I looked at her tiny face, but something wasn't quite right. Her eyes held a glow that I had hoped I'd never see again. Her grape juice splashed to the floor, no longer wanted. A cry tore from her lips, and she collapsed to the ground.

"What's wrong with her?" The man hesitated with tape still in hand.

"Nothing, she's fine." My mother stepped in front of Grace again, this time a little more cautious.

I distinctly remember the growl that filled the room before the chaos broke loose. A streak of fur flew at the man and knocked him backward. He tripped on the rug and fell to the ground. Before words could be uttered, they were ripped from his throat as Grace, my precious wolf, silenced the man for good. Blood gurgled to the surface and spilled to the rug beneath the large body. I wanted to speak up, to try and stop my baby girl from staining her muzzle further but the words were stuck in my throat. Watching as she eliminated our threat, protected us from harm, had me in awe. Her dark fur glistened in the fluorescent lighting, and the air seemed to buzz with excitement.

"Grace." My mother's voice cut through the air like a knife. She walked up to Grace, slow but steady. I had never seen my mother this way before.

"Don't get too close, mother. I can't lose you too," I pleaded.

My mother glanced at me, her eyes glowing amber. "Lillian, pull yourself together."

"Your eyes…" My whisper was so uncertain even I doubted what I had really seen. All I could do was watch as my mother knelt on the ground beside Grace. She placed a gentle hand on the wolf who was still lapping up the warm blood. Grace growled and looked at her grandmother with hunger in her eyes. Taking the wolf's head in her hands, she leaned in and looked deeply into Grace's eyes.

"Thank you for protecting us. You've done your job and protected Grace. She is so lucky to have you, but now it is time to let Grace have control again. She's young and was scared. She has much to learn about when to call upon you for help. I promise you'll be well fed, but for now, please let Grace regain control." Mother's eyes bore deep into Grace's, and just when I thought it was hopeless, the wolf lowered her head in submission and laid on the floor beside the body that was surely growing cold.

Fur began to recede, and I could hear the cracking of bones as they transformed back into their human shape. Where a wolf had just been, Grace's little body now laid. She grabbed onto her grandmother's legs and closed her eyes, a small whimper escaping her lips.

"It's okay, Grace," mother cooed. I struggled to my feet and ran over to her, searching her body for any wounds. I still wasn't familiar with the transformation, and I didn't know what had changed.

"She's fine. She just needs to rest."

"Mother, what's going on. Your eyes changed. How were you able to convince her wolf to retreat?" There were so many questions racing through my mind, but the one that stood out the most left me in wonderment. "Are you a wolf?"

The question rolled from my tongue before I could stop it.

Mother sighed and her now blue eyes welled up with tears. "No. I'm not a wolf. I'm just a giant disappointment to your grandmother. We never could figure out why I can't change. My wolf tries to surface, tries to force her way out but my body just won't let her. Nothing has been passed down through the family about partial changes, but all my mother saw was a broken wolf. She wanted so desperately for me to be able to accept the change, but she died before that could happen. But I felt my wolf tonight. It's been so long but the moment Grace's wolf started to surface my wolf wanted to join in. I felt the desire to share in the delight of ripping that man's throat out. To taste the sweet copper as his blood coated my tongue. But I also knew when the bloodlust was becoming too great for her young wolf to handle. I'm just glad her wolf listened to me." She glanced down at Grace and ran her hand gently through her hair. Small snores escaped her stained lips, and we couldn't help but smile. Not only Grace but her wolf had protected my family, and I was grateful. The beast that I thought lived within Grace didn't seem so bad now. I knew now that not only did I need to protect my sweet Grace, but I had to protect her wolf too.

"Help me out of this duct tape, please?" I did my best to hold up my hands, and my mother jumped back to reality.

"Oh, my goodness! I completely forgot. I'm so sorry!" She exclaimed. She gently rested Grace's head on the rug and raced to get a pair of scissors.

I glanced at the dead body on the floor and couldn't help but smile. A sense of calmness rushed over me, and I knew that everything would work out. I glanced out of the large picture window and saw the moon peeking from behind the storm clouds, its warm rays casting their bright glow on the wet world outside. I knew what I had to do. First, I was going to get Grace cleaned up and snuggled into bed. Then I was going to find a way to dispose of this stranger's body. Lastly, I needed to find a way to get blood and grape juice out of carpeting. It was going to be a long night, but I didn't mind. Everything was starting to look up.

***

"How's Grace doing?" I asked my mother as she walked into the bathroom.

"Passed out like a light. The change really took its toll on her small body." Mother glanced at the body in the tub and raised an eyebrow. "What's going on here?"

"Well, I figured that I couldn't pass up on the gift basket that was brought to our door, metaphorically speaking. If I can preserve his organs, maybe even some of his muscle, then I'll have enough food to feed Grace for a few months."

"It makes sense," she said. "Need help?"

"That'd be great. It's not like I've cut up a body and tried to preserve it before. I grabbed some of Charles' tools from the garage and have lined that clothes basket with a trash bag." I pointed to the basket that sat ready by the tub. "Could you go to the kitchen and get the vacuum sealer ready? I thought we could seal the organs to make them last longer. We just need to make sure and label them, though I don't think I'll be forgetting this night any time soon."

"Sounds like you've thought of everything," my mother said. "So, we're putting the stuff we want to keep in the basket?" She questioned.

"Yes. I thought that after I removed the organs, I could put them in the basket and you could take the basket to the kitchen and vacuum seal them. So long as we get them in the freezer soon, they should keep well. Should we keep the blood though? He's already lost a lot, and I'm not sure how we could drain the rest. I wish we could hang him up." My mind whirled with ways to harvest the body. This would be so much easier if I had the proper equipment. I wish I still had access to the hospital. That wasn't an option now, so I would just make do with what I had on hand. I grabbed Charles' hacksaw and took a deep breath. How hard could it be to saw through a human sternum? That had already been done for us in nursing school when we worked with cadavers, but it couldn't be too bad. At least I knew the locations of the organs. That would make this much easier and hopefully quicker. The sun would be up in about six hours, and I needed to get rid of this body before Grace woke up. I rested the shiny metal against the cold flesh and pressed with all the strength I could muster. The skin ripped, and blood began to collect at the incision site. *Here we go*, I thought to myself.

The heart, lungs, liver, kidneys, brain, and tongue had already been removed and were in the kitchen with mother being vacuum sealed and frozen. A nice pool of blood had gathered on the tarp that lined the bathtub, and I was currently using a turkey baster to suction what I could up and put into a Tupperware bowl. It would easily keep in the refrigerator for a little while, and I could use that as a supplement to keep Grace's wolf appeased. She saved my family, and I was grateful, but I wasn't looking forward to seeing her any time soon.

"That's the last of it." Mother came into the bathroom and rubbed a drop of sweat from her brow. "I cut most of them into smaller portions, so they will last longer. If you space it out, there should be enough to last several months. I'm proud of the work you've done." She smiled at me, and her eyes glistened with pride.

"Thank you, mother, but I'm just protecting my daughter. You would have done the same for me."

"Yes, I would have. I'll do whatever it takes to protect Grace too. We must remember to give her the opportunities to live a normal childhood too. Just because she has a wolf inside of her doesn't mean that she must give up being a human child. There's a balance, and we just have to find it."

"I agree," I said and reached for the knife. "I'm going to see if I can get some of the flesh from his legs. He has a ton of muscle here that would be good."

"I'll bring the basket back. While you're doing that, I'm going to roll up the rug from the entryway. I don't think we will ever be able to get the blood out. It's best if we get it out of the house just to be safe. While I don't think anyone will come around looking for this thug, I don't think we need to take the risk." Before I could respond, she turned on her heel and was out of the room.

I ran the knife along the bone, slicing off what muscle I could. It wasn't the best of cuts, but it was a start. Once the hunk of meat was removed, I put it in the basket. I'd have to skin it in the kitchen as I just didn't have the room on here to properly work. I sliced and sliced and before I knew it, I had found a rhythm for cutting the meat off. I thought I'd have a harder time processing the body in my tub, but I felt nothing — no remorse or thoughts about the family who would never know what happened to him. I was just prepping meals for my child — a nice rump roast, some sirloin steaks. The tidbits that were left over could always be ground up and put into spaghetti. Grace loved spaghetti, always twirling the noodles around her fork and laughing as they would fall back onto the plate. She hadn't quite gotten the hang of it, but thankfully she would have plenty of time to learn. I sighed a breath of relief. I knew everything was going to be just fine.

THE NEXT YEAR

I knelt on the warm ground and pulled weeds from the garden. A variety of flowering vegetables had sprouted, adding a splash of color to the green yard. All the neighbors asked what I had used to make my garden grow so abundantly, but I would just smile and say it was a family secret that my grandmother passed down to me. They would just chuckle and ask to have any extras that we didn't need. I always had plenty to share. The whole neighborhood enjoyed the juicy tomatoes, crisp green beans and leafy lettuce that I grew every year. They didn't need to know that the same vegetables that nourished them did so because they had been fertilized with human remains.

Giggling interrupted my serene moment, and I turned and watched as Grace played with a friend that she had met at preschool. It made my heart melt to see her growing so well. There had been no signs of her wolf surfacing since last year. She was never pale and always had energy thanks to the food in the freezer. I had made sure to space out when she received them, and even the vegetables seemed to help better than store-bought food. I believed that the homemade fertilizer played a part in that.

"The girls seem to be getting along well."

The voice startled me, and I glanced at the well-dressed woman standing in my yard.

"I hope you don't mind, but I let myself inside the gate. I heard the girls out here playing."

"Don't be silly, of course I don't mind, Mary." I stood up and brushed the dirt from my knees. "The girls are having a ball. Thanks for letting Vanessa come over."

"No problem. She really likes Grace. I think they will be friends for a long time. So, I thought that if it was okay with you, maybe Grace could come over for a sleepover this weekend? It's Vanessa's birthday, and so I'm inviting some of the kids from the school. The boys will have to go home, of course, but the girls can sleep over. I'll get pizza and ice cream, the works."

I paused at her request. I'd never let Grace go anywhere without my supervision before. It was hard for me to let her out of my sight because even though I knew there hadn't been any issues recently, that didn't mean they wouldn't pop up unexpectedly. I watched the girls as they played tag and pondered what to do. The words that my mother and spoken to me ran through my mind. *Just because she has a wolf inside of her doesn't mean that she must give up being a human child.* I knew that this was a chance to let Grace be a normal child. There was no harm in letting her spend the night at a friend's house.

"Sure, that would be lovely. Thank you for the invite. I know Grace will have a blast." I nodded to Mary as she awaited my response.

"That's great! We look forward to it. Vanessa!" Mary called her daughter over to her, and they both waved as they retreated through the fence gate. "See you this weekend," She yelled before disappearing from sight.

Grace ran over to me, and I pulled her into a tight hug. She was my moon and stars; my everything. "Would you like to go over to Vanessa's house this weekend?" I asked.

"To play?" She questioned.

"Yes, and to sleep too. You'll get to play with all of your friends."

"Yay! I can't wait." She wrapped her tiny arms around my neck and squeezed with excitement.

My heart swelled with happiness. I was honored that I could be her mom and that I could provide her with a normal childhood. I'd make sure to feed her well before going over there just in case, but I was confident everything would be okay. What was the worst that could happen?

DEMONS ARE A GIRL'S BEST FRIEND

BY CARMILLA VOIEZ

I T WAS ON THE DAY her mother died that Natalie began seeing demons.

"I'm sorry," Doctor Wills said, and his face did look sorry. Sympathy was his default expression. How many times had he repeated the same words to people like her? "All we can do is make her comfortable now."

Natalie nodded, unable to form sentences. The letters were in her head, but they were jumbled like jigsaw pieces, and she was certain some were missing.

"Maybe you should let your brothers and sisters know, if they want to see her before … Is there anyone I can call to sit with you? I know it's a shock. She seemed to be improving."

Was he taking the unformed words directly from her brain? She only realized what she wanted to say after the doctor provided the answer. Or was it experience? Did everyone ask the same questions when they knew that soon a loved one would leave them?

He made her feel much younger than her thirty-five years.

She shook her head. No one would come to share her burden. Natalie would summon her brothers and sisters back to their painful past, but they would arrive too late to help. Instead they would pull up to the front door in their huge cars and rush to the room that smelled of wilting flowers. She supposed she should get fresh ones. They'd forget Natalie was there. Forget she was anything more than a messenger, the bringer of sad news. They would be nursing their own grief, and would have no space to share hers. The burden of the middle child. Forgotten. Ignored.

"Please call me if anything changes," Doctor Wills said before he left.

What could change? Hadn't he said this was it? They could only make her comfortable and wait for her to die. Natalie's mother.

Natalie sat by the bed and held her mother's limp hand. She didn't squeeze, but rather cradled the claw of loose flesh over brittle bone. The illness had taken everything, but the doctors couldn't even give it a name. At least Mother was at home now. Unconscious in her own bed. The doctor's powerlessness had given her that at least.

Her mother grumbled in her sleep. A bad dream? Or had she heard the doctor's words? Did she know she was dying?

Natalie should call her siblings. They would expect her to, but they expected too much. Where were they when diapers had to be changed? Where were they when vomit soaked sheets needed to be washed? They had their careers – newsreader, beautician, lawyer and accountant. There wasn't room in their lives to nurse their sick mother. That fell to Natalie, the under-achiever. Forgotten. Ignored.

She pulled a wet sponge from a bowl that was the last remaining piece of a wedding set before the matching plates and dishes had been smashed in rage. She squeezed out the excess, the tears she couldn't cry, and gently wiped her mother's brow. A dribble of dark liquid ran down the sick woman's chin. The grumbling ceased and Mother was calm again.

Natalie would call them, but before they arrived and pushed her aside she would spend time alone, with Mother, chasing away the demons that plagued her fevered sleep.

***

"I came as fast as I could. I had to cancel an appointment with an important client. Am I too late?" That was Stephen's greeting. No, 'how are you', no, 'I'm sorry'; just an 'am I too late'. Did half of him hope he was? That he wouldn't have to linger in that old house for too long?

"She's upstairs, sleeping," Natalie replied, taking the coat that he seemed unable to hang for himself. "You're the first to arrive."

He snorted.

"Do you want some tea?" she asked.

He nodded and mounted the first step. "I'll be up ... there." He stared at Natalie for a moment, and she wondered what he wanted to say. But he must have decided against speaking. A moment later he turned his back to her again and climbed.

When Natalie brought the tea, Stephen was sitting in a chair, a few feet from the bed, watching the rise and fall of their mother's chest.

"Did the doctor say how long?" he asked, taking the cup and saucer from Natalie.

"I don't think he knows, but soon."

The doorbell rang and Natalie hurried away.

***

Natalie cooked dinner for them all. Perhaps fear or grief robbed them of their sense of taste, because none of them seemed to enjoy the food, even though it was a dish their mother used to make.

They talked around Natalie, discussing their various careers, their important clients, ignoring the elephant in the upstairs room, while catching up with self-congratulatory anecdotes. Natalie realized how much she hated every one of them.

***

"Is she ever awake?" Sophie asked.

Sophie's manicured nail dragged along Natalie's index finger as she took a cup of coffee from her sister the following morning. It didn't hurt Natalie's hand, but it grazed her heart as did the words. What had Sophie expected? A jolly family get together?

"Sometimes," Natalie answered. "But not often and never for long. Not for a month now."

"And there's nothing they can do?"

"Only make her comfortable."

"It's just ... I have to get back. Do you think she knows I came?"

Natalie shrugged, biting back the vicious words she wanted to scream.

"I mean if she doesn't know I'm here ..."

"Do you know I'm here?" Natalie asked.

Her sister looked at her askew. "Of course I do. You were always so close to her. I'm sure she appreciates it. We all do."

Well that's okay then, Natalie thought furiously, *as long as you can say you appreciate me, what more can I expect? Maybe you should all just fuck off and leave me to it then.*

***

Their mother died two hours after Sophie had driven away in her vintage Mercedes Benz. Stephen made the call to their absentee sister.

The death wasn't dramatic. One moment Mother's chest rose and fell and then it didn't rise again. For a long while they watched, all four of them – Stephen, Charles, Madeline and Natalie. It seemed like a held breath, but it was held too long.

Charles spoke first. "I think she's gone."

Stephen and Madeline nodded in eager agreement. A collective sigh was exhaled. It was over. They could get back to their respective lives.

To be certain, Charles checked her pulse.

"I'll call Doctor Wills," Charles said, fishing his phone from his jacket pocket. "Do you have his number?"

"I'll call Sophie," Stephen said.

Natalie sat, registering the flustered movements of her siblings in her periphery vision. She focused on her mother's face. There was a trace of a smile. Was Mother as relieved it was over as her brothers and sister seemed to be?

When Natalie glanced towards her siblings she saw their eyes flash red. Their features creased up into sharp grey and khaki lines below their eyes. A moment later their taut flesh softened and their normal skin tones were restored. She assumed it was her grief that caused the strange transformations, or theirs.

"Doctor Wills' number?" Charles asked again.

***

They took her away in a white van. Natalie's mother. Natalie wondered what she might do now.

The others huddled together in the sitting room, bent like crones towards a central point she couldn't see. She decided to make tea for everyone, but even the kettle looked different. The water wouldn't fall in right. It splashed her hand instead. The scene melted. She realized she was crying.

"Are you okay?" Madeline asked.

When had Madeline sneaked in behind her? How long had Natalie been bent over the sink, weeping?

Natalie rubbed her eyes. She straightened her back and turned to her sister, but Madeline wasn't there. It was strange that this thing used Madeline's voice. It might have tricked Natalie if her eyes weren't clear and dry. But this thing, touching Natalie's arm, was not her oldest sister, the beloved newsreader on national television. Not the special princess that their father used to call her. Not the smart one like their aunt Lucy used to say. Not the pretty one, as their mother had often crooned. This creature was not pretty, it was grotesque. Green and gray flesh hung in folds around its flame-red eyes. The strands of hair that clung to its scalp were knotted and matted like a nest of snakes. Its sharp teeth were black when it attempted a friendly smile. It was the disease. The demon that had haunted Mother's dreams and sucked her life slowly away. Natalie had to kill it. She had to avenge her mother's death and save herself. Thankfully there was a knife on the draining board. She only had to reach it before the demon sensed it had been discovered.

She curled her fingers around the handle. The demon seemed oblivious to her plans. Its soothing voice tried to console her, like an older sibling was supposed to do. Then the demon fled and Madeline stood there. The folded skin was replaced by crimson rings around tired eyes.

"Is it you?" Natalie asked, dropping the knife with a loud clatter.

Madeline's mouth formed an O. She reached across the breach and drew Natalie into an embrace. A few moments later, Natalie found she'd been marched to the living room where her younger brothers sat.

"Charles, can you call Doctor Wills again, please? I'm worried about Nat."

***

Doctor Wills gave her pills. He told her it was her nerves, but his long nose looked like a plague mask and his black jacket like raven's wings. Natalie knew she couldn't trust him. He'd let her mother die.

"One of us should stay," Madeline said, looking pointedly at the others. Obviously it couldn't be her.

"Maybe she should come with one of us," Sophie suggested. She'd returned at last, only wanting to leave again as quickly as possible. "A change of scene might be what she needs. This house is …"

"I'm not leaving," Natalie said. "This is my home."

Charles, the fourth child, the first son, the lawyer, piped in. "Nat, you know we're going to sell the house, don't you?"

His eyes flashed red as the demon surfaced. He made his living sucking from the marrow from all that was good, and now he expected financial gain from his own mother's death. How could he? Mother's mattress was still warm. She who had struggled to birth him for two days in agonizing labor. Natalie had only been three when Charles tore his way out from their precious parent, but she remembered the pallor that remained in Mother's skin for weeks after she came home. She remembered helping her older sisters to take care of the screaming parasite while her mother rested. Her sisters must remember too. Charles was a selfish brat. He always had been, and yet he was the favorite, the prince. His birth put an abrupt end to Natalie's childhood, and her life-long job as a caregiver began. Now he planned to kick her out of her home for a measly payout?

"Demon!" she screamed.

"Where are those pills?" Madeline asked. "Have you taken any yet? Nat?"

"This is ridiculous," Stephen said, the accountant, the pragmatist. "She needs care, professional care. It's a breakdown. We left Nat here with Mum. We should pay for her care. She just needs to rest."

They stood above her, wringing their hands and working their jaws, thinking on the one hand of the holidays and cars they'd buy when the house was sold, and on the other how they'd let their sister take the burden they should have shared equally. They owed her something, not too much of course, but something. Something that would help them sleep at night without guilt-ridden dreams. They said none of this out loud but, in their twisted faces, Natalie saw the truth.

"A breakdown?" Madeline asked, studying the bottle of pills. "Is that what these are for? I just thought she needed a sedative."

"How can a doctor justify leaving her here with us and a bottle of anti-psychotics?" Sophie said. "It isn't right."

"It's been a long day," Charles said. "Let's get Nat into bed, then we can talk."

***

One of the demonic siblings, Natalie couldn't tell them apart now, tucked her into bed. Its breath, as it said goodnight, smelled like a puff of putrid air escaping an ancient tomb. The narrow lips barely concealed its shark-like teeth. It shut the door behind it when it left, but she wasn't left alone. A terrifying face lurked in every corner of the room, plus the one above her who kept guard. She couldn't move, and she couldn't sleep. Her jaw ached, but she couldn't close her mouth. The demon wriggled against the ceiling. Its eyes never left her face. It didn't even blink. She tried not to blink either, but her eyeballs were burning, her skin too. She pulled the covers over her head and closed her eyes, praying that her dead mother was there to protect her.

***

She slept, albeit fitfully, and when Natalie awoke and the rays of morning sunlight which poured through the window cleansed her room. The demons were gone. Her siblings were gone too. They must have left in the night, while the demons trapped her in bed. None of their cars were outside and none of their beds had been slept in. For a moment Natalie wondered whether she'd dreamed it all, but when she checked her mother's bed it too was empty. Empty and cold.

As she filled the kettle to make tea, the sound of water drumming against metal calmed her. There was a note left on the kitchen table. She ignored it. Whatever the demons wanted to tell her could wait.

The phone rang. Natalie felt a lump in her throat. It would be someone for Mother. Anyone who rang to speak to Natalie used her mobile.

"Hello?"

"Good morning, I'm sorry to disturb you. Am I speaking to Miss Natalie Green?" The voice sounded formal, official. The funeral home maybe?

"Yes. Who is this?"

"I'm sorry. I'm calling from Severen and Wilde. We're your late mother's solicitors. I am sorry for your loss. I'm phoning to see if you can come into our office tomorrow at eleven, for the reading of your mother's will."

"Isn't my brother in charge of all that? I thought he'd be the executor."

"No, your mother wanted someone outside the family to handle her affairs. Are you available?"

Natalie nodded. "Sure. Eleven, right? Give me the address."

***

Sophie studied her nails while the others studied the menu. Natalie tried to hide her smirk. It served them all right. They could moan and groan, but their mother had left the house to Natalie and there was nothing they could do about it.

Madeline eschewed food in favor of green tea. She claimed she wasn't hungry. Natalie was sure she heard her sister's stomach rumble in protest.

After lunch they would head to the funeral parlor together to discuss arrangements. By three Natalie would be alone again. She didn't mind too much. She had expected their desertion, but she was surprised the subject of her mental health had been dropped so quickly, unless it was a subject they planned to discuss in her absence.

***

The coffin seemed extravagant for an object that was to be burned. Natalie suspected it was a final fuck you to a community who had pitied their mother rather than respecting her. The town had considered their family too large, too disruptive, full of wayward children and a dead-beat dad. They thought she'd married beneath her, and had never expected four of the five children to grow up successful and rich.

It was very different to the ceremony they'd held for their father a decade before. That was a quiet affair and only their mother had cried. The flames that ate their dad's remains were no doubt aided by the alcohol in his blood, or so they'd joked when out earshot of their mother. For some reason their mother had loved him. For many reasons the children didn't. Perhaps if he'd lived longer he would have found a way to crush all their dreams.

But Mother was different. Mother was loved, by her children and the wider community. The chapel was full and voices rose in song to wish her safe travels.

At the wake, Doctor Wills approached Natalie. She was busy making tea in the kitchen. She realized that making tea had become her default setting, but it felt healthier than the alternative. It calmed her and made her feel useful, while allowing her time away from the streams of conversations that echoed around both reception rooms.

"How are you, Natalie?" he asked.

"Much better, doctor. Thank you for coming," she replied.

She avoided looking at him. His hawkish nose was all she saw when she focused on his face.

"Do you need more pills?" he asked.

"No thank you."

"Can you come in for a check up next week?" he urged.

"I'll try," she replied, hoping to dismiss him.

It worked and with a long sigh he left her to it. She wondered which of her brothers or sisters had urged him to see her, and whether they'd been motivated by worry or avarice.

***

The demons kept Natalie company. Sometimes they brushed across the faces of people she met, momentarily changing their features, and at others they crouched in her bedroom waiting for nightfall when they could follow her into her dreams. She wondered whether she growled as she slept, like her mother, but there was no one to ask.

When she asked the demons what they wanted they were reticent. When she persisted with her interrogation they flitted away, but they always returned, normally when she was too tired to argue.

They spoke to her of other things. They were her advisers. They warned her to keep the house clean and tidy. They made her flush away the pills. They told her that her siblings were watching, waiting for her to fail so they could sell the house and lock her up.

They let her know when the doctor was about to knock on her door, so she could hide and pretend to be out. They painted beautiful pictures in her imagination of far off places full of vibrant hues that shimmered when she focused on them. They reminded her to shower, and bustled her out of the door each morning, telling her that healthy minds needed friends.

She began to see beauty in their creased flesh and ruby eyes, convinced that her mother had sent them to take care of her solitary daughter. She looked forward to night when they would play with her in her dreams.

She grew stronger. Less afraid of the judgements of others. Less in awe of her siblings.

She got a job. With her experience and two weeks of basic induction, she landed a position with an agency, working in community care. It was comfortably familiar. Something she was good at, taking care of the elderly and infirm. Her clients' demons swelled Natalie's retinue of friends. She gathered them to her bosom and accepted them. Sometimes they'd follow her home.

When Natalie was sad, demons stroked her hair. When she was angry, they smashed things. When she wanted affection, they caressed her skin. In return they were grateful to be seen and understood.

Fewer people called at the house. Outside, people smiled at her, but she always saw a sliver of fear in their eyes. Inside, she knew she was loved.

The demons taught her things, ancient languages, forgotten songs and poignant tales. They opened her eyes to her own beauty, no longer overshadowed by her older sisters, but fresh and bright. They encouraged her to take risks, experiment with make-up, dye her hair, wear more revealing clothes. The smiles of the outside world became hungry leers. The sliver of fear changed to envy. The jealousy and desire of other people changed how she saw herself, and her confidence grew.

***

A year, almost to the day, after her mother died, Natalie awoke to the sharp sound of shattering glass.

"Someone's inside the house," the demons warned her.

"Three men," they confirmed.

"It's okay. Go downstairs and confront them. We'll protect you," they promised.

She trusted the voices, but still felt afraid. She wrapped a dressing gown around herself and opened the bedroom door, silently. She listened. The demons were right. She heard voices and footsteps on the floor below. She considered calling the police, but knew they'd arrive too late to help. But the demons had promised their protection. She overcame the desire to hide and stepped lightly onto the landing.

Natalie crept down the stairs, avoiding the ones that creaked. Three men, that's what the demons had said. Instead she saw teenagers, so young they were more like children, gathered in the sitting room. They'd removed her grandmother's portrait from the wall and were staring at the safe. The closest one to Natalie shivered.

"Why's it so cold," he whispered.

Natalie smiled. She was warm enough. It must be the demons, messing with him.

"Read those numbers again," the one closest to the safe said. He kept his voice low.

"Twenty-three, sixty-seven, forty-nine."

The one at the safe tried the dial again. "No. She must have changed the combination. Who wants to wake her?"

Natalie slipped back into the shadows of the hallway and watched as one boy reluctantly climbed the stairs.

"Your brother?" one of the demons asked.

Natalie shook her head. No, her family wouldn't send people to rob her. That was insane.

She heard each of the doors being opened upstairs, then hurried footsteps descending. The boy returned to the others without glancing Natalie's way.

"Empty," he told them, no longer bothering to whisper. "But one of the beds's been slept in."

"Search the house," the leader, 'safe boy' said. "I'll work on getting this open."

Natalie fled to the kitchen. She grabbed the same knife she'd once raised against her sister, and crouched behind a cabinet.

One boy followed another into the kitchen, perhaps they'd heard the clatter of the cutlery drawer. One made eye contact with Natalie and shivered again. He was wide eyed with messy light brown hair, a Dickensian street cherub. He pointed in her direction but didn't move towards her.

"There," he said.

The other took three steps then stopped in his tracks. This one was less pretty, but no less scared. Natalie didn't need to ask the intruders what was wrong. She knew why they were afraid. She felt the demons surrounding her, bristling with anger, and knew the boys sensed them too.

With a shrug of her shoulders she was pushed from her body. Natalie dangled in the corner of the kitchen ceiling, as small and unnoticeable as a spider. She watched the boys shake with terror, and saw the object of their fear just as clearly. Natalie's flesh moved from behind the cupboard without any conscious effort of her will.

As her body rose to its feet, the two boys inhaled. As it spread her arms, they turned to run. Her hair moved around the serene face as though she was under water. Her dressing gown undulated too. The current puppet master of her flesh wasn't concerned about her modesty. It laughed, this body that was once her own, and with the air expelled from her lungs the demons stormed ahead.

She watched in horror, powerless. The cowering teens were children. But the demons didn't care.

"Nasty vermin invading our lair," one roared.

"Disrespecting us. Breaking in to steal what isn't theirs."

"No reaction would be an overreaction."

"Our fury is justified. Our anger is righteous. Natalie will be avenged."

They were rage, and Natalie's body was at the centre of it all. Without her interference, she was all powerful. The horror and powerlessness she'd felt at first, watching from above, changed to awe and acceptance. The boys' fear gave her power, and she revelled in it. The moment she felt the rightness of her body's actions she was reabsorbed by her flesh.

One boy screamed as he was lifted then thrown at the wall. Natalie heard bones crack. Blood dribbled from his lips as his crumpled body fell to the floor.

She turned to the other. His eyes were even bigger now and wet with tears. He was the sensitive one, the one who had shivered when her demons had touched him. He saw them all, every pulsing molecule, and his mind cracked.

"Who sent you?" she asked.

His slack jaw couldn't form a reply. Bubbles of saliva popped around his trembling lips. His pupils expanded to fill his eyes. She saw her reflection in them. She was terrifying.

She abandoned him and made her way to the sitting room.

"Who sent you?" she asked.

The boy jumped and removed his earplugs. He looked embarrassed when he faced her rather than afraid. As if a teacher had caught him misbehaving in class.

"Who gave you the number?" she tried again.

He looked behind her and saw he was alone. He shrugged. "Sorry, love, nothing personal. Just a man in a pub."

"What did he look like?"

"Blond hair, kind of ugly, bad skin."

The description didn't fit either of her brothers. Maybe they'd hired someone else to do their dirty work, or maybe she'd been right and this wasn't her family. But who else would have the number her mother had used for the family safe?

"My mates, okay?" he asked.

She shrugged. "So you need the new number, huh?"

He didn't know how to reply. He struggled to focus on her face.

"I'm sorry. We'll just go," he said, but didn't move a muscle.

"Just ask me," she said.

"Huh?"

"For the safe number. Just ask me."

His brow furrowed as if he'd forgotten his lines and needed Natalie to prompt him.

"Ask me!" she yelled.

"Umm, what's the combination?" he asked.

"Six, six and fucking six." She laughed. "Get it?"

He trembled, but didn't turn back to the safe. He stared at her while sweat dripped from his forehead and over his cheeks. His fear was delicious.

She let out a scream that forced the boy backwards and pinned him to the wall. She took a step towards him. He tried to make himself small by sinking to the floor. A greasy black smear stained the wallpaper. It had a head and arms. Natalie wondered whether his shadow self had entered the wall.

With his cocky confidence gone, the safe breaker looked younger still. For a moment Natalie hesitated. These children were no threat to her. She should let them go. They would not return, neither would their story, should they choose to share it, be believed.

The demons wanted to finish it now. Kill the kids, dispose of their bodies. Their venom shook Natalie, it frightened her. She'd been relying on their good counsel for twelve months. They'd kept her loneliness at bay. They'd made sure she ate, cleaned, slept and woke up again. Defying them, after they'd taken care of her, felt wrong, but so did killing the boys. It was messed up. She hadn't asked for any of this. But she wasn't sure she could make the demons leave, even if she wanted to. She belonged to the voices, her demons. They'd adopted her after her mother had died and she had thought Mother sent them to protect her. But now, she began to doubt this logic. What if they had been her mother's illness? What if they had left her mother's shell after she drew her last breath to join with Natalie. What if they were slowly killing her as they'd killed her mother, day by day, hour by hour. She felt stronger now, but she was less herself than a portal for the voices. A vessel to carry them around.

"Go now, and take your friends with you," she yelled.

The boy darted away. She saw gratitude and relief in his nervous smile. She had beaten the demons back, but for how long, and what would they do to Natalie when she was alone?

***

Natalie couldn't remember falling asleep, but the sitting room was bright with sunlight when she opened her eyes. She replaced the portrait of her grandmother, hiding the safe. She stared for a while at the silhouette safe boy had left behind and hoped it would fade. She moved a lamp in front of it to hide the stain. Order had been restored.

The kitchen would take a lot more effort to put right. A table had been upturned and blood spatter marked the spot where the first boy fell. He wasn't here, which meant he was alive at least, or had been when safe boy had taken him.

Wind howled through a smashed pane in the back door.

"Look what you've done," Natalie chastised the demons.

When she received no reply she felt both relieved and sad. The voices had been terrifying, but they were her only companions. She didn't know whether she'd survive without them. She told herself they were still there but sulking. This silent treatment was her punishment for spoiling their fun. They'd forgive her eventually.

She considered phoning the police, but knew she couldn't explain what they'd find. She wondered whether she should call her brothers and sisters, but they'd been campaigning to find her mentally unfit and would use it as an excuse to evict her from the house. The only option was to clean it up herself. It was obvious the demons didn't intend to help.

"Where are you?" she asked. Only the wind replied.

The glazier wanted her to inform the police. "If you've had a break in, or attempted break in, your insurance will cover it."

She thanked him, but paid in cash.

The house felt too big. She rattled around inside it. Its empty rooms echoed her hollow existence.

She called the demons again, but they were still ignoring her.

***

Weeks passed, then months. Natalie cared for the old and infirm, but she no longer encountered their demons. Her clients seemed like shadows, as if their vibrancy had been a symptom of demonic possession? Natalie was losing her will to endure. She didn't eat. She woke up in front of the television, having forgotten to go to her bed. Even incontinent old women remarked on her pungent smell.

When she lost her job she didn't have the energy to care.

It was then Natalie's family descended. Their sympathetic smiles did little to hide their glee at her demise. They'd expected this, but thought it would happen sooner. Natalie couldn't take care of herself. She needed to be looked after. The house was divided equally between the four siblings and Natalie was sent away.

***

"I miss them," Natalie said.

The therapist's room was warm. The low lighting seemed to dance on the walls. The couch was soft. Her body sank into it.

"Your family?" the therapist asked.

"My demons. I should have let them kill those boys."

The therapist scribbled something in her notes. Natalie closed her eyes and smiled. At least she wasn't alone.

AQUA VITA

BY A. GIACOMI

New York, present day

A KNOCK AT THE DOOR IS no longer a sound I welcome, instead, I dread it. The sound is loud, intrusive and knowing exactly what they've come for became increasingly exhausting and irritating. The frail boy at the door had been knocking for exactly three minutes and I wouldn't bother to greet him until the final drop from my mug had been tasted, time made no difference, he would wait. I could smell the desperation off him, it was deliciously curious. I no longer knew what it meant to be desperate, or to have time dictate my decisions. It had been nearly 120 years since I last tasted a breath of air, and I could barely remember what it meant to be alive anymore.

Sipping the last euphoric drop of liquid, I rise from my ottoman and begin towards the kitchen to rinse my mug, a simple routine, and the only constant I had now. However, before reaching the kitchen of my small apartment, the knocks at the door grew more desperate and a voice accompanied it now.

"I know you're there Sir. Look, I need to speak with you please. It's very important."

I could barely hold back a snarl as I walked up to the door and began knocking on it incessantly, like a mad man, trying to mimic how annoying it was to be disturbed in such a loud and obnoxious manner. My hope was that he would leave, but instead, he began to plead.

"I'm sorry for the hour, I'm sorry for my rudeness, but I wouldn't be here unless I was…"

"Desperate?" I say, completing his ever so obvious conclusion.

"Yes, Sir. I'm desperate. I have nowhere else to go."

With my hand over the padlock, I pause, and debate leaving it where it lies, but there was something about this boy that felt oddly familiar and I let my curiosity get the better of me and open the door to find the scrawny boy I had imagined. His voice matched his appearance; there was nothing grand or impressive about him, his clothes hung from him, his hair a tousled mess atop his head that one could mistake as a toupee if he wasn't so young. The boy appeared to be about 16, yet he was a giant, taller than I, and needing to stoop a bit as he entered my apartment.

Raising an eyebrow, I ask "So you haven't tasted it yet I take it?"

The boy shakes his head looking a little sore at himself, and then it dawns on him that we haven't met before.

"Wait, how do you know I bought some? How do you know I want to drink it?"

Placing a hand on his shoulder, I tell him that it's written all over his face.

"You're panicked, you've come here of all places, and you appear to know that I can provide some help to you. Therefore, you know what I am, and I know what you are, since you weren't invited in, yet here you are standing in my living room like a fool."

The boy takes a few steps back towards the doorway. He feels the error of coming here, he now feels fear, something I wish he could have refrained from feeling. Fear was tempting, fear was delicious.

"Look, maybe I should go. I'm sorry I've wasted your time."

Grabbing his wrist before he can leave, I bid him sit down, but often forgetting my strength I launch him towards the armchair rather than lead him. He's properly fearful now, he seems like the type who would get a nosebleed from the stress. I begin to hope for such a sight, it would be almost hilarious given the situation, not for him, but for me.

"I'm sorry about that son, it's not my intent to hurt you right now, but you have come here, and now I would like to know why." I say as I find a chair next to him.

"So, it's true then? You are?" He asks, his voice trembling.

"I am...but surely that can't be your question?" I say with a mild chuckle.

Riffling through his pockets nervously he pulls out a small vial of clear liquid, I knew what it was, he knew what it was, but he doubted its power, *why else would he have come.*

"Who did you get that from? I thought I was one of the only dealers in the area." I say with an angry smirk.

"Um, well, there's this guy, Thomas. He sold it to me, but told me that you were the "Tutor' and I have no idea what that means, other than the fact that he mentioned that you'll help me after I drink this. Only I haven't drank it yet, and I'm scared to drink it."

I find his fear of the liquid hilarious and can't help but laugh until it pains me. He looks at me in stunned silence as I continue to laugh at his expense.

"You fear a tiny vial when death is stalking you? Can you not hear Death's breath behind you? He stands there waiting, hoping you will not tempt fate. Why would you let him win when you can deny him the one thing he wants? It's a fun game to play, actually, he curses me daily for what I am."

The boy jumps from his seat, looking behind him fearfully, but soon realizes there is nothing there. I assure him it was a metaphor, but snicker knowing of the third guest in the room.

"I want to drink it." The boy confesses. "I got a shit deal. I'm just a kid and I'm dying. I haven't started treatment; I didn't bother when they told me my chances. Then this guy shows up, Thomas, and he tells me this stuff will cure me, but he wasn't too specific on what that meant and he breath reeked of blood. Maybe it's just my imagination and the books I like to read about bloodsuckers, but he sure fit the bill."

Laughing again I ask. "What is your name son? Let us begin there."

"I'm Sam, what's your name?" The boy asks timidly, not seeming to expect any answer back.

"I've had many names over the years, but I started as Eli, you may call me that."

The conversation becomes stale then and I motion towards the vial, asking if he intends to drink it now. He shrugs and I can understand the hesitation he feels, all those who have drank from the tiny vial have hesitated, have questioned it, have nearly thrown it away.

After some time thoughtfully looking at the vial, he asks "What is this stuff really? They call it Aqua Vita, but is this a trick? Just some scam to get dying people to give you a shit load of money? I bet most people just flush it, or worse it's just poison."

"Oh it's definitely poison, and it will definitely kill you Sam, but it is perhaps one of the most glorious deaths you can hope for. I have seen generations pass, I have seen the world evolve. It's strange and wonderful and I'm glad I drank that vial so many years ago."

Sam squeezes the vial, looking as though he would pass out. "Can you just tell me about when you drank it and why they call you The Tutor? This is just all so very surreal to me and I can't, I can't wrap my head around any of it. I feel like I'm going nuts."

"That's a rather long story Sam, are you sure you won't die on me before I finish the tale?" I nearly laugh, but Sam gives me such a look of disapproval that I decide it better to begin my tale.

Ottawa, 1900

I had been traveling for many days by horse drawn carriage in order to reach the city that would hopefully become my salvation. After watching my mother fall ill and pass on and my father slowly disintegrate until taking his own life, there was no way for me to stay at the farm where I had grown up. My father had dreams of me taking over his small farm that had been passed down from his father to him, and I would have gladly done so, after all I had been training for the role my entire life. But I feared living with the ghosts of my parents would eventually catch up to me, so instead, I opted for a fresh start in a city I had never been to. I had reached out to a couple on the outskirts of the city who were seeking a stable attendant, the role didn't pay very much, but there was room and board and it was a blessing to have regular meals tied into the deal, so I accepted it and all that it might bring.

When the coach stopped in front of a rather large iron gate, I was summoned by the coachman, "Lad, we're here. Let's get your bags and get you on your way."

Stepping out of the coach and making my way towards the gate with my few belongings, it seemed as though the gate became bigger with each step I took. The intricate metal vines were both beautiful and intimidating, on the other side of the gate lay a new life and it was somehow calling to me.

I thanked the man for my safe arrival and offered him some extra money as a way of proving my absolute gratitude for the long trip. He seemed a bit ashamed for taking it, but I had a sense that he may have needed every penny. He wished me luck and was soon on his way.

Standing at the iron gate I could see a stretch of road leading up to the manor. The dirt road was lined with trees that seemed to want to greet you. Soon there was a man rapidly approaching down the tree lined path, he was nearly out of breath after reaching me. "Sorry, the name's George, I was supposed to be awaiting your arrival but was called away for something, my apologies for your wait. The master would not be happy to know you've waited."

I waved my hand. "Not to worry, I had only just arrived" not at all concerned with time anymore, I had no rooster to summon me from my sleep, and no need for daylight to dictate my errands.

Walking towards the house, the trees seemed to lean in towards me, as if to keep myself and the grounds hidden from the rest of the world. It was an odd feeling but I pushed it away as nerves, a new place can shake you. The large manor amongst the trees was dark and looked a bit forgotten; some pieces of it looked crumbled away from years of neglect. I followed George into the house, and upon entering it, it felt as though some dark veil had been lifted. The inside was full of beauty, marble floors, sculptures, paintings, all the things that you would accredit to those with too much income and too much time with which to spend it. The house had this strange glow to it, it was beautiful, and although the home was filled with many things and trinkets, there was something still very hollow about it.

George quickly led me through the house and into the kitchen where maids had already made up a platter of food for me. As I was about to sit down and eat it, George urges me to hurry and follow him outside. Scooping up my tray and nodding to the ladies, in a quick attempt at gratitude, I hurry out the door after George who has spared no time in waiting for me. As I quicken my pace to catch up to him I notice a large stable, beyond the trees and George beckoning me to join him inside. Famished from the journey, I shove a few morsels in my mouth before entering what would soon be my working quarters. As I enter, I realize that George is not alone, a well-dressed man stands beside him wearing a very serious expression as he examines me very closely. I quickly swallow the food hidden in my mouth and bow slightly to greet him, I didn't know it at the time, but I hazard a guess that this was to be my master, Mr. Harrington.

"Oh dear, are you truly one of those? I'm not much for grovelers, so if that's your way, you best be off! These horses will train you if you're weak in mind, they can smell it! I was looking for a man with strong character as well as strong arms for this job." He snorts with disgust.

"I assure you Sir, I do not grovel, I do not beg, I do not whine, I simply do. I am looking forward to the work you'll set before me. I have worked as a farm hand all my life and I can assure you, your horses will be well mannered by the time I've finished with them." I reply, biting my lip so as not to say anything further and overstep.

The man grins and extends his hand to me. "Very well, I shall like to see it rather than have it said. They tell me your name is Eli, Eli Clark, correct?"

"Yes, I am Eli Clarke of Clarke Farms, but as you already know, the farm is no more, that's what brings me here and I am ready to work." I say as I shake his hand firmly, remembering that my father used to say that a good handshake meant a lot amongst men.

"A tragedy Mr. Clarke, but we are pleased to have you with us. This stable contains your horses and next door you'll find a small guest house, that is where you shall live. Seeing as it is late, I will leave you to your meal and allow you time to rest. Tomorrow I shall introduce you to the rest of the house at dinner. Until then." He says as he nods towards me and George and then slowly makes his way out of the stable.

There was something odd about my new master, the Harrington family was old money, but there was nothing very old about Mr. Harrington, besides his clothing, they were very old fashioned, and nearly royal looking. I felt that I could grow to like him, he was to the point and I liked that. Looking around the stable I see that George looks a tad shaken. Placing a hand on his shoulder, he nearly jumps.

"George, is something wrong?" I ask as he continues to look concerned about something.

"No, nothing. I am to show you the horses now and then the rest of the evening is yours."

George hurries through the tour of the stables and the horses that are nearly sound asleep. He then rushes me to my quarters and bids me goodnight. I shrug it off, I didn't know George well enough to assume anything was out of the ordinary with him, for all I knew, he was always in a hurry like that rabbit from Alice in Wonderland. I went to bed that night thinking of George with white rabbit ears and I laughed myself to sleep.

***

That night an odd dream crept over me, a dream I hadn't had since I was a boy. My naked self was standing upon an ice-cold lake, shivers crept from one extremity to the next and before I could fear dying from freezing, the ice beneath me began to crack and crumble, until I was submerged in the icy underworld. My limbs stiffen with cold and I struggle to scream, taking in more and more water, wishing it were air. Just as my body begins to go limp, I awake from my nightmare, panting, sweating and glad for the warmth of each bead against my forehead. I thought I would struggle to get back to sleep, but it comes quickly.

***

Up at the crack of dawn, I didn't expect anyone to be awake with me. Farmers rose at odd hours and I was sure that Mr. Harrington and his family were the sort to need their beauty rest. As I tend to the horses I can't fight off the feeling that someone's gaze was upon me, but as the day wore on the grounds were oddly quiet. No one ventured out of the house, nor in. After grooming, feeding and allowing the horses time to roam, I returned them to the stable. A snap of straw within alerts me to a hidden visitor, as I check the stable, I am shocked to find a girl hiding inside one of the stalls, looking very frightened at being discovered.

"Who, who are you?" I ask trying not to seem frightened, but her appearance was as wild as an animal who had been kept in captivity for far too long.

Nearly shivering, she begs me to hush, bringing her finger to her lips and slowly approaching me, or so I thought, instead she reaches for the reigns in my outstretched hand, and she takes them before I could protest. In a moment she's on the horse and bursting out of the stables doors. I try to call after her, but realizing it a waste of breath, I grab another horse and follow the little thief.

It doesn't take me long to find her, a scream echoes through the tree-lined grounds and I follow it to her location. She had fallen off the horse, but it's not the fall that seems to be bothering her. I hope of my horse and race to examine her as she writhes in pain, screaming upon the ground, arching her back and flailing as if something was fighting to free itself from within her. I press my hands to her shoulders trying to hold her still and see what harms her. What I find is her flesh, sizzling, the scent of smoke rising into the air as her flesh burns in an unnatural manner.

"Dear god!" I gasp, unable to make sense of what I was witnessing.

"The light, the light" she screams as she pulls at my shirt, begging for help.

Realizing the sun beaming down on her in the clearing, I drag her into the shade of a nearby tree, where her screams immediately halt.

"Thank you," she breathes before becoming unconscious and limp in my arms.

I place the young woman on one of the horses and take us all back to the safety of the stables. She soon awakens and I take the opportunity to question her once more.

"Who are you and what has happened to your skin?" I ask as I point to the wounds upon her face.

She pushes my finger away, "Do not stare at me, it is a skin condition that I can do nothing about. It's the sun, it harms me, my skin is delicate and unable to enjoy its rays. I assure you I will be fine, it heals, I just have to stay out of the sun and it will heal.

With that she stands and although limping slightly she goes to leave.

"Where are you going?" I ask, near insulted by the lack of gratitude.

"I am going inside. I need to rest." She replies.

"Wait, do you live in this house? Are you...are you one of Mr. Harrington's children?"

She nods "yes, the youngest and the oldest at the same time."

The girl was such a puzzle I couldn't even think of what to ask her next, instead of asking another arbitrary question, I watch as she leaves, sticking to the shade and enters the house. It was if that odd moment had never happened if we were the only two who had witnessed it.

***

A few hours later I am interrupted from my work by George, looking more frazzled than the night before. He glances at me from top to toe, examining me.

"Well what is it George, spit it out." I say with a grin, which he does not return.

"You're not ready for dinner."

Glancing down at my dirty clothes I realize that Mr. Harrington might not like to be kept waiting.

"Give me but a moment George. I can be presentable in a few seconds."

Racing to wash up and change my clothing stained from the day's work, I find that I am ready sooner than George expected because I startle him when I return.

"Oh my!" He jumps. "Come let us go, they're all waiting to meet with you."

"All? You mean the entire family?"

"Why yes, they've been quite anxious to meet you since your arrival, and they thought it best to give you a proper welcome dinner. It will be exquisite, you lucky little lap dog! I wish I could be new to this place again, for you only get the one welcome dinner and it is extravagant to say the least!"

George's tease thrills me and my stomach replies with an excited growl as well. Upon entering the home, I notice all the staff is lined up in the halls to welcome me and lead me towards the dining hall. The hall is grand, every wall is full of art and the ceiling filled with dazzling light from the chandelier. The dining table is already set, candelabras glowing, making the guests seem like shadows. Mr. Harrington jumps out of the shadows to greet me and shake my hand, welcoming me to dinner and bidding me to sit. He goes around the table, fist introducing me to his wife Mary, his son David and his daughter Caroline. My eyes fall upon Caroline who looked very different from the girl I had met earlier. Her wounds had healed completely, her dress made her seem refined instead of frazzled, and she actually knew how to smile.

I bow my head to acknowledge and greet them all and soon dinner is served.

***

As the months grew colder I found myself infatuated with Caroline, something about the mystery that surrounded her and her family was absolutely irresistible. I found her watching me as I went about my errands, she would smile shyly but never speak to me. Perhaps it was that my status was low, or perhaps it was the fact that I was employed by her father, but I never received anything more than a smile from fair Caroline.

It wasn't until the months began to grow colder that she would finally speak. I had been coughing for a few days, but with my strength still intact I thought nothing of it. I remember riding one of the horses towards the stable and then coughing so heavily that I blacked out and must have fallen off. The next thing I remember is water, this feeling as though I were drowning, and although I wasn't entirely sure I was conscious, I heard voices screaming. One of the voices belonged to Caroline, she was begging someone to "save him" and "let him drink." I could only assume she meant me, but it could have all been a dream. What occurred next, there was no mistaking, hands wrapped around my throat, softly at first and then violently as the hands pushed me beneath the water. I could feel my lungs filling with icy cold liquid and although I wanted to scream, I simply gurgled until I became still.

***

Bolting upright from a panicked sleep, I look across the room to see that it is nearly morning. I think it all a dream until I find a visitor by my bedside. "Caroline?" I utter in a pathetically quite voice.

"Shhh…all is well Eli. I thought I had lost you for a moment there."

She says as she strokes my hair, which I only notice then that it is quite damp.

"What happened Caroline? I feel as though death struck me down with his scythe!"

She laughs, "No darling, you are more alive than you can imagine." And with those few cryptic words, she kisses me softly on the mouth and I forget everything all at once.

The kiss would have lasted longer if I hadn't suddenly felt an awful burning sensation in my arm, it felt as though fire had engulfed me. I pull away, screaming and look towards the window as the sun rises and then to my arm that appears to be blistering rapidly. Caroline races towards the window and draws the curtains, saving me from my agony instantly. I shake as I watch the blisters erase themselves.

"What is happening to me? What have you done?"

Caroline looks almost fearful, perhaps my eyes were crazy, but I simply hadn't noticed that her father had entered the room holding a note in his hand.

"My word, it seems that Queen Victoria has passed, on January 22nd. How terrible to lose her majesty...but I see that you are well Eli, that is quite fortunate, you can thank my daughter for nursing you back to health. The winters here can be murderous."

His grin is almost sinister as he stares at his daughter. She backs away slightly, almost as if she fears being attacked.

"Sir, I feel as though there is something I am missing here. I don't remember how I came to be in this bed and something truly odd just happened when the sunlight hit my arm."

Mr. Harrington nods, "yes, I suppose Caroline has much to explain to you." He looks as though he was about to leave, but then turns back to stare at his daughter. "I hope you are happy with your choice young one, because you will no longer be under my protection now, you must leave at the first sign of night."

With that, he's gone.

I am left starting at Caroline as she paces the room, she opens her mouth to speak several times, but nothing comes out. Instead she decides to start with placing a small vile in my hand. The liquid inside is clear.

"What is it?" I ask as I examine it closer.

"It's life. It's why I'm alive, it's why my family continues to live, and it's why you're here now, with me."

"I don't understand? The water, is life?"

She comes back to sit by my side and takes my hands in hers. "Yes, the water in the lake behind my home is sacred. Once you drink, you must continue to drink, or you will die, truly die."

My mind races to make sense of all the nonsense, but it can't, so I simply listen as Caroline continues.

"I know this will all sound mad, but have patience with me. I know no other life but this. My family is part of an ancient clan of Vampires, we have survived for centuries on the water made of our own blood mixed with the sacrifice of a hundred men. This is the only way to create Aqua Vita, and when it is made, it cannot be unmade. The water must be protected, it must be kept a secret and we are never to share it with mortals, as I have done with you."

As she tells me this, the only bit of it I truly understood was that she had essentially risked her life for mine, she would now be an outsider to her kind, she had been disowned by her family, all for me. All this time, when I thought myself unworthy, Caroline had loved me.

I rise form my bed and for the first time I feel the strength that the water had gifted me with, I walk towards her and kiss her firmly, making her understand that I would not abandon her. I hear her sigh with relief, she must have thought I would abandon her too, now that I knew what she truly was, but I didn't and I never did.

New York, present day

Pulling out a vial from my pocket, I place it in front of the young man who looked rather hesitant after hearing my story.

"So, what happened after you left? What happened to the girl? She's not here is she?"

I lower my head, "no, she is not, we fled, we ran for many years together, lived more years together than humans usually get, we were happy, but in the end, they found us. They took her as a traitor and drained her of her blood. I wanted to die too, but instead they made me a healer, her blood runs through the Harlem Meer in central park and I was charged to take lives in order to create a pool of Aqua Vita to satiate the Vampires of New York. So, you see, I am a willing prisoner here. I am still close to her in some way, and in this vial, I offer you a small part of her. I do hope it helps you."

I see the boy's eyes grow wide. "Do you mean there is a possibility it won't?"

Everything in life and death is uncertain I'm afraid, the water only works for those strong in spirit. If you are strong enough it will safe you, if it thinks you unworthy of its power it will destroy you, but what choice do you really have boy? Are you not dying now? Haven't you been dying slowly for the past hour of your visit?"

The boy shakes as he takes the vial from my coffee table and slowly opens it. He whispers a little prayer before placing the liquid to his lips. He hesitates a moment and then throws the contents down his throat before he can change his mind. He waits a few moments before speaking, waiting to feel different, but nothing happens, he smiles faintly and begins to rise. His slight smile quickly fades as he retches and claws at his stomach through his t-shirt. I could see the look of disappointment on his face as he begins to gurgle and dissolve into liquid goop.

As I walk to the closet to grab my mop and bucket to begin cleaning away the wet pool that was once a person, I can't help but feel a little disappointment myself, what could have made this young man so unworthy of immortality? As I clean up the last bit of him, I wish him well in my own small way:

"Back to the waters that birthed you my son, may your afterlife be kind to you."

BLOOD MOON

BY FAITH MARLOW

L IBBY SAT IN THE LOBBY of a new medical office, filling out the booklet of paperwork on a clipboard. She was trying to ignore the gnawing pinch of the button on the waistband of her jeans as they creased her belly. Her good jeans were soaking in a bucket of cold, soapy water on top of the washing machine. She hoped she could get the bloodstain out because it wasn't in her budget to buy new jeans, especially after being out extra gas money for her thirty-minute drive one way to the office. A sneeze, a pair of soiled pants, the following emotional melt-down, and years of frustration had brought her here, to an address on the bottom of a newspaper ad. She was seeking help in the only place she had left. She was going to be a lab rat. She took the newspaper clipping from her purse and read over it again.

Participants needed for study

Medical study is currently interviewing applicants who meet the following criteria.

Must be female between the ages of 18-30

No pregnancies or miscarriages in the last 6 months

Experiencing any of the previous GYN issues: heavy periods, bleeding that last longer than 7 days, excessive cramping/ clotting/ strong to severe PMS

Participants will be compensated

"Elizabeth," a quiet voice called from the partially opened door, no more than ten minutes after turning in her completed paperwork. The petite young nurse led her down a short hallway to an exam room and cordially began taking her vitals. It was the usual banter, small talk to fill the empty space. "Dr. Gilbert will be in shortly."

The scarcely furnished exam room smelled musty, like someone had spilled a bottle of disinfectant in an attic. Libby wondered how long the building had been empty before the new occupants arrived. She had barely gotten halfway through an article on the effects of global warming on the Emperor penguins of Antarctica featured in the two-month-old *National Geographic* magazine, when she heard a quick knock preceding the door opening.

"Hello Elizabeth, I'm Dr. Owen Gilbert. It's nice to meet you," The gigantic, heavily bearded man thrust his long arm and wide hand out for her to shake. His fingers encircled her entire hand, almost touching as he heartily greeted her. Libby's arm felt like the tail of a kite flapping in the wind. Of all the mental images she had conjured in her mind, a lumberjack in a lab coat was not among them. Due to the nature of the study, she had expected the doctor conducting it to be a woman. To see a burly man, no less than six and a half foot tall with a bushy, salt and pepper beard, was certainly a shock. She wouldn't have cared if he had been a little green man from outer space if he could help her situation.

"Nice to meet you, doctor. You can just call me Libby for short, everyone does."

"Well thank you for agreeing to participate in our study, Libby. If you don't mind, tell me a little about yourself."

"Well, there's not much to say. I'm single, no kids, never been pregnant. Aside from *female issues,* I don't really have any health problems. I'm a cashier at Gas n Grab, evening shift."

"Do you like your job?" she could tell he was trying to be personable, but it seemed like being around strangers made him as uncomfortable as it did her.

"No, but I get by, mostly."

"Hobbies, other interests?"

"Not really."

"Okay... would you please tell me about your symptoms? What brought you here today?"

"Sure," she replied with a smile, but her soul was sighing in frustration. It had to be the one-hundredth time she had been over it. She had lost count of how many times she had described the unbearable pain and cramping, the heavy blood loss and embarrassing overflow accidents, the frequent and gut-wrenching blood clots and uterine tissue discharges, and the overwhelming exhaustion, depression, mood swings, and tender breasts. Everyone had essentially written her off and told her to take ibuprofen as needed. A hysterectomy was never an option that was discussed, even though she had begged for it because she was just in her twenties and had never had children. Due to an elevated risk of stroke, she was unable to take hormonal birth control. She truly felt as though she was out of options, that she would be forced to endure until menopause because she *might* want to have kids someday.

She was a single woman who lived in a small, single-wide trailer sorely in need of repairs that she could not afford with three cats, all of which had been inherited when her mother passed away. She could barely afford to care for herself, so why on Earth would she want to be responsible for a child?

"Well from what you have told me, and what I see in your paperwork, it looks like you have been under an extraordinary amount of stress this year. Have you attempted any relaxation techniques, exercise, yoga?"

"No, it doesn't really help me." Libby could feel her chest tighten, cheeks getting flushed. He was just another judgmental doctor, another person without a uterus telling her what she needed to do.

"I see you take ibuprofen. Does that help?"

"Not really, might take the edge off at most."

"What does help your symptoms? What are your typical techniques for managing them?" Dr. Gilbert asked, twiddling a pen back and forth between his fingers.

"Nothing helps me. That's why I'm here. That's why I'm offering to be your human lab rat, because nothing I can do helps. It makes me miss work, which hurts me financially. I can't afford to miss."

"What treatment options has your OBGYN discussed with you?"

"Are you even listening to me?" Libby snapped. All the pent up frustration and pain boiled over and burst out of her in tears and shouting. "I don't have an OBGYN. I can't afford to go to the doctor. I go to the Health Department to get my annual. I suffer, that's how I manage. That's what I'm doing now, and that's what I'm going to be doing because I've already missed one day of work this week. So if you're not going to help me, just say so."

Libby grabbed her purse and headed toward the door. She regretted going and spending money she didn't have on gas she shouldn't have to spend.

"Libby, I want to help. Please."

She stopped in her tracks, hand on the door handle. She glared at him over her shoulder. He sounded sincere but how much of that was an act?

"I *can* help you if you're willing." She turned around slowly, unconvinced, but at least willing to listen. Sincerity had creased his forehead into a wrinkle. "I think you'll be an excellent candidate for this treatment, but I must stress this *is* a clinical trial. There could be some side effects."

"My life is controlled by side effects right now." She sat back down, placing her purse on her lap. "What have I got to lose?"

"Nothing, but everything to gain if the treatment is effective." Dr.

Gilbert smiled, the ends of his mustache curling up in response. "Preliminary studies have shown that most women with symptoms similar to yours show a dramatic increase in their quality of life, even after just one dose. Phase one just started two weeks ago, so that is quite promising. However, they did experience some rather negative side effects, nausea, mood swings, even a couple cases of sleepwalking, but they were not severe enough for any of the participants to drop out of the program."

"It would have to be pretty bad for me to quit, I can tell you that. I could put up with a lot to not have to go through all this."

"That's right, Libby. We want women to be able to decide for themselves. After the initial three monthly doses, no further medication is needed unless the patient *wants* to become pregnant. Instead of tricking the body into believing it is already pregnant, like traditional hormonal birth control, we have found a way to make the body believe the patient is too young to have their period, so the process of menstruation never begins. The eggs simply wait until the body sends the signal to release, just like an adolescent girl getting her period for the first time."

"And later if I want to have a baby, I can just come back to you and take another shot, like an antidote?"

"Exactly, that's a very good way of saying it." The doctor nodded his head, impressed with her cleverness. "The treatment works much like a virus, sustaining itself in the patient until the *antidote* is administered. Within a couple of months, a regular cycle should re-establish, and the patient would be ready to conceive."

"What about the cost?"

"This study is free for all participants. Actually, we will be paying you for participating, keeping the logs and journals, checking in for blood work, and such. Hopefully, that will offset some of your lost wages from today."

"No, I mean later," Libby countered, knowing that she could be walking into a situation that could turn out being expensive to get out of.

"The reversal drug, or antidote, will be free of charge to anyone who has taken the treatment."

Experimental, lab rat, human guinea pig, test subject.

Libby's head swirled with every heinous scenario her mind could conjure. Her skin breaking out in hives, throat swelling shut, waking up covered in hair, or not waking up again at all. Her mother's ever-cautious voice clattered in her head like broken pottery in an aluminum bucket. Her mother had never taken a risk, had never been able to afford to. She had been born, lived, and died in the same town, probably never traveled even one hundred miles from home. She never got to visit the amazing scenic locations she longed to see, never flown in a helicopter like she had always wanted to do, never had a spa day, never visited a big city. She had lived a cautious life, and she had died anyway.

"When do we start?" Libby asked, speaking over the lump in her throat.

A few moments later, a nurse returned with a little tray of vials, a syringe, alcohol wipes, and bandages. A few more consent forms signed, the syringe filled, and then only a few moments and the quick pinch of the needle stood between Libby and the treatment that could change her life. She couldn't help but be excited for the sting when the nurse wiped a spot on her upper arm sterile for the injection, the scent of alcohol tickling her nose.

"We have had reports of mild to moderate stinging, like a flu shot," the nurse paused with the razor sharp end of the hypodermic just a breath away from her skin.

"No worries, needles don't bother me," Libby winced when the needle passed beneath her skin, a faint chemical smell lofting up from the injection site. It was a little larger than she had anticipated, not the tiny straw of clear fluid like in a vaccination. This formula was thicker like a penicillin shot. The nurse's hand trembled under the pressure she was applying to the plunger, as the viscous material pushed beneath Libby's skin. The area was getting hotter by the moment, burning as it spread out. Just when she began to grimace, the nurse removed the needle.

"All done," she smiled, rubbing the injection site vigorously. "It's a time released drug, so you may feel some heat, some tenderness, or a little knot on your arm but it should only be about a day or so. Anything more than that, you need to let us know."

"Like what? What should I be looking for?"

"Any allergic reaction, anything that you feel is *off.* You will need to plan to come back in a month for the second dose." The nurse kept any assumptions to herself, not wanting to contaminate her perception.

"Right, so keep my eye out for anything strange, but not so much that *everything* becomes strange and I convince myself that I'm probably going to die? Got it."

***

Two months later

"Good morning, Libby. How've you been?" Dr. Gilbert smiled warmly at his patient, his star pupil. She had gone above and beyond to document her experience with the treatment and had responded wonderfully.

"I'm in shock, honestly," Libby smiled broadly, relief evident. "Things could not be going better. I feel fantastic. I have more energy. I'm in a better mood. Everything has improved."

"What about the menstrual symptoms? How are they progressing? Any change?"

"It's like daylight and dark. The cramping and clotting have almost stopped entirely, and last month I only had two heavy days. I am due to start any day now, but so far I have only noticed a little bloating and some light spotting."

"Any other side effects? I know you may be happy with the positive results you are experiencing, but I would still need to know if you're experiencing anything negative, even if you feel like the benefits outweigh the drawbacks." He asked cautiously, fearing that she might hide information from him out of fear.

"Well, there is one little thing I've noticed, but I don't mind it really," Libby said reluctantly, and then quickly back peddled.

"I want you to report anything, good, bad, or otherwise. It doesn't necessarily mean you should stop the treatment." Dr. Gilbert reassured. "Many medications have some sort of inconvenience, but the benefits outweigh them."

"Well, I have noticed that the hair on my legs and arms, just wherever, seems a little darker, thicker." She pulled up the sleeve of her sweater to expose her forearm. The hair was present but didn't appear to be outside of normal. "See, it's not bad. It's just more than before."

"That's not so unusual even for traditional hormonal treatments. Increased body hair, acne, even mood swings, and cramping are fairly common. Usually, they subside in a few months as your body acclimates to the drugs. Do you wish to continue treatment? All your labs came back normal again."

"Even if it doesn't go away, it's worth it to me. I mean, I can shave and wax if I want. I can control that."

"That's excellent," Dr. Gilbert exclaimed, jotting down his notes in her file. He handed her back the monthly flow chart she had been recording, looked over his notes before closing her file, clapping his hands on his knees in accomplishment. "Well, unless you have any questions or concerns, I say let's get Mandy in here to administer the last dose and let you go about your day."

"That sounds fantastic, but I did have one question if you don't mind me asking."

"Of course, what is it?"

"What made you want to do all this, of everything you could have studied?" She asked, stumbling around her words.

"Why a man would choose women's health as their field of study?" he asked, raising his eyebrows over his thick, black-framed glasses. She nodded shyly, fearing she had asked something improper. "I gained an understanding of the struggle women face from an early age because I watched my mother suffer. Sometimes she would be bedridden by the pain. I saw the embarrassment she felt when we were in town and she realized she had bled into her clothes, the tears in her eyes. I watched her put shopping bags in the seat of our car so she could make it home without staining the upholstery. I saw her cry at the kitchen table when her doctor told her there was nothing they could do to help her. I saw that was unacceptable, and I promised her, and myself, I would grow up and become a doctor and help her."

"Were you able to help her?"

"Well, nature took its course, and she was in menopause before I graduated med school, but my mission was clear by then."

"I'm glad. Your mother must be very proud of you."

"I like to think so," Dr. Gilbert's full cheeks blushed, evident even through his beard. He made his way to the door. "Mandy will be right in."

"Thank you."

After a short wait, Mandy, the nurse that had been present for every administration of the treatment arrived with her usual arsenal.

"Last dose, ladybug," she said melodically as she prepped Libby's arm with the alcohol pad, cooling her skin as it evaporated. She squeezed up a thick pinch of the soft back of her arm and Libby braced for impact. The sharp pinch was quickly followed by the burn as the thick fluid spread out under her skin. In her mind, Libby could see a substance as thick as syrup and hot as fire, burning out a path out between the fat and muscle like lava scorching the earth. "You may notice some stronger side effects, now that the full treatment is in your system. Nothing dramatic, just keep your eyes open."

"Did anyone in the other study group?" Libby asked with obvious and well founded concern.

"No, everyone is fine." Mandy rubbed the injection site, finishing with a comforting pat. "You know the drill. Wait about thirty minutes, and if you feel okay, you're good to go."

"Will I need to come back in a month?" Libby asked, rubbing the burn from her arm.

"Yes, probably for a couple of months or until Dr. Gilbert gives you the all clear." Mandy looked at the calendar and raised her eyebrows playfully. "So I should be seeing you sometime around Valentine's Day. Or will your schedule be too busy that week with all this new freedom?"

"I doubt that. I will either be working or spending another cozy night at home with the cats."

"I hear that." The nurse gathered her items and made her way to the door. "Take care, Libby. See you soon."

***

The next morning, Libby woke with the appetite of two starving women. She grabbed her go-to breakfast, a pack of cold Pop-Tarts and a cup of coffee, and sat down at the kitchen table. It wasn't the breakfast of champions, and she understood that, but it was cheap and provided a punch of sugar and caffeine to get her day moving. One day, she hoped her fortunes would improve, and she would be able to eat healthier but for now, refined sugar and empty carbs would have to do. With her growling belly subdued, at least for a bit, she moved on to her next task. She took three cans of wet cat food from the pantry and as soon as the can opener sounded, she had three meowing and excited felines twisting and rubbing against her legs.

Piper, Paige, and Phoebe, named by her mother in honor of *Charmed's* Halliwell sisters, almost made it impossible for her to walk as she tried to get to their bowls just a few feet away.

"I think you girls eat better than I do," Libby snickered as she watched each of them enjoy their breakfast, purring as they ate. She rubbed her forehead, feeling the starts of a headache, and sighed. It seemed the last dose of medication was going to give her a little grief after all, in the form of cold symptoms, but it was nothing she couldn't handle.

Hours later and halfway through her shift, Libby struggled to focus on the cash register's keys and displays through a splitting headache. She had taken ibuprofen and over the counter migraine medicine both at higher dosages than directed and it hadn't even touched the pain. It had gotten progressively worse with each passing hour. The fluorescent lights stung her eyes, leaving them blurry and watery. Her sinuses drained down the back of her throat in reaction, like she had been crying. The revving motors, electronic doorbell, and nonstop Country music radio echoed in her ears like waves crashing against cliffs. And to make matters even worse, each customer carried in their own scent. It might be too much perfume, cigarette smoke, car exhaust, body odor, or work dirt, but regardless, each smell seemed to collect, condense, and then rattle inside her skull like ball bearings.

Libby hid her face in her hands as she felt a sickly cold sweat break out on her face and the nape of her neck. She grabbed the wastebasket just in time to throw up into it and not all over herself and the floor. She heard the doorbell chime twice between heaves, quickly back to back. Thankfully the customer turned right back around and went out the door. Hopefully, she would have a moment to run to the dumpster and wash her face before they came back.

She pulled the bag from the can and tied it up, hanging onto the side of the counter as she walked around it. The shop was chilly, as it usually was during the cooler months, but her face was scalding hot. Sweat raced down her back and soaked into the waistband of her underwear. She paused, feeling the darkness encroach on her peripheral vision like a heated blanket.

I'm okay, she said to herself after a few deep breaths. Two more steps forward and she collapsed to the ground between the counter and end cap of the snack aisle.

Libby woke with a disoriented gasp, struggling to get up and make sense of the bright penlight that was shining in her eyes and the disgusting odor of ammonia that lingered under her nose.

"Don't try to get up," a strange male voice said, pushing her shoulder back down and holding her there. The light was so bright that she couldn't focus on his face. As soon as she realized she was wearing a neck brace, she felt like she was being strangled. She tried to reach for it, but her hand was pushed back down. "You're okay, Libby. You are at the ER getting checked out. Just try to follow the light with your eyes for me, okay?"

"I'm fine," she responded, following orders as instructed. The fog had finally lifted from her head, and she was able to understand what was happening to her. "I just need to sit up."

The nurse assisted her to a sitting position, still inspecting her.

"Do you remember what happened?"

"Yeah, I threw up, and when I got up to empty the trash, I must've blacked out. Been feeling like shit all day." Libby answered as he checked her vitals.

"Well, you were pretty dehydrated and your sugar bottomed out. What have you eaten today?"

"I had Pop- Tarts this morning for breakfast, a hot dog from the Gas and Grab about halfway through my shift, some chips. I haven't had much of an appetite."

"That's not very much. No wonder you hit the ground." the nurse answered. "Try to rest. The doctor will be in to check you out soon."

Midmorning of the next day, Libby was waiting outside the emergency room with her discharge papers, the frigid January wind cutting through her jeans and t-shirt. Her coat was still at the shop. It wasn't long before an aging F-150 rumbling loudly as usual pulled up beside her.

"You require a ride, milady?" Brenda asked in a faux British accent, tainted by her southern drawl. She was Libby's co-worker and closest friend. A couple of hours each day, their shifts intersected, and it was always the highlight of Libby's day. Brenda laughed hardily at herself and Libby's expression, muffling the blaring Country music on the radio for a moment.

"Thanks, Brenda. I really appreciate it."

"No problem at all. Want to grab something to eat?"

"I don't…"

"My treat."

"You don't have…"

"Sounds good to me, too. I'm starved."

After a quick detour through the drive-thru, the drive to Libby's trailer was made mostly in silence. She leaned against the passenger side window of the truck, processing the night's events as the reflection of the road's white line zipped under her cheek. She wondered if Phil would have to file a worker's comp claim and how much grief he was going to give her for having to do so. Would he find a way out of it and stick her with the bill? The glass rattled against her face from the bad muffler, and the whole truck shivered as she rolled down the gravel driveway of the trailer park.

"You're sure you're okay?" Brenda asked as she slid out of the cab, looking even shorter than usual besides the elevated truck.

"Yeah, I just need to actually sleep. You know how it is, no sleep in a hospital." Libby hoped to dismiss Brenda's concerns, knowing she had enough on her shoulders without worrying about her. "Thanks again for breakfast and for bringing me home."

"You're welcome, hun. Take tomorrow off and rest up. I'll cover for you."

"Thanks, Brenda. You're too good to me."

The short walk from the driveway to her trailer and up the small set of stairs felt like climbing a mountain, and it must have shown because Brenda made sure she was safely inside before backing out. After her mother passed away, Brenda and Frank had proven to be the only people left in Libby's life that genuinely cared for her. Everyone else had been a lot of talk, a lot of "thoughts and prayers," but not very much follow through. Out of sight, out of mind.

"Hey girls! Did you miss me?" Libby sat her purse and hospital paperwork on the counter and slowly leaned down to pet the cats joyfully circling her legs, meowing with each breath. She didn't want to move too quickly or bend over too sharply for fear of passing out again. "I bet you guys are starving."

She portioned out an extra serving in each bowl and with each of her fur- children happily eating, Libby drug herself down the narrow hallway to her bedroom and collapsed on the bed, kicking her shoes off the edge. She had never been so exhausted in her life.

***

Hours passed before Libby even rolled over to get under the blanket, longer still before she managed to wiggle out of her jeans, unfasten her bra and pull it out the sleeve of her T-shirt. As soon as she dipped beneath consciousness, her mind raced with vivid dreams.

For a moment, she was a child at her grandmother's house with her mom, before anyone was sick, before they died. She remembered the taste of Sunday supper after church. She dreamed she was sitting in her favorite restaurant, the expensive place in the next town that was reserved for only the most special occasions. She could feel the steam on her face from the medium rare steak, hot off the grill. She cut into it, and the red juices filled the shallow of her plate, but it continued until it flooded the table. She happily cut away one savory bite after another, the taste filling her mouth as the blood-tinted juices trickled to the floor.

By the time she woke again, she was ravenous. She stumbled through to the fridge and guzzled down an entire sports drink before filling the bottle up with water and drinking it just as quickly, finishing it off with a burp. As usual, her feline companions were at her feet, anxious to see if she would be having a snack they could share. Her stomach growled so hard she thought she felt it flip, or perhaps convulse. Her selection was limited, as it was still two days to payday, so she settled off with a few slices of ham from the pack of lunchmeat, tearing off pieces for the swarming trio at her ankles. She ate enough to stave off the hunger and drank some more water before going to bed, hiding her head under her blanket to block out the sun.

***

The next morning, Libby woke feeling better than she had in days. She stretched, feeling the bones in her spine and shoulders realign. Her feet hit the floor with a bounce as she headed to the bathroom. Her dark hair was in tangles, bushed up around her head like an 80's hair band groupie. She giggled as she struggled to brush through the knots until something about her reflection caught her attention. She focused on her reflection a little closer, sitting the brush down and leaning over the counter to get her face close to the mirror. Her eyes, normally a rich brown, appeared lighter. She blinked hard and looked at them again.

They were definitely lighter; a yellowish tint had lifted them to an amber tone.

"Hmph," she puffed with a shrug. "Weird, but I don't hate it."

Libby danced her way through the house, immune to the chill that had settled in the air overnight. Typically, she would wrap up in blankets with coffee on the couch as soon as she woke up, unwilling to turn up the thermostat even a degree and risk raising her electric bill to take the chill out of the air. But today she was comfortable to relax on the couch in just her T-shirt and panties, watching the girls eat their breakfast. She looked down at the cold strawberry Pop-Tart knockoff in her hand and tossed it in the trash on her way to the fridge. Lunchmeat, half of a Subway sandwich from three days ago, some condiments, pickles, and a few slices of cheese was just about all she had left. Her high sugar, simple carb breakfast wasn't going to cut it today. Hell, even the wet cat food smelled better than what she had to eat. She wanted something warm, meaty. Something cooked.

Fifteen minutes later, Libby sat at the table with an entire family sized Salisbury steak freezer entree. No veggies, no bread, just a fork and the processed, sodium rich goodness of bargain priced mystery meat and gravy. She chopped up one patty and divided it up between her four-legged roommates. She smiled as the food warmed her belly. She picked up her phone, noticing that it was already noon, and dialed.

"Gas and Grab, this is Brenda."

"Hey boo, it's Libby. Can you let Phil know I'm taking another day? Actually, let him know I am taking the rest of the week."

"Are you feeling okay? Do you need something?"

"No, actually I'm feelin' a lot better, but I think I need a few days to get my strength up. All I want to do is eat and sleep."

"Okay... I'll let him know. Are you sure you don't want to tell him yourself?"

Nah, I don't feel like hearing him bitch. Oh, and tell Frank thanks for bringing my car home, and thank you too. I'm sorry I didn't hear the phone when you called."

Of course, hun. It was no trouble." Brenda replied, her concern evident in her voice. "Take care of yourself, okay? Let me know if you need anything."

"I will, and thanks. Bye!"

Libby turned the ringer off her phone an laid it screen down on the table and returned to her meal without a care in the world. When she finished, she sat the cardboard tray of leftover gravy on the ground for the cats, licking the residual taste from her lips. "I need to go to the store."

***

One week later

Libby showed up for her shift fifteen minutes late, her first day back since she collapsed. Despite the cold, she was only wearing a thin, off the shoulder sweater, leggings, and boots. It was a far departure from her usual jeans and hoodie.

"I was startin' to get worried about you," she said, sliding out from behind the counter as soon as she entered. She already had her coat on and purse on her shoulder, impatiently waiting. Libby realized that Brenda would be cutting it close to getting home in time to get the kids off the bus.

"I'm sorry, stupid cats. Phoebe decided to hide, and I spent half the morning trying to find her. She has stuffed herself in the top of my bedroom closet and will not come down. She's never even got up there before. I don't know what her problem is." She explained while putting her sunglasses down in her backpack.

"Cold weather makes them feisty, I think," Brenda said over the electronic chime as she stood in the doorway, purposely letting the chilly air in to watch Libby's reaction. She watched her brush her hair back, which had been stuck to her cheeks with sweat, and fanned her flushed face. It appeared she had lost some weight, and not in the way a person wilts after an illness or injury. She looked more muscular, toned, and even her hair looked healthier than it had a week ago. She wanted to ask her a hundred questions about her peculiar behavior but didn't have the time. "Keep your eye on her and make sure she's eating, going potty, all that. See ya tomorrow."

"See ya," Libby answered with the same smile she always had for her, but there was always a shadow behind it, a lingering sadness that had followed her since her mother was given her diagnosis. Today she seemed happy, genuinely so. And while Brenda was pleased to see an upturn in her mood, she couldn't help but wonder why.

The busiest time of the day at Gas and Grab was evening rush hour when everyone was trying to get back into town to their families. Libby often wondered why people with good jobs didn't just move away. Why did they choose to stay in their little pothole and lose a couple of hours of their day commuting every day? She knew without a doubt that if the opportunity presented itself, she would run away and never come back. With her mother gone, she had nothing to tie her to that place, aside from Brenda and memories.

Phil waited until the traffic slacked before coming to the front of the store. Libby knew what was coming as soon as she saw him, pretending to search for out of stock items on the handful of aisles.

"How ya feeling, Libby?" he asked, propping up on the counter by the register.

"A lot better, thank you," she answered as shortly, yet politely as possible.

"So, what was it, just more *female* problems?"

"Just?" Libby could feel the vein in the side of her neck start to throb as a hot flash of sweat misted the back of her neck. "What exactly do you mean by *just*?"

"Just that it wasn't nothing serious, you know. Wasn't like you had a stroke or something. Don't understand why you would need to miss a whole week of work *just* for that."

Libby locked eyes with Phil over the counter, grinding her teeth so loud that he could hear it but she didn't seem to notice.

"Well for your information, Phil, it wasn't *just* that. It wasn't *just* anything. It was a lot of things." She watched him step backward, looking cautiously at her grip on the side of the counter like he was afraid she was preparing to leap over it. "But I'm better now."

"Well… that good and all, but I am going to have to ask you not to wear those colored contacts back to work." He stated flatly, his courage seeming restored after he knew he was greater than arm's length from her. "Ethel Johnson from the Senior Center called and complained. She said they bothered her and she didn't think they were appropriate for someone working with the public."

Libby leaned deep over the counter, nearly climbing on top of it. Her scoop neck sweater fell low on her bosom as she closed the gap between them again. Phil swallowed hard, confused but not inclined to move.

"Do they look fake, Phil?" She said looking up at him, biting her bottom lip. She pulled it between her teeth slowly as she waited for him to answer.

"What happened to you?"

"Dr. Gilbert fixed my *female* problems. The eyes were an unexpected side effect." She answered, just barely louder than a whisper. "So tell Ethel to either mind her own damn business or just buy her Virginia Slims on Brenda's shift."

The rest of Libby's night crawled at a snail's pace. Phil went home with little more than a glance her way. The handful of customers that trickled in from eight o'clock until just before midnight was standard fare, a handful of travelers passing through to bigger and better places and a few usual locals. The radio behind the counter played Brenda's station but had switched gears at ten o'clock to taking listener requests. The sincere voices of love and loss and steel guitars of the country music station had been temporarily interrupted with a quick weather update from the local news channel. Clear but cold for the next seven days, perfect weather for the upcoming full moon everyone was going on about. January 31, 2018, was supposed to be a special one, only occurring every one hundred years or so, a super blue blood moon. It was supposed to look bigger than normal, and some viewers might see the hint of a ruddy color due to some astronomical reasons that Libby didn't quite understand.

Hopefully, she would remember to look for it on her way home from work that night if she was working, if not, oh well. Better luck next time.

It had been a pretty good night, considering she was in the most miserable place she could imagine, but it would be over soon. It was the ache in her lower back and in the pit of her belly that had her concerned. She had tried to ignore it, blame it on nerves from her confrontation with Phil, blame it on being her feet so much after being off work a week, but she knew that pain. She knew what it meant, and looking at the calendar only confirmed her fears. It was the week of her period, and by the way she felt, it was gearing up to be hellish.

She felt the tingling, static-like crackling of anxiety as it fried the ends of her nerves, out from her chest, down her arms, and exiting her fingertips. Her breath shortened as her lungs tightened. Dr. Gilbert said he could fix her, but now it's coming back. He said it should all be over, that the last dose would keep all this away until *she* was ready for it to come back. Tears began to flow, despite being at work, regardless of if she wanted them to come. A few gasps later and she was in full-blown breakdown, gasping and gagging against the tears and drainage down her throat. She looked at the clock, only ten minutes and she could close. She grabbed a couple of paper towels and hid her face in her hands, praying not to hear the doorbell.

Her symptoms seemed to intensify with her nerves, sending her stomach into rolling cramps. What if she had already started bleeding? Was it only menstrual pain or had she also come down with some sort of stomach bug? She slid off the barstool and was relieved the cushion wasn't stained, but now she wasn't sure if she could wait until she got home to go to the bathroom. She decided to lock the doors and turn off the lights five minutes early and rushed to the restroom.

There was nothing, not even pink tint on the toilet paper. She held out in the stuffy, moldy smelling single seat facility as long as she could, giving her gut ample time to execute an attack but she was unable even to pass gas. Confused, and still bent in half with pain, Libby finished closing up the shop and limped to her car. There was no way she was going to disturb Frank and Brenda, not with them both having to get up so early. She would make it if she had to drive ten miles an hour all the way home, which was only a couple miles away.

Finally making it home, Libby dropped her bag as she nearly fell into the trailer. The cats took off in a scurry, terrified by the racket. She collapsed onto the couch, wadded up in a ball, and prepared to ride out whatever was happening to her. Hopefully, she would have some relief by morning.

Hours passed in a delirium of cold sweats and cramps, waking her every time she dozed off. When she was able to sleep, her mind conjured vivid dreams, nightmares fueled by her raging body. Violent images that defined reason, ripping, biting, and tearing flesh, bones snapping, blood flowing like water. It was as though she was in the middle of the cruelest of slaughterhouses, where no respect for life or suffering was to be found. Each time she woke, she would be sick at her stomach from it, choked by it, but every time her eyes closed it was only another chapter of the same story. She could hear animals crying out in pain, yet she was unable to tell what kind. Human voices were screaming, cursing, praying, all while being consumed by shadow, drowning in blood.

Daylight brought a temporary respite from the dreadful dreams, but no relief. A headache worse than any migraine she had experienced threatened to crush her skull. She drug herself to the window and closed the curtains tighter, desperate to block out the sun. The time of day and the fact that she was supposed to be at work in three hours were the farthest things from her mind. She swallowed down a few ibuprofen pills with a drink of water and returned to the couch, hiding her face with a cushion.

Libby knew when the short winter day had ended and night began again because with the dark came the nightmares. The images were clearer, and the situations were recognizable now instead of yesterday's blur of carnage. She understood what she was seeing, what her mind visualized she was doing. She was a murderer, but more than that. She was a destroyer of life, of any living thing with breath and blood. It was like all her frustrations, all her pain, and all the circumstances beyond her control that had caused her to suffer had come together, and she was lashing out at anyone or anything in her path. Not a person, but a force of nature, a cutting wind that sheared flesh from bone. She was a plague from biblical Egypt. She was the kernel of truth in every superstition. She was no grim reaper, not a skeletal man in heavy robes but the mother of death, Kali in all her terrible beauty. She reveled in her wrath.

***

Wednesday
January 31, 2018

Despite her mind being so restless, Libby awoke rested and in better spirits. The cramps and stomach ache had lessened, and her headache was all but gone, so it seemed the worst of whatever she had experienced had passed. Some food and about half a gallon of water should hit the dehydrated and starved spot and set her straight. She scrambled up three whole eggs and threw a thick piece of steak on the hot skillet just long enough to sear the outside. Her stomach growled loudly as the delicious smell filled the kitchen. Surprisingly, her fur babies were nowhere to be found. She hoped whatever ailment that had caused Phoebe to act so strangely had not been spread to Piper and Paige.

The flavorful steak seemed to feed her soul, restoring her strength and spirit. She mixed her scrambled eggs in the blood laced juices that had leaked from the meat, enhancing their taste with the beef grease. Work was going to be a breeze tonight. She finished her meal with a smile.

A knock on her door startled her while she was rinsing off her plate, causing it to slip out her hand and crash against the dirty dishes that were waiting to be washed. It didn't appear that anything broke, so she wiped her hands on the kitchen towel and rushed to greet her unexpected guest.

"Brenda! Hey, come on in." Libby lit up when she saw her friend but immediately could sense that something was off. It was impossible for Brenda to hide when something was bothering her. She kept her hand to her nose like she was afraid it was going to drip. "Did you have to go home sick?"

"No, I'm fine." She moved her hand away from her face, knowing that Libby had noticed her. "I didn't leave early. It's almost five. I waited for Frank to get home and came over to check on you. Libby, where have you been?"

"What do you mean? I missed a day, but I was coming back in this evening. I didn't know it was so late. I need to call Phil."

"No, you don't, hun. He told me to tell you, if I talked to you, that you were fired. You missed three days without calling in. He let you go."

"No way! I was supposed to be off Sunday. What is today?"

"It's Wednesday, the last day of January. He replaced you today. Trish, Jim and Betty's daughter." Brenda picked at the dry skin around her cuticle. "I tried to call you."

"Wednesday?"

"Yeah… you were out a week from where you passed out, came back one day and worked Saturday, then you've been out ever since."

"That doesn't seem right…" Libby rubbed her head, pulling her hair away from her face and felt that it was noticeably oily.

Brenda sighed deep, worry written on the lines across her forehead.

"Libby, I'm gonna ask you this because I love you and because I'll help you. Are you on drugs?"

"Drugs? No! What the hell, Brenda? Drugs, really?" She couldn't believe that Brenda would even suggest such a thing.

"Are you hurt? Did somebody hurt you?"

"No, I've been sick, like really sick, but I'm feeling a lot better today. I actually feel really good."

"Maybe you should go look at yourself in the mirror, hun."

Libby walked to the bathroom with Brenda following close behind. She turned the light on for the first time in days and looked at herself. Her hair was dirty, stringy in her eyes, only partially covering the dark circles that nearly touched her sharply defined cheekbones. Her new eye color had intensified from brownish amber to a piercing tawny yellow. All around her mouth was stained by everything she had eaten for the last three days as if she were a baby. She hastily wiped her mouth, ashamed of her appearance, and became aware of her stained hands and bruises that covered her arms, mottling her skin in various shades of purple and green, striped with scratches and scrapes.

"What's happening to me?" She looked at her friend with tears in her eyes. She looked down at herself, only just noticing that she was wearing an oversized t-shirt and panties. She had changed into the extra large shirt when she came home from work, and it fit as it should, but now it hung off from her and was at least two sizes too big. She lifted it with trembling hands, her embarrassment overwhelmed by fear of what she would discover. She had shrunk, leaner and toned, muscle tone and bones now visible where she had been soft and full figured. Bruises covered her torso and even down her legs.

She sat down on the edge of the tub, her head in her hands. She could feel energy crawling under her skin, just like when static electricity would lift the fine hairs on her arms, but on the inside. Something had happened to her, something had changed, and even though she didn't understand it, she knew there was no turning back, no slowing down. Whatever had changed, whatever had begun in her would finish tonight. She couldn't mentally process it, but she could feel it, like her soul's intuition was explaining it to her. Instinct.

"Libby... honey, where are the cats?" Brenda's voice broke. "There's stains on the carpet, and it smells really bad in here, hun. Do you know what happened?"

Her mind raced through her memories of the last three days, in and out of consciousness like her brain was cooking from a fever. She remembered death, blood, and the sound of breaking bones. She remembered hunger, destruction, and satiation. She shut down. Her mind overloaded and rejected her memories as reality.

"Oh god, Brenda what did I do?" Libby sank into despair. She could barely speak as she gasped for air, panic seizing her. "Did I hurt my girls?"

"I don't know, honey, but none of this is your fault. It's that *treatment* you took." She pulled Libby into her arms, feeling the vertebra sticking out of her hunched back. "This is all *my* fault. I'm so sorry, Libby. I wish

I'd never give you that newspaper article. Maybe you should call Dr. Gilbert? Maybe he can help you. Didn't you say there was an antidote?"

Libby looked up from her crying, locking eyes with Brenda. The tears had stopped.

"He *did* cure me. I feel amazing. I can't explain just how good I feel right now. I told doctor after doctor what I was going through and it was like they didn't even hear me. I was just a weak woman. And not just that, I mean, I've been nothing my whole life, a nobody. Everyone just looked at me like I was trailer park trash, wasting my life working a dead end job. You and Frank are the only people on this earth that treat me like a person. Hell, my own body didn't even like me. But now it's different... now I'm *something*." Libby stood up and took Brenda's hands in hers, squeezing them tightly. She could feel the little bones beneath the surface of her skin, could feel how easy it would be to crush them into splinters. She lifted them to her lips and kissed them before releasing her. "I can't go back to that, to being in pain all the time and bleeding all over myself like some dying animal, to being ignored by doctors, by Phil, my family. I got nothing to go back to, but the future just got a whole lot more interesting."

"You don't want this, Libby. This isn't you."

"I didn't, but now I think I do. I love you, Brenda, but I think you should go home. It's getting late, and the blood moon is tonight. I don't think you should be here when it comes up."

***

When Libby knew Brenda was safely out of harm's way, she gave herself to the struggle that was taking place beneath her own skin. After so much self-hate, after so many attempts at medicating herself into submission, after so much self-help and home remedies, she finally just let go. She stopped worrying about it all and let the frustration and helplessness fall beneath the surface and let the darker side of her nature that was clawing at her rise.

She could feel every nerve ending, every muscle activating and releasing. She dropped to the floor, as the electrical signals were out of synch and unfamiliar. The uninformed eye would have thought that she was in the midst of an epileptic seizure, but it was far from the case. Libby was transforming, more like mutating, as the change was not fixed, but fluid. Much the way water could come to a boil, cool, and then be frozen, Libby was in the first stages of a transition that would follow the lunar cycle.

Her mind became flooded with what she had been made to endure, no offerings of sympathy, no consultations, no hope. Everyone but Brenda had thought she was exaggerating the grief her body had put her through. For months, she had experienced cramps that were more like labor pains, bleeding more days a month than not, exhaustion, chapped skin, and mood swings that had brought her to her knees and question herself. So long as she was still in her child bearing years, the medical field was fine with saying she would have to keep her baby making parts and deal with her issues however she could.

She might want kids one day. She might *want* to provide for a child when she was barely able to provide for herself. But if she did find herself pregnant, which would be difficult without a boyfriend anywhere on the horizon, god forbid she should ask for financial assistance from the government, because then she really would be living up to the southern white trash stereotype. She should have gone to college. She should have worked harder. She should have had insurance. She should have made better choices, so long as it was not considering an abortion. Libby screamed, pulling two handfuls of hair as she gritted her teeth. She was trapped in a life that she didn't want and surrounded by people who looked down at her, judged her. Not anymore. Not one day longer. She would get out. Then she remembered what Brenda told her.

Phil... that son of a bitch. She didn't even have a job anymore, thanks to him. She thought about all the times she had kissed his ass to keep that terrible job because it was all she could find in her shitty town. Now, what was she supposed to do? She was going to freeze to death in her run down trailer when the electricity was cut off. Even if she somehow found another job, how could she drive to it with an empty gas tank? She thought about his gutless last action toward her, sending Brenda to tell her she was fired instead of being man enough to tell her himself. Typical Phil. She felt her blood boil, her pulse knocking on the side of her head. He wasn't getting off that easy. Not today. Not again. She stood up on shaky legs and stumbled down the hallway. He was going to pay but first, she needed to put on some pants.

As the sky grew darker, the tingling static beneath Libby's skin intensified. She had chosen to walk to Phil's house, which wasn't far in a town as small as theirs. The spasms that were attacking her body were just too unpredictable to risk driving. But the one good thing about living in a small town on a cold January night was that after eight o' clock, the streets and roads were basically empty. To anyone passing, she just looked like any other junkie that might be out roaming the streets, hopped up on their mom's pain pills, looking for their next fix.

She knew what she needed and it sure as hell wasn't a drug. It was the pound of flesh Phil owed her, straight off his fat ass. She looked at the moon, covered by just a few lingering clouds. She didn't understand just yet what the moon meant to her now, but it had suddenly become the most beautiful thing in her life. Just standing in its shrouded light was to be touched by the divine, her new mother's cool embrace. She whispered to her on the gentle breeze. *Make haste, daughter. Your time is nearly here.*

Libby walked straight up to Phil's door, banging on it with the side of her fist. The street was quiet, no different than any other in town, but neighbors tended to mind their own business more often than not and never want to get involved in other people's issues. She waited a few seconds, a nervous jitter in her leg, and beat on the door even louder. She could hear the glass in the little windows at the top rattling in their casing.

"Libby, what the hell do you want?" He shouted as he flung the door open. She lunged at him with a growl and pushed him back through the door, slamming it behind them.

"What the hell do you *think* I want, Phil? I felt like we needed to talk in person since you had sent Brenda to do your dirty work. No surprise there. It's not like you can do anything for yourself. Brenda runs the store for you."

"Libby, what is wrong with you? Where are your shoes? Are you on something?"

"No Phil, I'm not fucking on something! Why is everyone asking me that? I'm just tired of the bullshit. You know what I mean?"

"Libby, you left me no choice. You didn't come to work for three days, no call no show. What was I supposed to do?" Phil was flabbergasted. Not in the three years that she had worked for him has he ever seen anything close to how she was acting.

"Maybe have some common decency, some understanding. But I guess that was too much to ask, out of you, out of anyone."

"Libby, if you had brought me a doctor's note, or given me something to go on, things might have been different, but you got undependable."

"Like that would have made a difference. You never believed me. I could hear it in your voice, but for your information, I *did* go to the doctor. Dr. Gilbert fixed me, Phil. Can't you see I've changed?"

"I don't know if I would call this fixed, Libby. I think you might need to talk to this Dr. Gilbert because you sure ain't acting like yourself."

"Wow... ya think? Thank you, Phil, for your astute observation." Libby screamed, her voice thick with sarcasm as she backed him away from the door and further into the living room, away from the windows. "Maybe I should have took you to the pussy doctor with me years ago? You would have solved all my problems, and maybe I wouldn't have eaten my cats!"

"You need to go, right now, or I'm calling the cops," Phil demanded, puffing up his chest, but not far enough to pass his bloated belly. Libby rubbed her face, his voice like sandpaper on her raw nerves. She grimaced, her lips curling back away from her lips. She dropped to her knees, on all fours, and arched her spine. She rotated her neck and heard it pop, cracking as the vertebrae had done. The change was happening in her spine first, shooting into her hips. "Libby, are you okay?"

She looked up to him, her yellow eyes glaring from behind her stringy hair, a devilish, crooked smile on her face. As in most things, the first attempt was always the most difficult, and painful. With time and practice, her joints would slip easier, tendons would limber, and muscles would relax through their paces, but this was not a night for gentleness. The overwhelming strength of the super blue blood moon meant that the changes were accelerated. What might have taken her body hours to do would be accomplished in moments thanks to a once in a lifetime lunar event in her part of the world. There would be other full moons, other blood moons, other dueling blue moons, but she would always remember her first time. Her first transformation. Her first kill.

The pain was almost cathartic, escaping with each spasm that shook her body, each cracking joint, each cramping muscle struggling to change position. It wasn't a beautiful transformation, no caterpillar turning into a butterfly. Full transition into a beautiful wolf would come with time and experience. This was a an in-between stage, a baby step, cutting her teeth. It was the beginning of her new life.

Libby stood with new strength, fear and weakness shed with her ripped clothes. Her new muscular body was covered in a dark, thick hair but she stood on her own two feet, still walking like a woman. The sleek form would remain, attractive and toned, but the hair would fall away at the setting moon. It would help her lure and secure her prey should she need to hunt between full moons. Her jaw clenched under the new muscle structure that supported it, sharp teeth hidden behind a beguiling smile. She licked her lips when she looked at Phil, not out of arousal but because he smelled like food, and she was starving.

Phil reacted like any prey animal, running scared. Libby reacted like any predator, chasing and overtaking him. Sliding across the floor on his stomach, she pinned him to the ground, her weight pushing into his back, and bit into the side of his neck. Electricity rushed through her body as hot blood and meat went down her throat. Her jaw shifted, skin stretched to allow her mouth to open wider. In time, she would have a lovely muzzle, perfect for digging into her kill, but she would have to make do with her more or less human body tonight. Another mouthful of his throat took the fight out of him, his blood trickling over her collarbones and between her breasts. She rubbed the sticky hotness into her skin, feeling it beneath the coarse hair the covered her body. It was like she was absorbing his essence, feeding off him inside and out. Primal. Ancient. Evolution.

She rolled him over and watched the flicker of life go out from behind his eyes. He was just a piece of meat now, and she wasn't used to wasting food.

***

Two months later

The electronic doorbell chimed flat and hopeless at the Gas and Grab. Brenda looked up from her clipboard with a smile, as usual.

"How can I help you?" her congenial manner hid the fact that she knew exactly who this patron was and that she already knew exactly what he wanted. She had been waiting for him to show up. He wasn't getting anything.

"I'm looking for an employee, Elizabeth Hines. Do you know when she will be in?"

"And who are you?" She wasn't going to make it easy for him.

"I'm her doctor, Charles Gilbert. She participated in a study a few months ago, and we would like to talk to her about her *experiences* since then."

"Don't you doctors have some kind of HIPPA confidentiality thing?"

Gilbert cleared his throat. "We um, yes, well. Under normal circumstances... we... well..."

"She ain't here."

"Do you know when she will be?"

"She ain't gonna be. She don't work here no more."

"Well... in that case, do you know where she lives? Maybe we can find her there?"

"That HIPPA thing doesn't mean much to you, does it? Is it because you made her a lab rat or are you just a rebel?"

"We have reason to believe Elizabeth might be in danger…"

"Well, you are about two months too late, Dr. Frankenstein. She's gone."

"Do you know where she went?"

"Last time I saw Elizabeth, she was getting in a truck with a long haul driver headed out of state. Your guess is as good as mine. I think she's hookin'." Brenda came up with the most elaborate lie she could imagine, whatever it took to throw him off Libby's trail.

"Hooking?"

"You ain't very smart to be a doctor, are you? Is that why you test on people, can't be a real doctor?" Brenda was done with him. He had transformed her friend into a monster, preyed on her weakness, turned a lamb into a lion. He deserved anything she could come up with.

"Oh… well, if you should see Elizabeth, please let her know we would like to talk to her."

"Well if I see *Libby*, I'll be sure to let her know."

***

Almost two months to the day since her first steps into transformation, Libby looked up at the beautiful full moon with new, lupine eyes. Her acclimation into her new life hadn't been easy, but it had been worth it. Her ochre yellow eyes beautifully accentuated her lush, dark coat, highlighted by silver around her muzzle, around her shoulders and chest, and near her paws. She thought it strange since she had not yet gotten any gray hair in her human form, but it was a small matter. Such things were of no consequence to her now.

She knew Dr. Gilbert had been snooping around the Gas and Grab. She could smell his cologne there hours after he had left but she wasn't concerned. Brenda sure as hell wasn't going to give him any information. Her friend blamed him for the way she was now. It grieved her because she couldn't understand, and probably never would. Libby didn't fault him. In fact, if she could speak to him without fear of being captured and taken to some secret lab, she would thank him for what he had done for her. But for now, she would keep her distance. She had more important matters at hand.

The nights were getting shorter and warmer, but considering she was now a mountain woman, she didn't mind the trade-off. The isolation had been one of the very things that she had hated about living in her tiny, southern town, but now it was something that she loved. The untouched parts mountain forests offered protection and nourishment. She could smell a human coming at a mile away, even when she wasn't a wolf, so steering clear of loggers and hunters was easy enough. Nobody ventured to the places she liked to roam and hunting humans for food was not something that interested her. Their meat was too salty and fatty, Phil's last lesson.

She walked into a small clearing, the branches separating just far enough in the breeze for her to see the brightly shining full moon, rustling her coat like waves of swaying tall grass. She inhaled deeply, smelling all the spicy, delicious scents of the forest, and released a long, steady howl. Tonight was the first full moon that the wave three participants would be experiencing. And even though she hadn't yet met any other women like her from the first two groups, and wasn't sure if there would be anyone else like her, if they were there she wanted them to know they were not alone.

ABOUT THE AUTHOR

Faith Marlow is a dark fantasy/ paranormal/ horror author with Vamptasy Publishing, an imprint of CHBB. Her stories stir emotions and explore the thin veil between human and the inhuman. Her books are dark yet inviting, and seek to deliver chills with a sense of class, and sometimes a bit of heat. With each story, Faith hopes to build exposure for fellow women authors and artists who create horror. Faith is a returning contributor to the Women of Horror anthologies. Her short story *Hair* is available in *Beautiful Nightmares*. She also has several books available on Amazon, namely the *Being Mrs. Dracula* series.

Links:
https://www.amazon.com/default/e/B00GOJ8X14
https://faithmarlow.wordpress.com/
www.facebook.com/authorfaithmarlow
https://www.instagram.com/faithmarlow/

ELEGANT ASSASSIN

BY SL PERRINE

A BLACK VELVET CURTAIN ROSE FROM the stage as the organ began to play hard and heavy. Every note vibrated in my chest while my pulse quickened with anticipation. The seat felt too far back, and I caught myself moving forward to the edge as the first dancer moved to the center of the stage. A tutu adorned with feathers, half black and half of it white, showing off silver and black sequence. The dancer's hair twisted into a neat bun at the nape of her neck where her headpiece was attached. The black and white feathers sparkled under the stage lights as she spun around on the tips of her toes.

Another dancer, a man came barreling out from backstage to the rhythm of the organ playing madly from somewhere unseen. He landed hard around the swan, her facial expression shown disbelief at the language the man's body was exhuming with the help of the music and the thud of his ballet shoes against the hardwood. I could see the sweat building along the line of his blonde hair, and the fabric of his leotard darkened at the apex of his chest, making the tan fabric turn to brown. Though, I was sure it was meant to look as if he were topless. I doubt anyone else cared much about the costumes as I did. They were caught up in the movements of the legs and feet. The gliding of the arms and hands as they moved swiftly across the stage.

Just as the music began to slow and quiet the man took the woman in his arms. The swan was about to change into a beautiful princess if it weren't for the blood-curdling scream from somewhere in the audience.

Red droplets fell from above landing on the man's shoulder and splattering the white of the swan in crimson. From their stunned faces, I knew the audience could tell it wasn't a part of the show. While everyone in the theater yelled and gaped at the couple on stage, I lifted the skirt of my dress, making sure not to increase the length of the slit in the side, and jumped up onto the rail of the box I sat in.

The dark purple blended well with the black curtain. So, when my dagger plunged into the fabric, and I slid down to the ground level, stage right, nobody even noticed. They were too busy pointing at what I couldn't see from my seat so high up. A woman's body hung from the catwalk by three ropes; one around her middle, one around her neck, and the last around her ankles leaving her body prone in the air. Her throat was cut, and the blood started to pour at a faster rate as the ropes moved to allow for her to turn face-down.

I stood watching the body move while using the tip of my blade to pick a popcorn kernel from my tooth.

"You going to just stand and stare, or are we doing something about this?"

"Just watch."

The ropes continued to move. Though the body was rocking side to side, still facing down. The swan and her prince were tucked away behind the curtain where the audience couldn't see them, but I could. The swan, Madame Céline had her face buried in Mr. Randal's shoulder. The one lacking blood droplets that smeared as he inspected the substance. While Mr. Randal stood watching the body swing overhead. The look on his face was fascination and disgust, but I could tell he couldn't tear his gaze away.

"What are we watching?"

My companion had no idea how it was I did what I did. He was the hurry up and go type, as I was a hurry up and wait kinda, person. Lifting the fabric, I slide my hand and dagger along my thigh until the tip was at the opening of the hip holster I wore. My companions' eyes following my slow movements while I kept a trained eye on my surroundings. It's strange how easily he can be conned into giving me a moment of silence. Of course, once the fabric fell back into place, he asked me once more.

"We going to leave her there?"

"I'm not the cleaning crew. It's not my concern if someone else had a score to settle. I'm here for that one. Keep your eyes on the target. Forget the corpse."

Three steps backward and Mr. Randal's eyes still hadn't left the woman in the air. The blood slowed before I tucked behind the canopy of the curtain, then slipped backstage where the usual commotion would be during a show. The theater was pretty much empty, by the time I reached stage left.

A tall round man barreled across the stage to where his stars were still huddled. His voice carrying throughout the large room.

"Céline, please. You must leave. The police are on their way." He took her from Mr. Randal and began walking her to the stairs on the side of the stage.

William Randal didn't so much as move. When he thought nobody was looking, I noticed the quick glimpse of a smile cross his lips.

"William, please. We mustn't linger. There will be questions." The fat man said as he and Céline descended the stairs and began the trek up the long aisle.

Before Mr. Randal could move, I was right behind him. I'd found a bread knife amongst the food laid out for the cast and crew. It slid easily against his skin. Like hot metal against a stick of butter. I didn't need to make it a long cut. One quick slice just below his Adam's apple did the trick. The blood didn't squirt out like in the movies. They always made it seem so much more dramatic. The knife was coated, but there was only a small trickle, to begin with. Mr. Randal flung his hands to his throat, but they wrapped around my forearm. I shoved the knife in his back for good measure. Not only was he a job, I never liked the man.

"Alpha." My companion scolded. I swear he only came along to keep me in line. It wasn't every day I got a job offer in my hometown, but I still had rules. Rules I followed and rules I created.

Mr. Randal. I knew him as well as Céline probably did. Though that was many years ago. Rule one was, never call a mark by the first name. You don't name your food. Rule two, never admit they are people. It'll just make killing them even harder.

"All good Charlie. Always good."

Never make things personal, but after the killing blow, it's okay to stab someone in the back, which was rule number three.

The doors at the end of the aisle opened. "Will," Céline's voice called. The shock seemed to be a thing of the past as she called for her co-star.

"Now, now. If he insists on gawking, then he can answer the damn questions himself." The pudgy man shoved his star out into the lobby of the theater.

I lowered Mr. Randal to the floor. His eyes rolled back in his head, but not in death. He wanted a look at his killer. Shock and an overwhelming need to scream, or maybe laugh shown on his eyes. Blood flowed faster now that he'd opened the small wound a bit more. It flowed up his throat, and he started to cough on it.

Momentarily, I failed rule number three once Charlie turned his back on me. I let the dying Mr. Randal see the smug look on my face as he tried to whisper my name.

I snapped back, Charlie turned back to me, his wrist up towards him. "Two minutes left. Time to fly."

"Puns are not your strong suit. We've been over this." My fingers looked for a pulse. Once we were both satisfied the man was dead, I snapped a picture of him on my phone and sent an encrypted e-mail message. By the time we cleared the building, our money was wired.

Another successful job completed, and payment received.

"That was risky. Maybe we should steer clear of home from now on."

I dropped the blonde wig in a trash can and pulled the seam of the purple garment free of my body. The slit I avoided earlier came clean apart. The dress landed in a dumpster three blocks away. Gloves, one at a time were dropped in an alley and then a sewer gate.

"Nonsense. It's great to be home again."

Charlie tossed a black vinyl bag at me from his back while I pulled my leggings down to my ankles, adjusted the tank top I wore and then tossed my shoes in the bag. I traded the silver heals for my black and white tennis shoes and threw on a green hooded sweatshirt.

"Why do you toss everything else, but keep the shoes?"

"What? They're Jimmy Choo's. You don't toss Jimmy Choo shoes. That would be a crime against nature."

"And what you just did wasn't a crime?"

"Mr. Randal's untimely demise was a public service. My entire graduating class will be over the moon when the news breaks in the morning. Trust me."

"We got paid for that job."

"How else would I be able to afford Jimmy Choo's?"

As always, we parted ways in the middle of the busiest intersection. Making sure to be seen in public once we were that far from the theater. I would go to one hotel, and Charlie to another. We'd both slip silently into sleep and wake, only to live the next day on repeat. The same job, different mark, and new exotic location. Or at least I hoped.

***

I heard what sounded like water running as I woke. My eyes not wanting to open even as I felt the suns rays against my closed lids.

"Evangeline!" The shrill voice of my step-mother broke through the serene quiet of my dream. It was the same as every other night. Someone

I knew, either from my life or from television was met with an early death at my hands. Although, it wasn't entirely me. I was older, I think. Much more sophisticated. And never the one being bullied. I was the one in charge. My sidekick, Charlie was the crush I'd had since first grade, Jason Randal. His bigot of a brother, William was my least favorite person. Well, after my step-mother, of course.

William spent the entire day before at school trying to get me to go behind the bleachers with him. When Jason heard him say it after the last bell rang, he punched his brother. I wouldn't doubt if he had a black eye today.

"Evangeline. It is time to get up. You have laundry and dishes before you leave for school. I'm going to work. I'll be home at eight. Make sure dinner is made this time." She slammed her fist against my door on her way through the small apartment. The front door opened and shut, and I breathed a sigh of relief.

There were only two things in life that scared the shit out of me. One was when I watched my father die. Cancer took him sooner than we had ever thought. Actually, the doctors said he'd improved. They still don't know what made his heart fail.

The second was being in the same room with Lydia. She was a monster alright. I just didn't have any proof of it. I wished one of my dreams would send me on assignment to get rid of her. At least I have the satisfaction of taking her out.

While I did the dishes, I listened to the news Lydia left on in the Livingroom. Some local boy was found dead behind the movie theater. One less body in the hell they call school. Not that I didn't empathize, but it was probably one of my usual bullies. I didn't care much for the kids at school, and none of them cared for me. Except for Jason.

The walk to school was harder than usual. Jason never showed up to walk with me. He was my best friend through high school, though I've had to watch him date every other nitwit in our class, I still wanted to be more than just his buddy.

When the first bell rang, our teacher held up her hands to quiet the room. She took attendance and then the loudspeaker came on. Being she was in a rush this morning, she must have known that would happen.

"As rumors fill the halls today, I would like to remind you we will keep you updated to this morning's activity as we get more information. Currently, the police are talking to the parents of the boy found, and we will get confirmation before the day is out. Anyone needing to stay after school today to speak to a counselor may do so, a sign-up sheet will be in the main office. That is all."

Of course, he was talking about the dead kid. Not that I would sign up, but I bet half the kids in the graduating class would since it would give them three days of bereavement. We were more than three-quarters of the way through our last year of high school. I just wanted to get it over with. Graduation day meant I would be eighteen and able to move away. I wasn't sure where, but anywhere without Lydia looked good.

The day carried on about the same. Rumors still flooded the halls. I paid no attention to any of it. Someone noticed Jason was missing from school and asked if I'd heard from him. I didn't know they knew we were friends, let alone knew of my existence.

"Yes, I spoke to him last night after work. He was fine."

Well, you know they say the dead guy was killed at four in the morning so it could have been him. Know anyone else missing today?"

"His brother's not in today either. Could be a coincidence." I said shooting down any possibility that Jason was gone from this world. Even as I stood I knew deep inside it was a possibility. He didn't show up to take me to school. His eye sparkled when we spoke, last. I was going to tell him then, that I wanted to date him but lost my nerve. He couldn't be dead. Not him.

My chest started to tighten. The knot I'd sometimes get in my breastbone started to throb. The room began to spin. My mind kept racing over everything we'd talked about. Everything we'd done together. Why did I never tell him how I felt?

"May I have your attention." The PA announced just before the last bell to let everyone go home for the day. "I have the identity of the classmate that was found dead this morning. While I know it will be hard for you to deal with, please understand the family needs time to grieve in peace. William Randal will be terribly missed on and off the field. Again, please see the counselors staying after today if you need to speak with anyone."

Just like that, the PA cut out, and the room erupted in chatter. Some were crying real tears since he was the heartthrob of Jennings High. I couldn't sit there. My heartfelt lighter knowing it wasn't Jason, but William... it was just like my dream last night. How is that even possible?

***

I woke with a start. Charlie peered over me. His dark hair tickling the skin on my shoulder.

"What are you doing here?" I sat pushing him away with the flat of my hand. I could feel the hard muscle beneath his black shirt. He was such good shape his abs had abs. I wish I had time to rub oil all over them in the Caribbean, but since we don't get much down time, we'd have to get sent there first.

"I want out of this town. Something about being here is upsetting my nerves."

"Well, it's not like your whole family isn't here. It's also not like they believe you're dead, as well as mine. It would be pretty bad if we were recognized."

"That's why we have to get out of dodge. Come on, Evie...we got a new mission anyway."

"Tropical?"

"Nope, far from it, but it's your favorite city."

"Oh...We're going to Seattle?" I jumped out of bed with his nod and ran a hand through my hair. "How long till our flight?"

"About three hours. We can sit in the airport and wait for it."

"Or," I pushed him hard towards the bed. "We can kill some time first."

"I suppose that's better than sitting in an airport. Nobody's going to see us here." He pulled me by my nightshirt, his hand moved to the back of my head, and pulled my mouth down to his. I greedily followed. The inferno inside me hadn't be released in far too long.

Just as he rolled me around the queen-sized bed, my head started to get dizzy. I tried to ignore it, but Charlie caught on.

"Another dizzy spell?"

"Yes. How'd you guess?" He sat straight up and helped me follow him to the edge of the bed. "That doesn't mean we can't..."

"I know, but I worry about you."

"I do too. I'm worried I'm never getting laid again. Why don't we ever just share a hotel room?"

"You know why. Besides, we're not official. I know you have your... fun."

"Just get me the bottles, and I'll show you some fun."

"I mean it, Evie. I'm not stupid."

"I'm not having fun. I have a brain tumor. Nothing besides you and my job could give me joy. Besides, when I'm not spacing out, killing someone or wrapped in your arms, when would I have time for anyone else?"

"Really?" He handed me the bottles from the dresser and then left to get me a glass of water.

"Yes, really."

"So, then why aren't we sharing a hotel room?" H asked my question back at me.

Before I could answer, I took my pills and forced them down my throat with a large gulp of water. Then another dizzy spell came.

***

It was the weirdest dream I'd had yet. Sure, I knew the other me liked Charlie, but I didn't realize he loved her back. What if my subconscious was telling me something? Something, about Jason and me. Or what if I was just getting my hopes up.

When I went outside to go to school, Jason was sitting on my stairs.

Lydia had already gone for the day, so I wasn't frightened about sitting down next to him instead of rushing us along.

"Hi." Was all I could think to say. What do you say when your best friends brother gets killed? Or when his death was just as it had been in a dream you had?

"Hi."

"How are you? What are you doing here?"

He turned and looked me in the eyes. "We did that. I know it was necessary, but it still hurts...ya, know?"

"What are you talking about?"

"The job, Evie. You forgot again, didn't you?"

I stood, not really thinking he was telling me my dreams were some kind of weird reality. That was what it sounded like he was trying to say. "We're going to be late for school."

"The funeral is today. You have to go."

My head whipped around and for a split second, I thought I was going to lunge at him. "Why?"

"Boss said." His eyes tilted, and he looked at me that strange way he sometimes does. "Alpha!"

My eyes glazed over and it was as if I was waking from a dream. The scene began to shift, and I wasn't the teenage self I thought I was. Instead of carrying a book bag I was holding my purse. My jeans were skin-tight, the shirt I wore hung down off one shoulder showing off the strap to my tank top. It was a different world entirely.

"Evie, you back?" he waved a hand in front of me.

"I think so. What's going on, Jason?"

"You reverted again. I'm telling you, it's the job. Maybe we should call it quits."

"Call it quits, are you crazy?"

"No, you are. You've developed some sort of split personality since we've been home."

The neighborhood was the same. The hotel doors stood behind us. Jason had never been sitting on the steps of my former home. He was sitting on a bench outside of the hotel after staying the night and deciding on a later flight.

"Your right, which is why I cannot stay for your brother's funeral. We're not even supposed to be here. How will it look if all the sudden we turn up before finding out Will is dead? Don't you think that looks suspicious? I told you we should have never taken this job. He's your god damn brother."

"My parents called me last night after you fell asleep."

"Great. So, they are expecting us?"

"Yes. We should get a room at the hotel in town. Staying here was fine when we didn't want to be seen, but now we have appearances to hold up."

"Fine, book us a flight to Colorado, and a return trip. Give your folks the info, and they can pick us up."

"Sure. In the meantime, you should call Doc. This problem your having won't help our cover if you revert while we are with my parents."

"It's been two days. What did I do yesterday?"

"I don't know. I didn't see you again till last night. You should have been sleeping. Do you think you went out?"

That was the question. The day I thought I was seventeen-year-old me trying to hide from Lydia, what was I really doing?"

***

We caught a flight out of town and then back again with our real names used this time. Jason was right, we should have never taken a job like this. We knew his brother was a creep, and we knew he was into dirty dealings, but I would have never guessed he'd come across our roster. Our boss was all about taking out the biggest threats to national security. So, just imagine Jason's surprise when Will came up on our list of targets. It was a nightmare convincing him we had to do it or find ourselves targets for being uncooperative.

Being a government assassin wasn't a part-time gig. You were in it for life. Sure, we were bound to be able to call it quits later in life. However, if they call on us for a hit, we had to comply. This was not a job you could retire from with benefits. So, if we declined a target, that would be the end of our career and our lives. They would just send a few of our peers to take us out.

Jason was the mastermind of our team. He managed to find every target even if they were in hiding. I was the firepower. He hated getting messy but didn't mind using far range tactics. It was my idea to be the killing blow that would take out Will. I didn't want him to have that on his conscience. It was bad enough he had to live with the knowledge that the woman he loved had done it. I was already a little worried he'd look at me differently. It was a necessary evil.

When we arrived at the airport in town, his father was waiting for us by the gate. I held back letting Jason give the man a hug.

"Evangeline, how are you? Lydia will be happy to see you home for a few days."

"I wish it were under better circumstances." I embraced him and he gave me a quick peck on the cheek.

"I don't get to see my favorite daughter-in-law enough. Thanks for coming with Jason."

"I'm your only..." I stepped back and folded my hands in front of me. "Sorry."

"Nonsense. We don't have to change our behavior, it's our thing. Even if I'll never have another daughter-in-law."

"We're really sorry about Will, dad," Jason said, probably to ease the growing tension. Though his father just gave him a shrug, Jason's face tells a different story to how he really is feeling.

The ride to the hotel is not long at all, and before we know it, we have deposited our belongings in our room and are back in the car on our way to Jason's childhood home. The entire last week is starting to catch up with the both of us. When we pass by the theater, I turned and looked out the other window, noticing Jason do the same. I just hope we are able to make it through the next two days without incident and get back to work.

The funeral was a blur. Will wasn't liked by many, though he was a celebrated local star with the ballet. They couldn't believe he just happened to be murdered while he was in town. Céline, his partner, and latest girl-friend was a ball of snot. She had black mascara flowing down her face, even while the body glitter she wore for the show still stained her skin.

"There you are," Lydia said after everyone gathered at the Randal house. "I heard you might be in town. How are you?"

"Hi, Lydia. I'm well. You?" I didn't care much to speak with her. She did after all make my life a living hell.

Her brown hair was tied up in a knot on the back of her head. She wore my mother's pearls on her ears and around her throat. A gift my father bestowed on her when they got married. She didn't even have the decency to wear black to the funeral. Instead, she wore a white chiffon blouse and a brown tweed print maxi skirt with flat sandals.

"I have a bunch of your stuff at the house. If you'd like to take it with you when you leave, it's boxed up in your old room. I just put the house on the market and need it out."

"Ok, I'll stop by before we head back to the hotel."

"Oh, and congrats on the nuptials. I wasn't aware you two got married."

I felt Jason wrap his arm around me protectively as he sidled up next to me. "Yes, we had a nice ceremony on the beach in Bermuda, about five years ago. We sent you an invitation and plane ticket, but never heard back from you."

"Oh, was that what that was? I just assumed I won a vacation. Bermu-da is too humid in the summer, so I cashed it in and went to Colorado."

"Why Colorado? We wouldn't have been home."

"To ski, of course. I wasn't even aware you lived there. I'll be sure to look you up next time I visit. I do love to ski."

"Sure."

"Be sure to stop by and grab your things. I'll just throw them in the trash if you don't." With a nod, she turned on her heel and left the through the front door.

We stopped by the house after the party, but Lydia wasn't home. As usual, the door was unlocked, and we let ourselves in and headed right to my old room.

It was empty, except for a small box of stuff from when I was in school. Jason picked up the box and carried it to the car for me. As I walked through the house, I noticed there was a picture on the mantle of a unique home. The house Jason and I had built to our specifications after our first year working together.

We were recruited and worked out of base for a while. Once we started doing assignments, Jason thought it would be nice to have a home of our own. Somewhere we could unwind between jobs and have recreational activities available regardless of the time of year.

The house was gorgeous; ceiling to floor windows throughout, stainless steel beams visible with fantastic lines. It was our home away from all the death. Seeing a picture of it on Lydia's mantel sent a shiver down my spine. Without thinking, I picked it up and threw it in the box Jason held.

"What's that?" Jason asked peering down at the frame.

"Just look at it."

He shook his head and carried the box to his father's car.

***

I woke up to the sound of pebbles hitting my window.

Tap, tink. Tap, tink.

My fluffy comforter was tugged up to my chin to block the cold air away from my body. When the season's changed in the fall, Lydia won't let me turn on the heat until snow stuck to the ground.

I threw my comforter away from me and ran to the window, pulling the glass up and stuck my head out in time to get a pebble to the nose. "Ouch. Jason, what are you doing?"

"It's Saturday. You were going to help me with the paper route this morning."

"It's five am," I noted looking at my clock. "Fine, give me a minute to get dressed."

"Don't wake Lydia."

"You think I care. I'm eighteen, she can't stop me." With a roll of my eyes, I duck back inside my room and close the window. I grabbed my warmest leggings and a thick sweater, pulled my boots up over my thick wool socks and headed downstairs to the front door.

"Where do you think you're going?" Lydia's brown hair was pulled back in a bun. A sure sign she was getting ready to go to the gym.

"I'm helping Jason with the paper route."

"You think you can just leave without saying anything? Do you think because your eighteen you can come and go as you'd like?"

"I think that now that I'm eighteen this is my house, and you can leave if you'd like. That's what the Will said."

The front door opened, and a heavy object hit the back of my head propelling me forward. I felt my hand push through the screen in the door, and my face hit the porch.

"Evie!" Jason called from the sidewalk.

"Get your ass off my property." A shrill scream came from Lydia as she moved closer to me. I felt a new pain slice through my back, and then again across the back of my leg.

Reaching to the back of my head I felt the sticky wetness of blood as it seeped from my head. Trying to move was painful, my back and leg protested. I reached behind my leg and was once again met with blood. It coated my fingers and most of my hand when I pulled it back in front of me. The color red forever engrained into my vision.

"Get the hell away from her." Jason came at me, and I heard the clatter of a baseball bat fall to the porch.

I couldn't let Jason get hurt. I knew what Lydia was capable of and wouldn't allow her to beat him. Reaching my arm out, I wrapped my hand around the bat, blood coated the metal and made it hard for me to hold on to. Screaming through the pain, I pulled myself up on my knees and pretended I was the girl from my dream. The one who felt no pain and feared nothing.

My feet finally planted on the porch and I saw Lydia throwing the patio furniture over the railing at Jason. He was dodging each piece of wicker that had gone his way and didn't look hurt at all. They were yelling, and people were starting to come from their houses.

I held onto the bat with two hands and swung it at the back of Lydia's head. Like the sound echoing throughout a baseball field, a loud crack sounded through the neighborhood. Lydia stopped moving, her hands resting on the glass top of the end table. Then her body slumped to the ground.

I stood still, wondering if I would need to swing at her again, but the pain in my back made me fall to the floor. The next thing I heard was the sound of sirens rushing down the street.

"I think she's dead." Jason rushed to me and whispered it in my ear.

***

I woke in a somber-looking room. The sofa I laid on was tartan. The walls a soft baby blue. A round black clock on the wall reminded me of the one I stared at in high school, as I waited for the last bell to ring at the end of each day. It ticked second after second. The noise is the only sound I could hear. Then, tuning my ears, I listened to the slow, steady breaths of someone else in the room.

Lifting my head, I felt the pulling of my scalp. The pain in my back wasn't as severe, but it still hurt. My leg was heavy, and when I looked down, I saw it was in a cast.

"Are you going to talk today, Evangeline?" A slim man with round silver-rimmed glasses spoke to me. He had a mustache that looked like it was glued on the top of his lip and a brown plaid shirt that matched the sofa.

"Why? You're just going to tell me the same things over again. I'm not who I think I am, and my step-mother didn't try to kill me."

"No, I was going to say you need to heal, and a part of healing is talking through all the things that have happened."

"Have they really happened?"

"You tell me."

"Well, I know this is happening. Or it might be. I could wake up in the morning and be a different person. I could be me. I could be this person from three years ago. I have no idea which is real."

"I'm pretty sure this is real. I'm sitting here, aren't I?"

"Yes, you are. How do I know which reality you're from if you won't explain to me what happened? Can I see Jason today, he'll tell me?"

"How often do you see Jason?"

"I don't know!" I turned toward the back of the sofa trying to remember. "I see him as often as you let me."

"When you sleep at night, do you dream?"

"Yes, of course, I dream. I dream of being an assassin."

"For a cartel?"

"No, a government assassin. You know, to take out the threats to the nation. Terrorists and such."

"What was the reason your brother-in-law was considered a terrorist?"

"I don't remember. He was a target. Therefore he needed to be taken care of. If we didn't take him out, then they would have sent others to take us out."

"That wouldn't have been a good thing would it?"

"Of course not but Jason understood."

"You mean Charlie."

"What?"

"Charlie understood." The man leaned forward, and I turned to face him once again. His glasses fell down his nose, and he peered out over top of them. "Your husband, Charlie, is your partner. He understood why his brother needed to be taken out. Why Jason had to die?"

"Jason? No Jason is... where is Jason?"

"Evangeline, you and Charlie killed Jason almost ten years ago."

"No. We killed William."

"Jason William Randal. Charlie's twin brother. He was smuggling heroin in the country from Cuba. He was your assignment."

"Yes, but...Will..." I sat up. "Please tell me what's happening."

The door opened, and a nurse stepped inside ushering Charlie in along with her.

"How is she, Doc?"

"I think I'll let her tell you. She seems a bit more lucid today." The doctor got up and left the room, the nurse following him.

"Charlie, what's going on? I can't tell my dreams from my reality anymore." My tears run hot against my face and stream down onto my arms in my lap.

"Awe, baby. Shh. It'll be ok. At least you finally got my name right. You've been calling me Jason for months now."

"I mean it. What happened to Lydia?"

"She's dead. The bat you hit her with cracked her skull open. It was nasty."

"At her house?"

"No, don't you remember? She showed up at our house and broke in while we were asleep. You grabbed the only weapon in the house and smacked her with it, but she pushed you through a window."

"What about Will?"

"Jason. He was a mark ten years ago. The movie theater back home. He was in town visiting my folks. That's when you found out Lydia was following us. That she's been working for the Russian government since before she married your father. You were her assignment, but she raised you instead of killing you. Then they found out and were going to take her out, but she decided to come to Colorado and finish the job. She also killed your father."

"The cancer?"

"All in your mind. Since Lydia pushed you out that window, you've been dreaming up all kinds of scenarios."

"And the doctor?"

"He's with the company we work for. Everything is ok here. You can tell him everything you remember. It'll help heal your mind. That fall did a number on you."

I tried to wrap my mind around everything I could recall. The job at the ballet, the funeral with Jason by my side, his parents, Lydia, my dad, and now Charlie. I honestly couldn't remember what was real and what was a figment of my damaged mind. It all kept coming back to me in bits and pieces.

Charlie walked me back to my room to rest. It wasn't padded, and there were no locks on the doors or bars on the windows. So, I had to believe I wasn't a prisoner anywhere. It wasn't until I laid down for a nap and woke again that things began to make a little bit of sense.

As my eyes opened, I remembered something Jason once said to me.

"I'll smack you around real good. You'll never even know it's not my brother you're screwing."

ABOUT THE AUTHOR

S.L. Perrine is a wife to a mechanic and mother of four crazy teenagers (3 are boys) who eat her out of house and home. Among writing, reading is another passion of hers. She also enjoys camping, fishing, and anything that means family time.

During the summer she can be found at camp with her laptop by the pool. She and her family reside in Troy, NY.

"I write stories to fill the world with imagination for those who have a hard time finding their own."

- SL PERRINE, 2016

Website - www.slperrine.com
Facebook – www.facebook.com/slperrine
Instagram – http://picbear.online/sl_perrine
Twitter - https://twitter.com/PerrineShannon

HOTEL KEY

BY L GAUTHIER AND P MATTERN

CHAPTER ONE

GUY REED WAS SWEATING PROFUSELY as he played the final hand. He was the only one remaining in a high stakes card game with celebrity card shark Benton Daley. These were private games, and Benton seemed to have be having most, but not quite all, of the luck.

As Guy placed a solid antique 18 kt gold hotel key on the table he saw Benton's eyebrows shoot up questioningly.

"Even if that key is solid gold it won't cover your bet Guy," Benton said flatly, "What are you thinking, man?"

Guy held Benton's gaze. He had to wonder about this man, the son of a well known celebrity with a notorious reputation as a gambler. Though Guy was as expensively dressed as Benton himself, and quite a young man, he walked with a cane and an obvious limp.

Guy must have been in some sort of accident, Ben decided.

"Not just the key," Guy told him, "But the deed to a historic landmark hotel is what I'm wagering. Worth 150k at the minimum. The Mandarin Arms Hotel in the West Central Area of town.

Take it or leave it."

Benton glanced over at his assistant, sitting in the half circle of bystanders surrounding the table. His assistant began typing furiously on his open laptop, then looked up and gave him a thumbs up.

"Okay I accept your wager. Let's get going with this. I have other places to be." Benton snapped.

Guy asked for two cards after he looked at his hand. Benton said he'd stay. In a stroke of luck, he had been dealt three aces. He was fairly certain he would win.

Benton was the first to lay his hand down. Guy's heart was pounding in his ears, and he laid his inferior hand down, saying, "I'm out!"

The hand he'd been dealt originally had been a royal flush. But he had turned in two of the cards because it was desperately important that he LOSE. Guy was happy to fold. He HAD to lose that key, and the hotel, to be rid of the curse that had almost cost him his life.

He'd only escaped by jumping out the 4th floor window of his suite. He had shattered his leg, but he had escaped with his life.

He was alive. That was all that mattered.

CHAPTER TWO

THE NEXT DAY BENTON DALEY asked his grandmother about the key and she recognized it as belonging to the Mandarin Arms.

"Oriental themed things were in vogue then, at the turn of the century. In fact, they were all the rage. The food, the lanterns, the jade jewelry and the fashion influence. I don't suppose the Mandarin had anything to do with the orient, but its exotic name promised elegance, adventure and mysteries of the far east, and it soon became a favorite with tourists.

I recognize this key because that was where my first husband, and your namesake, spent our honeymoon."

She stopped and sighed again, wheezing a little. Her face was a map of creases and wrinkles. There was no hint of the striking beauty she had been remaining in her time ravaged features. She had just celebrated her 89th birthday, blowing out all her own candles, and appeared to be good for another 80 or so.

"It's very beautiful. I'm sure that you didn't know whether it was 18 kt gold or not when you accepted the man's wager, but I assure you it is." She continued. Benton caught a whiff of her perfume. She smelled of violets, as she always had.

"At the time, just before the Depression hit, luxuries were commonplace and Boston was a favorite gathering place for the wealthy. All the hotels wanted their business, and all the rooms in the penthouse suite of the Mandarin Arms had a key of pure gold to each of the four luxury suites.

It was a different time you see Ben, a time when life moved more slowly so that you could appreciate it. And everyone appreciates niceties that go above and beyond the commonplace."

Ben smiled. "Did you and grandpa enjoy your honeymoon?"

"None of your business." his grandmother replied.

CHAPTER THREE

AS HE WENT AROUND THE bend on the road leading to the hotel, he saw an old, weathered and worn sign announcing The Mandarin Arms Hotel was just up ahead. He started getting excited at the possibilities his winning key could possibly hold.

He drove further on and came to the entrance of the Hotel. There were giant cast iron gates that were left wide open. He drove through the gates and looked around at the grounds that were covered with many years' worth of overgrown grass, weeds and wild plants. There was a large fountain in the center of the driveway that was chipped, peeling and cracked. It was run down looking. The pavement had cracks and potholes that weeds were growing through. His first thoughts were 'Well, it can definitely use some work. But it's doable.'

He got out of the car and walked up to the entrance doors. The stairs creaked under his weight as he climbed them. He pulled the key from his pocket and inserted it into the lock, the door didn't want to budge, so he bumped it with his hip and it popped open. His heart was pounding with suspense discovering the unknown condition of the inside of the building.

When he walked in he heard himself saying out loud, "What the…" He couldn't believe what he was seeing.

It was as if time stood still inside the hotel. It was glorious. Everything looked brand new. Nothing like the outside of the building. He found himself quickly closing the door, not wanting anyone to pass by and see what treasures were inside.

He stood frozen just looking around the foyer at the grand staircase and the chandeliers lighting the huge elegant entryway. The unique and intricate woodwork, the expensive decor was just amazing. He couldn't believe his good fortune.

'Was this for real?' he wondered.

"Hello. May I help you?"

The impeccably dressed man seemed to appear out of nowhere. His clothing was perfectly tailored, though it seemed a little dated, as though it was from an earlier time-perhaps the Victorian era. It was certainly in keeping with the atmosphere of the place.

"I'm sorry sir if I startled you, I am the caretaker. It's my job to be here and make sure the hotel is secure and clean and in proper working order."

Benton straightened up and said "No, I'm sorry. I thought the hotel was empty and I wasn't expecting to see anyone here. I was curious about this place. My name is Benton Daley. I see from the plaque on the outside of the building it's on the Historical Register. And you are…?"

"Reece Murphy," the man answered, extending a long clean hand toward Benton. "What brings you here this afternoon Mr. Daley?"

"Benton is fine," Ben told him, slightly amused at the other man's old-fashioned manners. "Say, I have an odd request. I won this key in a poker game last night. As far as I can tell I am the new owner. I wouldn't have known anything about it except that my Grandma remembered the Mandarin Arms because she and my Grandpa honeymooned here."

The other man chuckled and nodded.

"Many of our past guests retain fond memories of their stays here. It was quite the showplace in its day. Would you like me to show you around?"

Benton was delighted.

"Absolutely," he told him, "I was hoping for a tour."

The entire time he'd been talking with the man he'd been fingering the key in his pocket, ready to take it out, but he wanted to pick the right moment. What he really wanted to do was see the inside of the suite it went to. His urging to do so seemed to go way beyond casual curiosity.

After all, he had never owned a hotel before.

"Well Reece, I think I'll take you up on your offer of a tour, if you have time?"

"Sir," said Reece in his professionally polite manner, is there anything I can get for you, surely you must be hungry and tired after your trip." Realizing that he was indeed hungry he replied, "Reece, that would be great, I hadn't realized how hungry I was until you mentioned it. You don't have to go to any trouble, a sandwich would be just fine. Thank you very much."

The man bowed politely.

"First let me show you around. Your bag will be brought up to your suite. Though we no longer get the visitors we once did or have the tours, I am sure that with a few repairs, a little advertising and some local media coverage this place could become the talk of the town.

Urban renewal and all that! You could even have an open house and invite the Mayor!"

Benton was stunned. He hadn't thought of any of that, but the caretaker seemed to have business savvy and might be right about the Mandarin Arms becoming the "IT" place to stay. A surge of entrepreneurial excitement surged through him. Although he made a living, he had never felt as though he belonged anywhere.

Maybe this was his chance. His Grandma would be proud. And he could bring her here, and set her up in her own suite with a maid to cater to her every want and need.

He nodded. Looking down into the shorter man's eyes he noticed something odd. The man's gaze was glassy and flat, and when he spoke it almost seemed as if his voice was coming from behind him, rather than through his moving lips.

Ben shivered and dismissed his thoughts. He was likely overexcited and tired and needed a sandwich and a nap.

The first room he was shown was downstairs and directly forward off the reception area. It was stylish and impressive, with huge oriental mother of pearl lacquered screens placed strategically. A marble fountain tinkled in the middle of it, and the tables had high backed comfortable looking chairs for seating. The high backs assured privacy.

"WOW," Ben commented, "How do you keep up with all this. I haven't seen a speck of dust anywhere. And who takes care of the plants?"

He gestured to the giant ferns and bamboo plants placed decoratively around the huge room.

To his surprise the Caretaker chuckled.

"In spite of the skylight over the fountain letting in some natural light, it is fairly impossible to keep plants happy in here. Those are artificial I'm afraid. Some are silk and the others plastic. But you can't really tell, can you? Not unless you get up really close to them."

Ben nodded. At Reece's urging he took a seat at the brass bar on one side of the room as Reece disappeared through the swinging doors and emerged with a sandwich, chips, and a tall glass of iced tea with lemon and a mint sprig.

Ben found he was famished. As he munched, he continued to look around and noticed a curtained area at one end.

Before he could ask, Reece spoke up.

"A small stage-for announcements or a band. Politicians used to gather their supporters here. It's not a very large venue, but you could still close it to the public on occasion and rent it out. It has character after all."

Benton nodded. The more he had seen of the place the more he was thanking his lucky stars.

After his lunch he followed Reece for a tour of the Cigar Room (it still smelled like cigars and had been a popular congregating spot for politicians), the pool (which was drained and empty and very small compared to modern day hotel pools), the Mandarin Arms Tearoom (which had its own small fountain) and a ballroom on the second floor that took up half of the second floor and had its own orchestra pit.

Benton figured that he might rent it out for Weddings, Seminars and Conventions.

When they reached the Penthouse Reece informed Benton that this would be where he'd spend the night. That his golden key was to this suite of rooms.

The sun was starting to set and he was exhausted enough to turn in for the night.

Reece, the caretaker, escorted me to my suite of rooms and left me outside the door. He'd barely glanced around, other than noticing that it was tastefully furnished, clean and the bed had been turned down before he took off my pants and dress shirt and crawled under the covers.

And that's all he knew...for a time.

CHAPTER FOUR

HE SLOWLY CLIMBED OUT OF bed one leg gingerly placed on the floor at a time, realizing how sore he was. Grunting from the effort he stiffly walked to the bathroom when he thought he heard a soft moan in the adjacent room. He quietly walked toward where the sound was coming from and saw a naked woman just waking up lying on one of the damask covered, overstuffed couches. He quickly ducked back into the hallway, trying to make sense of what he had just seen. Totally confused, he couldn't figure out what happened last night. Could his dream possibly have been real? "No, it couldn't have been real. It just couldn't... Could it?" he said out loud to himself.

He couldn't even remember what he'd been drinking. As soon as he did he vowed that he would swear it off.

He pulled his pants on and once again walked out to the living room to see if he could get some answers.

"Hello there." he said to the naked woman who was now sitting up on the couch. "I know this sounds strange but, have you been here all night?"

She laughed and said "Sugar, don't you remember, we fucked every way possible all night long." She stood up and walked over to him and kissed his cheek. "I am just the last one to leave. The rest of the girls left earlier. I was way too tired to drive home." She walked around picking up her clothing that was thrown all about.

"Other girls?" He asked while taking a seat on the now empty couch." Are you saying that I had sex with all of you?" He asked in total disbelief. "I thought I must have been dreaming-it was real?"

"As real as hot monkey sex gets, you fine stud," She assured him, winking. "We had quite the night, all of us. It was amazing.

They say in a ménage a trios someone always gets left out-but you managed to service all five of us-myself, Renee, Gabby and the twins. I don't think you missed an orifice, either you naughty boy. And I was the one that finger fucked you in the ass as I was sucking you off-not something I do for everyone-did you like it?"

She had gotten all of her clothes on at this point. She sidled up to him and gave him a resounding parting kiss.

"Give me a call when you have your next little party." She purred,

"I'll definitely be here."

He got showered and dressed and called down to the caretaker for some breakfast. When Reece brought up his tray he said to Ben. "Did you enjoy yourself at the party last night? From the sound of it, the party was a success. I hope everything was to your liking sir."

Ben looked at him and said "You arranged that party? But, how did you know...?"

"How did I know what would suit you Sir? Well it's a specialty of the Hotel. We cater to our guests, more particularly if the guest is an owner.

It is a kind of talent I suppose. If you require anything, if we happen to overlook anything at all, no matter how minute, please let us know."

Ben found himself whistling as he dressed. Certain parts of his body were tender and sore, but it was a good kind of sore. It was something to remind him of his sexual prowess.

He had never had a sexual tryst with 5 women before. He wasn't quite ready for a repeat, but he thought he would definitely like a replay in the not too distant future.

CHAPTER FIVE

H E WAS BUSY WITH ERRANDS, another clandestine poker game, which he won handily, wiping out one of the heirs to the Fortini cosmetics fortune. Lady luck seemed to be with him, and he felt, for the first time in his life unstoppable.

Before he went back to the Mandarin Arms, he stopped at a flower shop and a confectionary to pick up a few gifts for his grandmother. She answered the door and immediately burst into a smile that melted his heart and made him gladder than ever for her company.

He tried to beg off after handing her the gifts. But ended up waving to the driver to wait while he had a short visit with her.

"Well well well my boy," she said, smiling as she prepared him a cup of tea he hadn't asked for, "I believe things are going well for you!"

"Yes, they are," he nodded happily as he sipped at the piping hot tea without tasting it, "I feel like my life has taken an upward turn, Grams, and everything seems brighter. I feel more optimistic...

The biggest difference is that I feel like I can finally relax a little, like I finally have the upper hand and I am not letting go!"

His grandmother chuckled.

"Yes, yes, I can feel your pleasure at the way things are going, and I am proud and happy for you. But because I am old and have experienced as well as seen many things, I must caution you not to fly too high in your emotions. Those who fly high eventually crash and burn my darling. I have seen it over and over. Maintain a sense of stability and keep your wits about you. Put money away for the future.

...Find a wife for god sakes Benton!"

Ben chuckled. He knew that his Grandmother was from a cautious generation, and he respected her advice. But it wasn't caution that had led him into the life of a gambler, and throwing caution to the wind had landed him the hotel, which so far had been his biggest payoff yet.

"I will pay attention to your advice as always," he told her, "But please allow me to celebrate a bit. This stroke of luck has been a long time coming."

Her eyes shining beautifully bright, bluer than he'd ever seen them, she captured his bearded chin in her wrinkled but still graceful hand.

"Just be careful," she urged him, "Sometimes it is better to quit while you are ahead. Fold even if you think you will win it all...that is my advice to you now. Think about it. It is advice from someone who loves you and wants the very best for you."

CHAPTER SIX

B EN ARRIVED BACK AT HIS hotel suite exhausted but in a state of happiness and well-being he hadn't felt in years. He had tipped his limo driver $300, and passed a $100 bill to a poor looking kid on a street corner selling papers. He felt like a millionaire.

He caught a quiet bite to eat in the dining room. There were smells coming from the kitchen area, and a murmur of voices, but as he looked around he noted that he was alone.

There must have been guests, or at least diners, present earlier, he mused. When the caretaker Reece appeared he motioned him over to his solitary table.

"So how is business?" he asked, I assume we have some guests?"

"Yes Sir," Reece replied, "With the downstairs renovations completed and some work on the upper levels, we are starting to attract a clientele-just the sort of patrons we SHOULD be attracting. Wealthy and aristocratic, travelers that are looking to stay at an out of the way but still 5-star establishment with a bit of history and character."

"Well we certainly have THAT," Benton agreed, taking a swill of his excellent 25-year-old scotch whiskey, "Any chance I could meet them? Are they early risers?"

"I am sure I don't know," Reece said, "But I can give you their names if you like. Sir Luis Mengill, Walter Platt, and Hannah Renauld are our current guests. They are occupying the floor below your own suite of rooms currently."

"Excellent! Benton chortled, tossing back another sip of his excellent whiskey, "There you go! Not one penny spent on advertising and we're already attracting a clientele!"

"Yes Sir," Reece agreed, attempting a rare smile that instead turned out to be more of a leer.

"I'm off to bed now," Ben told him, tossing his dinner napkin up onto the table. He'd picked at foie gras, sardines, smoked oysters and a tart made from persimmons with an amazingly tender and flakey crust, "It's been a long and fruitful day. Thanks for your hard work! I can see a raise in the not too distant future for you!"

"Sweet dreams, Sir," Reece said, bowing slightly.

They were sweet-Benton's 'dreams'. But first he encountered scenarios too visceral to be dreams.

CHAPTER SEVEN

B EN WAS ALMOST DISAPPOINTED WHEN he turned
the key and entered his suite of rooms. They were beautiful, of
course, but too quiet. He realized then that he had been half expecting his suite to be full of naked ladies.

Well anything would seem like a letdown after that-so he decided to
take a shower.

He turned the water on full throttle, and the heat of the streams of
water flowed over him like a benediction.

For a moment he drifted, then he startled as he felt another body
pressing into his from behind.

"It's me," a voice he recognized from that morning's encounter whispered against the back of his shoulder. He could feel her erect nipples
poking into his back.

"Just relax, I've got you Benton."

He felt fingers playing with his awakening organ, strumming the length of it as the water poured over them both. He was about to turn around when he saw the curtain move and another, blonde female joined them in the shower, giggling. Rubbing against them both she squeezed past the other two and knelt in front of Benton, taking his stiffened cock in her mouth and looking up at him adoringly.

More rustles of the curtain brought more eyes, more hungry mouths, and a flood of sensation. The women surrounded him, bending over and presenting their buttocks and genitalia so that he could stand and take turns shoving his greedy cock into one after another, enjoying the subtle differences in each of their willing cunts.

Some were softer than others, some tighter, some were like falling into wet velvet and others seemed to grab the length of him and not want to let him go when he tried to pull out, like Chinese finger cuffs.

Afterwards, as they toweled off and wandered arm in arm into his sitting room, he saw that a big fire had been laid in the fireplace and a feast was laid out on a long table that had been brought in. The centerpiece of the table was a whole roasted hog with an apple in its mouth.

None of his company bothered to get dressed. There was a fine wine, and Benton could hear seductive music playing in the background.

"We have a surprise," Tawny, the first of his guests said, "Something...different. I think you'll like it Benton."

A handsome young man, beautiful enough to be a girl, entered the room. The women led Benton over to a couch, and the youth knelt in front of him and began licking his balls and sucking on Benton's cock, the entire time not taking his eyes from Benton's own eyes.

He came hard into the young man's willing mouth, and then passed out on the couch

CHAPTER EIGHT

THE NEXT DAY HE HAD business to attend to. All the same he went through his working appointments with a smile plastered on his face. He couldn't wait to get back to the Mandarin Arms.

He had just fallen asleep when he started having the strangest dream. He was in his hotel suite and was surrounded by expensive furniture, extravagant food and beautiful, sexy women. They were dancing and enjoying themselves at some kind of party in his suite. Strangely, there were no other men in the room though. He grabbed a drink from the silver tray filled with crystal champagne glasses and walked over to join the women.

It took him a few flutes of champagne before he could mustered up the courage to actually dance with the beautiful women who were trying to pull him over to the makeshift dance floor with them. Once he started though he was actually having fun. This was really out of the ordinary for

Ben. Dancing and with beautiful women who were out of his league, this was one of the best dreams he ever had.

They decided to take a break and check out the delicious food that was set out for them. He had never seen such a banquet of fine food. Caviar, shrimp cocktail, lobster tails, huge porterhouse steaks, sushi, rice, pasta, and even a whole pig laid out on a silver platter with an apple in its mouth.

They all sat and talked and enjoyed their food. They went through bottle after bottle of delicious champagne, spilling it while they were drinking. Then they got started with the dessert table. There was a huge chocolate fountain to dip everything you could possibly think of in it. That was when the real fun started. He dipped his finger in the chocolate to taste it and the woman next to him put his finger into her mouth and sucked on it. She was making it look so erotic he just stared at her mouth. Her tongue was licking up, down and around his finger and he didn't know how much more he could take. The next thing he knew they were all touching him and kissing him as if they were all there just waiting for him.

Ben was never what they say 'Big with the ladies'. He was reasonably handsome but just never really what anyone would term a 'babe magnet'. So, he was feeling on top of the world having all the attention of these gorgeous creatures. They were at his beck and call no matter what he wanted.

Well since it's just a dream, I'm going to take advantage and enjoy every minute he thought. He looked around the room at the selection of voluptuous women to see which one he'd like to bed first.

There is one woman talking with a few others in the corner of the living room, she had thick, long brown hair with beautiful ocean blue eyes that just captured you when she looked at you.

He walked over to her and whispered in her ear all the things he'd love to do to her and with her.

Expecting a slap across the face for what was mentioned, instead she reached for his hand and pulled him into the bedroom and closed the door.

She started removing her clothing first, not that she was wearing that much in the first place. She walked over to him wearing a sexy bra and panties in the most vibrant red he'd ever seen. He was so engrossed in what she was doing that he could barely move. She started undressing him and slowly kissing every inch of him as she uncovered it. His excitement for her was very obvious when his engorged penis caught on the elastic band of his boxer briefs. When she finally removed his pants and underwear, she grabbed his swollen manhood so tightly he thought it would explode and everything would be over right at that second.

She licked the head of his penis gently at first then getting more aggressive she opened her lips and took all of him inside of her deep, deep mouth.

Oh, how he hoped this dream would never end. It felt so real.

The door suddenly opened and in walked a tall blonde woman with breasts so huge it was amazing that her strapless dress could even hold them in. It was a mind-boggling feat of engineering that they didn't burst free from their flimsy restraints. She took her time removing her clothing and walked over to where he was standing and where the brunette woman was still on her knees. She started kissing him and rubbing her breasts on Benton, eventually pulling his head down to suck on her nipples. She pushed him onto the bed and the two of them climbed up to join him. They started kissing and feeling each other's breasts and sucking each other's nipples as he watched. He started rubbing both of their asses and pushed his fingers between their legs to feel the wetness of their pussies. The blonde one started to take him in her mouth this time sucking him off while the brunette went behind the blonde and started licking her pussy. It was perhaps every man's dream to be an observer as women went down on each other, and it was certainly a top fantasy of Benton's. Just watching them go at it was making him want to come. The blonde then turned over from his penis and opened her legs wider and started touching herself and the brunette climbed on the bed spreading her legs and motioned for him to put his face in her swollen lips. Feeling more than happy to oblige he enjoying himself in her wetness, the blonde climbed over to join them again.

He never wanted to wake from this dream ever. He would have happily died face deep in warm, wet cunt.

As the night went on he had sex with every woman there, either alone or with multiple women at the same time. They did anything and everything he could have wanted. Until they finally all went to sleep from pure exhaustion.

When he finally woke up he did so with a huge smile on his face. What a dream, it felt so real. He sat up in his bed and looked around confused. The room was a complete shambles. The bed sheets, pillows and blankets were twisted in knots on the floor. Then he noticed there were women's clothing and underwear on the floor with them. 'What happened here last night?' he thought to himself.

Apparently, nothing, but it was the kind of nothing he wouldn't mind experiencing over and over.

CHAPTER NINE

WHEN BEN WENT BACK TO work the next morning his assistant was very inquisitive about his trip to the mysterious hotel that he won. Ben didn't know how much he should actually divulge, especially since he wasn't very sure of the happenings there himself. He told his assistant about the grounds and how much work needed to be done and that the inside was in great shape and full of wonderful antiques from when it was originally opened. This seemed to curb his assistant somewhat so that he could get some work done.

Ben sat at his desk and started thinking about the women he was with and all of their sexual talents. He couldn't concentrate on his work with the memories flooding through his mind like a pornographic movie. He was so deep in thought that he didn't hear his assistant come into his office reminding him of his schedule for the day.

"Mr. Daley, ahem... Are you ok? Your first client of the day showed up a few minutes early, are you ready to see them or would you like me to have them wait?"

Hmm, what, Oh, I'm sorry. I must have been lost in thought." Ben said as he quickly recovered his thoughts. "I just need a moment to prepare and I'll let you know when to send them in."

"Yes, of course Mr. Daley. Just let me know when you're ready," His assistant said as he walked through the doorway to get to his desk.

He needed to put the night behind him and get his head back into his work. He walked into the bathroom and splashed some cold water on his face and caught a glimpse of himself in the mirror. What he saw was a man with a satisfied look on his face but with dark circles from the very little sleep he got last night. He would ask his assistant for some strong coffee when he brings in his client. It will probably take more than one cup with the exhaustion he was feeling, but it was so worth it.

He thought he might drop some more gifts by his Grandmother's on his way home. She would no doubt chide him for the dark circles under his eyes and not getting enough sleep but, there was no need to tell her that he was the new Orgy King of the City.

CHAPTER TEN

B EN HAD TO GET BACK to the hotel.
He just had a nagging feeling that he needed to be there. It was like
a location addiction. It was driving him crazy. He had to see what
the hotel would have in store for him next. How could anything possibly
top the last two visits there he thought.

He would call in sick, that's the only way he could get to the hotel
now. His appointments will be rescheduled by his assistant and he would
be free to return to his own personal sexual playground.

An anxious feeling running through his veins. Like a small child
on Christmas morning, he just wanted to make sure all the loose ends
were tied up so that he could head down the road to his beckoning
destination.

He called his assistant and explained his fake illness and was reassured that it would all be taken care of so that he could rest and get better.
Now to pack up his bags and have something to eat before his ride to the

hotel. He couldn't believe how excited he was to get there. "Mandarin Arms, hotel of charms, I'm on my way!" He found himself saying out loud to no one in particular.

CHAPTER ELEVEN

THIS TIME WHEN BENTON WALKED into his suite of rooms it was filled with gracious music, conversation and beautiful women, the same beautiful women he had shared a long night of passion and lust with previously.

His first thought was 'this is going to be even better than last time.'

As he entered further into the room, he noticed that these women were not partying like they had been the previous times. There were no drinks in their hands or loud music and laughter in the background. It was pretty quiet as a matter of fact. Then he noticed how they were dressed. There were no sexy high heel shoes, no lingerie or revealing blouses or skirts. They were all dressed much more conservatively in fact. As if they were clients waiting to be seen at his office. Then he stopped short when he finally looked more closely at the women. They were all in various stages of pregnancy. But how?

'It can't be,' he thought, 'that would be impossible. Wouldn't it?'

"Hello ladies," he said cautiously but trying to sound friendly. "It's a pleasure to see you all again." He walked slowly into the group looking around for any friendly faces, but failed to see any. No one was smiling. He didn't know what to say or how to ask 'what in the hell is going on?' he thought. He felt off balance.

Worse than that, a sensation of fear was crawling slowly up his spine.

A woman standing in the back, beautiful brunette with chocolate brown eyes and luscious lips came towards him. He couldn't put a name to her face, of course he really didn't get any names during their first encounter. They were all a little busy with things other than introductions.

She walked slowly toward him, looking seductive in her walk even with the baby bump protruding from her hourglass figure. She reached out her hand gently toward his face and slapped him so hard he lost his balance and fell on his ass.

Quickly getting back on his feet he looked totally confused and asked, "What is going on, why did you do that?" The woman who slapped him answered first, "Are you serious, look at us all. Can't you figure it out? You got us all pregnant!"

Ben slowly looked around the room at each and every one of the women, and sure enough, every single one of them seemed pregnant. He nervously started to laugh, "This is some kind of joke, right? It has to be, there's no way you could all have gotten pregnant that night, could you?" Looking around the room there wasn't anyone else laughing or even smiling. "But that's impossible, come on really, how could that have really happened?" "I seem to recall I wasn't having sex alone, you all joined in willingly and no one seemed to be concerned about birth control at the time."

"You're a pig!" one of them shouted. Benton turned his head to the side and noticed the beautiful young man that had given him exquisite head. The youth was glaring at him balefully, pointing to his distended belly.

Apparently, defying all conventional wisdom, Benton had impregnated him too?

Something struck him from behind then, and for a blissful period of time he knew no more.

CHAPTER TWELVE

H E WAS COLD. ICE COLD. Numb in fact, and unable to get his limbs to work.

All around him raucous laughter erupted. As his blurred vision cleared he realized he was lying on a huge silver tray placed in the center of the long dining table. The table was filled with guests. He recognized all the women he had fucked and now seemed to have fallen out of favor with, as well as three strangers that seemed to be dressed in Victorian garb.

One of them stood up and offered his hand, quickly dropping it when he realized that Benton was hogtied and unable to take it.

"We were invited to the feast!" the man told him, "Such an honor, truly! We are guests at the Mandarin Arms invited personally by Mr. Reece!"

Benton squinted at him for a minute.

"You look familiar," he said with difficulty.

"Ah, well I'm not surprised that my reputation preceded me," the man said winking, "I owned a factory in this area over a century ago. I hired a lot of the local girls to fabricate our products.

Many of them disappeared after being asked to work late. Some I kept underground in dungeons for a time, to use at my pleasure. The machinery from the factory drowned out any noise they would make, and eventually when I grew tired of them I would dump their naked bodies in the canal that ran underneath our operation.

The Mandarin Arms was always my home away from home, so to speak."

The man took his seat and tucked his dinner napkin under his chin, smiling pleasantly.

A woman stood, giving him a little curtsy. She was neatly dressed, but her hair was a trifle wild looking.

"I want to introduce myself also. I am Hannah Renauld. I am a frequent visitor to the Mandarin Arms. I was a Baby Farmer for many years after my husband passed away and I was left with a farm just outside of the city and no money. I started taking in infants born out of wedlock for payment, but found I had no patience for raising them.

Some of their bones are still mired in the sediment along the edges of the river. So many tiny bones..."

The woman's face twisted in a gruesome attempt at a smile. All her teeth seemed to have been sharpened to razor points.

Fear twisted in Benton's gut. He kept willing himself to wake up, but he couldn't move.

Another dinner guest arose. He was wearing a bowler hat and had a mustache and a gray, pointed beard.

"Good evening Herr Daley!" he said jovially, "Sorry to see that you are 'tied up' at the moment..."

A titter was heard circulating around the table at this remark. Benton began sweating profusely. He realized that he was thirsty, and noticed an apple in front of his face, resting on a bed of parsley.

He leaned forward to try and capture it with his mouth, wanting to suck moisture from its juicy interior. But his sudden movement just caused his bindings to grow even tighter.

The stranger's eyes twinkled in amusement.

"Yes I can see you are in a tight spot!" he followed up, and this time audible laughter seemed to erupt from the dinner guests, "I just wanted to meet you and greet you before we...well, begin the feast. My name is Walter Platt. I ran the Castle Arms awhile back, unfortunately the estab-lishment burned to the ground quite some time ago, and I am forced to take lodging in other places.

Some of my guests left unexpectedly, when I was the owner of The Castle Arms...they always left their belongings, which I was legally al-lowed to claim after a specified waiting period. I grew very rich that way.

They ended up in The Castle Arms Incinerator, most of them. Some others had their skeletons sold for medical research. Many people don't realize it only takes a few hours for Hydrogen Peroxide to remove all the flesh from human bones, but it's a useful thing to know under the right circumstances.

Anyway, I can tell that you are getting bored. I want to thank you again for being our guest of honor at this banquet.

And if I may, I would like to carve the first slice!"

Even as Benton stared around at all their faces uncomprehendingly he began screaming as a large meat fork slid deeply into his left buttock, causing a bright, electric flash of pain to reverberate through his entire nervous system.

CHAPTER THIRTEEN

MR. REECE MURPHY, THE "CARETAKER", but in actuality the true owner of the Mandarin Arms, (after all he had sold his soul for it), yawned widely and smiled after he opened his eyes.

He could feel it. Another sucker had been snared and sacrificed. The Dark Ones were appeased, and he would be granted his reward....the only reward that mattered.

And with that he bounded out of bed to stare into his dresser mirror. He was not disappointed in the appearance of the face that stared back at him.

He was 35... again.

He looked refreshed and handsome, just as he had been when he'd first purchased the Mandarin Arms. He let his breath out in a long sigh of relief. He could relax and enjoy the next few years without worry. He knew the key would find its own way out into the city before long, and by the time the effects of the latest rejuvenation wore off, the key would bring him another victim.

The process worked like clockwork.

It always did.

EPILOGUE

SHE HAD BEEN PREOCCUPIED WITH work as she hurried along the busy city sidewalk, but looking down she spotted something that glinted dazzlingly even in the wan light of the early morning sun. She stopped short and bent to retrieve it.

It was a gold key. It looked like a fancy skeleton key. It was obviously an antique and was rather large. Instantly curious, she turned it over and over in her hands.

She wondered what it went to.

THE END

MARYANNA'S MIRROR
KATHY-LYNN CROSS

A set of keys jingled as the guard stepped around me while studying his collection for the specific one. Another male stood out of my peripheral vision, his lack of personal hygiene was accompanied by the stale stench of used chew and laced weed, triggering my gag reflex. When I coughed, a few sweat-soaked strands draped over my face, so I used the guise to glance behind. The name Ben was stickered, slightly crooked, on the brass name badge over his chest pocket. Both eyes were glazed and bloodshot, a sure sign he'd be crashing soon.

The hum and quick sessions of hiss-pops from the fluorescence's in the hallway I perceived as a warning, to not forget my place. Chewing on my lower lip, I played connect-the-rusty dots on the poorly painted blue door.

When the guard pivoted to acknowledge his co-worker, the glint from his name tag caught my attention. After a brief exchange of words, Cecil inserted the key, and the metal latch unlocked in protest. With force, he shifted his stance to wrench it open. Stale air blew past us, as though a collection of broken spirits had escaped. This prompted me to balance on the balls of my feet as I struggled to remain in control and force my vision to adjust to the multiple degrees of darkness. Eventually, certain objects began to form. The first was an outline of a chair in the middle of the room. It faced an ominous, one-way window. I wrapped both arms tighter around my middle to conceal the only possession that linked me to this era, unsure of what the outcome would be if it were discovered.

Fear was normally our drug of choice—in the right circumstances— but this rotted residue was from thousands of uncured and broken souls. The stench had rooted both feet to the floor. I fidgeted within the gray hospital smock to readjust the object in my sleeve.

Fingers pressed into my back and shoved me over the threshold. The action caused me to bite my lip. Instinctively, I began to suck on the puncture while stumbling to right myself. Taking two steps into the room, there was a click as the hanging bulb from the ceiling illuminated my invitation to sit. Even though the chair was bolted to the floor, it seemed to beckon for my presence.

High above my head, a male's voice with an electrical crackle tested the volume. "One, two, three. Can you hear me?"

I winced at the one-way window and noticed the seat's reflection. *This could be problematic*, I thought.

As if on cue a heated whisper penetrated my skull. *"Keep your head down."* There was a shift in the room as the presence encircled me. The oppressive bout of frustration turned into more of a complacent understanding. *"Keep your eyes roaming or fixed on a point in the room. Preferably, the floor. Try not to make eye contact with them through the glass, and we'll be fine."* There was a huff as the voice confirmed, *"We've been in worse situations. Keep them talking. I will figure something out."*

With a fleeting exhale, I nodded like a defiant child, lowering my head, and then clasping both hands until my nails bit into the skin. Once

I made my way to the middle of the room, a southern accent, much softer than before said, "Please take a seat, Maryanna."

Muscles tightened while fighting the knee-jerk reaction to respond. Instead, I locked onto a crack running along the cement floor. It stemmed from the bolt by my right heel. I realized there was more webbing spreading out from under my feet.

Clicks from the speaker above made my breath hitch. "Maryanna, did you hear me? Please sit down."

I complied.

"Ready? First session, November 3, 2020." The female's voice drifted overhead, indicating she was preoccupied. Probably filling out forms, I assumed. "Subject number 840236-Cambridge, M. Age approximately, twenty."

Internally, I scoffed. *Oh, if they only knew all of the historical events I've witnessed.*

"Birthdate unknown. Sex," There was a pause as I felt their eyes on me. I remained silent. Those C-cups pretty much indicated what I was. "Female." Echoed through the room. "Turn the volume down, Franklin."

"Yes, Ma'am."

"Caucasian. Black hair. Blue-gray eyes. Weight?" Papers rustled as the woman's voice became distant as she shifted her attention to ask an associate the question directly. "Her weight and height; did you get it?"

There was a terse set of mumbling from the back of the room, and then I heard an infuriated answer. "No, not yet."

Lips peeled back, exposing my teeth as I recalled fighting three men and the gratification when I latched on one of the guard's forearm. Then the pleasure was ripped away when pain from the back of my head reminded me of the outcome.

"I'll need her weight so I can prescribe the right dosage." She cleared her throat. "In case she needs medical help."

"Yes, Ma'am." Franklin's words were testy.

The doctor timidly coughed away from the mic before asking, "Maryanna, do you know where you are?"

I shook my head from side to side.

"This is Finite. An institution for humanity reprogramming and medical rehabilitation. My name is Dr. Sheila Worthington."

An asylum, how fitting. I couldn't recall the last time I was placed in one or admitted myself willingly. Our situation struck my funny bone, and I filled the room with my laughter. The pressure would have killed me a second time if I had held it in.

"Curious. Why do you find this humorous? You do recall why you are here?"

Greed and jealousy were two of the main reasons as to why I was here. Then I remembered two searing eyes, a room engulfed in flames, continuous screaming—maybe some pleading, mostly from my part. I found it surprising how death's melody can be beautiful depending on the person.

The repetitive clicking of a pen brought me back from my Shakespearean tragedy. I feigned innocence, using a scared child's demeanor. "No. No, I'm not sure why I'm here. Please let me go home."

"We found you at a murder scene. You were non-responsive and covered in blood. When you were brought to the hospital, they had to sedate you to check if you had any defensive wounds. Which, you did have several long gashes along your chest and a few shallow punctures across your abdomen, but no wounds on your hands. You were treated but healed remarkably fast. The doctors then believed your injuries might have been self-inflicted, which is why you were transferred here. That was three days ago."

I envisioned the knife sinking into my stomach several times before breaking her wrist. Damn curse. It was unfortunate the way things played out. I didn't necessarily regret the outcome, but the roommate wasn't my intended victim. If she hadn't broken what was mine, I might have left the little human alive.

"Maryanna, can you tell me what happened that night?"

Flippant, I replied, "No."

"Is it because you don't remember or you don't want to?"

"The latter," I mocked.

As though two iced fingers had pressed into my left temple, a command resonated within my skull. *"Keep talking. I have to figure a way out of this, for the both of us. You have to keep them occupied."*

At this point, the only way I could keep their attention was to retell my story. I've relived it, time and time again behind closed eyes, but listening to the sins of the damned slip between tongue and cheek made each scene etch deeper into my subconscious.

Cautiously, I glanced to the side of the one-way mirror and noticed a micro camera affixed four inches above it. That tiny lens would serve as my focal point. Breathing measured, I could feel my heart match the rhythm. Remaining calm would keep my true nature contained.

Transfixed on the camera, I stated, "The accounts about my life might come across as though I am seeking repentance for my sins, but this is quite the opposite, for I can no longer relate to empathy. I've accepted this existence of mine. The darkness beyond the reflective void is my comfort.

"It has taken many forms of pain, but in the end, I have come to terms with what I am, and now, I embrace the addiction, the challenge, the desire to allure and coax in the misinformed souls believing I can foresee their future. It is somewhat, unfortunate because I can see it, but if I choose to disclose this knowledge, it will be my undoing. We can't have that; I love myself too much, and many would miss playing the game if I were gone.

"Throughout the centuries, numerous stories of lore have changed, twisted, and altered to fit some wild tale to spark the sense of fear, dread, or anxiety for one's entertainment or amusement. But, speaking about this sweet torment—so openly—stirring the raw emotional cocktail for me to choke down once again, may come at a cost."

The mic hissed before the doctor stated, "I'm not sure where this is going, but if sharing your past can bring you back to the present, then please continue."

"This narration is from my perspective, and I will share this tale but allow me to start with a warning;

"If you look into the glass while whispering my name, and my reflection appears, do not gaze directly into my eyes... for I cannot guarantee your life will be spared."

A Soulless Trade

Year 1553

Hertfordshire, Southern England

My bones ached from maintaining the same pose during several flips of the head seamstress's hourglass. The new floor length gown seemed to be a newfound torture my aunt had come up with—punishment for my upcoming twentieth birthday.

The Duke of Hertford, Harold Hertford, was my mother's older brother. My uncle and father were childhood friends and spent many summers together. During which my mother, Lillian Hertford was introduced to my father, Lord Gallen Cambridge. Once his father passed, and he inherited the land along with the title of Duke of Cambridge, he married Lillian.

After my father's death last winter, my mother's health had declined while managing our affairs and the Cambridge estate. When word reached my uncle about his sister's grim condition, he insisted for me to visit until matters were settled and her health improved.

During my stay, he promised to host a birthday party at Hertfordshire in my honor. My aunt, the Duchess of Hertford, Serina Hertford, wasn't thrilled having been given the daunting task and I believed it was then her resentment toward me shifted from a light snowfall to a full-on blizzard.

It wasn't my fault he favored me over most of his kin, with the exception of his two youngest, Camryn and Kathline. They were twins, a son and daughter, almost ten in years. I held them in high regard, for both never treated me with contempt or disdain. A part of me wished they were my siblings.

I also had two older cousins, neither was on good relations with me. Lady Jane Hertford was my aunt and uncle's first born. She was about a year older than me. Her demeanor was rather shrewd in nature and deliberately avoided our family's religious beliefs. The only subject of conversation we could connect on was her upcoming engagement to a Duke from France, Monsieur Jamison Belmont.

Her brother, Lord Sean Hertford, was a few months shy from turning twenty following my birth month. He was a weasel, to put it kindly. Always making crude comments on my appearance and conduct. Whenever I entered a room, his eyes would immediately begin to covet my every move.

One of the seamstress' popped up behind me to position my arms straight out to either side. I huffed in frustration as the girl measured my arms from wrist to shoulder and then wrote down the information as I peered upon the reflection of a half-dressed female scarecrow staring back at me. Daydreaming, I envisioned myself standing in the middle of the King's royal gardens. Crows resting on each arm. But since I couldn't smell the roses or damp earth, the reverie swiftly vanished.

Tresses askew, several untamed inky curls bobbed before they tickled my face. I huffed at a few; unsuccessful from relieving me of their irritation. At the same time, my shoulders slumped forward. The head seamstress, Amithina, clapped to get my attention.

Twisting toward the sound, two bones popped in my neck. The relief didn't last long and was replaced with a dull throb. This exasperated my dark mood.

Using a superior air over a subordinate, I reprimanded the head seamstress. "Excuse me. I am not one of your dogs. You will address me accordingly, or I will have you and your staff removed and hire a new gown designer from Essex or Yorkshire." I started to drop my arms when the girl behind me propped them up again. "You touch me one more time," I threatened.

Blood drained from her face as she backed away, curtsied, and averted her eyes to the ground. It pleased me; she knew her place. Studying the petite girl, I toyed with the idea of requesting her as another personal servant.

A soft sneeze redirected my thoughts as I scanned the room to locate the sound. Two pairs of tiny shoes poked out from under the curtains to the far left of the room. I bit the inside of my cheek realizing the twins were spying on me, again. If I didn't establish my position how would that appear to them?

Peeved, I faced Amithina. "How much longer must I endure this mundane torture? I must bathe and dress for dinner. My aunt is very strict on punctuality, as you are well aware of." To affirm the warning, gongs from the cathedral bells resonated on the half an hour mark.

"Lady Maryanna, I beg your forgiveness, but if you want the best fit for your gown, we need you to hold still a bit longer." There was a hint of self-satisfaction in her voice. "We've toiled for five nights to keep to your schedule; and please permit me to say, your choice of material complements your fair skin and eyes extremely fine."

It pained me to admit; she was well versed with flattery. Temporarily forgetting the situation, I admired the gown made of pale-rose and pearl beadwork intricately fashioned in diminutive swirls around the bodice. It had a square neck adorned with an inch of silver, eyelet lace. The reflected pink frown that met my eyes reminded me of the argument the Duchess and I had over a week ago. I would have preferred a V-neckline to show off my best features, for I found delight when the frigid women would blush, and the tight-leashed males ogled. But to my distaste, Serina was a prude and insisted it wasn't proper for the occasion.

From the low waist to the hem, a sheer pattern of gold inlaid flowers draped in pinned waves, cascading to the floor, where the material pooled around my stockinged feet. I kicked out a pointed toe to inspect the pale white stockings my uncle had commissioned with the dress. Temper dissolving, I envisioned the footwear my mother sent me as a birthday gift.

Amithina's reflection saddled up to my own in the mirror. "Does the dress please you, my lady?"

Abruptly, I lowered my leg, huffed a few more curls from my face as a smile widened across my doppelgänger's in the mirror. In defeat, I answered her with an exhale, "Yes." An unexpected giggle escaped, and I slapped both hands under my nose right as the material down each arm made a tearing hiss from behind me.

All four girls moaned as my aunt entered the room. Collecting their composure each curtsied, formally greeting Duchess Serina Hertford. As if the head seamstress mentally commanded them, their attention shifted toward me as hands fluttered, tucked, pinned and repaired my accident.

An old woman stepped in between me and the mirror. I was met with two lackluster, black-brown eyes as they roamed down the dress and back to lock her gaze upon mine. I figured she was waiting for me to acknowledge her properly.

With a slight shrug, I used my chin to gesture that my body was being held against my will.

In a curt tone, she addressed me. "Lady Maryanna."

From years of conditioning, I straighten. "Duchess."

Pivoting to Amithina, she pointed at me, and then down to the panels of material. "She will be presentable by tomorrow evening, yes?"

The seamstress bowed with a tight nod. "Yes, my lady, the gown will be ready by sunset and delivered in the morn."

"Good. Once you are done with this task, please see to Lady Jane before you and your staff depart. Her bodice is stabbing into her lower back. I believe a pin or two was left in the seam. If there is a speck of blood on her dress, I will not compensate you for your time. Slapdash labor is not rewarded."

With arms folded she walked around the attendants, scrutinizing their work. Serina's last step placed her right in front of me. The air held a nip of chill as we mentally threw daggers at one another while several hands tugged, tightened, and pinned my gown to the timed beat of possible dismissal.

My aunt clasped both hands with a pop. "Well, Maryanna, I do have to say the color suits you well."

Shocked by the compliment, I was about to thank her when she added. "At least the color draws attention away from you and more on the gown. It will help you blend in as a conversational piece. Yes, girls that remain next to the walls must have something to discuss."

Unclasping her hands, she lifted the side of her dress. With a single nod, my aunt left me with a warning. "Maryanna, do as Amithina says. Natalie will be here shortly to help you change for dinner."

I didn't want to admit, but each icy remark was beginning to fester; hardening my soul. My aunt's oppressive nature made it hard to breathe at times, and I briefly wondered if others felt the same.

Pretending to watch the ladies work, I took a gulp of air and masked it with a yawn. "Yes. Five-thirty. I will be there."

I heard the rustle and swish of satin as she turned to depart. When the Duchess reached the door, from over her shoulder said, "Amithina, do not forget to fix Jane's dress," and then slammed the door.

A set of two frowns met my eyes from the mirror.

Kathline spoke first. "Mama can be scary at times."

Camryn nodded in agreement, but added, "I do believe she means well, sister." He tugged on one of his sleeves. "She does sound mad most of the time." There was a lack of confidence in his voice. "I have to say, sometimes you sound like her, Maryanna."

It stung. He thought I sounded like his mother. Ashamed from my conduct earlier, I swallowed my pride and turned to Amithina. "I'm sorry. It was wrong of me to demand and not take into account your work." With an airy laugh, I said, "My parents would have locked me in my room for overstating my place."

The twins bobbed their heads in agreement.

"The Silence Chair has seen my backside many of times for that." Camryn flatly stated.

Kathline blushed, and then playfully punched her brother's arm.

Amithina's grimace thinned into a line. Straightening, she smacked her apron, and grumbled, "No need to apologize. I know my station and my assistants know theirs. We will be done in time. Naomi, Debra, go collect Jane's dress."

Both girls scrambled to gather their tools and sewing boxes. Formality caused them to pause, and then curtsy, before leaving.

Altering my attention toward Amithina, all I saw were several long fingers heading straight for my neck. An involuntary gasp escaped but was timely matched to the others in the room. Panic controlled my body as it lurched backward which caused the stool to wobble. That's when two hands latched around the neckline and with a swift yank, the adornment was ripped away. After a few blinks, I watched a scrap of eyelet fall to the floor. Amithina slipped three pins between her lips. Teeth holding the pins so she could speak, said, "Now, let's see to this mishap."

***

"Subject is displaying signs of schizophrenia."

The blunt statement jarred my subconscious as Amithina's features melted, then swirled down the drain of reminiscence until I was left with an icy, numbness.

A disembodied voice, which only I could hear, clipped from behind me. *"You're on a one-way track to getting us committed."*

Exhausted from revisiting the past, I slumped forward not to draw attention while using my inner voice. *"Look, I'm doing my best. You know discussing certain events reopens old wounds, stirs the darkness, which sparks your hunger and sends me into a frenzy until we're satisfied."*

"You say that like it's a bad thing."

"I honestly don't care either way anymore. But if we split apart and there's blood-shed—I promise you—I'll drag you to the closest church and bathe in the baptistery until we're waterlogged."

He made a terse *humph* before diving into my subconsciousness. Like a snake coiling around its prey, he looped his masculine presence around my middle. Whenever he touched me this way, for the first century, it felt as though he was going to expel my spirit from this body. My demon calls it our snuggling time, but I figured it was his way to distract me so he could sulk without losing face.

His presence nuzzled against my ear, and joked. *"Maryanna, your confession, if you were really repentant, would take over a year. Personally, I could think of other ways to torture your existence. Besides, when the righteous speak about repentance, it gives me a headache—"*

Aggravated, I lashed out, "What are you doing? Shouldn't you be searching for a way out of here?"

Hands flew to my mouth in shock when I realized the people behind the glass had stopped conversing. All I could hear was me sucking air through my fingers and the demon laughing in my ear. Fidgeting, I readjusted the object in my sleeve and calmly placed both hands in my lap.

Teeth grinding, I glanced to the side and mentally intertwined my anger in between each syllable. *"You are purposely trying to rattle me. Stop testing the lock on my composure and go find what I need."*

The doctor's words were blunt. "Maryanna, do you need a break?"

I shook my head berating myself at the same time for the outburst.

"Do you want to continue?"

There was a difference in pitch between the males in the small room and the doctor. Once the disagreement died down, she asked again, "Would you like to continue?"

Seething, the demon gently cooed, *"Go ahead, answer the bitch before she strikes a match and lights my boredom."* This bout of tolerance he was displaying was out of character and a bit unnerving. He was planning something.

Stuck in the chair, unable to escape, I folded in on myself as my heart-rate spiked. The presence next to me dissipated leaving me with a slideshow of carnage flipping through my consciousness. It lit a chain reaction, and I had to struggle to contain my true nature.

A crazed bout of laughter resounded in my skull. The pressure was so intense that I had to grab both sides of my head and slam myself into the back of the chair. Then his laughter strengthened and ripped up my throat, filling the room with repetitive clicks and airy gagging.

Sweat beaded at the nape of my neck and temples. The air turned stagnant as it mixed with the heat from the hanging bulb and seemed to intensify with each mundane second. Mouth dry, I licked my lips and then reopened the small wound. Tasting my own blood was dissatisfying, like tepid water, but it would help to maintain control.

There was a faint snick of a key. Heavy footfalls accompanied the squeak of multiple wheels from a gurney. Hands grabbed my shoulders and upper arms. A light touch of fingers pressed into my left arm for a vein, followed by a sharp prick. The tingle of medication began to fizzle as I used my abilities to counteract it.

Frustrated, I berated my demon. *"You're not helping our situation."*

Phantom fingers traced along my jaw. *"I still enjoy it."*

Ignoring him, I pretended the drug was working, closed my eyes, and then leaned back until I was facing the hanging light bulb. Behind both eyelids, my world had changed. The raw color of red drew me in, and a soothing calm layered over the weighted memory from my twentieth birthday. With a hitched intake of air, I allowed it to drag me into the depths of my personal hell.

This is how the game began...

***

On the night of the party, three more attendants were helping Natalie with my needs, and I reveled in the attention. Natalie had filled the copper tub with warm water and different colored petals from the Duchesses prized roses. I soaked until the water turned cold while the four women fussed over me. The basket of petals was my aunt's present to me, no doubt insisted on by my uncle's request, but I gladly accepted them. Today, I was determined that nothing was going to ruin my day.

Natalie retrieved warm linens from a wrack by the fire. When I stood, she draped them around me to dry off with. It was heavenly. Two, much older women, I believed were Jane's attendants, directed me toward a chair when there was a harsh knuckle tap on the door.

There was a young miss, closer to my age, whom I didn't recognize, stopped fluffing the pillows to answer the door. After a brief exchange of words, she ended the conversation with, "I'll be sure to inform Lady Maryanna. Thank you."

When the girl turned around, there was a huge wooden box in her arms and on top was a smaller one tied with white ribbon. With a bright smile and words laced with excitement said, "My lady, this is from Amithina," and then placed both boxes on the bed. The servant lifted the smaller one and said, "This gift, I was told, is from the Duke of Hertford."

Then moved it toward the footboard.

Natalie held my robe open as I slipped into it. Bounding over to the bed, I cinched the robe closed. My dress had arrived. A pair of hands came into view to lift the lid. The young servant's eyes sparkled with excitement, and I found it contagious as we crowded around to see inside.

Firelight glinted off the beadwork, adding to its ethereal beauty. My fingers traced the bodice until I noticed the neckline. Stunned, I reached in the box, and with some effort lifted the heavy fabric and squealed. Amithina had recreated the gown and added the cut I wanted to the neckline. Material rustled as I jumped around all four girls.

"Happy birthday to me. Happy—happy birthday to me," I exclaimed in a sing-song.

The women laughed and clapped with me until the tacky, gold swan statue clock on the end table chimed five o'clock. The party was starting in two hours. A wind of haste swept through the room. Natalie bestowed certain tasks to each servant as I managed to hand the garment over to four outstretched arms.

A high back armchair was placed by the mirror, and another attendant directed me to it. The hustle and bustle of the evening was lifting everyone's mood. Once my hair was pinned and curls placed to my instructions, it was time to dress.

After squeezing into the corset and gown, Natalie told me to face the mirror. She inserted a spring of lilac into the top of my corset by the left breast and under the lace.

Awestruck, I beheld my form. Twenty agreed with me, even though my cousin, Sean, jabbed I would forever be an old maid and would never find a companion. Secretly, I believed there was more to his comments. Since he blatantly insinuated once, I would be his wife. Everyone in the dining hall had fallen silent, which caused me to choke on my after-dinner comfit. It was in that moment when our relationship took a nasty turn, five years ago.

With some extra effort, I shoved down the soiled memory. A pair of delicate hands placed the small box on the vanity. Caught off guard,

I stared at the petite female briefly as her smile widened. "Pardon, but I was told, per the Duke's instructions you were to be presented with this today."

It was hard to contain my excitement as my fingers fumbled to untie the ribbon. Surprised, I lifted the silver-etched hand mirror to face level. The servants included their remarks of splendor, gorgeousness, and thoughtfulness of my uncle. Studying my reflection in the oval-shaped glass, the eyes gazing back at me seemed as though they were judging my self-worth.

A tap on my wrist pulled me from the mirror's hold. Natalie pointed to the back of the mirror. "Did you see the inscription?"

When I flipped it over, an intricate open rose was in the middle. Five loops of thorny vines encircled it. On the edge was written, *To: My Maryanna — May the bonds of eternity never break — trap infinity within time's embrace.* Tension built in my chest as I studied my reflection long enough to watch a tear trail down my cheek. With a shaky voice, I whispered, "It's from my father."

A soft knock at the door made us all turn. The girl who answered it earlier hurried over, opened it and immediately curtsied when Jane Hertford pushed passed her in a deep blue satin and lace gown.

Cold blue eyes met mine before she took in my attire. With slight disdain, she curtsied before inquiring, "Lady Maryanna, are you almost ready? My father is requesting an audience with you."

Gently, I placed the mirror on the vanity. "Yes, I'm ready." When I stepped beside her, I added, "Your dress is beautiful. Amithina has a remarkable talent with a needle and vision."

Sniffing, she added some space between us and twirled a few times out in the hallway. Long brown curls bounced, adding to her spoiled demure. "Yes, I do believe it compliments my form." Pausing, Jane fiddled with something under the neckline of her dress. Her blue eyes narrowed as she tapped a pointed fingernail on her cheek. "You are going to get in trouble when my mother sees what you had Amithina change."

Irritated, because I didn't want the seamstress to lose her position, I allowed Jane to believe the change was my doing. "I am twenty. I do not need my attire to be picked out for me."

Prancing like a peacock, she opened her fan and held it over her mouth. "But I guess at your age, there's no time to practice modesty. Time is ticking, isn't it."

"I don't have my father here to arrange marriages for me." My retort lodged in my throat at the same time I realized my fist was cramping. Gradually relaxing each finger, I played the action off by smoothing out a few creases on my dress. Eyes swimming in anger, I marched past her. "You have no room to boast about your engagement to the Duke of Belmont. It's amazing how he appeared out of thin air. Handsome, titled, rich, and most of all, available."

Jane puffed out her chest, flesh darkening as she tried to remain composed. "Jamison and I are in love. We've been courting for well over two years."

"Yes, and I'm sure you look lovely from a distance."

The snap of her fan and scuffle of shoes made me pause to face her.

Slap!

Heat from the impact spread like venom from the sting. My arm flinched to return the blow but was interrupted when I heard Kathline and Camryn approaching from the east hall. Instead, I rubbed the other cheek to match the sore one so they wouldn't ask questions. I gave her my best, watch-your-back glower.

Jane straightened while pretending to fix her hair. It was then I picked up on an unpleasant aroma. I started to ask Jane if she detected it too when it instantaneously dissipated and was replaced with melted candle wax and hollyhocks. Her fingers slipped under the lace again to touch the object.

It was a dark-metal cross pendant. When my cousin noticed I was watching, she dropped both hands and regained her rigid composure. The moment made me uneasy.

Both kids came bounding toward us singing happy birthday. Each grabbed one of my arms and ignored their sister, giving me a smug sense of satisfaction as I turned my head to stick out my tongue. I was their favorite.

Camryn pointed out that my hair was different. Kathline was admiring the beadwork on my dress. We talked all the way to the main greeting room. Lady Jane kept her distance, strolling a good four, five feet behind us.

I reached out to open the door when my cousins tugged me down the hall toward the ballroom.

Camryn saw my confusion and explained, "No, no, father is in the ballroom. Mother is talking to the head of the house about the party. She will join us later." He dropped my hand and formally strode ahead to open the door for his sisters and me. Lady Jane disapproved of our banter with a little, *tsk*. Kathline and I giggled and then curtsied as Camryn bowed before we entered.

The room was draped in a deep red wine, and bright ember, with gold being used as an accessory. Dark curtains hung from ceiling to floor. Table covers, in the same shade of Cabernet, were decorated with a gold paisley pattern. Next to the cream and gold place setting were orange napkins. I was impressed and had to admit it was elegant, even though I would have never picked the colors. The kids left me to gawk at the dessert table.

My uncle was conversing with the musicians when I made my way to stand beside him. The man with the baton briefly acknowledged and addressed me while still speaking with the Duke of Hertford.

Startled, my uncle took a step back, then blinked a few times as he took in my stature. "Oh, for a second there you reminded me of Lillian."

Laughing, I replied, "You always say that. Do I really look like her that much?"

He grabbed my hands and held my arms out to admire my gown. "Yes, you do. If I believed in doppelgängers, I would say you were hers."

The musicians mumbled for redemption and a few made crosses over their chests.

"Uncle Harold," I scolded.

Then he took me into a fatherly side embrace. Laughing together, he spun me around while pointing certain party amenities my aunt had ordered for the occasion. My uncle was never one for formality among family unless my aunt was around.

We stopped at a table with different candied fruits and nuts. He popped a candied fruit into his mouth. "Go ahead. Try one."

I selected a slice of orange, and the sugar coated my tongue before the juice exploded. After savoring the last drop, I faced him, overflowing with pleasure. "Thank you for this. It is splendid. And thank you for the new gown."

Wringing my hands together, I felt nervous all of a sudden. There was a question needling me, and I had to know, but was afraid to address the bleak subject and cast clouds of sadness on my party.

Picking up on my vibe, the Duke motioned to the musicians. They fumbled taking their places and settled into their chairs. The first notes drifted into the air as an opened hand appeared before me. "Lady Maryanna, shall we take to the floor?"

A weak smile pulled on my cheeks as I slipped my gloved hand into his. "I would be honored. Thank you."

Dancing to a waltz, he whisked me into circles until my smile became genuine.

Uncle Harold cleared his throat. "Maryanna, I know things have been hard after your father's death. I didn't intend to cause you grief today. But, Gallen made me promise to give you his gift if he wasn't able."

Hearing my father's name carved out the hole that was slowly healing. I understood my uncle meant no harm by discussing his wishes. I shifted my gaze so he wouldn't see my sorrow.

"We were together when he fashioned the piece."

My head snapped up. "My father made it?"

"Yes. It was our secret. Both of us used to sneak away and watch the glassmakers and blacksmiths work. Eventually, some started showing us how to use the tools of the trade."

I snickered picturing both of them as impish children hiding and watching the common folk work.

"As you can imagine, it didn't sit with either of your grandparents. So, when we were older, we made a vow to follow our passion and created a private workspace. Since I married first and retained this land, I made the workroom here."

Astonished, this was a different side of my father. I wanted to know more. "Pray tell, why a mirror? Surely, he could have fashioned other trinkets."

He crinkled his eyes. "You don't like your gift?"

"No-no, the mirror is exquisite. It's just, well I'm not sure how to explain the sensation. I sense an uneasy stir from within me when I hold it."

"Oh?"

"Like something is tugging on my heart." I tried to brush off my explanation with a light chuckle. "Is that normal? Maybe, it was because I read the inscription and realized it was from him."

The Duke leaned in and whispered, "Maryanna, I have some private information about our family. You must listen with an open mind."

I nodded. "Yes?"

"The mirror was forged with blessed silver, and Gallen had used holy water to cool down the metal. It is special. The pull that tugs on you is from the other side. The mirror acts as a gateway. If for any reason, you find yourself without an escape, the mirror will keep you safe."

Slowing my steps, I stared at him in disbelief. "I do not understand. Gateway? A gateway to where? How does it work? Why would I need protection?"

Hesitant, my uncle sighed. "You are special, like the mirror. I might be able to explain our family's origins later, but if I rush through the details, it will sound absurd and hard to understand. Trust me, I harped on your parents to share this information with you, so when you found out the truth, you could accept your calling.

"I cannot discuss the specifics as of yet. But creating the hand mirror was Gallen's way to leave you with some protection if he could no longer keep you safe."

What he was implying couldn't be so. If both my father and uncle were practicing what I assumed, it would ruin our family. I tried to swallow my fear as I realized if this hearsay reached the royal courts of nearby kingdoms or even the Church of England, it could hang a death sentence on the House of Hertfordshire.

Alchemy was forbidden. Even if he said they were using it to help me. *You are special,* echoed in between my ears. *Why me? What was so special about me that they would risk everything?* I teetered; feeling faint. "I need some air."

The Duke harrumphed and stopped dancing. He let go of my right hand to dig into his right breast pocket. A smirk grew, which emphasized the crease forming in between his eyebrows. When he withdrew his hand, snaked around four fingers, was a silver chain. Dangling was a purplish-crystal pendant.

His face beamed with pride. "I made you this. It is a Spirit Stone. Think of it as a rare gem, specifically designed for you."

Dumbfounded, I stepped back, hesitant to touch it.

"Maryanna," my named rolled off of his tongue in disappointment, "it will not bite you. With this key, you can open a pathway in between life and death. Time doesn't exist within this space. One of the books we found the spell in, simply referred to this place as the Holding." His face hardened, when he added, "Once I put this on, do not remove it under any circumstances."

"Wh-what? What do you mean I can't take it off?" Instinctively, I raised a gloved hand to my throat.

His eyes glossed over as he asked, "Remember when the birds would nest beyond the gardens. You found a baby bird. It had fallen from a nest and broke its neck. Do you recall how you reacted?"

A scene from my past filtered into my mind, but the picture was fuzzy and muted. My throat ached as the vocal cords tightened on either side. It became slightly harder to breathe as I forced the memory to come in clearer. There was pressure building around my heart, as my lips parted. An eerie silence swirled from the back of my tongue. I clenched my teeth to the point of grating.

His eyebrows lifted in surprise. "Good-good. It is working."

Dizzy from breathing through my nose, my uncle took the opportunity to slip the chain around and fastened it. "Gallen and I had to find a way to keep your secret safe. Unfortunately, our skills weren't enough to maintain certain safeguards." The Duke's eyes filled with unshed tears. "Altering one's nature can come with a cost."

Uncertainties raced within my head making the room spin. It was too much to intake and accept as truth. The Duke shifted his gaze and straightened. Doubt rising like bile, our silence was interrupted as a finger tapped my shoulder. I craned my neck to see the Duchess glaring at her husband, lips ready to reprimand.

He interjected, "Darling, I only wanted a dance with my niece before her dance card was filled."

Lifting my hand, the Duke motioned to the tables. "So, eat, drink—enjoy yourself tonight. Happy Birthday, Maryanna."

My aunt scoffed, turned to criticize one of the servants while directing them toward one of the dining tables.

Once out of earshot, my uncle kissed my forehead and in a rush of gibberish said, "Ayh-na-drutia-blou-trit." Then touched the crystal and whispered, "Sce-cee-fotnia-nok-sleep. This is only temporary."

I was about to protest, when he winked at me. A wave of confusion swept over my questions making me feel that our conversation didn't seem prudent anymore.

"For now, forget. We'll finish our talk later. I promise."

***

The children ran over. "Maryanna, come look at this." In a daze, Kathline took my hand and dragged me to see a tower of sweetness. Camryn was right on our heels. The cake was white with buttercream frosting and chocolate shavings as a garnish. It was simple and perfect. My taste buds went into overdrive as I imagined the icing melting in my mouth, but resisted swiping a finger along the bottom. Voices arguing in the far corner distracted me further from the urge.

Lady Jane and a well-dressed man were in a heated discussion. I frowned while straining to hear one word. My determination was rewarded with a sentence. Jane sneered, "We have an agreement—I own you."

Lips quivering, I spun around and grabbed the kids' hands. *I own you*, echoed in my head as the emotions building between them seemed to overwhelm my senses. In a haze, the children protested from our abrupt departure, sounding far away. The only response my body could comprehend was flight. I didn't want to be a part of whatever was going on between that man and my cousin.

"Maryanna, where are we going?" Kathline's cry snapped me out of my one-track thoughts.

We were standing in the hall. I had marched us right out of the ballroom. Camryn pulled his hand from mine. "What did we do wrong?"

"Nothing. I'm sorry. I simply needed some air and didn't want to go by myself."

Kathline stood in front of me and meekly asked, "Mary, why are you crying?" It was their nickname for me when we were alone.

"I—I didn't know that I was. Sorry."

Small arms wrapped around my waist. Camryn looked at me in worry. "I didn't mean to upset you."

Wiping my face, I reassured them. "You didn't. I'm merely overcome by the splendor, and honestly, I'm missing my parents." The concern both of the kids showed made me smile through the tears. "I wish my mother could be here."

A flood of emotions swirled around me. Everything from the mirror, the hazy conversation with the Duke about my father, Jane's behavior, and that man. I wasn't sure if I could take any more unwelcomed surprises today.

Remembering my cousin and the heated argument, I asked the kids, "Do you know who your sister was talking to earlier?"

Kathline wrinkled her nose, and Camryn mimicked the gesture.

She spoke first. "That's sister's fiancé."

Pivoting on my heel, I whirled around to the door and peered into the room. A few more people were busying themselves with their duties.

Finally, I spotted the Duke of Belmont. He had a horsemanship's build. Wide shoulders, trim waist, wavy raven locks pulled back, angled features and a natural blush, which enhanced his dark eyes.

He was talking with my uncle and one of the musicians. But every now-and-then, he would glance my way. When our eyes met the third time, a zing of fervor brought a rush of warmth to my chest and neck. It almost felt like fingers on the skin. I wondered what stirred within Jane when she kissed him.

In my head, a masculine voice said, *"Would you like to know as well?"*

Disbelief swam in between my ears. This couldn't be. I left the kids and stepped back into the ballroom. Mesmerized, I found myself staring only at him. He couldn't have known what I was thinking, let alone for me to hear him from that distance.

Something was off about him and yet with all my senses screaming to get away, I was now standing two feet in front of him.

Glancing down at me, my uncle coughed and pardoned himself to pause and introduce Jane's fiancé. "Lady Maryanna, this is Monsieur Belmont, or recently titled the Duke of Belmont."

I held out my hand to him. "It is a pleasure to meet you."

In one swift movement, he latched onto my hand and feather kissed the top of it. When his lips grazed my glove, it was as though he was pushing his presence against my space. He then squeezed my fingers for half a second before releasing me.

My uncle smacked the young man on the back in a friendly gesture. It broke whatever was going on between Jane's fiancé and me. His once soft demure changed instantly to appear guarded and closed off. Jane looped an arm around his, and he stiffened.

Interesting.

I compared my cousin's pale, flawless skin, next to his slightly warmer tones. Her mousy hair, as opposed to his dark as a crow's after a rain. Jane's hardened blue eyes to his intense mid-night blue. It struck a chord, from afar they had appeared black and dull. Now they reminded me of a moonless night and how the darkness absorbs the star's light. Both portrayed to be from different worlds, and yet, I loathed to admit they did appear to be perfect for each other.

"Maryanna, it's time to take your place in the greeting line."

"Please excuse me." I followed my aunt to the door while fixing a few stray curls.

"Stop fidgeting, your hair is fine." The sentence knocked me off balance and I bumped into my aunt.

Once I righted myself, I glanced back at the Duke of Belmont. He patted Jane's hand in the curvature of his arm while conversing with a small group. Right before I lost sight of him, he winked at me but never missed the momentum of their conversation.

"Maryanna, whatever is the matter with you?" The Duchess waited for an answer.

"It's the excitement of the party, I guess."

"Well, try to contain yourself. It may be your party, but your actions reflect on the family. Do not forget that."

"Yes, Ma'am."

Eyebrows pinched, she narrowed her gaze on my gown. "You went behind my back and changed the neckline, I see."

I averted my eyes while she instructed the twins to stand next to me.

As the ballroom's doors opened, under her breath, she said, "We will discuss this later—with Amithina."

***

The party was amazing. People I didn't even know were being attentive, wishing me health, happiness, and birthday wishes. I had my dance card filled up within the first thirty minutes. My partners conversed about mundane subjects like the weather, fashion, and what music I preferred. It was pleasant, except for one thing. I hadn't seen or danced with the Duke of Belmont.

As the night lingered on, the rich food and wine started getting to me. I wasn't sick, but my vision had become a little blurry and my tongue tingled. For fear I would make a fool of myself I stopped talking. So, I resorted to adding to the conversations with a head bob, a smile, or a mumbled, "Mmm-hmm."

An ache stabbed in my stomach and I excused myself to get some air. My cousin, Sean, was in the corner, nursing his foul mood with drink. I kept my head down in hopes he wouldn't acknowledge my presence.

It didn't work.

Slurring, he said, "And how's the little debutante tonight? Enjoying yourself, I see. Who's your new conquest?" He motioned with the goblet toward my neck.

I didn't bother with an explanation, not that he would care. Instead, I left my answer short. "Yes, I am. Now if you'll pardon me."

In a flash of color, I was grabbed and pulled behind a curtain. Liquid splattered around my feet followed by the metal clanging of his goblet hitting the floor. Sean's breath trailed down my neck, like musty fog. He sniffed my hair. Inwardly, I cringed and tried to step out of his grip. The coil he had on me grew tighter.

"I don't understand you, Mary...," he took a drunken pause, "... anna." Reforming his words, he continued his rant. "You tease and flaunt. You giggle and smile at everyone but me." He belched a cloud of rancid wine in my face.

Gagging, I used both hands to press against his chest to create some space.

"The wine has impaired your judgment. Stop this, Sean."

"You're only allowed to address me as, Lord Sean." Teeth clenched, he leaned in.

Mind reeling, I had to think fast. Unfortunately, since I had had some wine earlier, I wasn't entirely thinking clear myself. Using my right arm, I wedged it until my elbow was pressing into his rib. He intertwined his fingers in my hair and yanked. I yelped, and then he slammed me into the wall so he could cover my mouth with his other hand.

Leaving soggy, "sh-sh-sh's," across my face and down my neck, he pressed his body against the side of my dress. Moving his hips seductively, he buried his face in my curls, and then traced sloppy circles with his tongue down to my shoulder while murmuring my nickname over and over. "Mary, you whore. Mary, you tease. Mary, touch me. Mary, I want you."

I only heard the name Mary burning into my brain.

With a hitched sob, I reared back, opened my mouth, and bit down on his index finger. He ripped his hand away in haste as I grounded my heel on the top of his foot. Now it was his turn to cry out. Hopping on one foot, his hand flung out as he tried to stop his fall with the curtain.

Between my breasts, the Spirit Stone glittered in the window's reflection. Vexed, my vision blurred with smears of red. Teeth chattering, my words gushed forth, riding on waves of fury. "You want to call my name. You want to play this game. I'll kill you for touching me."

Without even realizing what I was doing, I stumbled forward with enough strength to knock him backward. His head snapped back from the force and hit the corner of the nook. It connected with a sick, *thwack*. Eyes fluttering, he fell like a stone. Blood oozed from under his hair leaving a halo of crimson.

Breath held, I kicked under his ribs, then whispered, "Sean?"

Amazingly, no one heard our scuffle nor came to my aid. Not sure if he had passed out, knocked senseless, or worse; I fled out of the first open door. Racing past guests and into the garden, I passed the gazebo, allowing the fear of him retaliating pushed me further into the night. My skirts were heavy but opened enough that I could lengthen my stride. Heart pounding, and feverish I took off my gloves and tossed them. Next, came the combs holding up my curly locks. Hair flowing, the wind was liberating, especially after what I had been through.

The hedge maze was up ahead. It was my sanctuary. I would hide out there until Sean was found, declared drunk and taken back to his chambers. If he died in his state, the family would assume it was from the alcohol.

Walls of vegetation and crisp night air enveloped me as I flew into the maze's open mouth. I knew this place blindfolded and welcomed the cover of darkness. Even the sky seemed low enough to touch. Years of playing hide-and-seek with the twins had engraved its secrets into a mental map I kept locked within myself.

Running out of steam, my sprint altered to a steady pace as I held out my hands. The velvet leaves slapped against my palms. Right as I was turning into the bend toward the inner ring, a twig caught and slit the tip of my small finger. I reacted with an, "Ouch," and then sucked on the wound.

Irritation, had me openly expressing my woes. "Why did Sean do that? He deserved my anger. I shouldn't feel guilty." Feet cramping, I lifted a foot, admiring my grass-stained shoes. I thought, *not the best footwear to be running in.*

"No, not the best for running." His speech was so clear. I couldn't tell if the sentence was in my head or if I heard it vocally.

Startled, I pressed the ball of my right foot into the pebbles. Holding a swordsman's stance, with both fists prepared to strike, I faced the outline of a birdbath. I was in the middle of the maze.

Lowering my hands, I panned the area. "Who's there?"

Crickets, nightingales, and owls, filled the air, breaking the silence. I imagined Jane's fiancé. "Like he would be here," I grumbled, feeling dumb.

Nature quit talking. Then the Duke of Belmont's French accent curved around my name. "Maryanna, what are you doing here?" From one the adjacent pathways, he emerged.

Jaw unhinged, I just stood there gawking at the man that occupied my thoughts with heavenly and sinful ideas. Then like a bad nightmare, the memory of Sean tarnished the images. Lost in the moment, I whimpered, and as fate would have it, I full-blown sobbed.

Within seconds, there was a gorgeous male on one knee before me. Cautiously, he took my trembling hand in his. There was no physical desire—no emotion—only the coolness of his touch as he gently caressed my fingers until he came upon the one with the cut.

He brushed against it with his thumb. "You are hurt."

I withdrew my hand and curled my fingers. "It's fine. I'm fine."

He sulked. "You don't trust me?"

"No, it's not that. I..." I broke from his intense stare and backed away.

"Not all males act that way."

The gasp that escaped was brief as I covered my face, speaking into both hands, "How do you know?" Mortified, I cried out, "Oh my God, did you see?" Before he could answer, I was up on my toes ready to run.

My cousin's fiancé was next to me in between blinks. The man had also seized my upper arm. Whirling to face my captor, hot tears streamed down my cheeks.

Frowning, he touched one then rubbed it away.

I opened my mouth to protest that I'd had enough groping from men for one evening when he placed his finger over my lips. With a grimace, he removed it to retrieve my hand. The Duke of Belmont tugged me toward the birdbath. There was a white and crimson marbled carnation in his lapel.

Nervous, I asked, "What are you doing?"

"Well, I'm not sure how to say this without offending you, but you smell."

"What?" I shrieked.

"See, offended."

I turned to storm off when the spaced filled with his laughter.

"I don't see how this is funny."

"No, Maryanna, I guess you wouldn't. And do me a favor, call me Jamison," he said while tearing the petals from the flower.

"That wouldn't be right. We barely know each other, and you are my cousin's fiancé. How would that look?"

Jamison dipped the petals in the water and then approached me with his hands in a surrender gesture before pointing to my neck with the flower stem. "Please, allow me."

I angled my head and exposed the area where Sean had touched. He pressed them into my skin and softly rubbed. His voice was tender as he would ask if he could touch certain spots. Then he whispered, "Vous êtes si belle, ma chérie."

Shocked, I turned to meet him, face to face. "Why did you say that?"

"Because you are. I was merely stating a fact."

"But, I'm not yours. Lady Jane, she is your love and the one you are supposed to marry. Maybe the wine has gotten you confused."

Leaning in, voice laced with yearning, said, "It's an agreement with Lady Jane, nothing more. Besides, words like, love have no hold over me." His fingers trailed my cheek toward my ear and into my hair when he continued, "That is unless I give my consent to the one, I claim. Maryanna, you may find there is more to me than what you see. But for now, let us give in to the attraction; emotions only complicate what is natural."

Lightheaded, I could feel my will to fight him breaking.

Jamison purred my name. "Maryanna, be mine."

"Only if I can claim you?" I blurted the question without thinking.

His answer was a light breath against my lips. "Deal."

And like a moth to a flame, Jamison kissed me. The touch was gentle at first, fanning the first sparks of desire. This was nothing like how Sean had tried to take me.

As his touch became more demanding, I fantasized him lowering me to the ground, my fingers working feverishly to remove his clothes. Heat danced across my skin where his teeth lightly grazed my neck but was quickly replaced by an icy chill wherever the silver links touched in the same spots. Senses heightened, I wanted to scream, *mine*, over and over.

Remembering what Jane had said to him earlier, I pulled away and jokingly said, "Does this mean I own you now, too?"

Fingertips pressed into his chest, I detected a deep rumble before he jested, "You can try."

I parted my mouth to let him taste what I had to give. His tongue grazed over mine, and it kick-started a zeal of passion between us. I pulled on his lower lip. Jamison sucked on my tongue hard before he shuddered, breaking our kiss. Wiping his lips, he spat, and then hissed at me, "Blood."

Horrified, I backed away remembering the cut I had sucked on. "I'm sorry. This never happened. This never happened," I screamed.

"No, wait, Maryanna. Come back; you need to know something."

All I knew was this: I was twenty. Found out my father and uncle were dabbling in forbidden arts. Half of my extended family detested me. I was assaulted. And now, I allowed myself to care for a man who was spoken for.

Could this day get any worse?

***

The night torches cast their flickering firelight against the outer walls of the manor. Tears blurred my vision—at first—I believed it was on fire, but closing the distance the flames wavered to points of dancing light. A peculiar emotion pressed on my moral compass. Part of me wished it was engulfed in fire. Holy fire.

Guests were trickling out the front door, and I didn't want to draw attention to myself, so I skirted by the stables. Grumbles and harsh sighs from the animals warned me to work on my eluding skills. Edging around the corner, I managed to stay concealed within the building's shadow.

Two footmen were walking in my direction. Likely to retrieve one of the guests' means of travel. Hoisting my gown, I kicked off my shoes so they wouldn't alert them to my presence. I hugged the wall and quick-walked to the other side of the stables. Breathing shallow, I crept past an open window. Upon reaching the corner, I heard the men conversing. Their words were hushed and fast. I moved closer.

"It is too bad they had to end the celebration and send everyone away. It was such a splendid event." The first footmen said.

"Well, I'm sure they didn't want a scandal on their hands. After they found Lord Sean in his condition." His pause was a drawn-out tsk-tsk. "Lady Jane was furious when someone confirmed they had seen the Duke of Belmont leave right after the Duchess found her son." He huffed. "I would say it's safe to assume the two must have quarreled," said the second man.

"I concur, but of what is the burning question."

"Oh, God." The comment slipped past my tongue in haste. I chewed on my lower lip, praying they didn't hear me.

A horse nickered.

Inwardly, I thanked the animal for concealing my blunder.

The first male continued. "I have my own suspicions."

Protests from the horses layered over his words, as I strained to hear the rest.

"...and since Lady Maryanna is missing, The Duke of Hertford cannot leave without drawing questions," said the second man.

Tears threatened to release the emotional poison infecting my soul. My feet were cramping from standing in the wet dirt, but I remained grounded.

Then the first footman added, "After the fit Lady Jane made before heading off to find her fiancé, I'm sure someone will be paying a toll to Hell tonight." The last part of his sentence wafted into the night air.

I was alone, again.

Fatigued, I sank alongside the wall and took a few moments to collect my thoughts. No longer tipsy, but the web of incidents I had ensnared myself in was hindering my judgment. Nerves raw, I scanned the grounds until the servants' entrance came into view. That was my target, but my body didn't move.

"Dammit, Maryanna, you can do this," I chided.

Hiking my dress, I inhaled suddenly before sprinting across the yard in my stockinged feet. Within seconds, I made it to the bricked steps, taking two at a time. There was a fire in my chest, and swooshing in both ears as I grabbed the handle and pushed.

A servant opened the door at the same time my momentum continued through the threshold. Feet muddy, I slipped on the stone floor and then slam into a long table. Screaming from the impact, I puddled to the floor and hugged my ribs in anguish as people scattered, yelled and swore.

Protecting my middle, I rolled to position my knees under me and used the edge of the table to stand.

When the commotion stilled, everyone recognized me and immediately cornered me with an onslaught of questions, ranging from concerned inquiries to confirming scandalous accusations.

I remained unmoving, for I was trying to catch my breath. One of my ribs had to be bruised or broken. Wheezing, I motioned for something to drink.

A male by the open hearth understood my hand gestures and ladled some water into a cup. Lunging his lanky body across the table to hand it to me was comical. But to laugh right now would be unwise. *At least, that much I knew.*

Rust and grit swished in my cheeks before I gulped the concoction down. Thirst sated, my voice croaked like a crow's. "Could someone please help me back to my chambers?" Lungs quivering, I continued, "I don't believe I can make it on my own."

One of the cooks came rushing in with my attendant, and the head seamstress.

Natalie made an 'o' face and was promptly by my side.

Amithina exclaimed, "Oh, my lady!"

Using my forearm to protect my sore ribs, I leaned into Natalie's side embrace as she balanced our weight so Amithina could slip in on the other side.

My servant whispered, "Where have you been?"

The head seamstress spoke in a rush, "Did someone hurt you? Oh, no, your dress."

Losing my footing a few times, Natalie asked, "Where are your shoes?" She turned her head to look for them.

When I tried to answer, my tongue wouldn't cooperate. After several short coughs and whimpers, I managed to say, "Later." Another intake of air, I used the last bit of strength and muttered, "Please, get my uncle."

An oppressed weight of darkness crashed over me. I buckled forward, hearing the women respond in cries of fright and worry before I blacked out.

***

The two ladies had somehow managed to carry me to my chambers. Upon entering the room, the fireplace was lit, but it felt as though the windows were open. Eyes adjusting to the flickering shadows, I noticed chalk-like lines by the hearth. The women directed me toward the bed.

I tried to backpedal, but my body wouldn't listen. Voice airy, I pleaded, "No. Need to leave." Trying to catch my breath, I huffed, "Must leave. The air…" I paused, "feels wrong."

Natalie urged me to lean over the bed. "You're delirious and probably feverish from the injuries." She left my side, then reassured, "Let us take care of you. But first, I will fetch you some water."

Amithina began to unbutton the back of my dress. "My apologies, my lady, but we have to get you out of these soaked dressings and assess your injuries."

A splash of water.

Glass shattering.

A scream from behind.

Amithina jerked away from me. Panic was a temporary balm and managed to mask my injuries as I pushed from the bed to see what had happened.

The outline of two men stood on either side of a short, cloaked figure in front of the fireplace. It appeared as though the three of them had stepped right out of the flames and into my room. The blaze grew and danced higher adding to the assumption.

Frozen, I noticed the tall male held Natalie in an awkward one-handed hold by the neck. Feet kicking in the air, she struggled to free herself but was rewarded with a harsh shake.

Unspeaking, the tall figure paused briefly to capture the attention of the person standing in the middle. The figure moved slightly with an approval gesture, and then answered, "You may feed."

My heart stopped. It was Jane's voice.

Even in the dim light, I could tell he was straining to squeeze. A sickening pop came from Natalie's mouth before going limp. Pitch-black tears oozed from the corners of her unblinking eyes. A shimmery mist of gold and caerulean gushed from her nose and mouth. He started to inhale.

Frozen in horror, I processed the day's events—from everything I had learned about my family, to accepting what was truth, until the scene before me became surreal. In the recesses of my mind, I heard a single note. It grew in pitch until the bond confining my soul fragmented. A flood of information filled my head. The stone around my neck smoldered against my skin.

Answers bubbled from the darkness as I watch the man consume Natalie's life essence. Souls were meant to be summoned, and then ferried to the Land of the Dead where they would remain until their spirit moved on to Heaven or Hell. This was wrong.

Beyond the darkness the presence I detected earlier clawed from the emptiness. Chilled to the bone; my soul was trying to invade my living space. An excruciating throb grew between my ears. Pain shot straight down my body. Teeth began to chatter, so violently, I physically thought I was being split into two people.

A peculiar awareness of greed, jealousy, and rage possessed me, as I snarled, "That was mine!" Pointing an accusing finger, I inhaled past my normal capacity.

The wail that leapt forth was deafening.

A small row of teeth formed into a tiny tight smile from under the shroud. "Yes, my little waif. Sing for the dead, She-devil. Sing until your lungs bleed and your soul slips into oblivion."

Clutching at my neck, I intertwined my fingers through the necklace and tightened; hoping to choke myself into silence. My soul started to unravel. It was as though, hundreds of needles tied to several strings were being yanked out of my airway. *Natalie—Natalie—dead.* Those words repeated in my head as I continued to scream.

Several ribs reminded me I was broken as the pain flooded into my extremities. Lungs deflating, head pounding, Amithina seized my face; making me focus on her eyes. Unable to retrieve what was rightfully mine, my jaw unhinged; increasing the octave of my demand. Small pulsating lights drifted across the room. Panic consumed me as my greed turned to need. If I didn't refill my lungs soon, I was surely going to die.

The seamstress shouted over her shoulder. "What have you done? Maryanna's father paid the price to keep her sealed. Now that you've unlocked her human form, how will you contain this kind of power?"

A male's maniacal laughter erupted from under my continuous shattering note. "Watching her suffer is most gratifying. We are going to play with our new toy until she breaks." It was Sean. "Besides, my sister knows a trick or two to keep her in check." He pointed down at the white markings on the floor.

Seeing him, spiked both fury and dread. The rancid mix of emotions energized the volume of my wail.

This time, Amithina's fingers curved to the back of my skull. Her nails pressed into my skin with a bite of urgency and demanded, "Where is it?"

Unable to communicate, I blinked several times indicating my confusion. The tears I had held back dampened my cheeks. Amithina wiped my face and showed me her palm. It was smeared in black, like Natalie's tears.

"Your life is in danger. We must contain you. Where is it? The gift from your father." The last point of light was almost lost to the abyss where my soul used to dwell when my eyes darted to the vanity.

Following my gaze, she said in haste, "You must use it."

Compelled, I refocused on Natalie and kept screaming.

She left me to retrieve it, but Sean had blocked her path. He raised his hand. A flash of metal caught my eye. Then the dead weight of Natalie hit the floor. The second male spoke from the shadows. "Are you mad? Don't kill the woman while Maryanna cries for another. If you value yours and your sister's life, don't do anything rash."

Sean, dismissed his warning while swinging the blade in the air aggressively. "Demon, stand down. You are no different than this screeching whore. If it wasn't for my sister's devotion to the dark arts, and her promise Maryanna will be mine after the ritual, I would have already sent you back to Hell myself."

An ungodly snarl rose over my voice. Time sped forward as the man rushed Sean. They argued and grappled yelling obscenities. Amithina dodged the two men to run toward the vanity. Jane started chanting as an object formed in her hand, then attacked the seamstress with it. It was utter chaos.

Amithina pinned Jane underneath her body, grabbed her cloak and started to slam her head against the floor. In a panic, my cousin cried out. "Jamison, kill Maryanna."

His growl filled me with defiance. "No!"

Jane struggled against Amithina's hold as the seamstress tried to smack my cousin. Jane's voice turned hollow and commanding. "Bond by blood. Pact sealed by rite. Your vow and mine for life. I own you! Kill her now."

The roar he released cracked the stained-glass windows. A body was thrown against the door. It was Sean's. He slid down to his knees wheezing. Next, I heard the smack of flesh, a woman's cry, and then a crash. Amithina was laid out on the broken towel rack by the hearth. She cradled an object protectively. Her head lolled in my direction, eyes wide open, blood dripped from her nose and mouth.

"Not her," Jane shrieked.

Within that moment, I could sense the rhythm of a dying heartbeat. My knees buckled, but I forced myself to remain upright and screamed against the pressure building in my rib cage.

Streaks of darkness slithered over Amithina's lifeless body. A glint of silver caught my eye followed by my image. Except, it wasn't me. It couldn't be me. Wild strands of hair coiled and straighten like a nest of snakes. The coloring of skin was almost transparent. Lips dry, cracked, and agape. But what resonated to my core were the two empty holes leaking inky streaks down pale cheeks.

A deep purplish glow emanated from the pendant. The stone, my uncle, gave me was magically lifted from its spot. It hung in the air, tugging toward the mirror. The two were linked.

Warm swirls of air invaded my space. I barely felt the light touch of fingers, accompanied by a familiar scent. Carnations...

In my mind was a faint masculine whisper. *"Trust me."*

Jamison was standing in front of me. "Don't waste Amithina's sacrifice." There was a brazenness in his tone. "Accept it. This is your reality."

He snatched my hand and wrapped it around the mirror's handle. Cool air swirled into my chest, silencing my voice as the stone landed in between my breasts. The ghostly image in the mirror vanished and was replaced with a bruised and marred version of me.

Jamison's eyes shimmered like heat vapors rolling off of burning embers. The color pulsed around each black, horizontal, pupil. They were shaped like a goat.

A single tear trailed down his cheek. In my head, I heard his regret. *I wanted to tell you.*

"You fool." Jane used the vanity to stand. "You cannot disobey me. I'll send you back if you do that again."

"Requests must be specific." He snarled.

"You are a spell away from being banished."

He grimaced before taking my face in his hands. "Maryanna, breathe. Collect yourself. You'll have to fight. I cannot save you, again. Je suis ici pour te tuer, mon amour."

Regaining my bearings, I blinked at him in confusion.

He sighed and dropped his hands. "I was summoned to kill you, my love."

A whimper of betrayal escaped as I backed away, clutching the mirror. I imagined my father and forced myself to believe it would work.

"What? Unacceptable. You can't!" Her spoiled demure echoed throughout the room. "You swore your devotion to me—love only me."

Jamison's stance turned protective as he faced Jane. "Devotion yes, but never my love. I may be a demon, but certain powers, like love, are non-negotiable," sarcastically adding, "Master."

Firelight outlined her figure as she stepped forward. "Jamison, I command you to kill—."

"Sister, you promised me since we were little, the succubus would be mine." Sean's swift interruption was emphasized while threateningly waving his blade.

Affronted by his interruption, Jane screamed, "I saw your precious Maryanna with her tongue down his throat. He's mine—by blood—I will not lose his hold to the likes of her." She spat. "Maryanna cannot live brother. This banshee will ruin our family." Hands swinging from Natalie to Amithina as proof of her claim. "She will only bring death's swift touch to our door."

Flames rolled out of the fireplace. Orange and yellow flickers engulfed the furniture leaving angry streaks of red. Sparks rained down, landing on the rug and the bed canopy. Even the curtains twisted as if they were in pain.

My gaze latched onto Jamison's. The color in his eyes burned with the same intensity as the room's.

This time, I was the moth.

Jane seductively touched his shoulder and whispered, "Kill Maryanna."

The love he held behind those burning orbs, vanished.

Clutching the mirror into my sore ribs, I bounced off my toes toward the door. He was in front of me so fast that I crashed into him. It was like hitting a stone wall. Warm liquid dripped from my nose. I stumbled backward, then swung my weight in the opposite direction. It was a failed attempt. I fell into his outstretched arms.

Heat from the fire was making me dizzy. Jamison gathered me into a tight embrace, then pressed his full length against me. Lowering his mouth to mine, he brazenly kissed me. Mind spinning, I felt his desire for me, not physically, but on an altered level of control. When his tongue slid over mine, I tasted a mixture of honey and spiced wine. He did the same action again. His muscles hardened like two vices as he lifted my body. Beads from my torn bodice began to pop off in a shower of color. Breaking our kiss, he heaved me higher into the air and then flung me across the room.

I rag-dolled into the vanity. Searing jolts of pain exploded from the areas where my spine had gone out of place. Broken glass shards sprayed all around me. My hand mirror fell to the floor before I landed on my stomach, and smacked the side of my face on the stone floor. Fear gripped me when I saw the mirror, laying unbroken, mere inches from my fingertips. Not that it mattered. I couldn't move my arms.

Jane coughed and gagged a few times. "Well done Jamison, now put the fires out. I can't think in this heat."

Instantly, the room grew cold and smelled of sulfur and charred wood.

Pieces of mirror crunched under the demon's shoes. My soul silently sobbed. For he wasn't Jamison to me anymore. He was Jane's means to an end. My death.

Numerous tiny cuts and a few gashes where slivers of glass had embedded, were dripping blood. It pooled under my outstretched arm. Another set of boots stopped beside me. I laid there, unmoving when a hand yanked my head from the floor.

Sean studied my face then turned to his sister. "Your demon broke my Mary. You said I could have a demon too if I gave you some of my blood for the ritual." His words seemed to float above me, and I wondered when I would start screaming for myself.

Jane tussled her brother's hair playfully. "It's okay my dear, you'll see her soon enough."

Taken aback by his sister's acclaim, Sean dropped my head to pivot around and unsheathed his dagger wildly. The tip of a short sword was plunged between his lips and broke through the back of his skull.

Splattered in blood and bone, I listened to him gag involuntarily on the blade.

Lady Jane withdrew the sword with force. "Say, 'hi,' to your beloved Maryanna and no hard feelings, brother. I couldn't have done this without you."

Sean's body slumped forward in Jamison's path releasing a death rattle before going limp. The demon shoved Sean's body away and knelt before me. His eyes had transformed back to the midnight blue I remembered.

Jane took two steps back and assessed the room.

He moved a few soaked curls from my face.

My cousin yammered about what they needed to do next and wasn't paying attention to her demon.

I heard him in my head. *"I feel you slipping away. Don't give up now. Maryanna, give in to your banshee nature and free me; free us. We can work together. Live eternally; together."*

Leaning forward he whispered, "The woman believes you are dead. She foolishly killed the only link keeping me from disobeying her. Jane used her brother's soul to conjure me and his blood to bind me. I am no longer hers to command, and because of that, I will be pulled back into Hell if I do not link with a soul soon."

Sean's lifeless body came into view.

Jamison touched my cheek. *"I've tasted your soul, and you've tasted mine. The flavor of me is on your tongue. Claim me, Maryanna. Make me yours. I promise, you'll love it, and possibly regret it at times, but it is the price we pay to play, as demons."*

Using what air was left in me, I muttered, "How?"

"Let me eat your soul."

A wheeze was all I could muster as my throat strained to cry out. In my head, I answered, *"Either way, I'm dead."*

"You are dying now. Look, Jane told me all about the mirror, the Spirit Stone, and your banshee abilities. I can teach you how to slip in and out of the Holding, enlighten you about your family's history, and the Land of the Dead. Plus, you will have me at your beck and call. Does the price of one's soul seem so much?"

I closed my eyes, briefly mulling over the pros and cons. Then the coolness of smooth glass was under my fingertips. He had placed my mirror reflective side up. The necklace under me began to burn.

"First, you must agree to release your soul to me. Then we'll work together to unlock your true power."

With my last words and bloody fingers smearing across the mirror, I mouthed, "You may have all of me. I claim you, Jamison."

He disappeared from the room, filling it with his boisterous laughter. Jane stopped chatting and spun around to see me on the floor and bleeding out, but Jamison was gone.

She yelled toward the ceiling. "All right, enough games, come back and help me get rid of the bodies before others come to investigate. We've had enough bloodshed for one night."

Agony didn't even scratch the surface when my heart stopped beating with the final exhale. There was an inward pull, and my presence turned inside out before splintering into nothingness.

Opening my eyes in death was like a never-ending nightmare. The gates of the Land of the Dead loomed in front of me. Dry columns of air whipped around. I tasted grit followed by an intense need to drink. I needed to be sated. Throat tight, I looked beyond the iron gates and saw the lingering essence of the departed. They wandered about, bumping into each other.

Insides were burning and fueling an empty ache; I opened my mouth to call for them.

A hand appeared and cupped over my mouth. "Do not cry for them, my love. They have found their peace. Your kind only calls for those who cannot find their way to the gates. But, now that I have consumed your succulent soul, you will cry to feed our needs."

I spun to face him. "Demon, what have you done?"

Overpowering my space, he took my mouth until every thought was consumed with his touch. When he released me, I was back in my chambers and still on the floor. Jane loomed over me, kicked my hand away, and snatched my mirror.

Holding it to her face, she cooed, "Mary, Mary, Mary, your new dress is ruined. Covered in your blood, Mary. Look at you now, Bloody Mary." Removing the cloak's hood to free her hair, she spun while talking to herself. "Your father was a fraud, Maryanna." Jane flipped the mirror over and read the inscription out loud. "May the bonds of eternity never break — trap infinity within time's embrace."

There was a surge of power within my body, and then I disappeared from my reality to reappear in the mirror. Slightly alarmed, until I realized I was looking at Jane's face. My father fashioned it to work as a gateway. I placed my hand against the freezing glass pleading with her to say my name, to acknowledge me.

Her face twisted in disbelief. "Maryanna?"

The stone around my neck burned.

Lips quivering, she uttered, "Maryanna, is that you?" She whipped her head around looking for me in the room. "Jamison, if this is one of your spells."

"Make her say your name, one more time." Jamison's desperation to execute some revenge spiked my hunger.

With urgency, I pounded against the mirror. Jane yelped, "Maryanna," and released the handle.

I caught it inches from the floor.

Hovering, I lifted the mirror to eye level and was met with the banshee's face I saw earlier. My uncle's words held more meaning, *accept your calling.* I lowered my mirror and counted each corpse and gave her a wide smile, one I would only bestow upon the damned.

I clutched the stone around my neck, flipped the mirror around and held the reflective side for my cousin to see the demon standing behind her.

The first pains of hunger hit. "Jamison, let's play."

***

"Let's play," kept repeating in my head until it was replaced with the screams and pleas from the servants and the members left of my uncle's family. Kathline's and Camryn's empty eyes and broken husks tugged on old emotions.

I sniffed.

It was followed by Jamison's smug accusation. *"After hundreds of years you're still burning a candle for them, I see."*

Blinking back the tears, I was hit with an excruciating white light. "Where are we," I asked in a whispered rush.

"Examination room. They drugged you. You almost used up the last of our energy counteracting the toxins, but I charmed you before you let the cat out of the bag."

Edgy, I stated, "That is because you were only provoking me to change." Displeased, I tugged on the handcuffs on either side of me.

"Great. At least they didn't find the stone. After we get out of here, I want a new necklace. Did you find my mirror?"

His silence was loud and clear.

"And that's a solid, 'no.'" I tugged hard on the right cuff in frustration.

"Maryanna, a demon has to eat. I can't turn solid without it, and you can't change unless we've been charged. We are the equivalent of a poltergeist and a human."

Rolling my eyes, I hit the back of my head against the gurney, and sighed. "Give me some credit, four-hundred and sixty-something years we've been together."

Jamison purred, *"You are still as beautiful as the day I saw you."*

Testy, and not feeling overly romantic, I clipped, "Charmer."

The insertion of a key drew my attention to the door. Heart racing, I inwardly spoke to my demon. *"Plan?"*

"Yes. Give them all the crazy you can muster. Don't hold back."

Ben came into the room carrying a box. It had my name taped above the handle. "Well, little missy, the doctor's cleared you for temporary residency."

The stone by my elbow grew warm. Anxious, I scanned the countertops. Then remembered Ben's statement. "What?" I shrieked, and then kicked frantically, pretending to throw a fit. I figured this would buy Jamison a little more time.

The guard approached me as I twisted myself so that my foot would clip his jaw. Fuming, he used his mic to call for reinforcements and leg restraints.

Soon the gang was all here. Cecil and Ben were fighting to hold a leg. Dr. Worthington flew into the room with a clipboard and started giving medical instructions.

Franklin retrieved a vile from his table, and grumbled, "She needs to be punched in the mouth, not sedated."

Jamison yelled in my head. *"I found it."*

"I'm a little busy," I answered, continuing to thrash.

"It's in the box."

Comprehending my mirror was in the room, I amped-up the acting and shouted in Latin, for all of them to burn in Hell, as an added flourish.

Jamison coined, *"Nice touch."*

The male nurse pushed past Ben. As he bent down to swab my arm, I jutted forward, breaking his nose with my head. He cried out as blood gushed everywhere. Crimson splattered in different patterns on the bed, him, the doctor, and me. It was beautiful.

"Franklin, go to the infirmary," the doctor said in a deflated manor. She turned to me, wiping her hands on a used towel. "Really? If this keeps up, we might have to change things to a more permanent future." Heading toward the sink, she paused after noticing the box containing my things.

I smiled when I heard her exclaim, "This is beautiful, Maryanna." With a bloody hand, the doctor lifted my mirror out of the box. Admiring her reflection, she added, "Maryanna, is this yours? It seems to be very old."

The stone was on fire next to my skin. The key was primed as my demonic nature was being summoned into the mirror. Both men hollered in hysterics when they found themselves grasping for air.

Dr. Worthington stared at the empty bed, at the men, and then back at the mirror where I was waiting for her. I placed a hand on the reflective surface, anxious with anticipation. The doctor squinted, clearly questioning her sanity. "Maryanna, is that you?"

My demon appeared behind her and gave me a wink as I reappeared on top of the bed in full banshee mode. Picturing her throat torn out, I licked my lips watching the first traces of the doctor's soul slip past her lips.

"Jamison, let's play."

MISCREANT
A Miss Hyde Origin Short Story

BY KINDRA SOWDER

WATCHING THE YOUNG WOMAN, HER red hair swaying in the slight breeze as she walked in red-soled high-heeled pumps, I took another puff of the cigarette I had been allowing to burn between my fingers for far too long. She was beautiful, slim, and gave off an air of professionalism while something remained hidden. Something only me — and others like me — could detect, although I had learned to keep my own essence from those same people.

I puffed out the bitter smoke as I continued to watch the woman who held my interest even though I only knew her name, her occupation, and *what* she was. She knew what she was. I could see it in the way she carried herself, but there seemed to be a somber note just underneath that obvious pride.

She was a monster — just as sick and horrifying as I was.

While I was unrepentant, she seemed to carry guilt on her shoulders. The other entity inside of her lingered just under the surface, nearly shimmering like an aura that emanated from her pale, flawless skin. From where I stood, taking another drag of the smoldering cigarette, I could easily feel the sinister energies from that presence, and I focused on it — until the humanity in me began to pulse and beat against me, yearning for its freedom.

Clearing my throat, I threw the spent cigarette butt on the cement sidewalk, and stomped it out as I watched the woman — Blythe was her name — open the glass doors into the art gallery across the street, and disappear inside.

Seeing her, so normal and seemingly carefree, brought everything into focus. She was born into this, the monster inside of her slowly developing and strengthening until it surfaced. My own creation wasn't nearly as gradual or graceful. It was terrifying and painful, and lay waste to everything my life had once been.

The images of that horrific night pushed unbidden into my mind, and as I walked away from the gallery and the beautiful woman, memory pulled me down into its depths.

***

The night was dark in Sparta as I sat outside of the home I shared with my beautiful wife Eos, taking in the wonderfully cool night air that brushed my flesh and the sounds of the nightlife in the distance. We had planned to start a family, but it was difficult while I lived in the barracks with the other men. Finally, I earned my keep at the age of thirty and became an equal — making it so I could finally wake up to Eos' gorgeous hazel eyes that certainly any child we bore would inherit.

I looked over the broad expanse of Sparta, the tunic I wore light to accommodate for the coolness of the oncoming luke-warm months. It was typical, due to rising insomnia caused by worry, for me to sit outside and marvel at the blinking stars in the night sky.

Something large was just on the horizon. I could feel it.

Shuffling came from behind me, and I turned to see Eos gliding toward me, her long dark hair past her waist — beautiful and shining in the moonlight that filtered into the small courtyard. Her eyes glimmered, stunning as she watched me carefully when she approached. As I sat, she stood in front of me in her peplos, exposing just enough of her thigh for me to trace my fingers along the bare flesh.

Entwining my fingers delicately in her soft curls, I looked deep into her eyes — worshipping her without saying a single word.

"What woke you, my love? Are you all right?" I enquired, rubbing my thumb against the lock of deep brown hair. "I did not wake you, did I?"

She sighed -- her lips parted just slightly with exasperation.

"I'm all right. I am just not feeling well. What are you doing out here, Kallias? You should be resting in preparation for tomorrow evening. Is that what's kept you up?"

As she stared adoringly down at me, I had to tell her the truth under the stars that could never match her beauty.

"You know I can't lie to you. Yes, I am worried. I have no idea what to expect out of this," I paused, trying to find the correct word, "*ritual*. They are certain it creates much stronger warriors, but I have been told nothing about it..."

"Other than that a practitioner has come from Magna Graecia to perform it," she finished.

"Yes," I responded with a slight nod.

Eos reached up gingerly, tracing along my hairline with her fingertips, and then down to my jaw — leading up to my lips. I eagerly kissed them and leaned forward to place my forehead against her belly in surrender — to her and to the sleep I had felt pulling at me since the sun left the sky. It had been at least three nights and I had barely slept, the concern over the oncoming ritual playing over and over in my mind.

I felt her hands in my hair, and nearly succumbed to fatigue as I sat there with her. That was, until she spoke again — taking a deep breath that I felt deep within her body. She truly had no idea how much I loved and worshipped her, and now that I had proven myself, I hoped I could do her the honor of giving her children with the time we now got to spend together.

"Come to bed with me. I'll help you sleep," she said.

When I looked up at her again, I saw the desire in her eyes, and my own body responded readily to her and the fire inside of her. A devious smile played at her lips, and she took my hand in hers — attempting to pull me to my feet so I would follow.

Of course, I went willingly, and I finally slept.

***

It was night. Everything important and dark seemed to happen at night. The moon hung in the night sky and light reflected down on me as I approached the building toward the outskirts. It was the home of this great man that supposedly created stronger soldiers with just one spell — one enchantment. I was willing to do whatever I had to for Sparta. As a soldier we were conditioned to do so, but even I wondered just how far I was truly willing to go, and how this man would change me. Would it truly be for the better, or for worse?

When I approached the door, Anaxis — another soldier — stood just inside with arms crossed, waiting for my arrival. He had been through this not even six months prior. I had known him before and after — since the age of seven when we began training — and something had changed in him that I couldn't quite put my finger on. Except for the change in the hue of his eyes. They used to be a deep, chestnut brown, but changed to an almost glowing, sea-colored blue that left you mesmerized if you stared into them long enough. He was gritty, determined, and wiser beyond his years, but not only that, he was just . . . *more*. Something lingered just underneath that put my teeth on edge.

He came to attention, straightening his back and pushing away from the wall when I entered. I had been told prior that there was no need for formal introductions, or knocking for that matter. This man, this magician, had no secrets from what I knew of him.

"Kallias, thank the Gods. We thought we had lost you." Anaxis gestured toward the back of the small house and down a hallway that led straight into a courtyard half the size of my own. "Please, follow me. You are the only person taking part in this ceremony tonight and he wants to act as swiftly as possible before we lose the moon to the clouds."

I followed him quickly, sticking at his back as closely as I could. Despite the size of the home, I didn't want to become separated from my friend and comrade. I felt uncomfortable enough, and anxious. The sky opened up above us, and I took a deep breath of the barely muggy night air. It filled my lungs and settled there, taking deep residence that would have felt like drowning if the humidity was any higher.

An older man, long beard peaking past the folds of his cloak, stood in the short distance away on a dais with a small altar in the center. Something the height of a small infant sat on the altar, covered with a heavy cloth that barely hid a soft green glow underneath.

Curiosity spiked, and the closer we came to the figure of the man, my skin buzzed with anxiety and excitement that sang deep within my nerve fibers. It was then I noticed other robed figures stood around the dais in a wide circle, hands joined together in reverence. Humming echoed through the empty air, and when we came to the dais, Anaxis dropped to one knee in honor of the man. I remained standing. As a soldier of honor within the ranks of Sparta, I was not about to bow to an unknown whether everyone else did or not. Growing up, I had been know as *resilient*, and the same still rang true into adulthood. It had gotten me into some trouble when I was younger, but it helped me in these moments — when met with strange circumstances.

And this was definitely strange.

The man in the cloak turned toward us, reaching up to drop his hood around his shoulders. His fingers were slender and gnarled with age, his face echoing the same sentiments of his time on Earth. The wrinkles in his face were heavy, especially along his mouth and forehead, making him look more trodden than any patch of ground. His eyes were dark and sunken, nearly disappearing as he blinked down at Anaxis and myself from the raised platform. The expression on his face showed weariness as well as well-earned respect.

Leaning down with outstretched arms, he lectured, "Please, Anaxis, that is not necessary. Please stand with pride like the Spartan you are. You have been bestowed a gift and you shall not bow down to anyone. Do you understand?"

"Yes, Pythagoras," Anaxis responded, rising to his feet and standing perfectly straight.

Confusion bloomed in my mind and belly at the name. It ran rampant through Greece based on his practices, as well as those of his followers. Extreme as I felt it was, I had also heard of his brilliance when it came to mathematics, but why was he here? The last any had heard, he had been killed in Magna Graecia along with some of his followers — burned alive.

"Forgive me, but the last I heard, you perished. How are you here?" I asked, rather forcefully and completely skeptical.

"Or so, they thought." Pythagoras beamed at the mention of his supposed fate, the trickery in his eyes perfectly evident.

"Are you not worried you would be found out? Especially using your given name?" I asked.

"Oh, he is not bothered by such things," Anaxis cut in.

"You're right, Anaxis, I am not bothered by the prospect. I am a practitioner of strong magics, which cloak me from their awareness, even in name. Power which I have bestowed on your brothers — and that you are to receive at the behest of the state"

"Oh?" I said with the curious cocking of one eyebrow.

"Why, yes, Kallias. You are an excellent soldier, but they felt that you could benefit from the ruthless spirit I am about to gift to you," he explained.

"And that is?" I probed.

"The spirit of the succubus, dear man." He looked to Anaxis. "Is he always so skeptical?"

Anaxis nodded beside me, "Yes. Always."

"Maybe it is because I do not believe in such things," I responded. "No disrespect, of course."

"Of course," Pythagoras mirrored with a curt nod.

A beat of quiet moved through us aside from the humming figures surrounding the dais.

With a deep breath, the older gentleman continued, "Are we ready to begin?"

I hesitated, opened my mouth, and closed it again — really considering his question. I wasn't a believer in the fantastic, but what if I was wrong? What if this turned me into a dark creature that fed on women? According to what little I had been told, it would only make me stronger, and my observations of Anaxis had said just that. But what if that wasn't true? Especially considering the one physical change I did see. It was small, but who wouldn't notice suddenly blue eyes?

"Kallias? Are you ready?" Anaxis asked, irritated concern littering his tone.

Startled, my head swiveled to look at him, and our eyes met. That haunting blue dulled by the moonlight and the torches crept up my spine and wriggled into my brain, but I couldn't say no, could I?

The simple answer was that I couldn't, no matter how Anaxis looked at me. No matter how he had changed. The eyes may have been the only physical change from the man I grew up with — trained with — but his personality had shifted as well. Could I take this change, if it did take place, and show it to poor Eos who was so happy to have me in our home once I earned my favor? Would I fall out of favor if I walked away? And that was if the state would allow it.

No. I knew better than that. Soldiers, even those in my position, took orders and followed through. Taking part in this ritual was an order.

I nodded. "Yes, I am ready."

Anaxis clapped me on the shoulder and the hit reverberated through my back and chest. Pythagoras seemed pleased, turning back toward the altar while raising his hood back onto his head.

I barely caught a glimpse of the cloth-covered figure before Anaxis pulled my attention again.

He leaned into me, taking my hand in his. It was no secret we were lovers while in the barracks before mine and Eos' marriage, which made the change in him so striking. Eos knew, but she also knew the love in my heart was always meant for her. Clasping my hand tightly, he brought it into his chest and concealed the supportive squeeze with a gruff embrace.

"It will be all right, Kallias," he said.

"I'm not afraid," I replied, pulling away far enough I could see the fine scruff on his jaw.

"I can see the hesitation in your face, brother. I know you."

"I promise, I'm not afraid, Anaxis."

He studied me for a moment before glancing back up at the dais. I followed his gaze, and it settled on the sight of the green light coming from underneath the cloth on the altar. Pythagoras stood behind it, hands hovering reverently over the crown of the statue.

"This will change you for the rest of your life, Kallias. I can promise you that."

A deep, dark part of me believed him.

***

Standing on the dais, facing the moon, I stood as naked as a newborn babe — the slight chill of the night air rippling through my body. I shuddered slightly, but held strong. Pythagoras stood next to the altar just opposite of where I was, Anaxis having slid a robe over his own body and joined the mass of worshippers around us.

Every color was muted by the darkness — all except for one. I glanced at Pythagoras as he hummed, joining the chorus of the others, a green glow growing brighter and peeking out from underneath the cloth.

Fear took residence in my chest as I listened to their thrumming voices join in with the sounds of nightlife and insects, growing louder in concert as if they knew what was about to take place. I felt like my heart was beating so fast it would find its way into my throat. Swallowing hard,

I listened to the sounds as they grew ever louder. The humming turned into a mash of words I didn't understand — a language that sounded exotic, and terrifying all at once. It drew me in as I felt warmth begin in the pit of my belly. The rhythm began to pull at my mind, but I shook it away. I wanted to be aware of every moment, no matter what took place.

A soft tingling began in my feet, and snaked its way up into the rest of my body at such a pace it almost stole my breath.

I hadn't been certain of the magic before. I had been skeptical, but now, as I stood here and felt the odd sensations roll through me, I wanted to believe in it more than anything.

Pythagoras' words grew even louder, and then everything ceased — all sound coming to a halt. Even the animals and insects quieted in honor of such a ritual. Reaching out with his right hand, sleeve of the robe brushing the stone of the altar, his fingers took hold of the cloth and yanked it up, dropping it to the altar — figure underneath finally revealed.

I choked out the gasp that threatened to escape. What lie under the soft cloth was a small statue — a bust — of what I assumed was a woman, but this was different. The woman's form was slim, athletic, and seemed to reach out to the Heaven's, crouched down low with arms across her belly. Gray rock covered stone that resembled emerald, but much clearer. And it glowed, the light it emanated only growing stronger despite the silence as every practitioner around me focused on it. Even the warmth of the low hum inside my body, mind, and chest ceased.

Lightning cracked through the sky from out of nowhere, and the voices rose above the cadence of the rolling wind. Pain. Hot, searing pain shoved itself into my abdomen and lanced out through my entire body — splicing through my veins and each nerve-ending as though the lightning had slashed through me. The scream that built in my chest exploded through my vocal chords with such veracity it was startling.

I was fire — pure, cleansing, and shattering all at once.

The figure of the woman lit up the night from its home on the altar, showing through the small cracks if its rocky shell. The terror I felt before turned into the most intense wonder and amazement I had ever experienced. My mind was electric, and my heart beat so rapidly in my chest I was certain it would explode from within my ribcage.

All I heard was the roaring wind and the rising voices around me. Then my vision turned brilliant white before every part of my body went numb, my head swam, and everything went pitch dark.

My senses came back in crystal clear focus, especially the agony of whatever transformation was taking place. My knees gave out completely, causing me to fall onto the hard stone of the dais, scraping both knee-caps. A scream left my mouth unbidden.

Pythagoras came around the dais slowly, approaching me as if he were approaching a wounded predator. He pushed back the hood of his heavy cloak, and his eyes lit up with the emerald energy of the statuette. Then he did something I didn't expect him to do. He smiled. Why would he smile while I was in such agony? Tears began to stream down my face, taking every bit of strength I had with them.

"Don't fight it. Let the change take you, Kallias," he encouraged.

It was like those words opened a dam, and I let go of everything, sending everything that flowed through me out into the air and the rolling skies. Thunder rolled and the wind blew, cooling my blazing flesh.

I looked up at the dark clouds above our heads, and blue lightning streaked out from a central point and across the blanket they created. My entire body slackened, and the world quickly fell away. I didn't even feel the impact of my body hitting the stone.

***

I barely remembered anything after that, but flashes of images surfaced when I was half awake. I was in my own bed, Eos laying at my side with her body spread out, her beautiful curves beckoning. Blood, deep and warm, began to creep over her bare hip. Shaking my head, I knew it couldn't be real, but it remained. My eyes stung and exhaustion overtook me again, pulling me down into the deep, crimson-filled depths as image after image of blood, sweat, and screaming mouths forced their way into my dreams — turning them into terrifying nightmares.

Nothing would be the same ever again. I didn't need anyone to tell me that. I just knew.

***

I was dreaming — the only hint provided to me of it being that I stood on the same dais surrounded by nothing. Not even a cloud, or the clatter of thunder and lightning. Complete silence taking me down further into a deep void, like a vacuum.

Heart pounding in my throat, I took a hesitant step forward, just realizing I was completely nude. No tunic — no cloak — not even sandals covered my feet. The stone of the dais was rough against my soles as I stepped forward once more, even closer to the nothing now.

What was this place?

"Hello," I called out helplessly into the void.

No reply. Only the stunning, deafening quiet answered back. That and my breathing filled whatever kind of space I occupied. A part of me wanted to say it was my mind I was standing in, but the rest felt as if I were standing in a physical place. It felt finite and infinite all at once, bringing everything into sharp focus. Even the texture of my skin came to life in brilliant detail.

"Hello," I shouted again. "Is anyone out there?"

Nothing again, but when I turned the missing statuette that hadn't been there previously, suddenly appeared — glowing brilliant against the blackness.

A shrill, feminine scream shattered the silence into a million pieces. I turned as quickly as I could toward the cry, my body instantly crouching defensively — ready to pounce and to protect. As a Spartan, it was my duty. Another scream tore through the air, and I was caught off-guard by how familiar it sounded. When my eyes caught sight of two figures before me, I froze in pure shock at the sight of so much red. A man, large and intimidating, crouched over a soft yielding woman.

Eos.

Blood poured from the center of her chest, her gorgeous eyes dead as they stared up at me from the absent ground while her blood soaked into the startlingly white peplos she wore.

"No," I growled, turning into a primal yell.

Pouncing from the dais, my feet somehow connected with the ground that didn't exist, and I reached out toward the man harming my beautiful Eos. My fingers dug into the man's muscular shoulder, and forced him up to face me. When he came to stand erect, my own face stared back at me, and the terror I had felt to begin with replaced the need to protect. His eyes were wide, jaw clenched as he took me in — enraged by my interference.

Then I saw recognition in his eyes — the deep brown eyes that mirrored mine — and a sinister smirk took residence on his mouth. It took that moment for me to realize that Eos' blood, bright red against his tanned skin, coated his lips and ran down his chin. Almost like he had been tasting her, but I was too scared to look down at her lifeless form.

"What have you done?" I screamed at myself.

The grin on my face only grew wider as he stared back at me, a large, thick droplet of blood running down the bottom lip that mirrored my own. I felt my chin quiver, but still refused to look at Eos. She hadn't moved since I jerked the fiend away from her, which caused my heart to grow still in my chest with fear. The figure stood tall and strong, large muscles flexing as we circled one another like animals would in the wild.

"Oh, what have I done?" the man asked in my own voice, using my own mouth and throat to form the words. "What have you done?"

My foot brushed a soft lock of hair, and then flesh that had already begun to cool. I couldn't stop myself. I looked down at what used to be my beautiful wife who had been replaced with a corpse — her mouth hung wide open as she lay on her back, blood flowing from her open lips. Her eyes were nearly bulging from their sockets in terror, but I couldn't tear my eyes from the most glaring imperfection of them all. Fresh, glistening meat watched my every move from the gaping hole in her chest — heart missing where she had held it for me for at least a decade. Shock and bewilderment tore through my insides, immediately met with grief and absolute horror at what the other me had done. What *I* had done.

I was too startled to move. I didn't dare hold her again for fear of tearing apart her beautiful visage anymore than had already been accomplished. Her chilling flesh against my own warm skin was enough to stop me cold.

"This was not me," I whispered, more to myself than the mirror image of me standing there watching covered in crimson.

It ran down his chest and down to his thighs. I wanted to run from the vision, but I knew I couldn't. I was trapped in my own mind in the nightmare I felt I could never wake from. A chill ran down my spine and settled in the base of my soul, turning it black and dead.

"This was not me. You did this," I yelled, pointing at my own image standing in front of me.

He shook his head. "But you wanted this, Kallias. You thirst for blood and for violence. I see it in your mind and your heart. You can't hide that from me because I am you. I am a part of you that you can no longer escape from no matter how hard you try. It is the reason you did not walk away from the ritual. You wanted to be free from the confines of your morals, and now you can be."

"What are you?" I asked, my voice so much smaller than it had been previously.

The man that looked just like me laughed, loud and boisterous — so much like myself when I allowed an unhindered performance, which was typically only with Eos. The smirk that replaced the uproarious, bolstering laughter was horrifying, causing terror to rip through me like a torrent. We continued to circle one another, but then he stopped, and I stopped with him — with myself. We moved like a singular unit now, but it seemed unnatural.

"I know you feel it, Kallias. You feel it in your bones. *I am you*. We are one in every way — mind, body, and soul. I am the succubus. I now reside in your muscles and your bones. *You are me. I am you. We are one*."

My head shook without my permission. "No, I am not like you."

"You are not like me, you fool. You are me. If you do not accept this, your transformation will be most painful." My visage paused thoughtfully, and then spoke again. "Would you want to leave your beautiful Eos to fend for herself? For another soldier to replace you in her bed? Anaxis, perhaps?"

The image of friend and old lover flashed into my mind, his bright blue eyes taking over everything against his tanned flesh. Shaking the image away, I beat the side of my head with my open palm, refusing to let this creature beat me into submission with horrid thoughts. Anaxis would never betray me in such a fashion. We were brothers now, and our bond was strong as an ox. Possibly even stronger. But could it be over-powered by my resistance? Could he steal my powerful, beautiful Eos from me because I chose to struggle?

Could I take the risk?

My heart lurched in my chest and my stomach churned at the thought of leaving my wonderful wife to her own devices. How would she fair with the brutal Anaxis? Was this creature — the succubus — right?

"I see the fear in you, soldier. You know I am right. I will make you stronger as the old man promised, and you can hold onto your Eos," he cooed.

"What do I do?" I asked out of the same fear he saw in me — weakness, which I had never shown before. "How do I gain your strength?"

A smile crept onto his face, and his body smoothed out into a much less defensive posture. His shoulders relaxed and his arms slackened, almost as if he had expected me to attack. That would not be the case. I was weak, and the thought of leaving Eos in the hands of a fate without me ate at my mind and my heart.

"You must accept me into every part of you. Let me fill you and your existence, and you will have all that you desire," he said. "Can you accept me, Kallias?"

"Yes, I can," I breathed, the enormity of what I was saying barreling into me.

Moving forward, he put his arms out toward me as if to embrace me, and stepped into my chest. Face-to-face, I could see the crimson blood drying on his lips and down his chin and chest, but I didn't flinch away. I remained, ready to accept him — myself — in whatever way was necessary.

"Embrace me, Kallias. Accept me," he whispered.

I did as requested, wrapping my arms around myself with my heart hammering inside my chest. Closing my eyes, I felt warmth begin in my belly, rumbling and spreading outward from my navel. As it spread, I felt acceptance and calm wash over me.

***

I awoke to the feel of our bed, cool and comforting against my skin that was far too warm. Light filtered in from outside. I felt as normal as could be expected except for the solid pit of heat in my belly that seemed to live there now. Sitting up, I stretched out my stiff muscles, seeing that I was indeed naked like I had been in my dream. Eos' beautiful soprano singing voice floated in through the threshold. My ears pricked at the sound, and I turned my head to hear the sounds of moving of bowls and other things that hinted at the first meal of the day being set. Her voice was like a song, and I closed my eyes, taking the deepest of breaths my lungs could hold as if taking her into me as well.

Then I felt it.

The squirm of energy inside of me, the pit just inside stretching out and spreading like a living thing. My mind went back into the dream, realizing the sensation felt familiar. When the succubus had asked for acceptance, it was real. The succubus had to live inside me now. I knew it despite having never believed in it before. Placing my palm against my stomach, it squirmed even more, and there was a ping in my head that I shook away — trying to remain myself, even with the invading presence.

Swallowing, I tried my best to ignore it, and stood up — reaching out to pick up my tunic and shuffle into it so I was decent enough just in case. Walking out into the open space of our home, I was greeted with an amazing sight. Eos was fussing over a table filled with some of the most extravagant fair we had ever had in our home. Typically, we would feast on tagenias and olives, but there was so much more before me than usual. Tagenias were still there, but there were also figs and other fruits as well as wine and breads.

"Good morning, my love," I said, stopping just behind her as she busied herself placing a bowl of halved figs on the table.

I wrapped my arms around her, and she turned to face me, her eyes and face alight with a glow I had never seen in her before.

"Good morning," she breathed, her breath sweet like the figs. She placed a soft, loving kiss on my lips.

"You seem very happy today," I said. "And this is quite the feast. Are you celebrating something?"

"We are," she said, reaching behind her to pluck a fig from the table.

She placed it at my lips, the light in her eyes never extinguishing, and I opened it to take the deliciously sweet fruit into my mouth. The flavor coated my tongue, and as I swallowed, I twirled my fingers through the soft ringlets of her deep chestnut hair. The presence inside of me continued to spread out through my muscles, but I ignored it as best as I could. My lovely Eos was always of the utmost importance.

"I saw the doctor while you were sleeping before I went to the market."

"Are you all right? Are you ill?"

She shook her head with the smile still on her face. "No, I am not ill." She paused, seeming to think something over before parting her luscious lips. "I am with child."

"By the Gods, are you sure?" I asked, the smile taking control of my mouth before I could stop it.

"Yes, my love, I am sure."

Her smile was bright and wide, reaching her eyes and making them glitter with happiness. Joy and excitement caused my heart to race faster than if I were in battle, battling with my urge to slow its frantic beating.

Sinking to my knees, I rested my palms on her flat belly, wishing to speak with the life growing just within her flesh. The life we had created almost stole all breath from my lungs, my breathes hard and fast.

"Are you happy?" she questioned, looking down at me while running her fingers through my hair.

Not looking away from our child's resting place, I replied with a gracious laugh, "Yes, my beautiful Eos. I am happy beyond words." I planted a gentle kiss just below her navel and turned to lay my head against her softness. "You, my little one, will be the pride of the Gods."

Eos' hands continued to rake gently through my hair — lovingly.

"Now, don't put too much pressure on our unborn child, Kallias. Maybe he or she will only seek to bring pride to you as their father," she said.

"Ah," I chuckled, "I suppose that would be all right, then."

Stroking the most tender part of her belly with my thumb, I felt something swell inside my chest. Pride, joy, and anticipation resided there, but something else stirred within. The thought of the presence of the spirit Pythagoras brought to life within me flashed through my mind, bringing a twinge of fear in my chest with it. It almost felt like my heart gave a lurch, and then each valve clamped down and refused to let blood flow in and out in perfect rhythm. The shock of recognition ceased its movement for all of a moment, growing stronger as I remained with my cheek pressed against Eos, listening for the life germinating inside her — despite knowing I wouldn't be able to hear it or feel it just yet.

I closed my eyes and kneeled there before her as I silently worshipped her and attempted to dampen the rising presence that threatened to choke me. Gripping her, I just breathed and listened to the hushed sounds of our home and her body. The presence stirred and shifted deep in my belly, attempting to spread out through my entire body as I kneeled there and hold onto whatever sanity that remained. It was an odd sensation, kind of like something slithering through my intestines and winding through each and every organ. At first, it was almost imperceptible, but quickly grew in intensity — the harder I attempted to hold it at bay, the harder it fought against me. Of course, I wasn't certain what the result would be if I were to let it take over. A part of me was too afraid of it to allow it.

"Please, Kallias, stand and come eat with me. I bought all of this from the market to celebrate," Eos said.

Turning my face up toward her voice, I opened my eyes. The sight of her was breathtaking as always. Her long brown hair flowed down in soft curls and her eyes were alight with glee that penetrated the new darkness I felt.

"Can't I just stay down here and thank the Gods for the gift they have given us?" I asked, rubbing my palms on her stomach.

She laughed a rich, hearty laugh, throwing her head back slightly before looking back down at me — smile so wide I envisioned her face cracking in half. I blinked the image away, seeing only her beautiful face unmarred again.

"Not unless you want to feast on the floor."

"I am not against that thought in the slightest."

I reached up, grabbed her arms gently, and quickly pulled her down onto the hard stone floor with me — coming to hover over her. She let out a startled and excited yelp, but didn't stop me, laughing all the way down until our eyes met.

"My love, you have blessed me."

She didn't say anything, only smiled wider. No words would have done the light in her eyes any justice. The spirit of the succubus stirred inside me again, but I ignored it, kissing her hungrily. It was not long before I was completely short of breath, the desire for my wife flowed through my entire body like a hot tidal wave.

***

"Kallias," a deep, bass voice much like my own whispered to me in the darkness of slumber, pulling me from a dream I could not remember.

"Kallias."

It was the same animalistic version of my own voice I had heard when the succubus first introduced itself to me — frightening and visceral. Demonic. Something I hadn't believed in before that was more real than ever now when faced with it.

The air left my lungs as if an invisible force had sucked it out, and I awoke, shooting up to a sitting position in bed and gasping. Heart pounding, blood rushed in my ears and my temples throbbed, every muscle in my body screaming to run away from the presence taking over. It felt hot in the center of my belly, spreading outward through every part of me that it hadn't touched yet.

My eyes scanned the room, landing on Eos' prone form in our bed beside me, thin sheet draped over the beautiful curve of her hips — face serene with closed eyes and soft breathing. She was so peaceful, a stark contrast for the battle inside me.

I turned away from her, the sight of her naked body causing the presence to grow into a stronger force. I closed my eyes and took a deep breath as I sat on the edge of our bed, hands gripping it tightly, knuckles white and arms trembling. The presence felt vicious and angry and hungry for violence. So hungry for it beyond anything I had ever felt in battle as if it would take anything it could just to see spilled blood.

My leg jumped involuntarily, my heel tapping on the floor in a quick, steady rhythm. But I couldn't stop it, just like I couldn't stop the transformation continuing to take place despite my fight against it. Of course, even though I wasn't certain what this change would do to me, I did know that feeling was unsettling enough for fear to pierce my heart. Heat continued to pour through every part of my body, and swiftly, an odd sensation took over. I felt as if I were being pushed into the background of my mind, while something else was pushing forward to overpower me entirely. The edges of my vision became fuzzy and everything blurred like I was looking through a gossamer curtain. Anxiety spiked, and a cold sweat broke out over my skin as the heat continued to poured through me like a dam had been left wide open.

The sound of shifting fabric came from behind me, signaling Eos was awake. Had I woken her? Could she tell something was changing in me? I couldn't see a change in my body, but was there something else?

I felt her fingers lightly touch my shoulder, then her warm body pressed against me — her breath hot on my neck.

"Kallias? Are you all right? You feel feverish," she asked, placing her palm against my cheek.

The succubus stirred even more, spreading out even quicker as it pushed my own presence into the background. My flesh felt warm, fuzzy, and tingly. Sweat beaded on my forehead and upper lip. I felt a small voice in my mind, whispering my name again.

"Kallias, there is no use in fighting me. You accepted me. Now you must accept what I do. Resistance is useless," it purred.

And just like that, something snapped inside me, pushing me so far down into the darkness I could only see what my body did, but could not affect it. No matter how strong my will. It was as if I could only see from the bottom of a deep pit. I could still feel my body move, and the succubus' presence coiled there with me like a snake while using my body to strike.

Pounding against it, I cried out and screamed like a wild animal. I feared what this new presence would do to my beautiful Eos, but the only response to my terror was the succubus' horrifying laughter in the space around me.

"I am fine, my love," I heard and felt myself say, turning to face her while cupping her cheek with our shared hand. "I'm perfect."

It slid down to her slender throat, tracing her collar bones with light fingertips. Every instinct told me to fight, but I was beginning to see that the succubus was right. I could not resist and any urge it had would come to fruition no matter how loud I felt I was screaming. Fear and anguish lanced through me, and I knew that the spirit felt it because it chuckled in our shared mind, and almost purred in response to Eos as she placed her hand on mine. She was like a moth to a flame — easy prey. She always bent to me like I did to her so our love for each other was never in doubt.

Her eyes met mine, and she smiled playfully, her naked body leaning toward me as my hand continued to stroke her flesh.

"Is this your way of asking for more, my love? Because I will gladly give it," she said through obviously aroused, ragged breaths.

The succubus did not respond — only leaned forward, pressing against her to guide her back down to the bed where it positioned my body above her. My hand — our hand — moved up the length of her body to cup her neck, hungrily kissing her. At first, I thought maybe this would be the extent of the succubus' plans, but I quickly realized I was mistaken when my large hands reached up without my permission, and wrapped around her throat, squeezing tightly.

Her body stiffened, unsure at first, and then she stopped kissing me and attempted to push me off her. My shared eyes looked into hers, and I saw the terror and confusion that lay within. Her fingers clawed at my hands and her legs — wrapped around me — tried to come around to kick at me, but I was far too strong for her. A lot stronger than I had been before the transformation. Tears erupted and then spilled over her lids as she fought with all her tiny body's might against the succubus that had taken over. Crying out inside, I knew she could not hear my grief and apologies for what I had done. The spirit Pythagoras placed inside me, what the state believed would make me a stronger warrior, turned me into something that my poor Eos would fall victim to. I fought, trying to push my way out of the well of darkness that enveloped me to no avail.

It was that moment I wished I could explain somehow. That I could tell her I did not wish her dead. That I wanted our child to blossom inside her, and to grow into the Spartan the Gods would be proud of. Then anger at the Gods took over, driving the force of the succubus even further as Eos weakened and the light began to fade from her eyes.

Within mere moments, she ceased to fight, and there was a strange pride that bloomed in my chest alongside my grief that cracked the dark like lightning.

What the creature inside me did next shook me to my very core.

Letting go of her slender throat, bruises littering her pale flesh, it formed one of my hands into a large fist and brought it down hard into the center of her chest. A loud crack filled the air, resonating in my ears as I watched — horrified. It beat on the same spot again and again until flesh and bone gave way, blood flowing freely past my own fingers as the succubus reached down and pulled pieces of Eos' chest away — her heart, still and crimson, exposed for the world to see. My hand, our hand, reached inside and gripped the organ. Her chest cavity was warm and slick, almost as if she were still alive and breathing, and the muscles of her heart were smooth past the rigid sharp bone that once protected it from harm.

The succubus pulled it out, roughly severing every connection within her body with sheer force, and then brought it up to my lips.

I gagged and begged the creature to stop, but it did not hear me. That, or it ignored my presence completely, reveling in what I thought it was about to make me do. Lips grazed the meat of Eos' heart, and I gagged again, feeling the nausea burn its way into my throat — but it did not seem to affect the spirit. Absolute horror, grief, and disgust spiraled in my mind along with the pride and hunger from the succubus that threatened to take me over completely. It tried to wash me away with Eos' blood, but had not succeeded. Not yet.

But still enough.

My lips clung to the organ, and then my teeth bit into its tough exterior. The taste of iron flooded my mouth, coating my tongue in its heat. I felt my stomach heave, and I wanted to vomit, but I could not. I could not ingest the heart Eos had given me. Not like this. Not like a rabid carnivore with no sense of love or loyalty to its partner. The succubus was an animal, that much was clear.

"Kallias," I heard a strong, male voice echo through the room.

It was as if I slammed back into my own body, everything coming into crystal clear focus once again as control came back to me. Horrified, I looked down at what I had been forced to do, and a harsh wail left my throat to meet whomever had said my name.

Anaxis moved from within the shadowed doorway, the magician Pythagoras at his heels.

"What have I done?!" I screamed out, tears like liquid fire streaming down my cheeks.

I dropped the organ to the bed, watching it roll a couple inches and stop nestled in its original resting place — bite marks in it. Heart hammering in my chest and my entire body nearly collapsing with trembling horror, it took a moment for someone to speak. Some sort of shock had registered on their faces first, but then a sly grin plastered itself on Anaxis' face while Pythagoras only nodded in acknowledgement.

"You have made your first kill," Anaxis said — almost whispered.

"What? What is that supposed to mean?" I shrieked, rising from the bed.

Pythagoras took a step forward, moving Anaxis to the side in a rushed manner. "Did you accept the spirit, soldier? Did the succubus come to you?"

I thought about that for a moment, everything a blur over the last hours since the ritual took place. I remembered the important things — Eos telling me she was with child and making love. That was all I could recall.

Than it hit me like fist to the gut, and I almost crumbled to my knees and cried out. The dream. The image of myself that I spoke to that asked me to accept it so I could gain its power and strength. That was it, wasn't it? That was the moment that truly changed everything. My knees nearly buckled, but I held myself up, not willing to give into weakness in front of Anaxis. I could have cared less about the magician.

"Yes." The word barely left my lips. "Yes."

Pythagoras came to the edge of the bed, long robe moving around him as if it had a mind of its own, and looked down sadly as Eos' body — taking in the bloody scene before him. When he looked back up at me, his eyes were still full of the same sorrow, but nothing could compare to the disgust and grief I felt within myself at that moment.

"That was the spirit of the succubus. This," he motioned toward Eos, "is what it does. It kills indiscriminately. It feels no love; no matter how much its human shell may. And that is all you are to it now. You are a vessel for murder, Kallias."

"It made me kill my wife," I shouted, my tears mixing with Eos blood all over my face, neck, and chest — running down my legs toward the floor. "She is with child. My wife and child are dead!" Without even thinking, I vaulted over the bed and grabbed the magician by his cloak, pushing him up against the wall in an enraged frenzy. "You did this. What this thing is, you can take it back! Send it back where it came from!" I yelled into his face.

He remained calm, never once showing fear, and placed his old leathered hands on mine. "I am afraid I cannot do that."

"And why is that? You placed this spirit within me. Surely you can remove it."

"Because it's a part of you now, and will be as long as you live, brother," Anaxis said from behind me, his hands coming to rest on my shoulders.

I jerked away from them both, nearly toppling to the floor in shock.

"Do not touch me. You should have warned me. You are just as bad as the State. I am not some soldier that can be experimented on," I shouted. "The both of you are bastards! How could the Gods allow this?"

"It is your fate. Not even the Gods can stop fate, Kallias," Pythagoras muttered.

Falling to my knees, I looked up at the old magician and sneered. "And what do you know of fate?"

"What I do know is that fate is a cruel mistress, and this was chosen for you before your birth," he replied.

"Nothing can be changed now. You have no choice but to accept your new future," he paused, "without Eos. This journey is meant to be a lonely one, my friend." He kneeled beside me and clapped me on the shoulder.

"I will not live without her, you understand? I can't, especially knowing my own hands took her life and that of our unborn child."

I lifted my hands, the crimson on my flesh stark in contrast. Almost as if it were mocking me.

"You do not have a choice, soldier," Pythagoras stated. "The succubus will not allow you to die. You are immortal now."

The thought of living life like this, with no control over the murderous urge I felt rising up in me again, sent pure terror shooting through my veins. I saw Eos' beautiful visage in my mind, smiling up at me as we wed, and my heart ached. The presence rolled in my belly like fire, spreading out into each muscle and nerve fiber with my rage. I felt the same sensations again — my essence being pulled into the darkness.

"No," I hissed to the succubus. "No. Not again."

I fought against It, but just as before, resistance was unsuccessful. I could not stop the wave that crashed over me.

"Do not fight it, brother. Accept it," Anaxis said, placing a large hand on my back.

Just like that, it was as if everything snapped into place, and I was no longer in control. Everything had changed forever, and there was no going back. The succubus and I were one.

***

The acrid smell of blood tickled my nostrils, pulling my thoughts from the past and back to my latest kill spread out in front of me. It was as if the time outside watching the artist and then the kill passed in a flash, but I knew better. Images of her cries and body being ripped to ribbons slashed through me, making my heart ache —making Emmett's heart ache. The heart was not mine. Just the body and the mind.

Over the centuries, I — the succubus — had held onto control to this form. Kallias bounced from one identity to another, settling on Emmett Adler while, in this modern time, I became Adam Burnside. Emmett was an artist, and I was his 'benefactor.' And that was where all difference ceased to exist

Well, almost.

We later learned that this affliction was not truly supernatural, but the result of radiation morphing the original body's DNA — creating a new person inside the other. One with a murderous rage it could not help, and that every person who became either like we did or by hereditary misfortune could not overcome.

The reason for that, I could not tell, but it existed. It was uncontrollable, that thirst. Not even the blood of a million women could quench it, and now Blythe had caught my interest. The fact that she could nearly coexist with her other half was fascinating, and I needed her secret if I were going to continue on like this for what remained of eternity.

Standing before the body held up by chains on the large metal 'X,' I pushed her bloodied blonde hair away from what used to be a beautiful face. She yawned back at me, sightless since I had removed both blue orbs and devoured them. Her pale skin was blotchy, lips turning blue rather quickly after her death.

Not long after that, I had cracked her rib cage open, reached inside of her, and pulled out her beating heart as she screamed in agony. I had felt Emmett — Kallias — stir inside with disgust when I got down and devoured her heart as well. It was tough and the taste of iron had filled my mouth, still lingering as I stood there.

Reaching up, my fingertips grazed each protruding rib bone that glistened in the dim light. My stomach lurched, and I forced back the vomit that threatened to spill past my lips. Emmett's involuntary reaction to my actions.

I thought of the redhead again.

Blythe McAlister.

What a strange creature she was. It made me wonder — even more so than before — what secrets lie within her mind and body. What could I learn from the differences I had only sensed in her? What was different? What could I use?

What secrets could her particular brand of the same affliction tell me? There was only one way to find out.

MURDEROUS MERMAID

BY SHERI L. WILLIAMS

ACT I

HER BLUE TAIL SPARKLED IN the sun as she jumped out of the sea, slicking and twisting before diving back down. Her muscles burned in the best way possible. A quick trip to the land of humans had not been not productive, but she would not let the failure dismay her. She may not have any new toys to play with, but the ones she still had would keep her occupied until the new moon came.

The humans were a predictable lot. The King knew of her existence, but did not fear her. Every new moon cycle the humans threw a lavish celebration; a folly of waste and opulence. And during that celebration she would make her way to the shore and steal away with yet another human male. For more moon cycles than she could track she had done this. Aside from herself, and the toys she kept in her cave, only the King knew why she did what she did.

He knew her reasons and she sometimes wondered if he felt any guilt for what he had done to her. But she didn't wonder often, nor did she allow that wonder to stop her plan. She would have Vincent. He was the beginning of it all. He would be her crowning achievement. Perhaps when she had him she would stop. Perhaps not.

She dove deeper, flicking a fish that attempted to stay in her wake. She did not allow the simple creatures in her cave. She would not let them get near her at all if she had the option, but she did not. Instead she suffered through their annoying attentions. Once the fish went teetering off in the other direction she slid through a crack in some boulders and turned down the long tunnel that led to her playroom.

The orange seaweed parted around her as she pushed through the opening of her cave. The air was sweet and she gulped it in. Her lungs contracted as she made the shift from tail to legs. It hurt. More than she ever let on. The breaking of scales and muscle as one stem turned to two, you might as well have ripped her tail of completely for how badly it hurt. By the time she sat on the rock that jutted out as a platform, her legs were formed. The first few steps were clumsy, but then the grace that she had with her tail returned. As always with the conversion, pain raced up her legs as she walked. But she pushed it down and ignored it.

Many of her kind never made the transition. The pain was simply too much for them to handle. They let their innate magic fall away. Like the fish she loathed, Anahita found her own kind to be simple. She chose to be alone. Separated from the other merfolk, closed off from being normal, she reveled in her chosen isolation. Not that she was truly alone. Oh no, she had her toys.

She heard the moans as she moved deeper into the cavern. A burst of joy shot through her when she first caught sight of her five toys. The chains clanked and rattled as one tried to get comfortable. She wasn't a complete terror; she gave them beds of soft seaweed to sit on as well as enough room to move about. Yes she kept them chained, but she fed them and looked after them. And most of all, she played with them. She pushed and prodded, broke and ruined them. Strung them out with with pleasure that turned to pain quicker than they could wrap their feeble minds around what was happening.

It did not matter to her if their minds did not trust her or if their hearts hated her. Their bodies loved her and she reveled in that. She took notice that her favorite watched her warily. He had been with her long enough now that she practically knew what he was thinking. She'd had favorites before but this one was special. Maybe it was because he reminded her of Vincent, or maybe it was that even after many moon cycles he still defied her. He tried to deny his own body's reaction to her, but in the end she won. She always did.

With him watching her, she moved to the jars of cream she kept. Her human skin dried easily and in her vanity she had found an ointment that would keep her smooth and moist. Her skin was as luxurious as her tail. Voices murmuring behind her told her that another of her toys had awoken. Her favorite was arguing with his neighbor. As always, the sound of their voices sparked anger inside her.

She spun quickly, making a slicing moment across her throat. Her favorite glared but the other clamped his mouth shut. All her toys had learned quickly that she did not let them speak in her presence. Their human voices grated in her head. Her hearing was sharp and if she had to listen to anything she would not choose to listen to them. The younger of the two shuffled even closer to the rock wall, trying to make himself less. They all did that in the beginning. As if hiding would save them from her games. It left her with a smile; the thought of breaking in new ones.

With that in mind she walked over to the one who had spoken. She motioned for him to hold his hands out. If he hesitated it would only be worse for him; she knew he understood that. He held them out to her, knowing what to expect. She grabbed the key that was knotted in her hair and slipped it into the locked shackles on his wrists. Once he was free from the chains she led him to the edge of the rocks. He sat as he knew to.

She tied his hands behind him this time. Then with one well placed kick with her small foot the human fell into the water with a splash. With a grin she pushed off, leaping into the air with human feet. She arched in the air and when she dove through the water her tail was back. She found her toy sitting at the bottom of the sea cave. His cheeks puffed out and his eyes bulged. She swam forward and, using a shell as a buffer between her mouth and his, forced air into his lungs, giving him an extra precious few moments. She swam away again, slapping his face with the end of her tail. If he didn't gasp he might survive. The force of her tail slap disturbed the ocean bed. All around her toy the bones of his predecessors floated, before settling back down.

When she saw his eyes go wide again, she laughed. She made no sound but her torso rocked with the force of her mirth. When his eyes rolled back into his head and his body started to fall over she grabbed the rope that encircled his wrists and pulled him straight to the surface. On the ledge she pressed hard on his hair-covered chest. When he began to cough and rolled over on his side, she pulled herself up onto the rock. Her legs returned and she waved him back to his spot against the wall.

Once he settled she shackled him back to the wall, tying the key back into her hair. Then, disgruntled that the joy of playtime was waning, she left them in the outer chamber and made her way to her rooms. She had chosen this cave specifically because it had separate areas, and they all had an access point to the ocean. She lay down on the bed of moss and sea-weed, letting her legs dangle into the open pool. She closed her eyes and wondered what she would do now. Mermaids had a long life span, nearly thrice that of a human, and if she was already losing interest in the one thing that brought her joy, then she was looking at a long boring lifetime.

Sunlight filtered down into her cave. The beams of warmth rippled on the surface of the water. She surged up, throwing her hair to clear her face. Every day started the same for Anahita. A dive deep down in her own personal water hole, and then she saw to her toys. Today would see a deviation though. Today was the celebration on the land. The humans would party, and perhaps this time her plan would succeed. Perhaps this time she would grab Vincent, the only human to ever truly occupy her thoughts. Their history was muddled. Equal parts ecstasy and pain. Her heart pumped fast when she thought of him, but it raced out of control when she thought of the pain she would make him feel.

Thinking about what she would do to him, how she would make him pay, was enough to bring back the joy of her toys. She left her rooms in an effort to put it out of her mind until the appropriate time. Now was the time to be sure her toys were well maintained and ready to welcome a newcomer. She stood in front of them, motioning for them to prepare for inspection.

. One by one they stood, shackles clanking with movement. She thought maybe she heard the popping of underused bones, the imagined pain brought an evil smile to her lips. Her joy was coming back fully fledged now. Her favorite glared at her. She believed if he was able, his own arms would reach out for her with violence, but she had learned from her first toys. She had taken no time in killing the one who had marked her. Her temper had shown itself that day, but it had been long ago. Now she was able to control her emotions. She also knew that a swift killing did not fit her desires. She preferred to take her time, to make the pain last, to keep her toy lucid as long as she could. It was the fear she fed off. The fear and the exact moment their eyes rolled back until all she could see was her reflection in the whites.

All five stood in front of her. Their pale, naked bodies bowed in, each one in different stages of decline despite her care of them, but the last one appeared broken. One arm was hanging loosely, almost disconnected from his body, and half his face was purple and swollen. She pointed at him but none of them spoke. She walked over to stand in front of her favorite and motioned at his mouth, her way of permitting him to speak. He licked his lips and gulped hard. His voice angered her, but she had asked for him to speak and he did.

"He tried to escape. The one next to him did not allow him to. You slept through a fight, you abomination."

She ignored his insult, she knew that they thought poorly of her, but she would not ignore an attempted escape. Frustration coursed through her. The willpower it took to stay in human form ebbed, and the transformation had already started when she was finally able to gain control again. On painful legs that shook from the partial transformation, she made her way to the man at the end of the line. She paused before him, considering the next step. While she considered, he shook the chains that held him and broke into a hysterical laugh, sobbing at the same time.

The noise made her anger rise again, larger, darker than before, and she reached out with her delicate hands. Grabbing his head, she snapped his neck. When his body dropped to the floor she held still, letting the kill wash over her. It wasn't particularly satisfying, but done now, she could move on. Taking the key from her hair she quickly unlocked the shackles that bound him. Then, dragging him by his limp arm, she tossed him over the rock ledge. Turning to the rest of her toys she dared them silently to do or say anything. One by one they all sat, fear in their eyes. Even her favorite looked at her differently.

ACT II

WITH HER TOYS DOWN TO four and her anger still not pacified, she disregarded all her daily rituals. She dove into the water that lapped at the ledge. Her tail returned and she swam forcefully down. There at the bottom of the sea laid the body of her latest kill. His body already attracted scavengers and Anahita knew that soon his bones would be picked clean and left to be just another addition to her pile. Down there in the water the human's eyes had stayed open and the milky white was all she saw. It calmed her raging ire so she floated there for a few moments, staring at herself in the dead man's eyes. When she swam back up to her cave later, she was sure to grab fish for the rest of her toys.

As they tore at the fish ravenously, she cleaned the spot were the now dead toy had sat. Then one at a time she moved the remaining humans down a spot. When she was done locking the shackles back onto her favorite's wrists, she retied the key into her hair. His earlier momentary fear was gone and he was back to glaring at her as if he might possibly attack her. But she walked away with a swing in her hips, she would never let them know the pain she withstood to look like them, and prepared to leave. Now there was room for Vincent. He would be her new favorite.

She took time to run fingers through her hair. It would just get tangled again, that was what the sea water did, but she needed a moment of pure vanity to prepare for seeing him once more. She had changed, not only emotionally but physically, since they last saw each other. She could not help but wonder if he would still think she was the most beautiful creature he had ever seen, that's what he had said to her back then. Feeling more steady now, she dove into the water, kicking her feet out until they turned back into a beautiful blue tail. In her natural form she was unsurpassed in speed and agility, which she liked to prove by racing against the sharks and dolphins that others of her kind avoided. With her lungs bursting she pushes up out of the water. In front of her is the beach, and beyond that she can see the sun bleached stones of the kingdom.

Slower now, she swam toward the sandy expanse. Willing her transformation, she pushed through the pain and walked on wobbly legs. By the time she reached the outer ring of stalls of the market her gait was graceful. Her nudity bothered her not, but the gasps of the humans she encountered reminded her that covering her body was a requirement. She stopped by a stall manned by a short, stout female. The female's eyes went wide.

"I know what you are..." she stammered.

Anahita pointed to a vibrant gold and purple fabric. The human's hands shook as she handed it over. With only a few movements, Anahita covered her body. The silky fabric draped loosely around her, covering her breasts but leaving her middle bare. With a quick knot it was tied around her middle, allowing her legs plenty of room to move, and giving a tantalizing glimpse to any who would look her way. And many would.

Pleased with her appearance, she nodded her head at the stall keeper as a way of thanks. The female merely muttered, wringing her hands as Anahita walked away with a purpose. Walking through the market did not displease her. The wares the humans sell matter little to her, but she did snag a handful of olives from a stall before reaching the outer walls of the palace. With the salt on her lips that reminded her of her home in the sea, she passed under the curved arch in the wall that surrounds the palace.

As she walks she feels the gaze of the males on her. She hears the whispers of the females. But she ignores it all. She has a mission and she will not be waylaid. Her feet carry her into the interior of the palace. A cacophony of sounds assaulted her ears then; shouts of the humans, wheels of the carts and the whines of the animals that pull them. It was almost too much. The members of the royal family and the numerous humans who served them ran about preparing for the party that would happen once the sun started to set. They were all busy, not one single human paid her any attention, past a glimpse of all the skin she showed. She made it all the way up the flight of stairs before a guard stopped her. A shimmy of her hips and he was tricked into getting close to her. Close enough that she leaned in and pressed a kiss against his lips. He dropped where he stood. A mermaid's kiss was death to a human.

Leaving the guard she turned and followed the staircase up to the tower. Vincent thought he could avoid her simply by staying as far from the sea as he could. But she had learned about his place and found him, all thanks to her favorite. With purposeful hands she pushed open the ornate doors. Before he could react she had one of the many pointed rocks loosened from her hair. The long tendrils of hair held many secrets, a few tools, and more than one weapon. It flew from her hand and landed in the wall directly next to his head. She stalked forward, grace replaced with urgency.

"Ana please..."he began, but she stopped him with another sharpened stone from her long hair. She grabbed his arm with her free hand and jerked her head. He shuffled his feet, perhaps trying to get away from her. The sharp stone broke his skin, blood trickling from his neck. He moved then. He tried to head for the door she had entered through, but she shook her head and motioned to the door she knew hid behind the large wall hanging. It was an image of the sea and, again thanks to her favorite, she knew it hid a staircase down to where the servants lived and worked.

He grumbled, but complied when the point of her weapon pushed even harder into his neck. They descended slowly, but she had been correct in her planning. The cramped room they entered was empty. All hands and bodies were being put to work on the celebration. She pushed him out the door and through the kitchen garden. She urged him faster down the path that lead to another beach; a secluded strip of land where she stripped off the silk. The sun on her naked body felt glorious but she couldn't dawdle. She compelled him to strip as well, then pulled him into the surf. Dragging him behind her she paused for one moment near an outcropping of rocks. When she'd plotted this, she'd been sure to prepare. From a pouch she had hidden she pulled out a handful of weeds. Known to only those that dabble in the dark arts, this weed had one special use; to help humans breathe when they otherwise wouldn't be able to. She stuffed the weed in his mouth and he tried to refuse it, but the look she gave him persuaded him.

Even with the weed in his system she had barely enough time to get him to her cave. Just as her tail slapped at the top of the water for her dive she heard the alarms sound in the palace. She smiled hugely with the image of the bastard king setting every human to search for the prince. He would not be found. Not alive.

ACT III

H E DIDN'T STRUGGLE. SHE ALMOST wished he had. But when she pulled herself up on the ledge, braced for the pain of her tail separating into two pale legs, he held onto the rocks gasping for air.

"Sire, I'm sorry." Her favorite had spoken, and she reached out to slap him across the face. She started yanking Vincent up by one arm. Then, with more anger than she'd thought she'd feel, she shackled the prince next to his longtime servant. She'd expected to feel happiness, a sense of accomplishment, but she felt neither. Had she gone numb to the whole affair? At that moment the king was probably calling for his witch, the evil hag who had ruined her. He would be demanding that she work some sort of spell, but with the witch's reach was not so big that she could hurt her in the ocean. Even that knowledge didn't help with her apathy.

She left her toys. Their mumblings enraged her but she was tired from her trip to the palace and the onslaught of memories that hounded her once Vincent had said her name. She went to her quiet place, the cavern within the cave. She tried to quieten her mind, but the images blasted through every wall she had tried to erect in her brain. They flashed in pieces, only bits of a full scene but still enough to make tears rain down her face.

Learning to use her legs.

Running across the sand.

A laugh when she took her first tumble.

Being scared the first time she saw him.

Becoming friends slowly.

Pushing him away when he tried to kiss her.

The shock the first time he saw her tail.

Pressing a kiss to her hand, then pressing that hand to his lips.

The first time he touched her in a new way.

The ecstasy of mating.

The shame from her own kind

The fear when he told her his father knew

and then....

The agony when the King had caught her and had his witch curse her, stealing her voice.

She covered her eyes with her hands, trying to shut out the memories, but now that she'd seen him, touched him, breathed in the scent of him, she couldn't close her mind to the past any longer. He'd been her creator and she understood now that he'd be her destruction.

Her legs felt heavy so she slid off her bedding into the crystal blue of her own private waters. Her tail never suffered from heaviness and she swam down deep, under the ledge that she normally stood on and down to where the bones of her past toys lay. Anger coursed through her. Anger at herself for being so melancholy after her successful plan. Anger at Vincent for allowing his father to hurt her. Anger at her toys for not giving her joy any longer. The anger propelled her, digging through the bones until she reached the small chest they covered. She unlatched the chest and pulled out the only human thing she had ever held onto, aside from the chains and shackles that held her toys. A knife; sharp, golden, with a black stone adorning its handle. She'd found it many moons ago, washed up in a wreck. She'd used it to kill the three survivors; humans deserved to die after all, but she kept the knife. It glinted in the pale shafts of light that stubbornly made it that far deep. With no real thought as to why, she kicked off, heading back to her sanctuary, the knife still in her hand.

When she climbed back out of her portal she laid the knife on her bedding and went to deal with Vincent and her toys. She shook the water out of her hair. The jingle of the key and he weapons she kept there was enough to draw the attention of her toys. She sat, her legs crossed in front of them. Two of the toys stared, her nudity still a shock to them, but her favorite, he knew to be wary. Her body, though beautiful, was merely a tool for her. She admired him for that, she almost wished he didn't need to die.

Four out of five of the men who sat before her wouldn't speak, but that did not stop Vincent. With the others staring at him, he opened his mouth.

"Please Ana, let them go. You have me. That is what you want, is it not?" When she said nothing he continued. "Why do you not speak? Do you hate me that much?"

"She doesn't speak." Her favorite spoke out of turn. Before he could say anything else she let loose one of the sharpened stones she played with. It landed in his foot, causing him to scream and shout obscenities.

Vincent's eyes went wide. "Is that....my father's woman? The witch? Is that what she did to you? She stole your voice?"

It amused her that he wouldn't even say the word. A woman? No. An evil hag who dabbled in things she should not. Oh, the things she would tell him if she could. The things she could explain that would shatter his simple, sheltered brain. How she could have thought herself in love with him all those years ago was beyond her now. Tired of listening to his simpering voice, she slashed across her throat. The toys knew what this meant, Vincent however kept talking, going on about fixing her. But she did not want to be fixed. She wanted peace. After a few moments in his presence she knew he could not bring her that, no matter how she wished she could. She unfolded herself, then on her knees she crawled forward and slapped him. Once, twice, then his hand grabbed her wrist, his chains clanging in the effort.

"Sire don't," the servant said, moments before she slipped Vincent's grasp and grabbed him by the head with both hands. She slammed his head against the wall. With Vincent out, she stalked to to the natural shelf, grabbing an ointment and some drying seaweed. She went and doctored her former favorite's foot. He said nothing, but he did wince when she pulled the stone from his flesh. Satisfied that he would not die from infection she went back to her private space.

She sat down hard on her bedding. The knife glinted, drawing her attention. She picked it up, running the length of blade along her finger. The blade was sharp, drawing a thin line of blood. Intrigued by the slight pain, she ran the tip down the inside of her upper leg. The pain felt new and good. The sight of the line of purplish blood that emerged behind the blade's trail brought tears to her eyes. The tears continued to fall in unison with the blood. Though the blood soon stopped flowing, the tears did not. What emotion was this? She had known love once, but since then all she'd known was anger. Joy was rare, and only came when playing with her toys. Pleasure was something she swore she'd never feel again. But this new feeling, she could not place it.

Disgusted with herself and the path her thoughts were taking, she dropped the knife. With zero grace or finesse she jumped into her small portal. She didn't even wait for her legs to turn to tail. She kicked off, swimming hard. An unexpected pain in her freshly turned tail startled her. She paused to examine it and found a cut, barely healed. It was where she had run the blade along her human leg. It had stayed through her transformation.She didn't know it would do that.

She swam slower now, with more care for her injured tail. She was farther from her cave than she normally went when she heard someone hailing her. She turned to see a merman heading straight for her. She tried to avoid them, but had not been paying attention to where she was heading.

You will stop. He sent out. The pain of being merfolk was, you didn't need to be able to talk, not with your voice.

I do not listen to you, she replied.

You will. The Queen is displeased. Humans are in our waters. One of ours was caught and tortured. She has left you be long enough, Anahita. If you do not stop your twisted way of life, she will send the executioner.

You believe me to be scared of the child Queen?

I believe you know no fear, but that will not stop her from culling you. You jeopardize all of us.

And with that he left her. Rage like she had never known filled her. Even worse than when she had had her voice stolen from her. She opened her mouth and screamed. Though no sound came, the force of her rage pulsed out in a wave that knocked several fish dead around her. With renewed purpose she swam home. The Queen would not threaten her. She who had taken the lives of the humans who hunted them. Human ones lay at the bottom of the sea because of her, and now that infant thought to execute her? It wouldn't do.

She jumped out of the water, her legs screaming in pain as she landed. Four sets of eyes watched her as she went past them into her room. When she came back out she held the knife. Now all four sets of eyes grew. The first scream echoed through the cavern when she plunged the knife up to the handle into the first human. Twice more she jammed the knife through flesh and organs. The screams woke Vincent and he begged her to stop.

She did, but not for him. She stopped for her and for her favorite. He'd been her favorite for many moons, so when she stood before the servant, the one who had made it possible to get to Vincent, she did not kill him. She slid the key free from her hair, but before she unlocked him she slid the tip of the blade across his heart. Four times she marked him. Four red lines across his skin. Then she unlocked his shackles and dragged him to the ledge. With her eyes closed she pushed him into the water. If he was worthy he would survive. He could swim hard and break through the surface before his strength completely failed him, or a shark detected the fresh blood.

With the decision made, she would take away the joy the child Queen would get from her execution. She unlocked Vincent. He did not speak and she was thankful for that. Taking his hand, she brought him to her room. For the first time she wished she could speak to him like he were merfolk. She wanted to impress upon him how much their time had meant to her, but how much she blamed him as well. His cowardice had created a monster from beauty, and only he could end it. She placed the knife in his hand, turning him to face her head on.

"Ana..." he said, as she pulled his hand toward her middle as she kissed him. Her scream was silent. They died as one.

STRUCK THREE

BY R. L. WEEKS

ONE

YE OLD TOWN OF SKULL was one steeped with dark happenings. If it were a song, it would be a violin instrumental with a backtrack of inaudible suspicious whispers and church bells.

Mr Jones had lived in this town since he was a baby. He looked at the garden from behind the barbed-wire fence with tatters of crime scene tape still visible. The swing set once used by his children now looked like a permanent fixture amongst the overgrowth.

With a deep exhale, he walked up the uneven path to the front door.

Memories of the once pretty, homely house, thanks to his wife, crossed his mind as he looked at the peeling paint on the door. The wreath hanging in anticipation to Christmas, his wife's favorite holiday, lay on the ground, charred black.

He pushed the door open, which like every scary movie he had ever watched, creaked loudly. He had no fear of what was in the house. After all, wouldn't he soon be joining them?

His work boots, still caked with mud, thumped across the carpet. Pillars of dust rose into the air with each step.

He stopped and faced the clock, perhaps one of the only things left in the house that hadn't been fire-damaged. How? He wasn't sure.

The mechanical gears cracked as they slid together with a metallic click.

Each tick, each tock, drummed in sync with Mr Jones' heartbeat.

Suddenly, as if aware of his presence, a loud dong erupted from the grandfather clock. It was quarter past three, yet the clocked rang 3am, breaking the deafening silence.

Just as soon as the final dong sang, another set of four rang out, alerting anything in the house to his being there.

Then, five final dongs. The moment when time stood still. Five AM had been the time when his family had perished in the fire he had unfortunately survived.

He looked around. There was no more ticking to distract from the eerie silence. The worst part about an absolute quite is you could hear every single sound the house made.

Every creak from the floorboards upstairs, every shudder from the non-working fridge, and the sound of a key turning, and the lock clicking shut.

He felt something move behind him but didn't entertain it. Things always moved in the shadows, and you only gave them life by looking at them. He had heard many a time that when you see something in the corner of your eye if you let it stay in the corner of your eye, it will materialize.

He shuddered a little as he became aware that whilst he was busy watching the clock, something else had been staring at him through the darkness of the living room. Surrounded by whispers of the past, framed memories covered with shattered glass, and once-adored possession that lie covered in a layer of dust.

His gaze flitted over to a lone rattle at the bottom of the stairs. He could swear that rattle hadn't been there when he walked in, but then maybe he hadn't been looking properly.

In his peripheral vision, he could see a pair of tired eyes staring right at him. Dark circles under them, an angry expression in them.

Without looking at the figure, knowing that it was only an echo from the past, not anything he truly loved, he moved to the kitchen. On the floor, glass sparkled from the broken windows. Teenagers and the odd 'ghost seeker' had found their way into the house out of nothing more than morbid curiosity. Some of them had vandalized the already ruined house and graffitied their names on the cupboard doors.

Mr Jones sensed that something had followed him into the kitchen, but he did not dare look over his shoulder. There was more in that house than just the forgotten members of his dead family.

The walls and roof had survived the fire, although blackened and charred. It had been one year since the so-called accident. The skeleton of 412 Cherry Drive would always remain the final resting place to his wife and children. There wasn't anything left of them to give proper burial too.

The only good thing to come out of the catastrophe, and finally his own, would be the house would be a permanent reminder to everyone in that wretched town of their poor judgement, no thanks to the priest that was skilled at injecting fear in the small-town people of Stull. Paranoia was already burned into their minds from the horrific events and dubious reputation that Stull, and especially Stull cemetery had.

With precision, he hung the noose he had brought with him and tested its strength. His breath caught in his throat as he saw a small stool that was once his daughters, screech over next to him. Whatever was standing behind him, giggled just quietly enough that you could only hear if it if you were really listening.

With a deep breath, he pulled out his hip-flask and drank the golden whiskey inside. Liquid courage. He heard the sound of his dead-son calling out for him. He didn't answer, he didn't need too. He would be joining them soon.

TWO

REACHING OUT TO FEEL FOR a hard-surface in the pitch black, Mary called out for her boyfriend. "Billy?"

"I'm here doll." He replied with excitement. "Can you believe this place is still standing?"

She shuddered. "Yeah, I hoped they would have torn it down by now."

The house creaked as they stepped forward. She panicked as her foot slid over something round and hard. She grabbed the bannister, regaining her balance, and looked down. In the dark, she could just make out the white outline of the rattle. Her hand shot to her mouth. "There's a rattle here."

"Kids did live here, Mary." He said with exasperation. Her dramatic personality, however, was helping kick the adrenaline rush he wanted from breaking in 412 Cherry Drive.

The memories of Mary's seventeenth birthday came back to haunt her once more.

She and Billy had snuck some beers from his dad's and the gun from his safe. They headed out to the fields behind Cherry Drive and shot at cans. It was after a couple of beers, and Billy had got a bit handsy amongst the crops with Mary, that they saw the flames licking the walls of the Jones residence.

Billy wanted to get out of there, worried he'd get into trouble if caught with his dad's gun, but Mary insisted they go to help or at the very least call 911. He relented, only because taking Mary's virginity was something he had wanted for the longest time, and he was willing to do whatever it took to get her.

So he didn't seem uncaring, he shoved the gun in the waist of his pants, and ran with her to the tree line behind the Jones house.

Mary gripped the top of the fence, breathing heavily. "We need to call 911!"

Her brain was fuzzy from the beers, but the higher the fire soared, the soberer she felt.

Smoke clogged the air. Mary pulled her sleeve over her nose and mouth, and Billy zipped his jacket to the top, pulling it up over his nose. The sound of sirens rang through the air. Someone had already beat them to it.

Hours passed as Mary and Billy watched from behind the tree line, realizing that enough help was there. Half the town had shown up to watch. Neighbors gossiped as Mr Jones was the only person to be taken out of the house alive. It was only when the fire was put out that the horrifying realizing hit all of them.

The wife and children were dead. There were tanks and gasoline used, according to what they could overhear from the fire department. We all knew after the rumors about the Jones's that the fire was no accident.

***

Billy shone his phone light and saw Mary's vacant expression. He kicked the rattle out of the way and squeezed her shoulder. "I heard that they were devil worshippers, they deserved whatever happened to them. Probably messed with wrong thing and the devil burnt their house down," he said and shrugged.

Mary hushed her voice. "Two children died, one of them was one-year-old. They didn't deserve to die no matter what."

He shrugged. "Guess not, but it's the parent's fault. Especially the mother. She was seen at the cemetery practicing voodoo or something."

"She didn't deserve death," she whispered back. "She had her own set of beliefs, she did no wrong to anyone. Why am I the only one who cares about the injustice here?"

Billy smiled and ran his hand through her soft brown hair. "You care because of the same reason that I love you. You try to see the best in everyone."

She recoiled. "I just think there's more to this than we think. Houses don't just catch fire that quickly. Gasoline. Tanks. Come on, you can't believe what everyone says?"

Billy rolled his eyes. "You and your theories. Look, the fire department said it was an accident. They kept tanks of oxygen and gasoline in the house. How dumb do you have to be to do that."

"How dumb do you have to be to believe that story." She snapped back.

He bit his tongue, doing his best not to lose his patience. "Let's keep looking around."

She huffed. "I really wish we could go."

He moved along the corridor until the reached the children's bedroom. "our hand is freezing." He said as they halted.

Mary froze. "Billy, I'm not touching you."

Billy jumped a foot in the air and let out a scream.

Mary stepped backward, until she hit the cold wall behind her. "Let's go." She begged him.

Silence hung between them for a few seconds until Billy spoke. "Oh I get it. You were trying to scare me. Very funny." He said, choosing to believe that instead of the alternative. He didn't want to even think about the cold spot he could feel next to his face. Instead, he reached out, grabbed Mary's hand. "Let's go down to the kitchen. I just want to get some pictures. Jake doesn't believe that I'd actually do this."

"It really wasn't me." She said, but he wasn't listening. Instead, he pulled her out of the room. She would break away from him after everything he said, but he was the only body in the house that could protect her against whatever *did* touch Billy.

Once they reached the living room, Mary calmed down a little. The bedrooms upstairs were beyond creepy. Her mind flitted back to her earlier thoughts. "What if the townspeople did it? They hated Carrie Jones."

He shook his head. "They wouldn't have done that. Father Valgard said that the Devil comes to those who ask for him. He hurts them."

She pressed her lips together. "Right." She scoffed. "It wouldn't surprise me if they did kill them," she whispered and followed Billy as he made his way into the kitchen.

He stopped in the door frame, frozen.

"What is it?' She asked and pushed past him. A stool lay on the tiled floor, next to it an empty hipflask looking out of place from all the fire-damaged goods.

She first saw his feet, before moving her gaze upwards.

Mr Jones was swinging side to side, hanging from a noose. The ceiling beam above was splintering under his weight.

The rope had cut into Mr Jones's throat, and frothed blood covered his beard and top. His eyes were bloodshot and almost hanging out of their sockets.

A flicker of a girl smiling sadistically, like from an old projection movie, flashed behind the body before vanishing.

They screamed, turned, and ran out of the house as fast as they could. Mary felt as if her heart could seize up at any moment. Billy ran behind her and almost tripped over as the door slam shut behind them.

They focused on the end of the path, wanting to get as far away from the house as they could.

Once they reached the middle of the road, Billy headed off to the left. Mary paused only for a second to look back. Eyes watched her from the murky window. Shivers slithered down her spine and an impending sense of doom followed as she ran after Billy.

Once they were safely away, they called the police anonymously to alert them to the body of Mr Jones hanging in the kitchen.

THREE

T HE LIES WE ARE TOLD about death is that it is permanent." Father Valgard boomed out in the crowded church. "Our eternal soul lives on. We will be judged by our Father when we pass the threshold and our actions will determine if we will go to Heaven or Hell."

He looked out at the scared faces in front of him. They were lined-up in the pews, all with desperation etched onto their expressions. The church, small but historic, was the heart of their community. He had been told to move to the bigger space in Stull Cemetery where ruins lie of the old church there. The community would even foot the bill for the restorations, but he refused the offer. Evil lived in that cemetery, coiling its way around every headstone, and hissing into the ears of anyone who stepped foot into it. Valgard felt compassion for the deceased who were buried there. That's why he made his request to be buried elsewhere of paramount importance in his will.

The cemetery, as usual, was the hub of the discussion around the meeting called at almost midnight. Not only was the churching held for services, funerals, and weddings, but also as a meeting space for important community discussions.

He placed his hand on the bible. "They are playing with fire." He shouted, referring to the teenagers that kept sneaking into the cemetery, and into 412 Cherry Drive. "Stull Cemetery." He pronounced. "Is one of the gateways on Earth to Hell."

They gasped as the words left his mouth. Although that rumor had floated around for as long as anyone could remember, but that was the first time someone with standing had confirmed it aloud.

"No matter." He said quickly. "Evil cannot set foot on hallowed ground. We will protect this town against the forces trying to hurt it. Remember, evil only has a way in through you." His gaze landed over his people. "You are the vessel that evil needs to destroy our town. Your children are who they will manipulate. Repent, cleanse yourself from sinful thoughts, give not into temptation and see only the light for each sinful thought you have given evil an opportunity to latch on to you."

Some men shuffle uncomfortably as the words are spoken, and their wives flush red.

He finished the meeting with a sermon and closed his bible. As the cover slammed shut on the heavy book, a woman, Miss Naples, waited behind as everyone else left.

"Father." She began.

"My child."

She smiled in his presence. "What you said about evil... it made me think."

"Yes?" His interested was piqued.

"My daughter."

"Ah, sweet Mary."

She half-smiled. "Yes. She has been sneaking out recently, with Billy, her boyfriend." She paused. "I'm worried about her. She hasn't seemed herself."

His gaze latched on to hers with conviction in his eyes. "Bring her in to talk to me." He rests his hands on her shoulders. "You did the right thing by coming to me. No one is too late to be saved. Jesus did, after all, die for our sins."

Once Mrs Naples left, Father Valgard sat on a pew in the drafty, stone church, next to an arched stain-glass window. He thought back to his own experiences about the cemetery and the evil that pulsated beneath it. It was that, that kept him in the town. He needed to fight it, if no one else would.

He was younger when first stepped foot in Stull Cemetery. His back hadn't begun to ail him as it did now, and he even had a spring in his step. This was his chance, after years of training, to make a difference in his own church.

The building had not been torn down then. It wasn't in good condition, but it was repairable. The basement was what he remembered most about that place, if he had ever managed to reach it that was. He had walked down those steps for what felt like hours, but he never reached the bottom. When he finally decided to walk back up, it took him only seconds to reach the top of the steps again, making him question his own sanity.

Something down those steps called to him, even in his dreams. It was only when he realized what it was did, he steered clear of the place altogether.

He had been skeptical of the legends surrounding the small town before he came to live there. He had only heard whispers of the supposed Gateway to Hell, obviously a story told to bring in more tourism, or so he had thought.

He did believe in the Devil. To believe that God exists, one must acknowledge the existence of Satan too. However, he never truly believed when he came to Stull, with its small houses, lovely people, and pretty scenery, that he would come across Satan's work in the flesh. Nor did he know that he would one day be living just a mere three miles from one of the gateways.

What truly confirmed his theory was young boy he met when he was twenty-two and first at the church. His name was Edmund. His father was an active churchgoer since his wife died, but Edmund didn't accompany him once. Whenever Valgard asked him about his son, he refused to say anything.

At the time, the residents of Stull were dying mysteriously, all in ways that could not be explained by the fire department, police, no-one.

Father Valgard knew something sinister had happened when he had a run in with an incubus. A sex demon. He had only read of them, but every sign of Incubi possession was apparent.

A woman had rushed into the church, crying. She confessed to having sex with a demon in her dream and woke up to find semen on the covers. She fled town that week.

He heard a couple of years later that she had become a heroin addict, then died from an overdose, but she had birthed a baby boy which coincides with the time she confessed to her possession.

That was just the beginning to a series of very strange events.

Valgard looked through the stain-glass and out at the small, dreary town. Edmund's face came back to his mind.

The night after the women fled, he fell asleep after hours of searching through demon exorcism logs. In his dream, Edmund, the son of the churchgoer came to him. His face was unnervingly familiar although his eyes were black. Smoke pillared around him, and that's when he woke up to the screaming. He rushed out the door in his robe and saw a field, not far away, ablaze. Cinders danced into the blackness above as the flames roared impatiently. He called the fire department and ran to the field. The tree which was once used as gallows for witches was now a pile of ash.

As the fire was put out, more people came to look at the field and the destruction it had caused. Valgard did his best to keep everyone back, but it was too late. Edmund was dead, smoke still rising from his melted skin, his melted into his skull. Everyone was screaming, panicking.

From that moment, Valgard was left to deal with the growing hysteria creeping through the town, which was worsened by James, Edmund's father's, arrest. He was cuffed and found guilty. In his testimony, he told the court that he did because his son was possessed.

Now, aged seventy-two, Valgard was watching a similar hysteria happen again. Last time neighbor turned on neighbor and innocent people were killed for their beliefs.

The older ones and he still remember what had happened all those years ago.

Carrie Jones had sparked the fire, with her crazy beliefs and odd ways and now Mr Jones was found hanging from a rope. Everyone knew to take your own life was a terrible sin.

Valgard and a few others who had grown old with him, who knew the truth, thought by getting rid of her for the greater good would calm the hysteria, but it made it worse. He had tried to get the children out of the fire, not realising they were home already with Mr Jones, but he was too late. The fire spread and the children died.

With Mr Jones's suicide, paranoia and fear were mounting again. He was worried, not because of the house, but because of what he knew would happen next. Stull may hold evil, but from what he had seen, most of it came from the residents. They would turn on each other again, and in doing so, the town would be open to more possessions.

The reason the gateway to hell existed in Stull was because of the hundreds of massacres and evil acts, ironically brought on by their belief in God, attracted evil to the town, and that evil would continue to grow until it swallowed the town whole.

FOUR

MARY NAPLES LAID ON HER bed, playing with ringlets of her chocolate-colored hair as she mulled over everything that had happened in the last twenty-four hours.

Her window shot open, making her jump. "Billy." She breathed. slowly 'What are you doing here. You scared me."

Billy walked over, grinning, and placed his index finger over her lips. "Shush." He hushed. "I think you were right about everything."

She batted his finger away. "What part?"

"The fire not being an accident. Strange things are happening."

A pang of sadness shot through her. "I had hoped I'd be wrong, but I know that it wasn't an accident. Those poor children were murdered in cold blood."

"Mmhmm." Billy said dismissively. "I did some digging. I think it was Valgard. I think he did it!"

She gasped. "But he's a priest?"

"I was wrong about so much," Billy admitted. "They didn't deserve to do like that. They were only realizing the truth."

"What?"

"The truth." He looked at her excitedly. "Lucifer was cast from Heaven simply for loving God too much? He's not the one condemning us for doing things are simply enjoyable."

She furrowed her brows. Billy was a devout Christian. This was unlike him. "You look surprised?"

"Uh... this is insane." She looked down at his shoes. They were covered with thick mud. "Where have you been?"

He grinned. "Cemetery." He touched her hand softly. "Have you heard of the Devil's mark?" he asked.

She frowned. "Yes. Why?"

He ripped his sleeve up. She pinched her eyes shut. "Please no Billy. Tell me you didn't."

"Please, look." She heard him say.

She opened her eyes and gasped in horror. "Billy, how could you?"

He grinned more, looking more excited than he ever had. "Mary, don't you see? The Devil isn't evil! In fact, he says rape is wrong among many other things. A complete confliction to the bible which is one big contradiction. You tell me how rape, among many other horrible things, is okay in the bible?"

"I..." She stuttered. "All I know is the Devil can manipulate you. Don't let him. So what if some of the bible is wrong. I have faith in God. I believe everything happens for a reason." I pause. "So don't shove this down my throat. I don't know why you're even acting like this. The way I feel when I go into the church, when I wear my cross, I feel safe."

"Gullible more like," Billy retorted. "But I love you anyway," he said and ran his hand up and down her arm. "Either way, do you still love me?"

She sighed. "I always have but...I just didn't think you were capable of any of this. What deal did you make?"

He stood up and stretched out his hands. "Promise not to freak out?"

She bit her lip. "What did you do?"

She prepared herself for what he would say next, but instead he did something she never expected. His face warped. His eyes were coated with blackness, like another eyelid, except for the golden slit in the middle.

He leaned in to her, and against all her better sense, she couldn't help but be intoxicated by his scent. As if it was made for her.

He brushed his lips against hers. Electricity shot through her, and her lips curved into a sensual smile. Billy pressed his lips to hers and it was too late. She was at his mercy. It was unlike any other kiss they had ever had. It was... new.

He ran his hand up her night shirt until he reached her nipple. "I thought we were going wait." She managed.

His lips curved up. "Do you want to wait." He licked his lips and for a second, it was like every part of her was on fire.

He pinched her nipple which sent shock waves through her. She moaned with pleasure as he brought his lips down to her breasts and rolled his tongue around and around.

Her eyes rolled into the back of her head as he ran his hand up her leg. He pulled her panties down and caressed his fingertips down to her slit. She knew what she was doing was wrong, but it felt too good to stop.

Nothing else mattered in the world, just that moment in time when care and morals were discarded like his boxers on the red carpet.

"You're soaking wet, baby." He said, his greedy gaze locked onto hers. He pressed his fingers inside of her throbbing vagina and moaned. He reached back and stroked his length with his other hand.

Waves of pleasure pulsated through her. She closed her eyes as he pushed deeper.

"Baby," he said silkily. "Join me, baby, come down to the cemetery and we can do this forever. It will never be wrong. I promise."

She pushed her bottom into the bed, pushing his fingers inside her even deeper, and bit her lip.

Without another thought, she pushed him down and climbed on top of him.

She took his hard cock in her hands then put it between her legs. He pushed just the tip in, teasing her gently.

"I want to hear you say it." He said.

"Fuck me, please!"

"Agree to join me first," he said.

She ran her hand up to his face and wanted to look at his sweet, brown eyes as she lost her virginity.

Then, as if a bucket of cold water hit her, she woke up. When she opened her eyes she was faced with a disgusting, black-eyed man with bumpy skin and long fingernails.

Her eyes widened as she saw traces of blood on the blood from when it's fingers were inside of her. She recoiled. "What are you?"

"You still want it, I can feel it," he stated, smiling creepily.

She tried to push him off her. His midnight-black gaze sunk into hers. "No!" She shouted. "Get off me. I will never join. I said NO!"

As if a dream inside of a dream, she woke up again, covered in sweat. She jolted upright and looked around the room.

"It was a dream." She said thankfully, to no one in particular. But, as she felt the wetness between her legs and blood on her bed, that delusional quickly disappeared.

FIVE

FATHER VALGARD WALKED DOWN INTO the basement of the church. He loved his church and would live there if he could. It was the only place he felt safe.

He reached the draft basement which was filled with boxes, discarded old crosses and other items piled into one big mess. He had been planning on organizing and clearing it all out to make more space, but time was precious, and he hadn't had much of it as of late.

Amongst the dusty clutter, a brown chest with brass fittings stood out. It looked so new and out of place. He rubbed his hip that was giving him trouble and climbed over a stack of books to get to the chest. "I've never seen you before." He said to the chest and ran his fingers along the polished wood. "Where did you come from?"

He tried to open it, but it was locked. Across the room, in the gothic, cracked mirror that faced him coated in a film of grime, a flash of something caught his eyes. Something black.

He looked around, panicked, wondering if someone had followed him down to the basement.

Looking back at the chest, wondering if there was a crowbar, he could use to break it open, he sighed. "Looks like I need to find a way to get you open."

Finding different objects lost in the history of the church was fascinating. He remembered back to when he found an 18k gold cross under an old box, which now swung around his neck.

"Don't look in the mirror." A voice in his head said.

Panicked, he turned around and instinctively looked at the mirror. In the reflection was a woman's face, smiling sadistically as she started out at him.

He looked behind him, searching for the thing making the reflection, but nothing appeared.

Quickly, he looked back, and the mirror was empty of all but his own frightened expression.

Something tapped him on the shoulder, something that felt icy cold. He froze, not daring to move, but instead looked at the reflection in the mirror showing on a pale-white hand on his shoulder with no body attached to it.

He started to sweat, tremble, his heart beating faster.

He turned to run out of the basement, looking desperately for the way out. He wanted to cry out for someone to help, but the church was empty, and no one knew he was down there. The walls stretched out in a never-ending basement. Sweat dripped onto his robes. He reached for his cross and closed his eyes. "God save me from Evil."

A laughter echoed around the basement, one that sounded far too excited for where they were. Something was excited, watching as Valgard said God's name.

The sound of a lock clicking open made him jump. He turned and looked down at the now open chest. Inside of it were small dolls. They looked like they belonged in a doll-house. Two were children, and two were adults. The two child dolls and the woman doll were burned to a crisp and the male doll had a rope wrapped tightly around his neck.

His gaze widened as he saw the words scratched into the lid of chest 'The Jones's'. He gasped, his mouth covering his mouth, and fell backward. He stared up at the ceiling. How could he not notice it before? Written in blood on the ceiling were the words *'God can't save you here."*

SIX

THE HOUSE PHONE RANG LOUDLY. Billy jumped up and grabbed it, hoping it wouldn't wake his dad who had passed out on the couch after having too much wine.

"Mary?" I asked the voice on the end of the phone. She was crying. She kept asking him if he was okay. "Do you want me to come over?"

She sobbed. "Yes."

He looked over at this dad who was snoring lightly. He'd get grounded if he was caught sneaking out again, but Mary was so shaken up he had too.

"I'll be there soon sweetheart."

He hung up the phone and snuck out of the front door into the frost-bitten night.

He reached her house and looked up at the ivy wrapped around the drainpipe. He had climbed up to her window too many times to count and had only fallen once. He climbed with easy and tapped on the glass.

She pulled up the window and he pulled himself over the windowsill, landing softly on the carpet. She looked at him with bloodshot eyes. "Are you really you?"

He furrowed his brows. "Who else would I be?"

This set her off crying again. Her honey brown hair was knotted, and strands flew off in all directions. "Bedhead?" He laughed, but his smile quickly vanished on her solemn expression.

She sniffed and wiped her nose with the sleeve of her nightgown. "I am so sorry Billy! We... We did stuff. Sexual stuff. Well, not you and I... a-"

"Wait, what? You... you cheated on me?" He stuttered, shocked. Mary was the least likely person to cheat in their relationship.

She nodded. "I thought it was you."

He scoffed. "Of all the excuses with cheating, that was the worse! How could you mistake someone for me?" He paced around the room, running his hand compulsively through his hair as he processed it all. "After all this time of you telling me you weren't ready you go and slut it up with some other dude?"

"I was dreaming." She stated.

His eyes widened as he took in her words. Then, he let out a small laugh. "You called me up because you dream cheated?"

She cried hysterically. He sat down next to her on the bed and wrapped his arm around her waist. "Come on Mary don't cry. You can't help what you dream about."

She threw his arm off her and stood up, crossing her arms over he chest. "Wipe that grin off your face! This is not a joke. It was a demon, Billy. It was you, you had the Devil's mark,

you made a deal with the devil. Then, we... you know. Almost had sex." She bit her lip. "But then it wasn't you anymore. It was this guy, about our age, but he had bumpy pale skin, and black hair, and dark eyes.'

He arched an eyebrow. It struck a nerve, but he wouldn't let that show. "I think," he started in his calmest voice, "that everything that has happened has affected you. I shouldn't have taken you to that house. I'm sorry baby. It's made your imagination go crazy."

"No," she shouted. "It's not like that. I woke up and it was real. I was... I was wet and his saliva was on my chest and..."

His mouth opened then shut again. "Shall we go and see Father Valgard? He would know what do." He said, feeling at a loss. He was sure it was all a dream, but she was clearly very worked up about it and everyone knew the Devil preyed on the weak. He looked at his sweet, innocent girl and sighed. She was the perfect prey indeed.

Mary got dressed into her jacket and jeans and snuck out the window after Billy. He helped her down and they made their way over to the church.

"Do you think he'd still be there?" She asked.

Billy shrugged. "Guess so, He practically lives there."

'Bills,' she said slowly, drawing out the word with a sweet tone.

"Yes...?"

"Can I wear your jacket?" She eyed up his leather jacket, the one she loved to wear.

It was heavy but warm.

He looked at her thin jacket and sighed. She could have worn something warmer. Rolling his eyes, he handed it over.

She glanced at his arm. "What's that?"

He covered his arm with his hand. "What?"

"That!" She said desperately trying to pull his hand away from the mark on his skin.

"That mark..." she said, tears filling her eyes. "It's the same one the demon had in my dream."

She stepped backwards. He took a step toward her, but she almost toppled over. He put his hands in the air. "Okay hun, relax. It's just a tattoo."

He showed it to her. "No one knows I got it done yet. I didn't want to scare you after you told me about the dream and the mark in the dream. I promise, it's nothing."

She was scared, terrified even. He hated seeing her like that. "Please, believe me."

She shook her head. "It's a bit of a coincidence, isn't it?' she said through clenched teeth. "What have you done?"

"I..." He paused. How could he even begin to covey the truth after all the superstition surrounding this town?

How could he tell her that everyone was falling apart? A creeping hysteria mirroring that of Salem in the old days, was happening in Stull. People were turning on each other, and murder was becoming a norm. He saw the chain events and knew he had to join the winning side before he too ended up a corpse. He loved living far more than faith or loyalty. He knew being a Christian wouldn't save him. He saw the markings on all the walls, the demons in his dreams – God can't save you here – whispered again and again until he had enough.

He went to the cemetery. He did what no one else would and took action instead of running scared.

Stull had a secret as all small towns do, but this was a town with a big secret. Under it really was a Gateway to hell. Evil was rearing its ugly head once more, and the people there were fueling the fire. It started with act of murder. It turned out Mary was right after all. That fire had been no accident.

He waited until twilight and the son of the Devil appeared next to a gravestone engraved 'Wittich'. The boy with black eyes stared for a second at the headstone before looking at him. He gazed into Billy's eyes like he was reading his soul. Then, he knew everything that needed to be said.

He offered Billy a deal and gave him the mark to protect him and protect the ones he loved. In return, Billy was a soldier of Satan.

He looked back at Mary. His sweet girl. He'd never let the Devil take her. She's too precious and he intended on keeping her intact. "It's nothing." He looked deep into her eyes. "I won't let anything happen to you!"

SEVEN

FATHER VALGARD JUMPED FROM THE banging on the door of the church. He managed to find his way out of the basement after he finally could think clearly again. He disposed of the chest and smashed the mirror for good measure. He held onto his cross tight until the corner cut into his palm.

He hurried over to the doors asking God again to deliver him from Evil.

Had Edmund come back from the dead after being burned alive in that field? His eyes black from being burnt out, his skin bumpy from the burns. The image of the dead boy sent a shiver through him. He was the son of the Devil. He told everyone that, but few believed him until now. Carrie Jones was trying to contact him using a Ouija board, one of the many reasons she had to go. He was doing God's work.

He opened the door and breathed a sigh of relief. It was just Mary and Billy.

Billy looked around uncomfortably.

"Everything okay kids?" Father Valgard asked.

"Sorry to bother you so late," Mary said. Billy scratched at his arm. He looked in a lot of pain.

"Do you need a doctor?"

He looked up at Valgard and held his gaze. He felt something twist in his stomach.

"No," he answered in a deadpan tone. "We're here about Mary. I think an incubus has been invading her dreams." She flushed red. "A what? But yes, something did come to me in a dream but that's not important…" She grabbed Billy's arm. "He's been marked, Father."

He looked at the pair confused so she elaborated. "The Devil's mark. I had a dream that a demon visited me and tried to…" she blushed and looked at Billy nervously. "He tried to have intercourse with me, asking me to join him. He looked like Billy and then turned into this boy with black hair, black eyes, and bumpy skin."

Suddenly everything felt colder. Valgard gulped. It was Edmund. The dream and the sex sounded too similar to that poor woman who was lured by the incubus.

"Did you complete the act?" He asked, nervously.

She blushed again and shook her head. "I realised what I was doing and refused. That's when I woke up, but it seemed so real. There were traces… of him being there."

He nodded. "I'm glad you refused. Don't give in to the temptation, Mary. You're a good girl. So, this mark, tell me more about it." He looked at Billy. "Is it really the Devil's mark?" He asked because kids those days said anything to create drama.

Mary ripped up Billy's sleeve. The black markings moved, twisting and turning around a serpent. Above it's head was three small sixes in a row."

He knew he'd put his hip out with the quick action, but he didn't care. He grabbed Mary and pulled her over the threshold and into the church, whilst slamming the door.

"What are you doing?" She cried. "Billy!"

"It's too late for him." Valgard stated.

Mary tried to go after him. Valgard placed his arm out, blocking the door. "No. He has made his decision and he will pay for it. Stay away from him Mary and especially from Stull Cemetery. You're a good girl. You should leave town for a while."

Her forehead creased. She looked like she was fighting a losing battle. She looked up at the ceiling and gasped in horror. "I don't think we're safe." She said, pinching her eyes shut.

Blood dripped down from the ceiling onto the wood boards below. Behind them, a giggle sounded from the basement.

"What's that?"

Mary asked, horrified.

Valgard froze as he heard the laughing grow louder, and footsteps climbing the steps up into the church.

Valgard looked at the door. "Run!" He shouted at Mary who didn't need to be told twice. She fled out into the night and saw Billy waiting for her at the end of the road.

Valgard was left alone.

A whisper carried through the wind outside the open doors. A child's scream rang through the church. The church wasn't safe anymore. He ran out into the night, hoping to get away from whatever was inside. As soon he was outside the doors, the blood, the giggling, everything just vanished.

That's when it hit him.

There was nothing in the church. It was tricks placed into his mind to scare him into leaving. He hurried to run back inside, but the doors slammed shut and locked. He needed his sanctuary and prayed, but honestly, he had never felt so far away from God.

The time-chiselled oak tree that towered over the church cast a shadow over where Valgard stood. Beside it a form began to appear in the shape of a little boy. The toddler that had died in the fire that he had set. His heart jumped inside his chest. The guilt swallowed him whole as I stared into his little face. "You weren't meant to be there." He cried.

The boy walked over to him, unsteadily, like a toddler would walk. The closer her got, the more his appearance changed. His clothes were singed. His eyes melted onto his cheeks making bile rise in Valgard's throat.

"Help me." The little boy said just before he vanished.

Valgard dropped to his knees, sobbing as the wind pinched at his cheeks, drying his years instantly.

"You can't help them." A voice said from behind him. Valgard got to his feet and turned. Infront of him was Edmund. "Why did you kill them? They were just children?"

As he opened my mouth to talk, a sob escaped. "I was doing it for the greater good."

Edmund laughed. "No. You killed them. Murderer." He hissed. "Now, you're ours."

It felt like someone had stuck a hot poker through his back. He tried to escape but he couldn't move, held in that spot by invisible forces.

Until he couldn't move at all.

Tears stung at his eyes, but he couldn't blink them away. Just two more years until he could retire. He had always been loyal to the citizens of Stull. He had always been loyal to God. He pinched his eyes shut and prayed silently in his head, but it felt as if God had abandoned him.

Demons pulled at him, tearing his skin from his bones. He could feel their cold, slimy hands dragging him down. "No. Please. NOOO!"

In an instant he was at the same steps in the cemetery, the ones leading down to the basement that never ended, but this time they did end. He could feel the heat, hear the tortured screams. "God won't abandon me."

"He did. "Edmund said. "He abandoned you the second you took three lives."

Vlagard screamed as he was dragged further down, in a sea of never ending walls with no way out. What he had felt in the church basement earlier that day has just been a taste of Hell. Greeting him in the never-ending maze was a sadistic looking woman – the same woman that he had seen in the mirror.

In the distance, the town clock struck three. Another house was on fire and just like last time., it had begun.

ABOUT THE AUTHOR

R. l. Weeks is an international bestselling author of the Willow Woods Series for Young Adult, Raven's Shadows, a Victorian Mystery Series, and Haunting Fairytales Series for Adults.

She has several standalone books releasing throughout 2019. Her mystery/thriller, Dead Girls, releases in September 2019, as well as two other co-written standalone books.

She lives in San Antonio, Texas with her husband, and is originally from Devon in England. She enjoys doing graphic design for other authors, crafts and jewelry making, and planning book signings.

You can also follow her here:
Email: authorrlweeks@gmail.com
Twitter: https://twitter.com/authorrlweeks
Facebook: facebook.com/rlweeksauthor1

Get a free book when you sign up for her monthly newsletter packed with her latest releases, contests, giveaways, and great deals. You can sign up here:

http://bit.ly/RLWeeksNewsletter

THE FINAL GIRL

BY SAMANTHA ALLARD

TO SAY THAT MY SOCIAL life was abysmal would have been an understatement. My eighty-year-old grandmother's social life was better than mine. She invited me to bingo, but I politely refused. I'm twenty-one, and I was dangerously close to being older than my actual age. I switched the kettle on, the house blissfully quiet since everyone had either left to go to work or university. It wasn't like I didn't have options, but I blamed it on the work load, and I needed every brain cell that I had. As soon as I finished making my coffee, I went to the door to check for mail. A flyer on the doormat was the only thing there and I retrieved it, keeping a tight grip on my cup. Coffee's life and all that.

I flipped the flyer over and checked out the front. It took a minute for it to register in my sleep deprived mind. The Majestic cinema was doing a late-night showing of the 'Sleepover Murders'? I couldn't help the smile which spread across my face. Damn, I hadn't seen that movie in years. I took the flyer back with me to the kitchen and sat down, continuing to look at it as I drank my too hot coffee. That film had inspired my love of horror and even my course. A dual major in Film and Criminology. Even my DVD collection was bordering on obsessive.

"I can't believe they're showing this." I doubled checked the time, midnight. It would certainly be an experience to watch a movie at that time. I'd have finished work by then and by then I would be able to figure out the poor excuse of a map. It had to be a small cinema, probably hidden away off the beaten track. There was a multiplex, but I doubted the showing would be there. "I didn't think anyone knew about the movie but me."

"Ruby, who are you talking to?"

I screamed as I spun in my seat. Tessa Coulson, our resident art student, stood in the doorway rubbing her eyes. Dressed in a pair of tight tartan trousers and a black vest, which clung to every curve, she was effortlessly beautiful. "Damn, I thought the house was empty."

She checked her watch. "I just need to grab my bag and head off to class."

"You've been out all night?"

"You know how it is." Tessa disappeared from the doorway probably heading to her room. A minute passed, and she reappeared, this time wearing a jacket and with her red hair brushed over her shoulder. It was distinctly unfair how she managed to look refreshed after little or no sleep. "You got plans tonight?"

I shook my head. "No, I've got work." I don't know why I didn't mention the showing. The others thought I was weird as it was, letting them know I planned on going to a late night showing of a horror movie would only confirm it.

"If you're up to it, message me when you're finished, maybe we can meet up. You really need to start embracing the university lifestyle a little. You know, let your hair down, drink some alcohol and make some mistakes."

"I'll see how I feel."

She nodded. "See you later."

The house was quiet again before I looked back down at the flyer. The kitchen lights caught the metallic sheen of the graphic, an axe in a downward arch. It shimmered as I moved it, it was almost hypnotic. "Sorry Tessa, I've got plans."

***

When my shift finished at Yates, the pub was still busy. Dalton, the manager on shift had practically begged me to stay and help. Any other night it wouldn't have even been a question. There wasn't a time when I didn't need the money and I could tell he thought I was going to say yes, until I said no. His eyes went wide in disbelief and when I mentioned I had plans, for a second, I thought he was going to call me a liar. I never had plans before. If anything, I was the girl who never said no.

Pulling the flyer out of my back pocket, I hitched my bag up on my shoulder and went in search of the cinema. Being brought up in a small town, Derby intimidated me with its sheer size and how busy it always seemed to be. Halfway in my first year of University and I doubted I would know where everything was by the time I left. "At least there's a map on here." Tiny, with barely any detail on it, but there. I knew where the library was and apparently it was near there. In full swing, the streets were full of students on a quest for another drink. I pulled my hood up and kept my gaze straight in front of me. It wasn't like I thought I'd attract trouble, considered unassuming at best and mostly ignored but it was better safe than sorry.

The library was cloaked in shadow, an early Victorian building converted into a small but packed library. I spent a lot of time there and it was my favourite place besides my room, and the library at the university. I glanced at the map again, using the light of a streetlamp and looked for the alleyway next to it. I'd never noticed it before but since I was now looking for it, I found the steel gate hidden behind low hanging branches. Excitement built in the pit of my stomach, not just for the movie but the trip to see it. The long alleyway winded and diverted off into different directions. I half expected to see others looking for the elusive cinema, but I was the only one in the alleyway, maybe the others had gotten there earlier? I was looking forward to meeting people who liked a movie I thought only I remembered. There had to be a few, or they wouldn't have made the decision to show the film.

I found the turning I was looking for and went down that way. The alleyway opened into a courtyard. A building that I'd never seen before was dead centre. In fainted paint, the sign read The Majestic. It looked like it had been abandoned a long time ago. "This can't be the right place." It looked like something out of a horror movie and excitement gave way to apprehension. It was easy to picture the cinema being the home to ghosts and ghouls or a creature which lived behind the walls. Maybe I should leave. Did I want to watch the movie so much that the need bypassed all ideas of common sense?

The door opened and a girl walked out. Black hair pulled up in a messy knot, pale makeup and thick black lines circled eyes I couldn't make out the colour of. A look of surprise appeared on her face and I noticed the ring of keys in her hand. "Can I help you?" I feebly showed her the flyer, too spooked to talk. "You're here to watch the movie?" I nodded as she reopened the door. "Come on then. I thought that tonight was going to be a bust but that's the downside of being in a place few people know about." I walked up the steps and entered the building. The inside looked much better than the outside. Red and white tiles on the floor, a selection of chocolates and popcorn behind the counter. The vending machines looked like antiques.

The girl disappeared through a door and reappeared behind the counter. She dumped her bag on the ground and shrugged off her jacket. "Welcome to the Majestic. I'm Dottie." She offered her hand and I shook it. She was a little odd but who was I to comment on that? I was hardly considered normal on the best of days.

"Ruby."

"Nice to meet you, Ruby. I turned off the machines, but the popcorn should still be warm. What can I get you?"

I gave her my order. "Nobody else showed up?"

She shook her head, her silver hooped earrings rattling as they knocked against her face. "It's an old movie. I told my boss that it would be hard to get people interested in it, but he was adamant. We only have one screen which seats about 150 people." She pointed to one of the doors. "I hope that you don't mind being the only one in there. I don't expect anyone else to be coming."

"I guess it was too much to assume that anyone else liked this movie but me."

Dottie laughed. "It's hardly a classic."

She wanted to argue the reasons why 'Sleepover Murders' was a classic, but she had the distinct feeling it would go over the girl's head. "What are you going to do?"

"I'm going to be running everything behind the scenes." She reached down and pulled out a book, she showed me the cover. It looked familiar, a man spread out like he was on a cross. "I've also got to read a chapter for class."

"What class is that?"

She paused. "Art. I like the drawing part, but we also cover art history. Can't help but think that clients won't be hiring me because of my knowledge of the classics."

That was why it looked familiar. I'd seen that book before, Tessa carried it around with her. "The hoops we have to jump through, to just get a degree with the hopes that a degree will make it easier to get a job. I wish I was that easy."

Dottie burst out laughing and nodded. "Exactly. Go through to the screening room and I'll get the movie fired up. I might even join you later. Art history is a hard slog to get through on the best of days."

The first time I watched 'Sleepover Murders' I'd been eight and too young to watch it. Hettie, my babysitter had watched it with her boyfriend and as they made out on the couch, I watched it from the stairs. At the time it terrified me but as I got older and my own copy, I realised how bad it was. In the eighties it faded into obscurity because of much better films. There was every cliché in it. A bunch of kids spending the weekend in a cabin, drinking and having sex. Every stupid mistake in the book. Running up the stairs instead of out of the door. Going for a shower and splitting up. Many of them met the sharp end of an axe. The bad guy turned out to be the long-lost brother of Lene, jealous of the life she got while he'd been given up for adoption. In a decade of memorable masks, Pale Face wore one which was shaped like a face painted white.

Not terrifying.

I opened the two large doors using my butt since my hands were full. For a second all I could see was blackness until light exploded, chasing all the shadows away. Everything about the cinema harked back to a time long forgotten. Chequered carpet, this time dark green and black covered the ground. The chairs were dark red and as I found a seat, I felt the velvet material underneath my hand. There certainly weren't many places like this anymore or maybe there was. Maybe like the Majestic, they were hidden and only the most avid cinema fan knew about them? A secret which only a few people knew about? It was a little unnerving to be in there by myself, but I had to remember that I wasn't. Dottie was around here somewhere. I looked over my shoulder to see a tiny bead of light in the wall. She was probably in a room sorting out the film.

I took my jacket off and put it on the chair next to me. Could she see me in there? There had to be cameras, at least, for security? I glanced up at the ceiling, but I couldn't see anything. If the Majestic had them, they kept them hidden. The thick red heavy curtains which hid the screen, took up most of the opposing wall and I sat down. I picked up my popcorn and waited.

After a few minutes there was a whirling sound and the curtains opened. The screen looked like it had seen better days and I spied a tear near the bottom. Was it possible to arrange for viewings with my class? All our films where shown in a small classroom in a forgotten part of the campus. The Majestic would be an awesome place to view the films for our course instead. The screen burst into life and I snuggled down in the chair and threw some popcorn into my mouth, I missed, and I fought against the urge to giggle. I wasn't usually such a terrible shot. I'd have to talk to Dottie later about renting out the space.

***

The car moved along the windy road. Lene watched the scenery as the car zipped along. There were a lot of trees and they had left civilisation behind a long time ago. The weekend had been planned weeks in advance but there was an underlining tension in the car. Sally called her the night before, her and Brett had an argument and while she promised that it wouldn't ruin the weekend, it wasn't making the atmosphere any better. Lene sneaked a peek at Victor. She didn't know him very well, but she was hoping that the weekend would change that.

Jasper, the fifth wheel, had been trying to talk to her for ages but she wasn't even vaguely interested. She kept her replies to one word, three at the most and kept her attention on the horizon. Him being there was going to make connecting with Victor next to impossible. Brett took a left and drove deeper into the forest. He slowed the car when they went over the bridge. The small glimpse of the sea showed that it was dark and grey, the weather man had said that there would be a storm.

They travelled for another half an hour before Brett pulled up next to a cottage. They all got out of the car and collected their bags. Lene stood next to Victor who studied the cottage with a cynical gaze. "You've been here before?" Lene shook her head, both of her hands on her bag. "Have you?"

The corner of his lip kicked up in a half smile. "No but I've heard their parties can get wild."

Her cheeks burnt, so had she. "I haven't."

Victor pushed off from the car. He stopped a fraction before passing her and leaned towards her. "You're a terrible liar."

Lene watched as he walked to the cottage. Jasper knocked against her hip making her stumble. "You're too good for him."

She fought against the urge to scowl at him. The smile she flashed at him felt forced on her face. "Thanks for the words of advice."

He shrugged as he smiled at her. "He collects hearts and breaks them with surprising ease. I would hate to see that happen to you."

"I'm a grown woman, I can make my own mistakes just fine." Something moved in the corner of her eye and she turned to face it, trying to get a better look. Jasper followed her gaze and she caught the frown. "I thought I saw something. Brett?"

Her best friend's boyfriend pulled his bag out of the boot. "What?"

She glanced back at the forest and back at him. "There isn't anything in the forest is there? Bears or wolves?"

He barked out a laugh. "The only scary thing in those woods are weasels and squirrels." He hitched his bag over his shoulder and walked towards the cottage. Lene couldn't look away from the forest. It had been a large shadow that darted out of her vision as quickly as it had entered it. It couldn't have been a weasel or a squirrel. There was no way.

"Maybe your eyes are playing tricks on you?" Jasper suggested. "I can't see anything." He stepped closer to the trees but Lene reached out, stopping them.

"You're probably right." Lene didn't want to admit defeat but she wanted to be inside with Victor more. Jasper opened his mouth to say something else but Lene cut him off. "Don't let it go to your head. I said that you're right about this. Everything else? You couldn't be more wrong."

***

Why had the screenwriters written her that way? She was supposed to be the character the viewer identified with, but it was difficult to like a character who was too dumb to live. All of them were that way. There was a storm on the way. They were in the middle of nowhere. The only thing which would have made it too obvious was if they had a big neon sign above the house saying, horny teens are here, please kill us. There was also the fact of the anniversary of the guy who killed a bunch of people. Surely it should have been a day where everyone stayed inside their homes with double padlocks on the locks?

But nobody believed in monsters until they found themselves in their sights.

***

Jasper didn't know why he left the cottage. All it had taken was the sight of Lene cuddling up to Victor for the bad mood to hit him like a dark cloud. He muttered something about getting some air and left the laughter behind him. He liked the outdoors. There weren't many opportunities for him to spend outside in the big city but when he'd been a kid, his dad would have taken him to spend weekends in the woods not far from their house. He made his way deeper into the forest, making sure that he only moved in a straight line so he wouldn't get lost.

What did Lene see in Victor? Okay he was tall, ridiculously good-looking and a smoulder gaze that could stop a person in their tracks and steal their breathe. He laughed. "Damn, maybe it isn't about Lene? Maybe you want to date him yourself?" He stopped, gave it some serious thought and shook his head. "Lene's pretty cute, if the whole situation goes that way maybe you can just ask to join in, there's worse ways to spend a weekend."

Something rustled in the trees and Jasper's heart skipped a beat. "Just squirrels and weasels, you heard Brett. Nothing out here is going to kill..." A brief stab of pain went through him and he dropped to a knee grabbing at his throat. He tried opening his mouth, to shout out for help but thick liquid gushed out of it. He fell onto his face, a pair of black shoes crept into his vision before everything went black.

"Where do you think he went?" Lene edged closer to Victor, who put an arm around her shoulder. A fine misty rain, which seemed to seep into their skin made their clothes stick to their bodies.

"I'm not sure but he's been gone for a while. The storm is going to hit us soon. We all need to be inside."

Jasper might not have been her favourite person but in that moment, she was torn between hugging and slapping him. The night was going better than she thought that it would. Brett and Sally had finally finished arguing and disappeared upstairs. The noises they were making where as distracting as hell and Lene had caught Victor looking at her. She'd wondered if his mind was on the same track as hers, then he had noticed Jasper was still outside and suggested they go look for him.

They walked deeper into the forest, calling out for Jasper. He couldn't have gone far but she guessed there was a chance he'd fallen and hurt himself. Lene stopped and rubbed her arms, Victor pulled her into a hug, and she bit back a sigh of happiness. A bolt of lightening filled the sky and she jumped. "Where do you think he is?"

"I'm not sure. We can't stay out here for too long looking for him. None of us thought to bring a torch or anything."

"In our defence we weren't thinking we'd need to leave the cottage." She shivered.

"Cold?" She nodded against his chest. "We'll have to see if there is any hot water and take a shower to warm up."

"Together?" It took every ounce of bravery to even suggest it, but she knew she had to be clear about her intentions. His hands on her back stopped in mid rub.

"I guess that'll be one way to conserve the hot water." Lene glanced up at him, raised herself up onto her tiptoes and kissed him. For a second, she thought he'd push her away, but his arms tighten around her and he deepen the kiss.

Another bolt of lightening cut through the dark sky and Victor broke contact with her. She glanced up at him to notice that his attention was no longer on her. Instead it was on something in the trees. She made to follow his gaze but before she could get a clear look, he turned her away and started to lead her back to the cottage. "What's wrong, what did you see?" Instead of answering her, his pace quicken and Lene started to run to keep up with his longer stride. "Victor, you're scaring me."

With the cottage in sight, Lene tore her hand free. She might have liked him and even a part of her was thrilled that he seemed to want to get her back to the cottage quickly but even in her lust filled gaze, she knew something was wrong. Victor skidded to a stop. "We need to get back inside."

"What did you see in the trees?"

"Jasper."

***

I sipped at my drink as I watched the scene unfold in front of me. Damn, I'd had such a crush on Victor as I grew up. Brave, heroic. It was a shame how it ended for him in the film and when I tried to follow the actors' career, I found out Brandon Henderson died. 'Sleepover Murders' was his first and only movie. I never liked Lene, the final girl, but that probably had more to do with the fact she got to kiss Victor. One thing which I would never admit was I use to pretend to be her. I knew every line, every mannerism. What would it have been like to feel Victor's lips on mine?

***

Lene dashed up the stairs to the bathroom, slammed the door shut and sank to the ground. She heard the bedroom door open and Sally's voice asking what was wrong. After a brief pause, she heard Victor telling her to get some clothes on and come downstairs. He mentioned an accident. How could it have been an accident? Jasper climbed the tree himself and cut his own throat? Had he committed suicide? That didn't make any sense. He might have annoyed the hell out of her but there was nothing to suggest he would have taken his own life. Lene touched her face, parts of it felt sticky under her fingertips and she crawled towards the mirror. She slowly got to her feet and braved a look at her reflection.

Red droplets, now faintly pink because of the rain dotted her face. Oh Christ, it was Jasper's blood. She turned on the tap and rubbed at her face. Why did he leave in the first place? He had found a way to ruin her night after all. There was no way she would be sleeping with Victor tonight. Even in his death, Jasper had made sure of that. She glared at herself in the mirror. Was she really that desperate to get laid that she just put the blame on a dead man?

"You are a horrible human being."

There was a knock on the door. "Lene, are you okay in there?"

She opened the door to see Victor standing there. A door opened and closed downstairs and she looked at Victor. "What's going on?"

"Brett and Sally are going to get help."

"What about the phones?"

He shrugged. "None of us bothered to see if they were working when we got here but they're dead. Brett thinks something knocked out the phone line."

Lene stepped around him and heard the unmistakable sound of a car engine firing up. "Why can't we all go? I mean, what if it wasn't an animal that killed him?"

"It couldn't be anything else."

"Unless those weasels are on steroids there's no way it could have carried Jasper up there."

The corner of his lips kicked up into a smile. "Is it such a bad idea to spend some more time with me?" Lene was halfway to the stairs when she stopped. Victor closed the distance between them. "It'll be alright. I find it easier to believe that Jasper died because of some sort of freak accident, then something killed him and dragged him up into the trees. But I'll tell you won't, if you're still scared, we can go down into the basement and locked the door behind us. It's the safest place in a storm anyway." He offered his hand and Lene took it, lacing her fingers through his. "I'll keep you safe from the squirrels." He said deadpanned and Lene laughed.

"My hero."

"Do you really think that Victor saw Jasper in the trees?" They'd been driving in relative silence for a few minutes before Sally thought to ask. "I mean, that's silly isn't it?" Brett was frowning, she knew that he didn't like to drive in the dark, but they really didn't have a choice.

"I don't know but we should report it, get an ambulance. If he's wrong than at least we got help. The worse thing that could happen is we get into trouble."

"And if he's right? We just left Jasper there. Shouldn't we have checked?"

"You saw Victor's face when he described it, he was pretty sure that Jasper was dead."

"But how?"

Brett frowned. "I don't know."

"Do you think that they'll be alright in the house maybe we should have brought them with us?" Brett slammed the steering wheel and Sally flinched. Maybe it was time to finish the relationship? They weren't good for each other and the only time they seem to get along was when they were having sex and even then. She absentmindedly rubbed the bruise on her wrist.

He took a deep breath and released it on a sigh. "They'll be fine. We'll be back before they get into any real trouble."

There was a loud popping sound as the car bumped and rocked as it hit something on the ground. Sally screamed as the car skid out of control. Brett kept both hands on the wheel and tried to keep it straight, jamming his feet on the brakes. Sally's body shot forward as they collided with the tree. Pain exploded across her face and shoulders as she burst through the window screen. She hit something hard and after that felt nothing at all.

Brett struggled with the seatbelt, his chest hurt bad, he must have broken some ribs and it made breathing next to impossible. With effort he managed to open the door and fell to the ground. Sally was gone. There was no way she would have survived going through the screen like that. He should have told her to put the belt on, should have refused to drive without it but he hadn't been thinking about that. The woods were safe. There was nothing in them that would hurt them. He pulled himself free of the car and stopped by a tree.

"Sally?" He called out her name, not expecting a reply but knowing that he needed to at least try. His girlfriend was silent.

How was he going to get to the town without a car, with broken ribs? He looked the way they'd come. They'd only been in the car for about ten minutes but that was still about 5 miles. The heavy rain blinded his vision. What had he hit? A tree truck on the road maybe? It had to be something sharp to pop the tyre.

"Just catch your breath. You'll be okay." Words of encouragement that he didn't really believe. Even through the rain he heard the twig snap. "Hello? Is anyone there? We've had an accident." He coughed. "We could really use your help."

A shadow appeared next to him. "That was easy than I thought it would be, thank you Brett."

Brett feebly tried to get away from the shadow when he caught sight of the axe. "Wait a minute, I'm not..."

***

For all of it's faults that scene always hit me like a punch to the gut. I popped another piece of popcorn into my mouth. Suddenly there was a burst of muted light behind me and I looked over my shoulder. Whoever it was, was perfectly framed by the light behind them. It made making out their features next to impossible. They found a seat near the back and sat down. It had to be Dottie, I decided as I turned back to the screen, she said that she would watch the movie if she got bored with the book. I checked my watch, there wasn't much left of the film and then I would head home. I had classes in the morning but at the rate I was going I'd be asleep for most of them. At least if I was there. My attendance wouldn't go down. It was just be a case of a sleeping student rather than an attentive one.

***

Lene didn't know where Victor got the gun from. She didn't have much experience with them, but she knew they were dangerous. That people were more likely to shoot someone or something they weren't supposed to. She sat down on the makeshift bed and watched as he walked down the steps, the gun pointing down at the ground.

"Where did you find that?"

"It was in the living room, above the fireplace. There's even a bullet in it."

"Do you think you can hit someone with that?"

"I think it'll scare off most people." The bed dipped slightly as he sat down next to her. "They'll be back before you know it and then we'll leave here together. Maybe I was wrong, maybe my eyes were playing tricks on me and it wasn't Jasper in the trees."

She knew that he was trying to make her feel better, but he wasn't doing a good job of it. The blood on her face, what she washed off was proof enough that something terrible had happened in the woods. "Let's hope you don't shoot him by mistake." Victor put the gun down onto the floor and pulled her onto his lap.

"I've got some interesting ways to pass the time."

There was no telling how much time passed before she heard the footsteps from upstairs. Lene pulled her clothes back on and tugged on Victor's arm. He rolled onto his side and for a second, she thought he was going to ignore her but then it was like he remembered where they were, and he sat up. Lene put a finger to her lips and pointed to the ceiling. There it was again. The sound of footsteps and whistling? It was high pitched and there was something distinctly feminine about it. Sally? No, her best friend didn't whistle. She never sounded that cheerful. Victor pulled his boxers on and picked up the gun from the floor.

"Be careful."

He nodded, sighting down the barrel of the gun. His finger poised on the trigger.

"I know where you're hiding." The handle on the door moved but Victor had remembered to lock it. There was a smashing sound and the doorknob fell to the ground with a thud. The first thing she saw was a pair of black shoes, jeans and jacket both the same dark shade and a girl. Not very imposing, almost forgettable in appearance. In her hand an axe swung.

Victor fired but something terrible happened. There was a spark, an explosion and Victor yelled in pain before he collapsed to the ground. Lene glanced from him to the girl on the steps. Her eyes were wide and then she started to giggle. "A misfire, seriously? Oh my god, you guys really have the worse luck. I only thought that happened in the movies."

She walked down the steps. Lene edged away from the dead body of Victor. She couldn't look at him. The smell of cooked flesh turned her stomach. The knowledge that he was gone, talking one moment to being dead the next was just terrible she wouldn't be able to function. "Who are you?"

"I'm the Pale Face Killer, but you can call me Ruby."

Lene burst into tears. "Why are you doing this? I don't know you."

She moved her head to the side, studying her. "You were in the wrong place at the wrong time, Lene. You're not the final girl. I am. I wish Victor could have lived but that's not how the story goes."

"You've got the wrong place. I'm not Lene. My name's Alyson." Maybe if she knew the truth, maybe she would leave her alone.

"In my story you're Lene." A smirk crossed the girl's face and Alyson knew that she was going to die. The girl was insane. She got to her feet. There wasn't much of a size difference between them and there had to be a chance that she could get pass her. "Lene, Victor, Sally, Brett and Jasper. Five kids in the woods, murdered by an axe wielding manic. That would be me."

Alyson, Derek, Bonnie, George and Steven. All her friends gone because the girl was trapped in a fantasy? "You killed all of them, didn't you?"

Another smirk. "It's how the story goes. Except Victor and Sally died in different ways. They weren't supposed to die that way." For a second the girl looked sad but then she smiled. "I'm sure I'll get it right next time." She darted forwards and swung down with the axe. Alyson tried to move to the left and out of the way. All she needed to do was get to the door, but she wasn't fast enough. The blade cut into her shoulder and she screamed. "I promise this will not hurt for long."

***

The movie never changed. That was the point. It was how I liked every encounter to play out. I wasn't a monster, I was a perfectionist. There was a possibility that they were the same thing? One day the bodies would be discovered but who would put two and two together and not get five? Who would think that a serial killer would be inspired by a film from the eighties? I wouldn't be caught. My course helped me, I knew how not to leave a trace behind and all the conventions of a horror movie. I collected my bag and hitched it over my shoulder. My phone buzzed in my pocket and I pulled it out, answering it.

"Hello?"

"Ruby, where are you? I thought you said you would be meeting me." I bit my bottom lip. She sighed. "You really need to start living a little. I mean, you're the quietest person I know. You couldn't get into trouble if you tried."

That made me smile. She really didn't know me at all. "You know what they say, it's always the quiet ones you have to watch out for.

The End

FIRE, WALK WITH ME

BY SJ DAVIS

LOOKING BACK, IT'S EASY TO see that my world had changed from what it once was. But what happened, and how it happened, that is the mystery. Some say desire is like a bright sun beating down through holes in an old rusted tin roof, but it isn't like that at all. Not until you feel the blunt force of what you want, or what you think you want, it isn't yours to hold. And soon, I found something that pierced the armor of my heart.

Perhaps it was the smell of his sweat that had my heart beating so fast that I thought it would lodge in my throat, I don't know. The music was loud, so loud that the bass thumped like a metronome in my chest. The smoky haze of lights shone upon his dark hair and eyelashes. There was no talking, but conversation wasn't what I wanted anyway. I went with one purpose - to find someone. Someone who wouldn't text me the next day, making me regret they existed. Lasting relationship? No thank you. Not again. Never again.

Ice was frozen on the outside of the windows, unaffected by the heat of the packed club. On the inside of the windows, steam and condensation oozed from the walls. Staring, I walked past this new man; my red vinyl boots protected my feet from the drunken sway of the hypnotic dancers. My hip grazed his thigh and he turned to look at me. Blue eyes, cold and unblinking. This one wouldn't bother me later, I was certain of it. I smiled. He did not. And that, dear reader was a very good sign.

He placed his pale hand on the front of my shirt and gently slid it down to my waist. I tensed and looked down at the wet floor, slick with drinks and sweat.

"Hello," I muttered. "I'm Sophia." He ignored my words, which was fine with me.

I leaned back against a brass railing to a spiral staircase leading to a darkened bar. He pressed against my body, the smell of him made my eyes close. He stood so close, his feet surrounded mine as he played with my earring – twisting in between his fingers, pulling it almost painfully as my head rested on his chest. I looked up at him, sideways. It was only then that he smiled. Slightly.

His teeth reflected the limited light of the dance floor. So white, they seemed to glow in the dark. I stepped away to go to the bathroom but he grabbed my wrists to stop me and turned them up to the strobed light of the ceiling. My already short skirt rose way above decent standards when he pulled my right hand to his mouth and I could feel the pressure of his teeth graze my skin.

"What are you doing?" I pulled back, though his hands grabbed mine with a vice like grip. He held my arms against his chest and looked down at me, studying me.

"Whatever," he whispered, almost hissing over his shoulder as he turned away.

I inhaled deeply and smoothed my clothes back to submission. Shaking my head, I ran up the staircase to find my favorite bartender, a friend of mine since elementary school. He saw my face and handed me a cigarette, smiling through a curtain of blonde dreadlocks. I slowly took a drag and let the smoke roll from my lips. I looked over my shoulder for the strange man with the wrist-sucking fetish, scanning the balustrade to the lower level.

"Avoiding someone?"

"I think the freaks are out tonight," I answered.

"Freaks are usually right up your alley."

"My freak days are over. I want uneventful...satisfaction," I smiled as I French inhaled.

"Well, you're dressed for freaks. Your ass is hanging out and I have a pretty good view of the front too."

"Shut up." I tossed the cigarette on the floor and stomped it out with the heel of my boot.

I looked downstairs and watched two girls dancing together, one platinum blonde and the other a redhead. Both were rubbing against the other and significantly increasing the sex factor on the floor. A damp smell, almost moldy, hit me at once – mixed with the scent of sex and desire. I looked at the DJ and I saw him again, against the wall next to the speakers; his crimson shirt was damp. I could make out his features better from afar as the light hit his face directly. His hair wasn't long but his bangs were. They were damp too and swept to the side. His hair was dark, almost black - and very shiny.

Suddenly I felt a crushing pain in the back of my neck and pressure from behind as if someone was pushing me. He looked up the stairs towards me as I squinted back, frozen in pain. Still, he gave no expression. I blinked and bent over, reaching around to the back of my neck. My hair stuck to my skin and my breathing staggered.

I felt a hot flash of breath waft into my ear as the pain ran down my spine. He was behind me. *How did he get here so fast?* I turned and tilted my head to question him, but there was nothing to be said. I could make no noise. Everyone and everything around me was frozen in place. No sound, no music, no movement. It was as if I lived in a painting. Cigarette smoked froze in place, white swirls stagnant and still, unmoving in the air. Before I could bring forth a serious scream, my legs buckled and he balanced me with his arm around my waist.

He turned me with a brisk force to face him. I closed my mouth and his palm pressed against my lips to keep me quiet. *Cold, so cold.* He leaned in and slid his hand to my throat and squeezed it slightly as he bent into my neck.

"Enoch. I am Enoch."

That's all I remember until I woke up on the damp cement floor of the bathroom with two blondes snorting coke by the trashcan.

"Nice," I said as I arranged my skirt that was twisted around my hips. My head pounded and my mouth tasted like blood and metal.

"We're not judging," said the blondes in unison and in identical squeaky voices. The white powder dusted on their nostrils matched their hair.

Freaks.

***

I walked to my favorite coffee shop the next day, pulling my hair and twisting it into frayed ringlets until I finally gave in and gnawed on the ends. I sat in my favorite spot under the Hemingway portrait while my nervous hands clutched the red cup of my eggnog latte. I sensed the heat of eyes darting around me, as if everyone knew a secret. *Maybe it's just me.*

As the sugary steam from the holiday latte hit my skin, the motions of the customers and baristas slowed as if they existed in super slow motion. Each of them moved like they were weighed down by time and gravity. With each second passing, they slowed further. Some halted completely. Frozen, staring eyes, gaping mouths surrounded me. The music slowed to a monstrously slow sound, low and warped. I stood up quickly to leave.

Should I run? Damn it! My coffee is tipping over. As I grabbed my ridiculously overpriced beverage, the light brown froth stilled to a motionless drip, clinging to the table's edge. Tears stung my eyes. I could still move, as others around me froze.

"What is going on?" My voice cracked above the heads of the crowd as my chest tightened and I began to hyperventilate. No one noticed, most of them still moved in quarter time, as if in a drug-induced waltz. The barista's dark red lips, stained in a cranberry hue, dragged across her teeth slowly, forming words that slowed with each passing syllable. Her crimson-black fingernails gestured slowly up to the menu until they hung still in the air above her head. Still, silent, like a statue. *Just like at the club. What is going on?*

The air in the shop popped with electricity. I felt a sucking feeling pull me back to my chair as I collapsed into the faded wood. Invisible chains held me in place. *I can't move! Get me out of here!* I squirmed to the side, twisting. Then all was still. My heart pounded through my shirt when I saw him. Enoch, the man from last night stood outside the glass wall. He wore a black trench coat, tortoise shell Ray Ban sunglasses, with large droplets of rain beading on his shoulders. His hair hung wet over his forehead as he pressed himself into the glass window. Then, as if the window was made of water, he walked right through it. The glass did not crack nor did it shatter. First his foot and left leg shifted through the glass, then the rest of him pushed through the solid glass pane as if it were a gelatinous liquid. The window was undisturbed in his wake. The sound of a flutter of wings clipped through the air, whispering and blowing.

Watchers! An old crone's voice crackled in my ears for only me to hear. The sound smacked like thunder. *Watchers!*

My mind buzzed and my mouth felt dry. I tried to scream as he held his hand out to quiet me. Even though he wasn't actually touching me, I could feel the icy heat of his hands along my lips. Enoch was pale and seemed tired but he still exerted a strong force. The shop was filled with the sounds of rushing wind, as if air whistled through a tunnel. I tucked my head down as my scarf flew from off my neck. Next my brown sweater, an oversized warm cable-knit, slid roughly from my shoulders. I felt like I could no longer breathe on my own.

He stared and pointed to the floor at my feet. As soon as I looked where he indicated, he stood in front of me. It was as if he teleported or flew through time. His white face was drained of any color and his blue eyes were dilated in the brightness of the fluorescent ceiling lights. He crouched in front of me and rested his hands on my thighs. My sharp, and pained, intake of breath made him look at me. His nostrils sucked in air like a vacuum. A breeze filled the room, and again I heard the sound of wings.

It's hot, so hot. I feel like I'm on fire. His eyes closed as he kissed my shoulder and neck. *I'm cold ... I can't breathe ... I'm empty.*

I sucked in more air and opened my eyes. The walls of the room bent and warped in rhythm with my pulse. His lips rested against my chest. Then, painlessly, he laid his hands on my heart. I could feel the pressure of the palms, but a numb stillness ran down my body. *It's so quiet. It's so still. But at least there is no pain.*

"Who are you?" I begged. "What are you?"

Watchers. The syllables hung in the air as the room and its occupants swept back in motion. Sounds of coffee brewing and foaming, the sharp laughter of the customers, and the coughing and throat clearing of the bored baristas, all returned as if nothing was amiss. No one was the wiser. But I knew. I knew there was a change. Yet I wouldn't know what it was for many days to come.

***

I moaned. Damp sheets of sweat twisted around me. I tossed and turned as my heart fluttered. Flashes of the Enoch kissing my neck burned into my dreams and seared my thoughts.

I'm sorry... a deep voice whispered through the curtains. I heard a loud car alarm along the street below, but it didn't even startle me.

Why? I asked the voice in my sleep. *Who are you?* I didn't want to wake up. I finally enjoyed feeling again.

Feeling something, anything instead of the empty anger I'd grown accustomed to. Anger had lived inside me for so long. Ever since, well, ever since awhile. An incredible vibration filled the room and suddenly I felt cold. The window was open yet I was shimmering with sweat. I sat up, letting the silk sheet slide from me and I walked to the window.

How did this window get opened? It's freezing outside! It's winter for fuck's sake! The crisp wind kept me tense and alert while I tugged the window closed. The man in the building across from mine stood in his window in a wife beater and holding a Pabst Blue Ribbon; a perfect redneck combination. He put down his beer can and then looked at me again; a cigarette barely clung to his bottom lip as he smiled. *That's right, pervert. I'm naked. Enjoy the show.* I yanked harder on the window. *Yes, my boobs jiggle. It's quite normal.* He closed his curtains behind him as he pushed his hair from his face, staring at me from across the night sky.

He didn't stop staring, which pissed me off, so I decided to give him a little show. I jiggled my breasts in an exaggerated sway, then I squeezed them together, sticking my tongue out. He pointed at his chest and then to me, as if inviting himself over. *No way, buddy.* I jerked the curtains closed behind me. *No way.*

I lit the candles along the edge of my bathtub and ran the water. The surge of water echoed loudly over the cold tile of the floor as I dipped my toes in the water to test the temperature. *Too hot.* The candles flickered for no reason. I slipped as I stood back up. Two strong and slightly rough hands grabbed me from behind - one hand around my waist and the other around my neck. I wasn't afraid; I also had no intention of screaming. I knew who it was. It was Enoch. Part of me wanted this stranger just as he was – unknown and unresponsive. Another part of me wanted to know everything about him, especially who or what the hell he was. I felt his hands on my body. And then I felt nothing at all.

***

"Sophia!" a little girl's voice yelled from the back of my mind. Her voice sounded muffled but full of fear. "Sophia!"

Who is that girl?

I jerked awake and looked around, spitting water out of my mouth as the water splashed around me. I had fallen asleep in the bathtub.

"Who's here?" I sat up quickly, completely startled as I woke up from under the water. *And when did I get in the tub? Nothing makes any sense!*

I rubbed my eyes and ran my hands through my wet hair. I splashed from the tub, leaving a river of lukewarm water behind me. I leaned against the door for a moment, and then locked it. Suddenly I heard music. Old music, an orchestra with a big band sound yet with an almost carnival quality, complete with the hiss and pop of vinyl.

The music stopped as soon as I opened the door, wrapped in my pink bathrobe. Water ran down my legs, making wet marks on the carpet. I felt motion in the air. I felt the cool breeze of someone's presence. He must still be here.

I'm everything you wished for. Everything you could want. I'm here to help.

***

I rolled on my side with Michael's face still clear in my mind. I turned on my iPod, techno and loud. The beat thudded in my chest and I let it vibrate in all the places I needed it. He's gone, missing, dead. I missed him every day and every night, as I lay paralyzed on my pillow. Sometimes, I never slept at all.

"Michael," I whispered into the darkness. "Michael. Come back to me."

I closed my eyes and his beautiful face appears behind my eyelids. His tanned skin, bright blue eyes, chestnut hair. He wasn't much taller than me; we were often eye-to-eye. He said he loved that the most. As dark and foreboding as his music was, he released me from my boredom. A box I had built, and to which I now returned. It's only been one month. I can't listen to any of his songs anymore. I might never be able to again.

Dead. Like my lover and my heart.

***

"You don't remember the Watchers?" asked Georgia. "Mom used to scare us with them when we were little so we'd behave at communion?"

"That old Fallen Angel tale?" I asked. My twin sister was visiting from Ponchatoula, Louisiana, my hometown – a place filled with swamps, voodoo, Catholicism, and catfish. "You came to visit me, not make me crazy. And you're crazy too if you believe that old voodoo hoodoo."

"I'm not saying the Watchers are coming to get you for not following the rules of The Blessed Mother. Even though they should."

Georgia was always the obedient religious one. But she was also the last to be kissed, the last to be with a man, and I am certain the last to touch herself. I'd had almost enough of her self-righteousness in my life. "The Watchers exist only to make children obey the Church," I blurted out. "And I've never been one to adhere to a religion that manipulates people through fear."

"Angels," said Georgia quietly, "Angels are not to be feared."

"Angels? The Watchers are *Fallen* Angels. *Rejected* from a *cruel* God."

"After this time passes," Georgia's eyes seemed to cast a dark glow, "you will see the error of your ways." Georgia's accent thickened and her head tilted awkwardly as she spoke, almost twisting too far. She walked jaggedly to the bathroom. She turned as she closed the door, staring at me with blank, almost yellow eyes. I could have sworn I saw her pull the blade of a knife from her purse.

"There is darkness and there is light," hissed Georgia from behind the bathroom door. "And there are only two kinds of souls, the good and the evil."

"What are you talking about Georgia?" I shivered. "You're freaking me out."

"You have always been on the wrong side. There is nothing I can do."

"What is wrong with you, Georgia?"

"Your grave was dug before you were born, Sophia." She smiled in the doorway, the light from the sun radiated around her silhouette. "You were born bad."

There is a moment in time for everyone, when you see yourself in a mirror and realize you are exactly who you should be. I glanced at the looking glass next to my galley kitchen. I leaned in and saw blood splattered on my face. Tiny red dots decorated my reflection. I touched the blood and smeared it into my skin, but my hand was clean. My sister laughed. For the first time in my life, I realized my sister hated me.

And so I knew. Everything, as I had always thought it to be, never really was.

***

"Don't do that," he said as walked down the front steps of the brownstone.

"Don't do what?" I asked instinctively. "You again? What's going on?" I looked at the passersby; everyone appeared to be normal. "Is everyone going to freeze in place soon? Because that really freaks me out," I whispered up towards Enoch.

"Don't hold your keys like that," he instructed. "Anyone can grab them from you."

"Why do you think you can tell me what to do?" I countered. I looked up at him. His tall body blocked the strong sun from blinding my eyes. Sparks flew in my brain and caused a rush of adrenaline that I felt down to my toenails. I didn't expect it, not in the daytime, but I wanted and needed it. "Are you my new advisor?" I asked sarcastically.

He stood at least six inches taller than me, and I'm not short. Each beat of my heart pulsed in my neck as he stared down at me.

"My eyes are up here." He looked into them. I see blood in his eyes. I saw blood dripping down a wall. Next I saw curtains blowing from an open window.

I shook my head to clear my thoughts. *Silly visions, none of it is real.*

"Ready for our date?" he asked.

"Date," I reply in a flat tone. "Date? I'm on my way to work."

"No, you are coming with me." As soon as he finished speaking the world stopped. We walked through a maze of pedestrians, frozen in place on their way to work.

"How do you do that?" I snap with annoyance.

"It's not me doing it. It's you." He leaned into my ear and whispered lightly.

As I look at him, I can't remember who I am. He lowers his eyes to the ground and I reach to him. He takes my hand and I feel a vibration inching into my fingers and up my arm.

"Do you feel that?" he asked.

I say nothing to him. I don't know whether I am mad, scared, or intrigued.

"I'm sorry." He looked genuinely disturbed. He pushed me against the cold metal of the ATM machine. I tried to feel something other than this empty feeling, so I let him push me. Then I let him kiss me. He seemed so hungry with my mouth. His hand touched my face.

"What do you want from me?"

"It's about your sister."

"My sister hates me."

"So you say."

"Why are you bothering me?" I demand. *But is he bothering me?* My bag falls down my arm. "I am just trying to go work."

"You are trying to hurt yourself."

"Really." My eyes roll. "I'm trying to get by."

"Really," he said, mocking my tone. "If you hurt yourself, you think you are protected from other's hurting you." He smoothed my hair away from my eyes. "But you aren't." His hair fell into his eyes, slivers of blue cut through the dark fringe of his hair.

"For someone who knows nothing about me, except in clubs and coffee shops, you think you're pretty smart."

"I know what you need. Michael is gone. But you are still here. Stop wishing yourself away. Hurting yourself won't bring Michael back to you. Ever."

He put my bag strap back on my shoulder and turned to leave. As soon as he turned the corner, the crowds of people walked, cell phones vibrated, and coffee was poured. My world spun on a very strange axis. *How did he know about Michael?*

***

Georgia greeted me at the door. Her hair was dry and coarse, sticking it all directions. The fireplace cackled behind her. Her teeth looked strange and her mouth was clenched as if she'd been gnashing at something all day. But it's not her teeth that upset me the most. It's that her eyes were silver with dilated pupils. Her skin looked damp and almost blue.

"Are you sick?" I asked. She retreated to the kitchen and cleaned the table. She dumped the dinner plates into the sink and scraped off the spaghetti from last night. Each scrape of the plate screeched like fingernails across a chalkboard.

"Please, stop it," I said. "Just let them soak."

I stared out the window above the sink into the dark woods. The moon was full and made the room glow with a cool shimmer.

"You brought this on yourself," she hissed. "You had Michael, a nice man, for the first time in your life. Now you are back in the gutter, alone, just like before."

"Shut up, Georgia. You know nothing about Michael. And I don't think you really know me either."

Go look in the mirror. The voice of an old woman, cracking and harsh from years of smoking, whispered to me. *Go now and look. See your secret. She is not who you think. The answer is in front of you.*

Georgia laughed and picked up a glass of wine. She smiled as she turned away from me. Her back was covered in blood.

"Georgia!" I yelled. "You're bleeding."

"Am I?" She looked over her shoulder with a snarl. "Am I, really Sophia? Or is it you?"

"I am *looking* at you, Georgia."

"Look at *your* hands." She walked to the guest room and shut the door. I looked at my fingers, red with dried blood. Flakes of blood coagulated under my fingernails.

Georgia normally stays close enough to me where I can at least see her but now she was fading from my eyes.

I stumbled backwards and felt a body behind me. It was Enoch.

"Stay strong," he whispered in my ear. "Face her."

I pulled away from him and grabbed a knife from the table. I raced to the elevator and rushed in, backing up as people ran out the slowly closing doors. The brass doors reflected my insanity back to me. My clothes were splattered with blood and my hand clasped the knife against my thigh, digging at it and making tiny cuts.

"Call the police!" I heard someone yell as the door closed, separating me from everyone else. Enoch rammed a metal rod, a yardstick into the crack and opened the elevator door, following me.

"I'm scared," I whispered. "It's as if I don't live in the right world anymore. Nothing is right. Even the owls are not what they seem."

"You make the world what you want it to be. We are the ones who hurt ourselves."

"And why are you telling me this?"

"When man faces a loss, he can live in a backwards world. Or he can dig his way out."

"Are you talking about Michael?"

"I'm talking about you. You need to let go."

"I'm fine."

"You're killing yourself. You're killing yourself to be with a man that is gone."

***

My mobile vibrated in my pocket. My parents.

"Hello, dear!" My mother chirped happily.

"Mom," I yelled into the phone. "Something is going on with Georgia. I can't figure it out though."

"Georgia?" my mom sounded incredulous. "I haven't heard that name in a long time from you."

"What do mean? She's my sister, your daughter. I talk about her all the time."

"Sophia. She's not real. You know that." Click. She hung up.

***

I am five years old. My father drives with the windows down and cigarette ashes fly into the back seat, landing on my new dress. He waves his hand recklessly outside of the window, with a death's grip on his cigarette. The Rolling Stones *Tattoo You* album blares into the air.

You wouldn't think the music would still play after the accident, but it did. I sat in the backseat, locked in place by the seatbelt. My father was halfway ejected from the front window, his skin skewered back over whitened bones in his shoulders, glass stuck into his abdomen. His neck was twisted backwards and the whites of his eyes were completely red. His blood seeped through his shirt and made a puddle on the dashboard, mixing with dust and cigarette ash.

I heard a small knock on my window and saw only a small child's fist. Then I saw the rest of her.

"Hi," she says. "Let me in. It's Georgia." And I did. I let her in and we became inseparable, more than I could have ever imagined. "We'll be together forever from now on."

***

When I woke up again, it's the afternoon and I'm wearing the same clothes that I'd worn the day before. I slept more than twelve hours but I don't feel rested. How could I? I miss Michael. I wish I were dead. Nothing is new about that. The air around me felt crushing and I could taste the coldness in my life. The dark feeling of descent settled in my heart. I knew that I was near my end. I even hoped for it.

The memory of Michael hung on me like a heavy wet cloak. I tried to ignore it, but it dripped from me as I walked through my days. I want to be free.

The stairs to my apartment felt like they tilted and bent. The carpet moved under my feet. I ran back into my apartment, straight into the bathroom, hoping Georgia wasn't there. It felt like fangs sunk into my skin as a humming fear rung in my ears.

"Let go of me," I cried into the dark room. "Free me!" The mirror twisted and my reflection contorted back at me.

Eyes flashed behind me. *They are my eyes!*

"Georgia," I gasped. She stood behind me. Her profile glowed in the moonlight shooting through the window. She rubbed her arms and neck with her bony hands, her fingers reached into my hair. "What do you want?"

"I want what you want. I want to end your misery. That's why I'm here."

"Don't listen to her." Enoch's voice shouts from the other side of the door. "She has no power over you unless you let her."

"Don't listen to *him*," she countered. "He's a Watcher."

"There is no such thing as a Watcher," I said.

"There is no such thing as Georgia," he said.

"What?" I ask. Tears stung my eyes. "She's right here." I looked at her and I looked at myself in the mirror. She wanted to help me end my pain. I wanted to let her.

"You are the only one here. Look. Look very hard."

"What am I looking for?" I plead, biting my lip and flinching under his gaze.

Blind girl. There will be blood soon. You see me, because you are weak. Give yourself to me. I stared into her eyes and heard a cacophony of howling noises in the wind. I gasp. "It's me or it's you," she hissed. She stared at me through the bluish light coming through the window. Smiling, her mouth was hungry and feral.

"She finds you when you are weak."

"Michael..." I looked into Georgia's eyes and I saw Michael. He was walking backwards, waving at me. His mouth moves but there is no sound. I am lost inside her eyes, trying to find him. But the more I fought, the smaller he became.

I fumbled for the light. Georgia is gone. I felt like I walked through a pane of shattering glass. Tiny cuts burned my skin.

"What now?" I asked him.

"The rest is up to you. It's all in here." He pointed to my temple and brushed my cheek with the outside of his palm.

"What about you?"

"I come to you with what you want, but I leave you with what you need."

"Are you one of The Watchers?"

"A Fallen Angel?"

I nodded, tears falling from my eyes, dropping like mercury into his upturned hands.

"I am. I am here to keep you from falling further."

"I can't stop. I don't know if I want to."

"You can." He looked at me and tilted his head. "Let go of Georgia, and she'll be gone. She is nothing but a fire... a fire that starts by your own match."

And in a gust of wind, he faded from view. I smiled and looked up to my balcony across the street. Georgia, dressed in white, sat on the patio, wringing her hands. The sun came out and the world began to move around me again. I looked again at Georgia, and she too faded away.

KITCHEN WINDOW

BY P MATTERN

I WAS DOING THE DISHES BY hand, same as I'd been doing them for the past two months since the dishwasher had gone on
the fritz. At night time when it wasn't raining I could see over the
back fence and into the dining room window of the neighbor behind
me.

I live in a nice quiet neighborhood, with homes in the 140K range,
the kind of homes that might sell for 350K on the East Coast, where I am
originally from. Here in the Midwest the cost of living is lower, at least
as far as housing is concerned. I had nearly 3500 square feet in a ranch
built on a slab that I had paid under 120K for.

Pretty damn sweet.

I was a widow and had been for years. On the rare occasion when
I let the dishes go until after dark, it kind of comforted me to see the

couple enjoying their evening meal in their dining room. It made me think about Bob, my husband, and what it might be like if he had lived.

I was in my early 50's, but they looked to be in their late sixties. Both had white hair that shone silver in the sunshine when they would tend their flowers in the back garden. The only other time I ever saw them was when they had cookouts, and their kids and grandkids came to swim in the above ground pool they must have bought specially for them. I never saw either of the older couple in a swim suit.

In the winter I never saw them at all.

The weather was turning finally from a pesky, temperature record breaking Indian Summer that was rare for the tail end of September to more comfortable weather. Fall was my favorite time of year, and I welcomed in the cooler air by cranking open my kitchen window.

The couple was seated at their dining table, I couldn't tell if they were talking or just eating, their heads were bent over their plates. A single pillar candle was between them, the flame glowing steadily as they ate.

The lady was still eating but I guess her husband finished, laying his fork on his plate and pushing back from the table a little, as if he were stuffed. Perhaps he said something complimentary to her, because I saw his wife look up and nod. Then she just kept eating.

As I kept watching, the old man got up and went around the end of the table until he must have been behind his wife. I couldn't see him, but then I saw his arms, and his hands were on her shoulders, as if he were giving her a massage.

'AW' I thought. How sweet. Again, my thoughts went to Bob, and how we'd always said we'd grow old together. Now I was getting to grow old alone, and it kind of sucked.

I shifted my vision to a pan I was scrubbing. I was almost finished with the dishes. I finally loosened the stubborn spot of stuck on food from the frying pan, rinsed it off and placed it in the dish drainer.

What I saw when I peered through the window again changed everything.

I could still see the old man standing behind his wife, but his hands were now around her neck. She was attempting to push back from the table and it must have been shaking because even the rustic chandelier above the dining table was swaying crazily. Her hands were up at her throat, trying to pry his fingers away.

I froze. I kept squinting. I heard myself say, "What the hell...?"

I was frozen, and time seemed to be frozen as well.

After an indeterminable amount of time, all the shaking stopped. A few moments later I saw him let go, and watched as her head fell to her chest, rolling slightly.

That's when I saw him turn his head in my direction. I knew that just as surely as I could see them, he could see me staring through my kitchen window.

The next thing I knew, their house went dark. First the dining room light, then a light in whatever room was next to it. Their outdoor lights hadn't been on, and as I continued to stare all I saw was the dark silhouette of their house, backlit dimly by the street lights on the front side of it.

I kept running the scenario of what I just witnessed over and over again in my mind, asking myself if I could have misinterpreted what I saw. Maybe his wife had been choking, maybe she had some condition that was only alleviated by tension around her neck. They were really old after all.

But the more I reflected on it, the more I was convinced that I had seen something that was off, a scene that would have been viewed as disturbing, even if viewed objectively.

Up until I finally turned in to go to bed, I kept glancing out my kitchen window.

Their house lights never came on again.

TAP, tap...tap tap, TAP tap...

I couldn't place the sound at first, it seemed like hammering. Glancing over at my digital alarm clock I saw that it was a minute past 8:30. Eight thirty was the morning hour, according to the neighborhood association bylaws, at which home maintenance hubbub was allowed to commence. This included the mowing of lawns, car repair, home improvements and the like.

Apparently my neighbor had familiarized himself with the bylaws. As I got water for coffee I could see him squatting down and hammering away at the corner of his white barn shaped storage shed. I wondered what kind of repair it needed.

But mostly, I wondered where his wife was.

I had to admit that in the light of day my interpretation of events seemed less likely than ever. I regretted not interacting with my backyard neighbors more. The neighbors I interacted with the most were the ones on either side of me, and the couple directly across the street. I barely knew anything about the ones I shared a back fence with.

I woke up the next day convinced I had misinterpreted what I'd seen. Days get long when you live alone, which is my choice by the way. But I hadn't anticipated the kind of lonely you get when your kids are located halfway across the country. As time had gone on I was hearing less from all of them, and I missed the semiweekly Skyping we used to do.

I became aware of a banging noise. Hammer on wood, coming from the direction of the back yard.

As I yawned and ground coffee, I peered out the kitchen window and saw my neighbor banging away on the corner of his shed, his snowy white hair being ruffled by the summer breeze.

I decided I had to talk to him, just conversationally, so I slipped on cropped khakis and a short sleeved tee, grabbed my coffee and slipped out the back porch.

"Hey there!" I said loudly as I reached the fence. I wasn't sure he could hear me over the sound of the hammer. I wasn't even sure he could hear me, given his age and all.

The second time I said it, he looked up. He'd been kneeling on a gardening pad. He had a wary look in his eye.

"Is the hammering disturbing you?" he asked, "I'm within the codes you know. It's after 8:30 am!"

"No, not at all!" I reassured him, "I just wondered how you and your wife are doing. How are you getting along? Do you need anything?"

The last bit I had tacked on as an afterthought. I think he picked up on it because his eyes seemed to narrow.

"No we're fine," he said, "Thanks for asking. I thought I'd get out here and do some minor repairs I've been putting off."

"Oh," I said, growing bored with the conversation already, "I usually see her out watering her flowers in the mornings before the sun gets too hot. Is she around?"

"No no," he told me, "She's gone to visit her sister in Vermont that just had her hip replaced. She'll be out there for a few weeks. I guess I'll be batching it while she's gone."

I think he tried to finish with a chuckle, but it came out funny, sounding more like a wheeze.

"Well keep cool!" I told him, "Supposed to hit 90 today again! If you need anything let me know, Mr. Smith."

His last name had popped up out of nowhere, probably left over in my brain from some back fence conversation I'd had with his wife months before. That year we'd had record snowfall, and I'd seen her in her yard filling up the three bird feeders she had, talking to her little feathered friends as she did it. I remember thinking she had a knack for nature-the birds, cardinals, blue jays and wrens mostly, didn't seem afraid of her, coming in close and flying in circles around her like they were her minions.

"I forget your name," he told me, "Something with an r-Reynolds was it?"

"Yes," I answered surprised.

"Well it was in the papers you know," he said, looking pleased with himself for recalling my name, "Photos of the accident your husband was in after the semi hit him..."

"Attorney, wasn't he?"

I felt all the air being expelled from my lungs. I hadn't seen that coming.

"Yes, an attorney," I told him, recovering. It had been more than two years, and was probably the reason I was practically agoraphobic. My husband had been involved in several community projects and was thinking of running for the City Council when he was killed. Half the town had attended his wake-the receiving line had been so long that the gum I had been chewing disintegrated in my mouth before I had a chance to spit it out.

I didn't know gum could even do that.

Suddenly I felt naked, exposed, and unsociable.

"Well have fun with your projects!" I said gaily as I turned to go back into the sanctuary of my home. Just as I was turning I saw several large bags of lime propped up against the side of Mr. Smith's shed.

One of them was nearly depleted.

It was a couple weeks later I was startled to see Mrs. Smith bending over in her garden the way she usually did. She was in a housecoat, with her gray hair in a bun on top of her head. It looked like she was pruning the rose bushes she had along the fence right outside of her screened in porch on the back of her house.

I had just finished baking toll house cookies. I scooped about a dozen and a half onto a printed paper plate, and wrapped cookies, plate and all in pink cellophane and tied it with curly ribbon at the top so that it looked more like a gift.

I was feeling good about it as I hurried down the back porch steps.

"Mrs. Smith!" I called as I crossed my yard, "Welcome back! I have something for you!"

I saw her straighten up from her bent over position at the top of her yard, and expected that she would turn around, but she never did. She bent to gather her tools up quickly and hightailed back into her house before I got to the fence separating our two properties.

"Maybe she didn't hear me," I muttered to myself.

I really didn't feel like walking around the block but since I had gone to the effort of fixing a plate of cookies, with a ribbon no less, I decided to do just that. It was hot and I was sweating in spite of being sleeveless and in shorts but I headed up the street behind my own and rang the doorbell.

When no one answered, I opened the screen door and knocked. After the sound of my own breathing subsided I tried to listen for sounds of life from within the Smith's house.

I couldn't hear anything. No tv, no music, no vacuum cleaner running. Nothing.

I left the cookies on the porch, and walked back to my own house more slowly, puzzled. I couldn't come up with a single reason why Hedda Smith would be avoiding me.

Unless, of course her husband had told her to. I tried to remember if during my conversation with him I had come off as too nosy. I didn't think I had, but it wasn't out of the realm of possibility. People were pretty twitchy nowadays.

I spent the rest of the day binge watching one of the Real Housewives series and working on the novel I had always promised myself I'd write after the kids grew up and moved away. I'd won a couple writing contests when my husband was still alive, nothing major, one was 'A Christmas to Remember' contest for a local magazine. The piece had to be exactly 500 words long, and I won it with a memory of a Christmas spent with my Grandmother on her farm in the Shenandoah Valley of Virginia.

The first prize was a camcorder, and my husband had been convinced that I had enough writing chops to hit the New York Times Bestsellers List.

So far I'd had no such luck and I was currently amassing a remarkable pile of politely worded rejection emails. Still I powered on, eventually publishing my first two novels on Amazon, and working on a third.

The next day I had medical appointments all day and I didn't even think about the Smiths until I returned home. As I clambered up the front porch I saw a white paper sticking out from between the storm door and the door to the house.

It was a thank you note, briefly worded, from Hedda, thanking me for the cookies.

I washed dishes again later, but didn't see either of the Smiths in their yard. It was a temperate evening for a Midwest summer, and the locusts raising their usual droning, chittering intermittent chorus was about the only noise, apart from the distant traffic from the thoroughfare closest to our subdivision.

That's when I noticed something new. There was a mound of dirt to the side on the gardening shed, and I didn't see the bags of lime anywhere. The last time I'd seen Mr. Smith he'd been working with a hammer.

I didn't have a vegetable garden that year. The previous year so many rabbits and squirrels had attacked it in spite of the fencing, that I'd given up, but I did know that the ph of our soil in the neighborhood was pretty much on target.

Even if the older couple had been preparing the soil for a garden, they wouldn't have needed the lime. I scanned their back yard to see if anything looked dug up or disturbed, but aside from the portion of the yard blocked by the shed, there didn't seem to be anything new.

I raised my eyes to their house. The windows were open and there was a fan in one of them. There didn't appear to be any lights on downstairs, which seemed odd, but someone was home because there were lights coming from the upstairs windows.

All the same I couldn't shake any uneasy feeling that came over me every time I looked out of my kitchen window, across the backyard and at the back of the Smith's house.

***

The weather turned cooler. The neighborhood kids had returned to school a couple days earlier, and the cooler nights were a harbinger of autumn. One morning I saw Mr. Smith raking leaves and since I'd already dressed in jeans and one of my husband's old shirts to do the same, I set my coffee cup down, grabbed a rake from against the wall in the mudroom and hustled out the back door.

"Good morning!" I called out, noting that there were already quite a few leaves under our ancient maple.

Mr. Smith turned to look me up and down before he spoke. He held an old fashioned looking rake in his gnarled hands, and he managed his version of a smile.

"Good morning Mrs. Reynolds," he said, "Getting a jump on the fall yardwork I see."

"Yes," I replied, "How is your wife? I saw her the other day but she went in the house before I could say hello! How is her sister doing?"

Mr. Smith stopped what he was doing and came to the fence line so that he could continue talking in a lower voice.

"Well, not so good," he said, looking down and shaking his head, "Hedda no sooner came home than she was called back. Seems things went south and her sister developed an infection."

He leaned over more closely, close enough that I was shocked to realize he'd been drinking.

"You know they use that cartilage that they harvest from cadavers for these operations!" he said in a conspiratorial tone. "From damn cadavers! Now you tell me if that sounds like a good way to fix something wrong in a living person!"

I recoiled a little, not just from his breath but from what he'd told me. I'd heard about it of course, the way the medical establishment had gotten approval to use certain parts of the deceased for different applications. It sounded kind of macabre to me too. I was pretty sure I'd have to be desperate before I had a knee or a hip replaced using dead people parts.

"Anyway, she won't be back for a while," he said shaking his head regretfully. "That's the thing about getting older. Past a certain point in time things start to go downhill fast, and all bets are off. That's why I never take a single God given day for granted."

Our eyes met. I knew what he was talking about, and felt the same way. I had planned on growing old with my husband. I knew growing old together would be a rocky ride, but I also knew that when he was alive nothing bothered me because we faced everything together.

I expected a meeting of the minds when my eyes met my neighbors, but I found myself looking into two dark voids. I'd never seen irises so dark, and I shivered involuntarily.

I decided then that I didn't trust him.

***

I was out in my yard again a few days later I when saw him hurry out his back door, not even glancing my way. I'd started to raise my hand in greeting and stopped when it was at half-mast. His truck was parked in his driveway facing toward the street he lived on and he pulled out of his driveway with a squeal.

I wondered why he was in such a hurry. That was my first thought. My second thought was that I should take the opportunity to snoop around. I'd been meaning to take some brownies over anyway as an excuse.

I hurried into the house, shucking off my gardening get-up and grabbing a blouse, sweater and my high waisted Mommy jeans from a peg in the mudroom. I loosed my short ponytail from the scrunchy that had been holding it back from my face and shook out my hair, feeling it fall softly down in a curtain to my shoulders.

A paper plate of brownies in hand, I went to the far end and opened the little used gate into my neighbor's yard. It had rusted, I noticed. I was sure that my neighbors had forgotten it was even there.

I went up the steps to their back porch. We lived in a neighborhood where people rarely bothered to lock their doors if they ran out, and when I tried the back door knob it made a grating sound but opened easily.

I was in the kitchen. The inside of the house was dim, and the kitchen sink was overflowing with dishes. I wasn't surprised because I was sure that Mr. Smith was of the generation of clearly defined roles between the sexes. I doubted that he had ever done house work at all.

I moved through the dining room, looking around. I decided to leave the brownies on the dining room table while I checked out the rest of the downstairs.

The front room was a shocker. There was a big screen and several pieces of furniture. The ancient looking couch was covered with plastic, in the same way my grandmother had left a plastic covering on her furniture. But what captured my attention were the magazines thrown all over.

They were all pornographic. Different titles, some I was familiar with and some I wasn't, all featuring busty women in provocative poses. There were two empty beer cans on the coffee table, and some of the centerfolds were pulled out and on display.

In a way I was amused. I was sure Mr. Smith was making a holiday out of his wife's absence, and it seemed like the old goat had life in him yet.

I became worried about how much time was passing. I circled through the small foyer with the antique mirrored coat tree with the storage seat built in when something glinted and caught my eye.

It was a ladies wig tossed onto the seat. A gray wig with a bun, and above it I saw a housedress, an apron and a handmade knitted sweater hanging on pegs.

I stopped and frowned, trying to make sense of it. Did Mr. Smith like to dress in women's clothing? Pretend he was his wife? Did his wife own wigs because she was bald? I didn't know what to make of it.

I decided to leave. I also decided, given the circumstances, I'd be better off leaving the brownies on the back porch so that Mr. Smith wouldn't know I'd been inside his house. I did that, and I was halfway across the back yard when I happened to glance at the garden shed.

The door was closed but the latch with the lock on it was hanging open. Without really thinking I pulled it open.

Immediately the scent of ammonia hit me in the face. After recoiling I pulled the front of my shirt up over my nose and looked around the shed so my eyes could become accustomed to the dimness. I pulled the door open to get a better look and stepped inside.

The shed was empty. Completely empty.

There were some pegs along one wall where a few pairs of differently sized shears were neatly hanging. The floor was dirt, and I could see that the corner to my right looked like it had been dug up recently. I moved over and stepped there, and my sneaker sank in a little.

I couldn't stop myself. I pulled the door behind me in and began digging there with my hands. I can't explain to this day what drove me to do that. I think it was some instinct born of the general feeling of unease that had been building in my gut since that evening I had observed the Smiths at their dining table through my kitchen window.

It didn't take even 45 seconds of digging before I felt something round and soft beneath my fingertips. In the half light it looked gray.

I recognized it immediately as the bun that Hedda Smith wore on the top of her head.

I opened my fingers as wide as they would go and felt around just to make sure it was what I thought it was. My heart was racing and unmindful of the dirt clinging to me I brought my fingers up to my mouth to stifle a gasp.

I turned as the door behind me swung open. Squinting at the brightness of the light and unable to make out the silhouette of the figure standing there.

As I stared, frozen and still on my knees, something made a whooshing sound through the air and the last thing I was conscious of was the sensation of the top of my head exploding.

***

I was cold. Cold enough to feel myself shaking. My eyelids felt so heavy just opening my eyes was a struggle and my shoulders and neck hurt.

I looked through slitted eyes at my surroundings. I was in the Smith's living room, the one I had been in on the last day I remembered. The curtains were drawn, and I was disoriented.

The room had been tidied up, all the magazines were put away. The television was on and as I glanced downward I realized that I was naked.

My hands and my ankles were duct taped together and I had duct tape over my mouth. I could already feel that it had loosened, but something told me not to try to scream.

My head was pounding, probably from where I'd been hit.

I heard a commotion outside the room. Some kind of shuffling and then, turning my head with difficulty, I saw Mr. Smith emerge from the short hallway outside the room.

He was wearing a sleeveless wife beater tee shirt and wiping his forehead with a stained and yellowed man's handkerchief.

He didn't look well. I could see long sweat stains under the armholes of his shirt, and his face was bright red.

"Oh, there you are," he said gruffly. "Sorry about your head. Sorry you couldn't mind your own business too. Living alone as you do now, I think it'll take awhile for anyone to miss you.

I took your clothes so that you couldn't run so easy if you got loose. Don't worry I ain't gonna rape you. I have to say I don't mind the view though....these days all I can do is look."

It was surreal listening to him ramble. Clearly he had a few marbles loose. He stood staring at me as if waiting for me to respond in spite of the duct tape across my mouth.

"Oh," he said, as if remembering. He came over with the shovel still in his hand and bent down to look me sternly in the eye.

"Now I will take the tape off your mouth, but if you make so much as a peep I will hit you in the head again. You understand?"

I nodded. As soon as he took the tape off I said, "Water."

He grabbed a partially empty bottle of water from an end table, unscrewed it and held it up to my lips. I drank greedily, and immediately felt more in focus.

"Are you going to kill me?" I asked.

"Afraid so," he answered shortly, "I can't do anything else now that I know you saw her. What made you come snooping around, anyway? We've been backyard neighbors for going on 20 years. The most contact we ever had was exchanging Christmas cookies."

"I saw you kill her," I said bluntly, "I saw you strangle Hedda from my kitchen window. It didn't seem real, but I wasn't seeing her after that, so-"

"So you thought you'd play detective," he said with a note of disgust, "I see. Well, what do you think now?"

"I think you are a murderer," I answered. I was trying to buy time. He had duct taped my wrists together in front of me, and there was a chance I could get out of it. I had already loosened the sloppy job he'd done of trying to bind my ankles around the chair legs. One of my feet was already outside of the bindings, and he hadn't even noticed.

"I guess I am," he said, looking down for a moment, "But somehow I don't care. I don't know whether it's my age or the fact that Hedda and I were 20 years past tolerating each other. She had a weak heart you know. She was supposed to have passed long before this."

"I think it's one of life's ironies that the weak can linger so long. I never could see the point, you know? It may not have been of her own choosing, but in a way it was a mercy that I took her life. I think I did us both a favor. I'm sure she was as sick of me as I was of her."

"We'll never know now," I said.

Mr. Smith looked at me contemplatively.

"I have some pills," he said finally, "I think you should take them and go to sleep. I will smother you then, and it's about the gentlest way to go that I can think of. It will be painless. I already dug another hole to plant you in, and you can keep Hedda company."

"And if I don't take them?" I asked.

"Then it's shovel time again," he told me, "But I don't want that, and neither do you I bet."

I thought for a moment.

"Okay, I'll take the pills," I told him, "DO you have any milk? I always take pills with milk."

"Sure thing!" he replied, almost cheerfully, and hurried off to the kitchen again.

As soon as I heard him banging cabinets I lifted my duct taped hands until they were slightly behind my head and brought them down as hard as I could, making sure my elbows stayed wide past my hips and bringing my wrists into my hipbones.

The tape split, just as I'd been assured it would when I took the self defense classes at the Community Center last fall..

Mr. Smith came back into the room again. I had placed my hands back together in my lap. He held out a pill with one hand and brought the glass of milk close to my lips.

"Which do ya want first?" he asked, "The milk or the water?"

When I reared up out of the chair the look on his face was priceless. I knocked the glass away and milk seemed to arc out of it in slow motion as it rotated through the air and landed without breaking on the carpet. I could feel adrenalin pumping. I was prepared for a fight, and I thought I could take him.

Instead he staggered back, holding his left arm and shaking. He fell backward onto the coffee table, displacing magazines and causing one of the corner legs to pop off as his body descended on the end of it.

He made burbling sounds, white foam appearing at one corner of his mouth. His legs jerked. It almost seemed like he was getting electrified by an unseen and unrelenting force.

And then he was still, lying there with his eyes open and fixed.

I found my clothes. I knew what I should do, but I also knew what I wanted to do. I was just grateful I hadn't killed anyone.

Months passed. There was an investigation eventually. It was the talk of the town when the bodies of both Mr. and Mrs. Smith were found planted vertically in their garden shed. The mystery of how they got there was never solved.

I saw articles in the paper occasionally. The Smith house took a while to sell but eventually a nice younger couple purchased it.

I waited to feel anything—guilt, remorse, a sudden urge to run down and confess to one of the local detectives at the downtown precinct...

Two years have passed, and I am still waiting.

The End
COPYRIGHT 2018 BY P.MATTERN

ABOUT THE AUTHOR

Author P.Mattern is an Amazon #1 Bestselling, RONE award nominated, multi award winning author of over 30 books, cowritten books and novellas. She publishes through CHBB Publishing, Tell-Tale Publishing and Dark Books Press and her award winning FULL MOON SERIES was cowritten with her adult children, J.C. Estall and Vincent Price Award winning son Marcus Mattern. She began composing stories in utero and was born with a stylus clutched in her tiny hand. She is currently involved with one of her characters.("It's complicated").

AMAZON AUTHOR PAGE
https://www.amazon.com/default/e/B0756ITMiP

ON FACEBOOK
https://www.facebook.com/patricia.annette.3

NEWSLETTER
http://bit.ly/FMSNewsletter

ORIGINS

TALE OF THE RED DRAGON

RUE VOLLEY

No legacy is so rich as honesty.

~William Shakespeare

Love.

The worst of all four-letter words.

Nothing trumps it, but loyalty.

Just as treacherous. Just as devastating.

Both have ruled over me for as long as I can remember.

Love.

I stared down at my hands and spotted the slight tremor.

He always does this to me. Always.

My name is Dorin. I'm a vampire. I'm a slayer of the king of all vampires.

Dracula or as I knew him, Vlad the Impaler.

But before I killed him, I loved him.

More than anything. More than salvation.

For that, I traded my soul...

THE RED DRAGON

MERCY, DRAGON!" THE MAN SCREAMED. I stood above him with my sword raised and eyes burning with the fire of battle. My chest rose and fell in the chilled air. With a sudden jolt, I could feel it in my lungs, bringing me back to life and out of my bloody stupor.

War does this to a man. It will turn you into an animal. Fighting to survive amongst dismembered body parts and deathly moaning. A disgusting display of what we're capable of when forced to choose survival over civility.

My wild eyes remained transfixed on my mortally wounded prey. The man fell to his knees on the ground before me. My compassion fought for him. I tried my best to ignore my weakness.

Mercy. I cannot afford it. I'm not tasked with mercy. I'm tasked with destruction.

The muscles tensed in my arms. Tearing at my will like a rabid dog. My blood coursed through my veins, swelling my heart when it should be shriveling. The weight of my sword felt heavier as my adrenaline faltered. Failing me, when it should drive me forward.

His muddied hands shook in front of me. His eyes were filled with tears. He was discovering his faith. The stark realization was settling into his weary soul. The end was near. I've seen this over and over again on the field of battle.

Men foolishly rushing in with no education to serve as their guide.

I knew exactly what my fate was, and I'd made my peace with it.

I noticed his wedding band, forged of cheap metal on his left hand.

Was he a father? Would his children mourn him? Or was he abusive as mine had been to me? I hated my father and in between his drunken rampages and offensive nature I had become callous when it was needed. My father had made me worthy of war. He had created me, not only in the flesh but stone. He had beaten the *gentle nature* out of me. The same gentle nature that he was desperate to extinguish inside of me. He claimed it would cost me my life. That I could never survive in this world if I found so much beauty in it.

The truth was, he feared me. He didn't understand me. He didn't realize that I enjoyed dolls and dressing up in mother's clothing. He couldn't wrap his mind around it, so he did what he felt he had to do. Ignorant of my true nature and unwilling to accept me as I am.

This sent my honesty into retreat and my life into turmoil.

I hated him and it fueled me with each battle. I drew upon his brutality to do what I had to do for my King. Vlad the Impaler, sovereign King and master of my sword.

My eyes wandered as Vlad slay his twentieth man and let the body drop before him. He paused and let his manly gaze settle on me. My enemy cowered before me with his fingers intertwined and lips quivering. I won't disguise my feelings. It filled me with power. Should I embrace it and with it my true nature? Will it devour me, as fire devours everything in its wake?

Perhaps the word *dragon* is fitting for me. Not that I doubt my King's ability to see through the shroud of deceit. I could never hide from him. I just don't possess the fortitude.

If I have one true weakness in this world, it would be him. He brings me to my knees.

Vlad stood tall on top of the hill, covered in our enemy's blood. His long sword was dripping with our victory. My eyes glossed over as I cried out and it echoed above the battle ground. My sword came down with all of the strength left in me, cutting through bone and muscle with ease. The man grabbed at my sword, now buried deep in his chest. I watched his lips part, blood bubbling up and seeping out onto his weathered skin. I took a short breath and released it. White smoke poured out of my mouth like a dragon. It is what Vlad calls me, and perhaps I am. A dragon of *death*, an instrument of destruction.

A dragon, but loyal and loyalty is the true king.

I jerked my sword upward, and blood spewed out. It shot across my tightly fitted armor and strained facial expression. It reeked of iron. A stench I was growing accustomed to. I quickly turned and raised my sword with honor. Vlad smiled, then he laughed as he held his sword up high and rejoiced in our victory. Our triumph over yet another piece of land he wanted to absorb into his ever growing empire. I cannot blame him for he was orphaned as a child, and I think that his lack of paren-tal guidance ruined him. He was thrust into sovereignty. Robbed of his childhood. Of his innocence. I could see this in his eyes.

Sometimes I wonder if he has a soul and then I remember who I am. I kill just as he does. I have no right to judge anyone or anything.

I'm an assassin, my name known far and wide as a bringer of death.

I raised my sword as high as I could to honor him, my King and a man that I would do anything for. I love him, as a loyal subject loves their Lord and Master, but as I stand here and watch him, my heart fills with something more. An old feeling that I cannot allow to overtake me. It is a sense of want and need for his attention, and I know this is not how it should be. I should be grateful to be in his company and the trusted few who fight at his side.

This feeling first tried to overtake me when Vlad was gracious enough to allow me to stay within the castle walls. My parents were servants of the Dracul family. My father, a blacksmith, my mother, a chamber maid. When plague took them, I was left orphaned. Vlad had taken a liking to me. Probably because our King and Queen, his mother and father, had only produced one heir. His was a lonely life, filled with training and schooling. He was being groomed to rule as he should be.

The library in Castle Bran rivaled all others in the region, and I was confident that Vlad had read every book available to him. I would have killed to have access to it and with Vlad befriending me, I suddenly did. In fact, I had access to everything. To his library, to his private lessons, to his chamber at night.

His advisors tried to end his friendship with me, but Vlad refused. He fought for me, and that fight stayed with me. It seduced my heart.

He seduced me.

Days turned into weeks, weeks into months and then two years had passed by. Those two years were the happiest of my life. Two years of pure joy as Vlad befriended me and trusted me with his deepest desires.

He wished to one day be King and make me the head of his royal army.

I had laughed at the time, thinking about my true nature. How could I possibly lift a sword, or better yet, take a life?

All I wanted was his attention and love. A love I knew I could never see to fruition.

But one summer day, amongst the cherry blossom trees in the royal garden, Vlad had leaned in and kissed my lips. Gentle, soft. Quick and sweet. I had parted my lips, ready to speak. Ready to profess my undying love for him.

That kiss was my invitation. A welcomed release from my prison.

Just as freedom started to become a reality, we were interrupted by guards with grave news.

We raced back to the castle, only to find that his father had fallen ill, along with his mother, and three weeks later they were both claimed by the plague. The same that had taken my parents away from me.

Vlad was thrust into power, robbing him of his childhood and his fledgling love for me.

The kiss haunted me to this day.

I closed my eyes and could still smell the flowers in the air. The warm sun upon my face. His soft, rosy red lips resting against my own. Then the stench of the battlefield overtook my senses and ate away at my memory, bringing me back to this hellish reality. To the spoils of war.

I lowered my sword as he started to walk toward me. He glanced at my slain victim on the ground, taking very little time to honor the enemy with any of his attention. His eyes quickly locked onto mine. Blue, blue as sky and heaven above. Mine, a chocolate brown. His eyes engulf me every single time. He stopped and placed a hand on my shoulder, and his grip was firm and flooded me with pride. To watch him once again lead us, this small group of Romanian trash, into the battlefield, and always find victory was a miracle that only God had bestowed upon us.

God was who Vlad fought for. His faith was unwavering, and his love for our God complete.

He had blessed us with a warrior and sovereign King.

Worthy of my allegiance. Worthy of my love.

He spoke calmly with a tinge of adoration. "Dorin, my loyal dragon." His hand continued to grip my shoulder. I nodded to him, watching his eyes light up with pride. I know he cares for me as a King should for his loyal guard. The leader of his army. But I hoped in my heart that he could care as he had for me that summer day.

So long ago, so far away. A dream of another life that I could never have.

"My King," I replied, lowering my eyes. He gave me a manly shake.

His voice held steady. "Shed the formality my dear friend, how many battles must we win before you see that I fight at your side as an equal, and not as your ruler?"

My eyes lifted, and I studied his face. He spoke the truth, and it fed my need for him, but I quickly corrected it. "I know my place, if I did not, there would be anarchy."

Vlad smiled. His smile mesmerized me. His lips full, inviting. The laughter escaped him, forcing me to blink. The roar was profound. He is so passionate about everything that he does. It is a contagion, a welcomed virus that is the heartbeat of his people, and for me.

I would know no other life worthy of living if not in his company.

"We ride for home. Then we celebrate, we celebrate as victors once again, my dear friend."

He forcefully pulled me into his embrace. I closed my eyes. He smelled like sweat and blood. His body felt firm against me. It made my heartbeat speed up in my chest. I felt the shame of wanting him in an unnatural way once again. I try to control it, but it becomes harder every single day. My lust disgusts me. My body and mind betray me.

This love that I have for him must die, it must make way for duty. My duty to him is to keep him safe, help him in his conquests and stay at his side.

Vlad's mischievous grin consumed his expression. It was a look not to foreign to me. One that amused, when amusement could be a distant memory at best. We had been fighting for so long. Killing without mercy, expanding this empire.

He winked at me. "You can have as many women as you can fit into your bed, Dorin. Take your pick of mine. I offer that to you. You've more than earned it. This shall be your prize when we return home, victorious. Our people shall be grateful, and the fruits of war shall be ours." I pondered his generosity and the word *ours*. He often referred to our people as *ours*, the victory, *ours*. I wish that it brought peace to my heart when I knew that I should be grateful, too. Thankful that he included me when there was no obligation.

Vlad was the true King. I, his loyal friend and companion. I should not be so selfish and want more.

More would be my ruin.

More kept me up at night.

More had kept women out of my bed and my heart.

He shook me one last time, and I allowed the fake smile to part my lips. I nodded to him.

I lied, as I should. "Thank you, my Lord."

He tapped me one last time and laughed under his breath.

"Now to only convince you that you are welcome to use my name as you did when we were young. Do you remember, Dorin?"

I bit my bottom lip a little too hard. The pain was coming in a distant second to that pain which festers in the dark recesses of my heart. Of course, I remember when we were young. Every blissful second of it. Every night he allowed me to crawl into his bed and stay warm at his side. Every smile, every look he gave to me with those piercing blue eyes. Every time he spoke my name. Whispered into my ear. Let his hand brush up against mine.

And the kiss, the one I longed for yet again.

That was the paradise I stole away to in times of turmoil. A haven where a naïve boy once believed that he could find love within the walls of Castle Bran with its future and now King. Such hopes dashed such dreams folly.

I am but a fool.

"I remember many things, my Lord. Mostly I remember my place and that you are my King."

He shook his head and pulled me closer to him. His breath hot, his eyes filled with fiery passion. My imagination about to run wild. If only the men could fall away, leaving us behind to be alone together once again. Perhaps then he could honestly remember me. Remember how he felt for me, or how I wished he had when we were young. I longed for that more with each passing day. It held me prisoner here. An unwilling participant in a love affair never fully realized.

I cling to fantasy when reality should be my real salvation.

"I suppose I should practice restraint." He laughed. "My bachelor days have come to an end."

I swallowed hard. My throat felt so dry and his words wrapped around it like an iron fist, tightening its icy grip. Choking the hope of renewal from my battered soul.

Vlad had many women in the castle who did his bidding. He was a man who had a reputation for sexual conquest, but over the past months he had slowed down, and one woman had risen above the rest. A woman who I adored and yet envied now. A woman who would bring his bachelor days to an end. Should I be gracious? Should I be thankful that she would bring his conquests in his bed to an end? I wasn't sure if it would be easier to know that he belonged to one, or if I preferred to know that he cared for none that had come and gone.

Regardless, her name was Illona, and she was as kind as she was beautiful. Or so she seemed. She was of royal blood and held herself in a much different way than the concubines who roamed the halls of Bran Castle. My home, or as Vlad would say, *our* home, built in the Carpathian Mountains. She stands as a protection for our people here in Transylvania. A stronghold that had held for generations. A place I felt most secure and yet least loved.

A place that once held my dreams and aspirations.

A lie.

I would never be his. He would never be mine.

Vlad was birthed within her walls, as was I. I, born to servants, Vlad born to royal blood. Yet he treated me as his equal. That was his charm. Making me believe that I was equal in all ways. Stripping away my insecurities and allowing me to be myself. Well, as much as I could afford to allow.

Illona was sent as a goodwill ambassador from a neighboring land. Her father hoped she would woo Vlad and make him take her homeland under his protection. She had been with us for a year now. At first, she appeared shy, homesick, and it eventually drew Vlad in. I can't be certain if she honestly felt uneasy or if it was her goal to attract him to her with her innocent nature.

Regardless, she appears gentle and kind. Unlike any other woman I had ever encountered before. Not that I had bedded any, although I paid a few to spend the night with me to appease Vlad's unwavering need for me to be with them. It seems as if he remembers nothing of our youth. Nothing of me or us.

Vlad spends all of his time now in the cathedral and taking long walks with Illona. Leaving me to watch and prepare for what I know may come...a wedding.

His wedding to *her*. I swallowed hard and accepted it as I have to accept my place in this world. A place at his side, but never *with* him, as I desire.

That seems to be my fate. My Hell. My payment due to our God above.

I collected myself. "Thank you, I appreciate your generosity." He watched my expression with curious fervor. Vlad is not one to miss many things. He was a creature of detailed habit, and it made me nervous each time he studied me.

"You shall find happiness." He whispered to me. "As have I." It seemed like a compromise, a strange admission coming from him.

His words pained me. He sounded so familiar. Just a breath away from allowing his true nature to emerge. But his eyes hardened and the moment slipped away as it always did. He had buried his youth on the battlefield amongst blood and tears. Duty and circumstances beyond his control.

I so wished that I could do the same. My strength fails me in love. I fear this weakness will be my downfall. I feel it all around me, seeping into my dreams at night, confusing me, taunting me.

Do I look like a sinner? A man who would go against God and his will that I lay with women and be grateful to plant my seed? I know I should settle down, or at least consider my legacy, but standing here in this field of the dead and dying holds more weight for me than the thought of living forever.

Here I am. Exactly what he wants me to be, here I get the opportunity to stand at his side. That, to me, is worth more than my name enduring forever. More than a legacy. More than my seed carrying on my name.

My name means nothing next to his.

He saved me yet again by interrupting my thoughts. "Come." He let me go and turned back to the gruesome scene surrounding us. The buzzards circled high above the battlefield. I shielded my eyes from the hazy sun. This was our legacy as we spread out across the known lands, leaving a trail of destruction in our wake.

A warning to all those who would refuse Vlad's rule.

His voice boomed across the battlefield. "Bury the dead, kill the wounded, and then we ride for home." They listen to him without question. Swords rose and fell all over the field as the dying were released to heaven or hell.

The choice made by each of them with how they had lived their lives. With honor or treachery.

SNAKEBITE

THE RIDE HOME BECAME TREACHEROUS. The weather quickly changed from chilled to freezing cold, two days in. Romanians can endure this, and it solidified our ability to fight in whatever circumstances God bestowed upon us. Our victories rested in *his hands,* as well as Vlad's mastered ability to outwit our adversaries.

Only this was a harsh winter. The most brutal that I had ever remembered. Unforgiving, as is my wicked desire. I could hear coughing behind me. The men were exhausted. Some had injuries that needed to be attended to before they became infectious. This could be a devastating blow to our march toward victory. Rest is a necessary evil. We had been fighting for three years, this time, we had been on this campaign for three weeks. I missed home, as I would assume they all did. Regardless of the ferocity of our campaign, we are still flesh and blood.

Our army is small but fierce in nature. Loyal to a fault. As am I.

Ignoring need was something I was used too, but it wouldn't serve to garner success, where success was so desperately needed.

I stared up at our flag as it waved against the gray sky. Stark white with a red dragon engulfing it from corner to corner. It's claws were protruding and fire cascading from its gaping mouth.

I glanced down at the same emblem on my chest. It was beaten and bloodied, but it stood for something more. It gave me a purpose in life. One that I cherished. I needed to focus on this more. The preservation of our people and not my wants and needs. My happiness was nothing next to that. I had given my oath to him, to my homeland, to its people. To fail now would be a tragic reminder of the frailty of men. The weakness of my character.

Something my father would spew at me as he beat me, claiming I was more feminine than manly. Unnatural. He knew me better than I knew myself so I buried that deep inside of me. It wasn't until Vlad entered my life that the old feelings returned to me. Something I could do without.

It weakened me. *He* makes me weak. I can't seem to control it any longer, but I must find a way. I need to pray. I need to ask God for forgiveness and strength.

I held the furs close to me as I gripped the leather strap between my legs. The horse had slowed, and I knew it was hungry and needed rest. I kicked my feet into its thinning sides, and he sped up. I was able to get next to Vlad as he rode with his chin high in the air. Proud as always. His profile so handsome against the bleak backdrop of the countryside. He turned to stare at me. I was shivering, and he laughed and shook his head. It wasn't the cold wind that tore through me. It was him. Always him.

His voice lowered as he spoke to me, careful to keep it between us. "Cold, my brother?" I straightened up and tried to act as if I wasn't.

"I'm all right, my Lord, but the men are tired and hungry...not to mention the horses, we need to rest, or we may face sickness."

"Dorin, please call me Vlad. I think you've earned this right by now, would you not agree?"

We stared at each other for a moment longer than needed. I longed for these private moments with him, yet I hated them. It was a constant reminder of what we felt for one another, even though his feelings for me were wrought with confusion. He could switch from gentle too harsh in the blink of an eye, so I constantly felt at odds.

I took no time to counteract his statement. "I prefer to call you as you deserve, my Lord."

His eyes lowered, and his gaze rested on my lips. "Do you remember when we were young?"

I swallowed hard, and my horse shifted beneath me. It became an extension of my uneasiness.

"Of course."

He sighed, and his breath came out in puffs of white smoke. It escaped his tender lips. I peered at his mouth until I realized that he was watching me. Studying my expression.

"I miss those days. I miss peace." He sounded remorseful.

"My Lord?" I asked, and he laughed and shook his head.

"Dorin, I will break you of this habit. I swear to our God above."

I gave into his request. "Vlad," I murmured as he looked at me. His blue eyes nestled in deep black lashes. So beautiful yet wild, just as he had always been.

"It's nice to hear my name on your lips." He sounded flirtatious.

My breath caught in the back of my throat. His words soothed me, brought me the peace he spoke of. I did remember that peaceful time. A time when we spent our days learning, bonding, sharing our dreams with one another. I longed for those days with bated breath.

I longed for him. I couldn't help myself, as much as I prayed to keep it at bay.

I cleared my throat. "Perhaps we need to suspend this campaign, just for the remainder of the season. Rest."

He tilted his head and stared up at the sky. His eyes scanned the graying clouds and then returned to me. Bright blue and forcing my heart to skip a beat in my armor laden chest.

"I do miss home." He added. "And you." he quickly cleared his throat and turned his horse to face the men. "I mean, the friendship we had outside of battle and blood."

I nodded to him. His words were confusing me even further.

Vlad reached down and touched the deep black hair of his Stallion. He patted it on the side of its neck and talked to it as if it were human. Some men have a relationship with their horses that surpasses that of any human. That is what Vlad felt for his horse, which he called *vânt moarte*, which translates to *Death Wind*. This horse had been with him for years and eventually he will have to set it out to pasture, but for now, it is part of his strength and will. An extension of himself.

Just as I seem to be now.

"Perhaps we should camp for the night and continue on in the morning."

"I do think it would be best for everyone, horses included."

Vlad tapped the side of his horse's neck again and stopped. He turned and called out to the men following behind.

"We rest here. Build shelter, gather wood, and hunt game. Let us eat, rest, and then tomorrow we return home victorious with God's grace upon us." He lifted his fist and shook it high in the air as a few large snowflakes gently glided down upon us. I stared up at the sky and let my breath rise into it. I hadn't eaten for two days, and it was finally catching up with me. I could feel it in my bones.

The murmuring that rose up amongst the men told me that I had made the right decision. I watched him dismount as I caught sight of something in the woods. I jumped down and knocked Vlad to the ground as I had nothing in mind but his protection. I called out to the men.

"Enemy! There!" I cried out.

Arrows flew into the thick woods as I lay on top of Vlad and he stared up at me. I gazed down at him, and his lips looked so inviting. Large and slightly red. My body ached to taste him and yet I knew it would be certain death if I even attempted it. It was torturous to be this close to him. I cleared my throat.

"The thought of battle makes you hard between the legs, Dorin." He said to me as he started to laugh and I rolled off of him. I was mortified that my cock had hardened as I lay on top of him. It was such a disgusting thing for me to allow. I pushed myself up and then reached down to Vlad as he took my hand. I pulled him to his feet. He leaned into my ear, his voice low and his breath hot against my skin.

"I often get hard when the thought of death is upon me. I'm happy to know I am not the only one." He leaned back and winked at me.

I sighed as he walked away from me and a woman was drug back to us, kicking and screaming. She was tossed forward and fell at Vlad's feet as he looked down on her.

He leaned down to study her face. "What is this?" he asked as she looked up at him with hatred. She quickly spat at him. It hit him in the face as I stepped forward and drew my sword and placed it to her throat, but Vlad held his hand up, and I stopped as he wished me to. He reached down and jerked her up to her feet and held her shoulders tightly.

She hissed at him. "You filthy animal."

"Are you alone?" he asked as his voice held steady.

"You killed my family, my brother…my blood. You disgust me." She struggled to break free of his hold on her.

His grip held firm. "So did you come to slay me? One woman, alone?" His eyes scanned the woods behind her and I stepped forward and pointed my sword at the trees.

"Go, search it all. Leave nothing unturned."

Five men ran past me and quickly disappeared into the thick woods. I watched it swallow them whole and then I turned my attention back to her. She reached down and expeditiously produced a knife, raising it high and crying out as she buried it into Vlad's shoulder before I could react. I screamed at her as he stumbled back, shocked that he had been wounded.

I spun on one foot and beheaded her without a second thought. Her head fell to the ground, eyes still open before I dropped my sword and ran to Vlad just as he started to collapse. I rested in the snow, holding him close to me as I called out for help. Our two doctors on the battlefield had now been reduced to one. The master had been slain. The apprentice was all we could rely upon.

I was terrified that he may not be enough for this. I pressed my hand against Vlad's shoulder as he smiled up at me. I could feel his heartbeat in the blood that escaped his wound. It bubbled up between my fingers, hot and sticky. I grit my teeth in horror.

"Always there for me. Always, my dragon." He whispered before he passed out.

***

I stood outside of his large tent. I heard moaning. *His* moaning. It tore at my heart and every fiber of my being. All I wanted to do was rush to his side and help him. However I possibly could. But my place was standing guard, outside of his tent, making sure that no one entered that shouldn't, and that my protection of him would not waver again.

This is why I hate my feelings toward him. They do make me weak. They ruin me. They force me to focus on the wrong things. I feel as if this is my fault. I was right there, standing so close I could smell the stench coming off of her wretched breath. Yet I had allowed her to wound him. Perhaps fatally. I could never forgive myself for this.

I closed my eyes and lowered my head. Gripping my sword firmly in my right hand and ready to kill at a moment's notice. I needed to push these emotions aside and return to my rightful place. I would never have him, not as I fantasized that I could. I needed to accept this just as I needed to accept that he had a future bride and queen waiting for him at home.

It was my job to return him to her alive, not dead. Widowing her before his lineage could carry on. That would curse me forever.

The loud cry escaped the tent from behind me. Then I heard him call out, but to my surprise, it wasn't for who I expected it to be.

"Dorin! Dorin!" He yelled with desperation in his voice.

I quickly entered the tent and could see him lying there on a pile of soft furs. A makeshift bed for a King. The apprentice attended to his wound with herbs as he struggled to sit up. Another man tried to hold him down, but his strength and will was strong. I sheathed my sword and rushed to his side, staring down at him in horror. His skin was pale, his lips cracking from dehydration. This seemed more than just a flesh wound. He looked as if he may be dying.

I fell to one knee as he reached out and gripped my hand in his. His eyes pale and glossed over. "Tell her that I love her."

I narrowed my eyes and held his sweaty palm against my own.

"You will tell her this yourself, my Lord."

He shook his head and arched his back. The pain was tearing through him like nothing I had ever seen before. I looked at the apprentice and shook my head.

"Surely you can remedy this."

He looked back at me and his expression spoke volumes before he used the words I did not want to hear. "It appears to be a poison. That demon poisoned the blade."

"What?" I leaned forward and could see the black streaks running from his wound and across his shimmering shoulder. He was burning up. An internal fire was consuming him.

I placed my hand on his forehead and quickly removed it. I pushed the apprentice aside and scooped him up into my arms, rising as he leaned his head against my shoulder. I peered down at him as he started to mumble to himself. I couldn't understand a word that he was saying, but I knew the onset of death all too well. I had watched my mother and father both succumb to this feverish state, and all be damned if I would allow Vlad to suffer the same fate.

DREAMS OF YOU

I RUSHED OUT OF THE TENT and into the cold snow. My legs ached, and my muscles strained as I carried him in my arms. I fought back my terror and the tears as I reached the edge of the shoreline and blankly gazed into the slowly moving water. I could see the ice chunks floating by in the slurry. I took a deep breath. Calming myself. Focusing on him.

"You will not die this day. I won't allow it."

I walked into the water, crying out in pain. The cold inched its way up my legs, over the base of my back, and finally, I stopped with it resting just beneath my chest. I lowered him into the water. He screamed out to the heavens.

"Illona! My love."

He opened his eyes and glared up at the sky. The snow descended upon us. My teeth chattered, my bones ached. The life force was slowly being stripped away from me. I felt dizzy and just as I started to lose my grip on him two men rushed in and grabbed me by the shoulders. I watched him sink below the surface of the water. The terror of losing him tore through my heart, filling me with fear and hopelessness. He was quickly retrieved and lifted up. He took a deep breath and choked up water from his lungs, along with a small amount of blood. It trickled from his blue lips and over his pale chin. If it weren't for his intense eyes locking onto mine, I would have sworn that death had taken him and me along with it.

I was dragged ashore as he was carried back to his tent. I struggled to break free and pushed myself up to my feet, swaying as I walked toward him. His head fell back, and my heart fell along with him.

"Live! Live!" I called out to him as I fell face first into the snow and lost consciousness.

***

Dreams of blue sky and flowers floating down from above me consumed my mind. I rolled onto my side and could see Vlad lying next to me. Happy, smiling. Gentle and free. He reached toward me and touched my cheek. I closed my eyes, allowing his touch to consume me. Then I felt the warmth of his lips pressed against mine. It engulfed my senses, and I let the shame and sorrow slip away from me as he took me to a place that I had only dreamed of.

One in which he returned my affection just as I had desperately hoped that he would.

The kissing became harder, needier. I felt his hand lower and press against my abdomen. It excited me and my erection followed without any control. I groaned and rolled onto my back as he climbed on top of me. I grinned at his lips, wanting more. Wanting him to take me.

He gripped me firmly in his hand. I let my lips part, sucking in a much-needed breath. He started to stroke me, forcing me to race toward a climax. His chin rose with each slow pull. My chin was rising along with his. Eyes locked, mouths open. He studied my expression, allowing my pleasure to ebb slowly and flow with each delicate movement of his hand.

He took such great care to preserve the moment.

I twitched, every muscle in my stomach becoming rock hard. He looked down and then back up to me. His mischievous grin teased me. He lowered and before I knew it I could feel the warmth of his mouth engulfing my strength. My power. He pulled back, toying with me. Flicking his tongue and then taking another long stroke with his lips pressed hard against my aching flesh.

His moan rose in the back of his throat. His pace quickened. I felt a slight brush of teeth and hissed uncontrollably. The twinge of pain was only adding to my excitement. He pushed forward, forcing the length of my cock to the back of his throat. He paused, moaning, sending waves of pleasure through my entire body. The vibration was taunting my inevitable eruption. I bit my lip, arched my back, and turned my face. I buried it into the tall, thick grass. I could smell the seasons changing, the renewal of life. He was allowing me to set my soul free. To be reborn into this glorious realization of who I truly am.

His lover, his true soul mate. Now and forever.

A lifetime of his love would never be enough.

I wanted forever. I needed it as desperately as I needed him.

***

I let his name escape my lips and reached down, feeling long hair at my fingertips. I opened my eyes and focused in on a youthful girl who peeked up at me from under my fur blankets. I cried out as if I had been stabbed and pushed her off of me. My erection quickly retreated as the horror of the situation sank in. No woman had ever had me, and the thought of it was repulsive.

I shook my head and looked around to see candles lit in a familiar room. We had returned home to Castle Bran.

She sat up in the bed. Her small breasts erect. Pointed nipples aimed at me. I swallowed hard and shook my head.

"I was dreaming."

She grinned at me. "I'm well aware, brave dragon."

I took a slow breath and let it out along with some of the uneasy tension that held my body in suspension. I shook my hands out and looked around the room. I hadn't realized that I left the bed and frantically ran from her. Placing distance between us.

Her eyes lowered, and she bit her lip. "I would be happy to finish if you wish it so."

I bit my lip and grabbed my pants that lay on the ground. I nearly fell over as I scrambled to pull them on, but I quickly regained my composure as I stood up and pushed my shaggy black hair out of my eyes. She rose up onto her knees and stared at me. Her hand lifted and cupped her breast. She toyed with her nipple and sighed.

I cleared my throat. "Food...I need food. Would you mind?"

She narrowed her eyes as her small hand lowered. Her face relaxed, and she grinned at me.

"I only meant to help you. Our King sent me here to warm you up and bring you back to the land of the living."

I stammered and placed my hands on my hips. "I appreciate the effort, now could you, I don't know...perhaps you should get dressed and tell the cooks that I need food. I'm sorry, but my health and strength mean more than pleasure."

She slid from the side of the bed and slipped her white nightgown back on. It was sheer and held nothing back by way of her naked form. I kept my eyes on hers as she stood there in front of me and adjusted her hair. She pulled it back and out of her gown. It flowed red like a lake of blood. The candlelight was capturing the hue in perfect shades as she moved.

"Perhaps you would prefer that I send a boy back with your food, my Lord? Would that please you better than I?"

I paused. Obviously, I had let it be known to her of my true nature. I straightened my shoulders and shifted from one foot to the other. Her words bothered me. I had never been confronted with the truth.

My voice cracked as I spoke. "I don't care if it is you or someone else. I simply require something to eat, nothing more."

She winked at me. "Very well."

Her strange acceptance of me was unnerving. It was the last thing that I needed to ponder. But perhaps it was a blessing in disguise. Her calm attitude helped to ease the tension that had risen inside of me. Something I was accustomed to handling on my own.

She walked to the large wooden door and opened it up, straining as she did so. It must have weighed twice what she did, but she refused to allow it to stop her. She paused and let her long red hair cascade over her shoulder. She spoke with an innocent tone to her voice.

"We welcome you home, Lord Dorin. King's protector and red dragon."

I rubbed the palm of my hand with my thumb and swallowed my insecurities. There was no need to elaborate on what had just occurred between us. I shifted my thoughts and focused on more important things.

"Our king, he is okay?" I asked, lifting my eyes and staring at her ever so intently. My words true, my intention, sincere. Regardless of anything, Vlad was my only concern. His welfare, my responsibility.

She tilted her head. "Of course, he is, Lord Dorin. You kept your word and returned him to his kingdom." She started to turn, ready to take her leave of me.

I held up my hand. "Wait, what is your name?" I asked.

She turned back and looked me over. "Angela." She said, without hesitation.

"Messenger of God," I whispered.

She took a small step toward me. "What, my Lord?"

I lifted my head. "Your name, it means messenger of God."

She laughed. "Well, I have been called many things, but that is not one of them, my Lord."

"Dorin," I added.

She tilted her head.

I continued, perhaps out of a need to bond with this girl who now knew my secret. "You can call me Dorin. It is my given name."

"My Lord…" she paused. "Dorin." She added. She looked back at me. "Our King will have you seated next to him at this evening's celebration. I just thought you should be aware."

I nodded to her as she smiled and slipped into the faintly lit hallway.

I let out a huge sigh of relief and ran my hand through my bushy black hair. He wanted me at his side at the Kings table. It was an honor to be asked. I paused and stared at my bed. I shook my head and tried to release the memory of seeing her staring up at me as she…the thought of it disgusted me. I couldn't help it.

Then the reality settled into the core of my being. *Vlad had sent her to me. Vlad.* The man that I would die for, the man that I adored and placed above all others. The same man who had kissed me in the garden so long ago.

Tempting me. Forcing my awakening.

Before war.

Before responsibility.

Before Illona.

SHARPEN YOUR KNIFE UPON MY MISTAKES

I SAT IN MY CHAMBER AND fussed with my jacket. My hands shook again, and I had to press the center of my palms with my thumbs to calm them down.

I had not been allowed to see Vlad all day. I was informed that he was resting, and it worried me. I had been assured that he was well, but not seeing it for myself left an uneasy feeling in my chest. Something felt wrong, off...amiss. I couldn't place it, but then again, my feelings for him had a way of blinding me to reality.

My vivid dream had proven this fact to be true. I allowed a woman to toy with me. I could not force myself to want them, even though I should try. It just seemed so unnatural to me, foreign. The sin pained me.

I took a deep breath and pushed the memory from my mind. I guess I return to it if needed. It certainly jerked me back into line when it served

me best. The thought of her lips wrapped around me, erect and aching...
thinking it was *him*. I shuddered.

Perhaps I should remember the beatings that my father had given to
me. His hope only to change what I was. What he knew I could never be.

A man who preferred men.

An abomination in the eyes of our God and Savior.

An abomination in the eyes of all we knew or would ever know.

I tugged at my jacket once again with more force. My disgust and
anger now guiding me. I despised dressing up, but I was beginning to
detest myself more. I just wished that I could see him. Lay eyes on him,
confirm his health and well-being. It was torturous to feel this way. I felt
lost without direction, lost without a war to give me purpose. Without his
hand on my shoulder and reaffirming stance.

A direction governed by the sword and his will. Without a battle, what
am I? A sad creature allowing frivolous dreams to consume it. Dreams
that will never be. Love that is forbidden and sacrilege. Love that only I
have designed.

I tried to shake the uneasy feeling from my bones. Vlad loves cele-
brations. I could not blame him for that, in fact, I knew it was not the
dressing up that had me on edge, but the fact that he had asked that I sit
at his side. He had never done so in the years I had been loyal to him. I
had been to many a feast of celebration in his honor, but I had always sat
across the room, with the other barbarians who fought at his side. His
table was reserved for his royal court.

I heard a tap at my door, and I turned as it opened. A guard stood
there in his silver armor. A red dragon etched into it on his chest. The
red dragon. Vlad's beating heart. He had called me his dragon...*his and his
alone,* as I held him in the snow. The vision flustered me until I snapped
myself out of it and straightened up.

The guard stepped aside as I nodded to him and she appeared like
an angel from heaven. I know that I do not prefer women, but Illona was
stunning. She had a beauty beyond anything I had ever seen before, and I
knew that if I felt this way, then Vlad must be consumed by her. Her hair

was long, black, pieces of it running down her back into a V and resting at the base of it. It lay in long curls, natural. The splintered fragments of daylight played off of it and made her look otherworldly.

Her skin was pale, almost white as snow and her naturally crimson lips rest on her face full and soft. One small indention in her bottom lip, making them even more desirable. Her eyes were large, brown. Profound and warm. She looked so very youthful, but her eyes told the story of an old soul. Someone that you could easily confide in. Her eyebrows gently arched and her nose was small. Everything about her was appealing. She was built for ruling the masses, from her appearance to the tone of her voice.

Royal, a Queen in waiting. My Queen.

She rushed in and hugged me. I swallowed hard as her sweet smell engulfed my senses. She always smelled of fresh flowers, not too over-powering, but just enough to please. She leaned up and whispered into my ear.

"Thank you for bringing him back to me, Dorin. I worried so. For both of you, as always. I prayed to our God to bring you both home, safe and sound. I should never doubt his love for us, for you, and for our King."

I closed my eyes as her words stung me. I knew I should be grateful that she thought so highly of me, but I was not. Her presence was a con-stant reminder of what I could never be to Vlad. I could never be *her*.

She leaned back and placed one small hand to my cheek. I lifted my hand and covered hers, reassuringly. I could not deny her the pleasure of seeing me appear grateful for her attention. I gently kissed the inside of her palm as she grinned at me. My lips lingered a bit longer than I meant to and then I heard Vlad's voice behind her. I let her go as she spun around and smiled at him. He eyed me and then his eyes went to her as they always did. Regardless of what he may do to any other woman, she would always have him, his obsession with her was absolute. I straight-ened my shoulders as she ran to him and hugged him, kissing him on the cheek as he locked his gaze upon me. I took a breath as he hugged her back and then let her go.

"He is to thank for my return. As always, he is my protector, my dragon. I would have died this time without his quick response to my fever, or so I am told. I remember very little if anything at all."

She turned but remained at his side. They both looked at me, and the awkward bit of silence in the room was finally swept away when I decided to speak.

I placed my hand over my heart and spoke with sincerity. "It is my duty to serve you my Lord, you and only you. I am grateful to see you well."

Illona laughed as she tilted her head at me. "Only for him? What about me, Dorin? Am I cast aside as your love for our King clouds your vision?"

My heart rose into my throat. If she only knew how her jesting words had fallen upon truths sword.

Vlad laughed as he stared me down. I cleared my throat and stepped forward. "Of course, I serve you as well, Lady Illona. My loyalty is yours to keep." My eyes went from him to her and back again. I studied his eyes and noticed the dark circles that lay beneath them. His skin was still a bit paler than usual and his lips rosier. I parted my lips. Prepared to ask him if he was feeling better or just putting on airs to appease the masses, and perhaps Illona.

She interrupted me before I could say a word. "Well." She stepped up to me and started to adjust my collar. I kept my eye on him as she straightened it and centered the red dragon medallion in the middle. She let her fingers linger on it for a moment and then spoke to me in a soft tone.

"You are the dragon of Bran, the heart that beats at the center of all things. Kings protector, leader of his army."

I shook my head. "I'm no leader, I follow."

"Dorin."

I looked at Vlad with adoration. He straightened his shoulders and stared me down. He looked as strong as ever, and I felt foolish for doubting his health.

"Did you not question as to why I asked you to sit at my side when we returned home?"

I paused and shook my head. He laughed and looked at Illona, then back to me.

"I trust you with my life. Tonight you take your place as general of this army and my most trusted friend and brother. You will be known as Dorin Dracul, a member of the House of Draculesti.

"My Lord." I choked out as he bestowed a great honor upon me. It was unheard of for the house to take in anyone of peasant blood, but here he was, accepting me as one of his own.

"I guess you are now his favorite, Dorin Dracul," Illona said as she grinned at me. Her eyes wandered from mine to my lips. I felt a bit flush.

Vlad rushed up behind her and picked her up as she yelled out. Her laughter was so full of joy. It engulfed the room. He spun her and then set her down. She tapped him on the chest as she looked up at him. "Behave, my Lord." He nodded to her and kissed her on the cheek. His lips lingered. My eyes locked onto the two of them. They looked perfect for one another. As always.

Perfect and it pained me.

She had brought him nothing but joy. I will not lie and say that I did not feel jealousy. I wanted to bring him that kind of happiness, that kind of peace and tranquility. My train of thought was broken when Illona spoke to me again.

"I am so proud of you, Dorin."

I nodded to her and then looked at Vlad. "I'm grateful for all I have been given here." She stepped toward me. "Well, we are thankful for you. Again, thank you, Dorin. Thank you for bringing him home to me, and to his people, of course."

I watched as they left my chamber and I was bothered by her use of the term 'we'. She had never used that before when it came to referring to her and Vlad. I knew that I should stop torturing myself and be glad that he invited me to sit at his side. I knew that I should take pleasure in our victories and just forget his mouth upon mine. I touched my lips and sighed.

If only I could have him love me as he did her.

If only.

PUT OUT THE FIRE AND MAKE IT
RAIN

I SAT AT THE MAIN TABLE, waiting for Vlad to arrive. Illona
sat at the other side of his large chair. I reached up and grabbed my
drink. Gripping it tightly as my fingers turned white from nervous
tension. I took a small sip, and so did she. She glanced over at me and
grinned. I nodded as I pulled my cup down, but immediately stood, as
did the entire room, when Vlad entered.

He had changed, he had on all red, which always looked incredible
on him. His pale skin, black hair and red lips a perfect match for the
color. His hair was now neat again. Pushed back, slick against his head.
He had shaved the sides shorter since returning home, as he often did.
In battle, it often fell into his face. It was something that caused me to
harden beneath my armor, this look, the one he had when we were home
and civilized, was incredibly mesmerizing. But I preferred the animal.

The glossy eyed demon who cried out with his sword raised high. The beast.

That was who I fought for. Who I fantasized would one day take me. Brutal and savage.

My eyes remained locked onto him. He was beautiful in all ways. His face, his jawline, his lips. His eyes always had a shine to them as if he was full of life, and truthfully he was. He was the beating heart of Romania, the rightful Lord of Bran. His royal blood stretched back to the beginning of time for us. No other had held the throne, but his descendants. He was perfection, a rightful King...to me, and too many others.

Vlad had many a painter sit down and create portraits of him. I always found it amusing because he would sit and then get up, grab the man who was the royal cook of Bran Castle, and have the painter capture his image. Not one enemy knew what Vlad looked like.

He was also brilliant, doing this with his portraits had probably saved his life on the field many a time. The enemy was expecting a man with long hair, a mustache, small build and he was none of that. I am all of 6'2 and he had at least an inch on me. His shoulders were as broad as my own, and his body was sculpted. He was, for lack of a better term, perfection. I was average, although I had been called handsome. My hair was straight and jet black. My eyes large, lips plump.

I watched as he walked the hall, his stride steady and his facial expression that of contentment. I was happy to see him this way, for I had always known him to be restless. Something in him had changed. It was welcoming to see it as he stepped up to the long table and stared at me and then at Illona. I nodded to him and so did she as he made his way up to his large black chair that sat in between the two of us. The throne was constructed of black wood. Spiked and hardened with steel at the two tall points that rose up behind it. Built for a King. Built to intimidate and yet Vlad made it welcoming and noble. We had stayed up many a night when we were young, playing in this hall. Taking turns sitting in that chair, handing out mercy and reprieve.

It intimidated me less than my love for him.

I stood there, shifting from one foot then to the other as my collar irritated my skin. I would be so happy to undo it and be casual later on, but for now, we needed to be prim and proper, just as he wished us to be for this celebration.

He stepped forward and grabbed his cup. He lifted it up into the air, and everyone in the room did the same. He stared at it and then glanced over at me as I joined him and raised my own. He brought it to his lips and took a long drink from it, longer than I expected. I was sure he would make one of his infamous speeches before he took the cup and slammed it down. But he drank it all as the room remained transfixed upon him. He lowered it from his lips and grinned as he snapped his fingers and a boy ran to his cup and filled it again. He nodded to him and then raised it again. The room was silent, waiting for their King and ruler to allow them to partake in the night's festivities.

"Loyal and proud people of Romania, I stand here before you a beaten man."

I narrowed my eyes and glanced out into the crowd as they looked to be as puzzled as I was. He didn't hesitate to go on with his speech, but my confusion lay on my face as it did so many others. Vlad admitting defeat was like watching the sun fall from the sky.

"I have fought for land, I have fought for freedom, but mostly I have fought for something I have always desired. That of legacy, an enduring flame, one that will always shine brightly upon the house of Bran and on Romania as a sovereign nation. I have done this in my father's name, in yours and in the name of Bran to live on in the hearts of every warrior, every kingdom...every heart." He paused and then looked at me. He placed a hand on my shoulder as he continued. "In life we are blessed, it is a blessing from God himself when we find someone who completes us, who we know to be an equal and that you can always trust in, rely upon, and stand beside with pride. I am a lucky man, very lucky." His eyes locked onto mine, and my heartbeat was racing in my chest. His words meant everything to me, and his expression was filled with something I had never received from him before...*one of love.*

I nodded to him and then he grinned and took his hand from my shoulder. "So, here before you tonight I want to say that I have decided to settle down, for I have found one person who is worthy of the legacy of Bran and of whom I want at my side forever." He glanced at me again and then turned to Illona and took her hand. "Will you do me the honor of becoming your husband and King, Illona, as you will become my Queen?" He lowered to his knee as she stood there with a look of pure pleasure on her face. I gripped my cup in my hand and let it tilt at my side. The wine spilling to the floor not so unlike blood as if I had been pierced through and bleeding out to my death.

Death. For that would be the only thing that could nullify this pain and set me free of this torment. .

The thunder rang out and echoed in the hall as lightening lit up every window. The fire in my heart, making way for the rain.

***

I sat in the chapel and stared up at the large brooding cross suspended from the cathedral ceiling. Bright paintings of our Lord and Savior flanked the walls and angels held their swords high overhead, protecting their King, as I did ours. But I was no angelic soldier of fortune. I was cursed, a wretched creature with dark intention, dark desires.

My eyes lowered, and I stared at the symbol of our salvation. The cross was black, black as night and as black as my heart felt after hearing Vlad's words a week prior at the celebration.

I was so foolish to think that it was for me. He never even announced my new place at his table until the moon was starting to fade and the sun was making her way back onto the broad horizon. He had toasted me then, in a hazy wine-fueled stupor. I had nodded and taken leave of his company, no intention of returning, and yet here I sit. A broken man, shackled to him with pathetic memories of what could have been.

I was sinking deeper into a black abyss of which there was no escape. Lingering, when I should be packing my things and moving on.

But I couldn't. I was spellbound, held in place by the mere thought of him.

My love would marry, plant his seed, and carry on as if we never existed. Erasing all traces of me and what I could have been to him in this life. A life I didn't ask for and was now starting to regret ever living.

I suffered from a hatred for Illona, a hatred I could not quell as hard as I tried. I did not want to hate her, she did not deserve it, but I could not help myself. She was, in effect, taking something from me, something I wanted more than anything else in this world. I wanted Vlad to love me as he did her. I wanted his thoughts to be consumed with me.

Then I felt the guilt in my heart. I fell forward onto my knees in the pew. I tightly clasped my hands together and pressed them against my lips. My eyes filled with bitter tears. I closed my eyes, and they streamed down my cheeks as I did everything I could to forget him. To erase how he felt against me. How I yearned for him. His taste, his touch. All of which was being stolen away from me.

I jumped as I felt a hand on my shoulder and looked up to see Illona standing there, like an angel from heaven. The slivers of light in the chapel room lingering behind her head and creating a halo. I sighed and slid back into the pew as she sat down next to me.

"There is no shame in having a passion for him." She whispered as she looked up at the cross. I turned my head and stared at her in horror, wondering how she could have known. Had Angela told her how I raced from my bed, impotent and pathetic? I parted my lips to speak and thankfully she continued, interrupting me.

"God's love is absolute in all things, Dorin Dracul. His passion for us should be matched tenfold. I often find myself in tears when I truly allow his light to enter into my soul." I nodded as I stared at her beautiful profile. Her eyes locked onto the cross and her words full of conviction. She did love God and his blessings he bestowed upon us. I closed my eyes and beat back my lustful thoughts of Vlad. I opened them, and she was staring at me. She placed a hand on my face, and her gentle smile soothed me. As did her touch. She leaned in closer to me.

"You have killed in his name and for the glory of your King. Vlad will always be grateful to you for protecting him and for protecting this land.

Your deeds will not go unnoticed. You will always be royalty here, Dorin, regardless of your blood line. Vlad loves you, as do I." She leaned in and closed her eyes. Her lips pressing against my own and I allowed the kiss to linger. It was so bittersweet. The taste of it laced with a slow poison that would surely kill me over time.

Her presence was a poison in my life.

I nodded to her as her lips left my own. She grinned and let her hand rest a while longer on my cheek until we both turned at the sound of Vlad's voice in the cathedral. "Should I be concerned?" he asked as we both stared at him. His words were soon followed by laughter as he walked down the aisle and then he lowered to one knee. He lowered his head and kissed his closed fist. He made the symbol of the cross and then rose up, his eyes locked onto the large black cross hanging there in front of us. He turned to us and nodded, his mischievous grin the only thing calming my nerves. Any other man may have seen this as treason and demanded blood.

Of course, he knew better, but I almost wished that he didn't. Death could find me. I would no longer hide from it. It seems it may be easier than accepting my truth, one that would forever haunt me.

"I would like to go ahead and have the wedding, next week, if you would allow it, Illona."

She stared at him and then jumped up, throwing her arms around his neck and hugging him. A kiss followed, but she quickly stopped when she remembered where she was. I sat there and controlled my temper. I felt the heat rising in me as I wanted to scream out. *"No, don't do this!"* But I would never. I could never say what was in my heart. The darkness that lurked behind my reason for fighting at his side. If I did, then I would have to leave and to leave his side would be worse than death.

I did not enjoy war and killing. I enjoyed protecting him and proving to him how much he meant to me. I knew this now as much as I knew that this wedding would kill me. It would kill off any hopes I would ever have of being with him, convincing him that love does not have to be the way the book says. It just does not. I turned my head and stared at the cross.

For the first time in my life I started to feel betrayal. I felt as if God was the one who was betraying me, for as much as I begged and pleaded for him to wipe these thoughts clean, he allowed them to linger. I sighed as I tried to maintain my faith, but honestly, I felt it slipping away with each breath that I took. I cannot say that to be Godless would be a bad thing. In fact, it may offer up a small token of salvation. I blinked as I felt a hand on my shoulder. I looked up at Vlad, who appeared as beautiful as ever, even pale.

"I will need your help, my friend."

I nodded to him as he led Illona from the chapel and I sat there as a traitor to God and all that I had ever believed in.

SECRET ESCAPES

THE METAL CLASHED, AND TEETH ground together. My footing slid a bit as the young warrior before me tried his best to push me back. He was all of eighteen, a royal, Illona's brother, Stefan, who had arrived for the festivities and the impending wedding.

This union would bind our nations. It was something Vlad knew he had to do but relished the thought of it until Illona had arrived. Once he laid eyes on her, his opinion of it changed. He had complained for weeks prior to it happening, and I had listened to it all, trying to reassure him of how good it would be politically, but now...I wish I had been silent.

Perhaps if I had been he would have second guessed it and canceled it before she even had a chance to come and bewitch him with her charm and beauty.

Bewitch was correct. I had never seen him this way. It seemed so unfair.

I knew he enjoyed her when he rushed our last battle, sacrificing more of his men than he needed to, but he was able to cut it all short by weeks. He had done this for her, and I wondered now if I had fallen there on the battlefield if I would simply be remembered in song by drunken warriors. Would he have mourned me as I would mourn him? I could not be certain now.

I pushed back, and Stefan cried out as he lost his footing and fell onto his back. He scowled at me. He was not gentle like his sister, his eyes were darker, his tone and attitude the opposite of her own. He was being groomed to lead, not follow in any way. It concerned me as I reached down to him and he slapped my hand away and stood up on his own. He was arrogant, and I did not know if he would eventually become a problem for Vlad. If he did, I would be there to stand in between them. A shield, a protector, until the end. I would never allow anything to happen to him, as long as I drew breath into my lungs and could still wield my sword in his honor.

Stefan stood up and looked me over. "You are the warrior, Dorin? The red dragon?" I laughed and switched my sword to the other hand. Giving it one quick toss and catching it with ease. Surely he wasn't mocking me, was he? I had struck down many a man with dirty nails and bloodied scalps. *Men*, not boys.

"Some call me this, most call me death." He grinned as his stance stiffened and I knew he would fall easily. His training for battle had been weak if he had received any at all. I thrust forward as he turned and I hit him in the back. He stumbled forward and onto his knees. His sword slid across the floor and a black booted foot stopped it dead. Stefan looked up as Vlad stood there grinning down at him.

"I see you have met Dorin. He is the greatest warrior in this kingdom."

I placed my hand over my heart. "Outside of you, my Lord," I spoke with sincere conviction.

Stefan pushed himself up and glanced back at me and then at Vlad. "My Father says you have peasants fight at your side, including your dragon. Our guard only consists of royalty, as it should be. You cannot trust the lower class. The breeding is weak, as is the mind." His eyes looked me over with such disdain. Now I understood his bitterness. He was prejudice toward my place in this world. If he only knew that I had earned everything I had received. His lack of knowledge amused me. He may be of royal blood, but his life experience was lacking.

I heard his words and had to laugh. He turned and walked toward me. He lifted a hand and shook his head. "No one laughs at me, peasant."

Stefan stopped dead as Vlad was now behind him. He had one arm around him and his sword to his throat. He swallowed hard, his eyes wide. I would bet he was pissing his pants. Vlad winked at me and then spoke to him in an intimidating tone. One he often used in battle.

"Now listen little one. I will soon be your Uncle, and Dorin, well... seeing that I value him as family, he will be your Uncle, too. So why don't you practice by saying, Hello, my Uncle, I am grateful for your service to King and country. I welcome everything you can teach me, seeing that I know so very little."

Stefan said nothing, so Vlad tightened his grip. He pressed the sword closer to his skin until the boy could feel the cold steel against his throat. He stammered and repeated the words. Vlad smiled at me. He let him go as he stumbled forward and turned to look at Vlad with hatred in his eyes, but he said nothing, knowing better, as he should.

"See...humility is not so hard to find, now is it, Stefan?" Vlad asked. Stefan glared at me and ran from the hall. I laughed as Vlad stood there and shook Stefan's sword in his hand. He turned it and gazed at his reflection in it. He lowered it and peered at me, his expression one of trust and admiration.

"He will hate me, perhaps even wish me dead," Vlad spoke with certainty.

I nodded. "I think we should be weary of him."

Vlad smiled and dropped his sword to the stone floor beneath us. He looked down on the metal and shook his head. "His kingdom is weak, his father likes to appear as if he is a warlord, but he is not. He knows that if he had not sent Illona to bind us, then I would have overtaken him and ruled his lands as I could any other. The only thing I admire about him is his ability to produce a Queen to sit at my side. Someone worthy of

Castle Bran and her legacy. With Illona, I will secure this kingdom and its future, forever."

I stepped forward as his words pained me. "Future?"

"Illona is with child. Before we left for battle I laid down with her, and now she will bear me an heir to Bran, a future King. I didn't know if we would return, my friend. The legacy of my bloodline must endure."

I couldn't speak. The thought of it infuriated me. He had said nothing about this, nothing about bedding her for this reason before we left for battle. It now made more sense as to why he wanted to speed up this marriage. This union with her before she would start to show. An early birth could be easily explained, but not if she began to show before he wed her and made her queen. Right now she carried a bastard, after the wedding, she carried an heir to the throne and the future that he dreamed of.

"So is this why you are marrying her?" I asked without thinking of how it sounded. I can't say that I cared. My emotions ruled over me for a split second. He passed me by then turned back and shook his head at me. "I would marry her with or without my child. She is the sun and the moon...the stars for me. I love her, Dorin. I loved her from the moment I laid my eyes on her and to have her is to have everything. Everything I desire."

I watched him turn and leave me there in the cold hall. My armor suddenly felt heavier than it ever had before and my heart shattered into a million pieces.

God had indeed abandoned me, and I made a decision right there to return the favor to him tenfold.

***

I sat by the fountain in the royal garden and stared at the water and my reflection. A reflection of a man that I no longer recognized. One who had damned his soul as he renounced God and everything that he offered in the so-called hereafter.

There would be no paradise for me. I wished it gone. I had no hopes of entering heaven's gates. Deemed unworthy by the books word. Left damned by my lack of faith.

I reached toward the pool to scatter my image. A rock preceded me and turned my reflection into a distant memory, breaking the surface and shattering it. I turned and stared at Stefan. He had changed out of his armor and was now dressed in a blue shirt and pants to match. His hair slicked back and muddied cheeks washed clean. He was a striking boy who would one day be a handsome man.

"I wanted to apologize." He said without taking his eyes from mine. I could respect this, at least he was willing to admit his wrongs, even if I still knew that he held prejudice in his heart for those not born of royal blood.

I stood up and adjusted my sword at my side. His eyes lowered to it and then he grinned.

"May I?" he asked, taking a step toward me.

I hesitated but then unsheathed it, certain that he posed no real danger to me. He could barely hold his sword, which weighed less than mine.

I placed the hilt of it in his hand and his eyes widened. It lowered until he lifted his other hand and gripped it firmly. He raised it up, and the sun's light skirted across my eyes and made me blink. He laughed as he swung it out and the tip of the blade landed right in front of my face. I grinned at him and peered down the long metal blade. His expression never changed. The smile sat upon his lips and the blade firm in hand.

I reached up and pushed it aside with ease. It lowered as the weight of it tired him. The tip hit the ground, and I stole it back from him. I quickly placed it back in the holster on my side. He shook his head.

"I'm ashamed." He murmured. He walked toward the fountain and sat down on the edge of it. He gently placed his hand on the surface of the water and waved it back and forth. I slowly approached him and took a seat next to him. He glanced over at me, and I at him.

"What has brought you to this conclusion?" I asked. He adjusted himself and faced me.

He leaned in close to my lips and whispered to me. "I prefer men and sometimes women. You would be surprised what secrets they will relieve themselves of while you bury your cock deep inside of them. Angela, especially. Hers is sweet and tight. You should take advantage of this. She is very fond of you, in fact, she cries out your name as pleasure overtakes her."

I swallowed hard and adjusted on the stone beneath me. "Why tell me this?"

"You intrigue me, red dragon."

I bit my lip and straightened my shoulders. "I have no idea what you mean."

He smiled. "Oh come now. Like I care that you cannot remain hard inside of her. I only came here to let you know that you are not alone. I thought that you would find this comforting."

I looked down and then decided to stand up and take my leave of him.

"I have all the friends that I need to confide in."

He stood up and stared at me. He took one step forward. "You could have more. You could have a friend in me. Someone who understands you as you are and not what you try to appear to be. I would even be willing to allow you to call me King if it pleasures you." He reached toward my face.

I cleared my throat. "I will find a suitable replacement to help train you, Stefan."

"Dorin." He called out to me as I left him behind. My heart was pounding in my chest and my skin shining with sweat.

He had now become a liability as had Angela. I wasn't sure how I could correct this without the sword.

SILENT ENEMY

I DREAMED OF BLOOD AND BATTLE *that night.*
My skin shimmering from sweat and my heartbeat racing inside of my chest. I clutched at my bedding, thrashing my legs. I was in an epic battle, one I felt as if I could not win.

Just as I lifted my blade to stab it into the heart of the enemy below me, he morphed into Illona. I hesitated and then thrust my sword downward, through her chest and cutting into her heart. I felt no shame until the act was done.

I stumbled back as she held a trembling hand toward me, her mouth open, and a small amount of blood trickling from the edge of her full lip. I cried out as I fell to my knees and stared up at the blackened sky. I could see winged angels behind the clouds as the lightning lit up sections of the sky above me. I lowered my head and saw her standing before me. Blood oozing from her chest and my sword in her hand. She walked toward me, and I held my arms out, closing my eyes as she swung the sword to cut my head off...exacting her revenge upon me.

I sat straight up in my bed, crying out as my head detached from my shoulders in the dream. The last of the vision was of her looking down upon me. Vlad stepped up to her side, touching her stomach and then kissed her lips.

My life ending as theirs began.

***

"My Lord?"

I turned quickly in my bed to see Illona standing there in her white nightgown. It was translucent, and I could make out her erect nipples. She stepped up and allowed the slivers of moonlight to expose more of her lovely frame. I narrowed my eyes and looked her over. She let it drop to the floor and my eyes took her in. They landed on a small crescent shaped birthmark on her inner thigh. It reminded me of the moon.

"Illona, why are you here? Are you ill?"

She slowly approached the side of my bed and then climbed into it. The look of confusion on my face could not be hidden. She touched my cheek, her hand warm and inviting. Then leaned in, allowing her lips to press against my own. I closed my eyes as she reached under the fur and started to stroke me. I reached down to try to stop her, but she would not. Her grip was firm. I pulled my lips from hers as she lovingly gazed into my eyes.

"I...we cannot do this." She slowed her hand. I hissed, becoming erect in her firm embrace.

"I know what you desire, dragon. I know it isn't what I have. Do you think that your secret will be kept for long?" Then I screamed as I felt the blade slice into me, taking my strength and separating it from my body.

I sat up in my bed and gripped the furs tight. It had only been an extension of my treacherous dream. I tried to catch my breath as a figure walked toward me. It was Angela. She slipped out of her nightgown and stood there with her nipples hard from the chill in the air.

I shook my head as she continued to walk toward my bed then another figure appeared from the shadows. It was Stefan.

I adjusted on the bed and pushed myself backward until I felt the cold frame against my shoulders.

"My Lord," She whispered. "We have come to please you."

I wanted to protest, but my cock stood erect, and I ached with desire.

Angela crawled into my bed and slowly pulled the furs off of my body. The candlelight played off of my skin, each curve shimmering with sweat. Stefan stepped up to the side of my bed as Angela reached down and started to stroke me. His eyes lowered and then returned to mine. His expression was soft and inviting.

He crawled up next to me and leaned in. Gently kissing my lips. I moaned as he pushed me down onto my back. He let his hand glide across my chest, stopping only to play with my nipple. I hissed as he twisted it with too much force and bit into my bottom lip.

"Let me pleasure you as you should be." He whispered into my ear. "As only I can."

"Please, stop," I adjusted on the bed and felt Angela's hand moving up and down my rigid shaft. Short bursts of pleasure inched their way down my legs and across my abdomen. My flat stomach contracted. Stefan grinned, letting his fingers move across it. I flinched.

"It seems there is something that I possess skill in that the great dragon does not."

He straddled me and placed his firm cock in front of my lips. He reached down and I could feel his hand under my chin. "Take me." He cooed. The temptation was too sweet. My needs had gone unanswered for so very long. I closed my eyes. I could envision Vlad in the garden, a distant memory, brought to life before me. His skin soft, mouth swollen. His nectar begging to race across my lips and down my throat. I let out a growl that began in the belly of the beast and escaped with unbridled passion.

I gave in.

Tired of fighting.

Tired of wanting and never receiving.

I parted my lips and felt his girth fill my mouth to the brim. He fisted the stone wall and pressed forward, shoving it to the back of my throat. I moaned, deep and abiding. My tongue slithered along his shaft, memorizing each valley, every peak. Committing this long sought after conquest to memory. Replacing his presence with Vlad's, without shameful regret.

I glanced up and imagined my King's strength before me. It begged for my attention, so I gave it all that I had, without restraint.

I gave it my sword, my allegiance, my loyalty.

I gave it my love.

He moved his hips back and forth, a slow pace, pleasurable, allowing me to savor it. Angela toyed at the tip of my cock, and it twitched in her hand. She ran her tongue the length of me. Making it shine from what little light played havoc in the room. It hardened with each passing moment, aching to explode with years of built up frustration. Her feminine form did not hinder me. I focused only on the task at hand, just as I had in battle. It kept me erect and strong. Willing to accept that a woman's mouth lay upon me.

Sex is not so unlike that of war.

To survive it you must give into the basic instincts that tear at the heart of thee.

Enjoy each long stride, each stroke taken with the tip of your blade.

Pierce flesh, offer relief. Let the fire consume you.

I cried out for a split second before the length of him quieted my tongue with a deep moan.

She crawled on top of me and slid my extended dagger deep inside. Pushing past her folds and settling into her wetness. I reached up and grabbed his hips, helping him thrust forward. I swallowed everything he had to give, resisting the urge to fight her off of me.

She ground her hips against me. Making my cock ache for release. Stefan thrust harder and harder, moaning with each movement. His strength shook against my tongue, begging for his seed to spill out and down my awaiting throat, but he pulled back, a string of shimmering spit connecting my lips to his throbbing heat.

He quickly moved down and pulled her off of me. He lifted my knees and positioned himself between my legs. I nodded to him as he spat on his hand and rubbed his shaft to a glistening sheen. He placed it against my opening, and I ground my teeth, preparing for what was to come.

He reached over and grabbed the back of Angela's head, pushing her mouth down upon my shaft as he shoved himself into me. I cried out and grabbed at the furs, feeling his massive cock fill me up and force me to submit to it. My ass tightened on him, and he growled like an animal. Each time he thrust into me he would shove Angela's swollen lips down and over my hardened cock, filling her mouth up until I could feel the back of her throat teasing the tip of my sensitive head.

He thrust again and again until we all found ourselves shimmering in sweat and moaning like beasts in an orgy of pleasure. He suddenly tossed her aside, jerking her mouth off of me and grabbing my shaft tightly as he ground into me as hard as he could. With each stroke, he pushed his hips forward, again and again, burying himself to the hilt.

"Take it all, all that I have to give, my dragon." He whispered with a raspy tone. "Yes, yes."

I watched through tear-filled eyes as my cock twitched in his firm grip and my seed escaped me. He rotated his hand, capturing it on his palm and stroking me even further, gliding along with such ease...extending my release and bringing me to a second climax. My ass tightened around him with such ferocity. He groaned, deep and pleasurable. His cock shook like thunder inside of me and his seed spilled out, warm and lustful. He dug even deeper, giving it all to me as Angela fingered at herself and cried out on the bed next to us.

I could only choke out one name as my vision blurred.

I could only see my true love before me.

"Vlad." My lips parted and the last bits of pleasure raced away, bringing me back to a bleak reality. His face morphed into Stefan's. Ending the fantasy as quickly as it had begun.

He collapsed upon me, breathing as hard as I was. His girth was receding as he pulled out.

I quickly pushed him away and tried to regain my composure.

"Well..." he started to say. I raised my hand and interrupted him.

"Leave, both of you. Leave my room and do not return."

He sat up and tried to touch me. I didn't hesitate to slap his hand away from me. The look on his face one of pain and rejection. Angela said nothing as she quickly put her nightgown back on and headed for the door.

"Dorin." He started to say. I couldn't look at him. I was filled with shame for what I had allowed to happen. This was against everything in me, but I had succumbed to it like an animal, a beast...nothing more and nothing less.

"Go," I said as my jaw tightened then relaxed.

He left my bed and quickly made his way to my door. I allowed them to both leave without saying a word. I pressed my face into the furs and the tears came, hot and unforgiving.

"What have I done?" I whispered, feeling so lost and alone.

AS HATE GROWS

I WATCHED AS ILLONA WALKED ALONGSIDE Vlad in the garden. She smiled, looking so young and innocent. She glanced back at me as I stood my post. Stefan stepped up next to me and stared at them too.

"So Uncle, are you happy about their union?"

"Don't call me that," I muttered. He laughed under his breath.

"Why? Does it fluster you as you remember what I can do for you?" He reached toward me. I grabbed his wrist and stopped him from touching me.

"That will never occur again."

He sighed and looked back toward his sister. "You hurt me, Dorin."

I blinked and lowered my head before I glanced at him. I ignored his admission. No one had hurt him. He was a very skilled predator in his own right. "It is not about happiness it is about a binding treaty and peace."

He grinned and lifted an apple to his lips, biting into it and the juice rolled down his chin. He let it drip onto the ground as he chewed. He swallowed and then pointed at them with the apple in hand. His fingers shimmered from the sweet nectar in the sunlight. I felt like we may be standing in the Garden of Eden. He offered it to me and I shook my head, refusing him.

"I want to tell you something about my sister."

I watched as Vlad and Illona stopped and he touched her face. He leaned down and kissed her just as my eyes turned to Stefan. He studied my expression.

"She can have any man she wants."

I nodded to him. "Her beauty is unwavering."

He shook his head. "Not as treacherous as her will."

I paused and turned to him. "It is unkind to speak ill of your family."

He looked me over and took another bite of his apple. He stopped chewing and then laughed at me. "Oh no, don't tell me that she has bewitched you, too. My dear dragon, was it she who had you ready to go in your bed?"

I shook my head, and my expression hardened. "Don't."

He grinned and swallowed his mouthful of fruit. He cleared his throat and crossed his arms over his chest.

"Our Mother died when I was born. I never knew her, but I heard stories. I know *her, her kind*...and Illona is just as she was, manipulating and seeking power. Like all women are. They seduce for power, and she will take Vlad's strength as her own."

"Who told you these things about your sister?" I asked him as he tossed the apple into the grass. I looked down at it as a large black bird swooped in and pecked at it.

"No one has to tell me anything, all I am saying is the next time she tries to crawl into your dreams...kick her out. She is poison. Don't think that it was by mistake."

"I never said...she didn't...wait, what do you mean by that?" Stefan winked at me. His eyes lowered and rested below my belt.

"Not to say that I would blame her. I mean look at you. I can only hope that you will not always refuse me. Temptation is the true King, and my sister, she practices a dark art. Sorcery. Just as mother did."

I felt flush. "Stop, we are never going to speak of that night again, and stop lying about Illona."

I parted my lips, and he reached down and brushed his hand against me. I made a small noise in the back of my throat. He laughed under his breath. He leaned in and whispered into my ear. "For a man of such stature I am stunned at your naivety when it comes to women, but what should I have expected when you prefer something like me? Just let me know when you're ready...again. I will come whenever you call for me."

Stefan smiled as Illona spotted us and waved in our direction. Dark arts? Illona a sorcerous? Surely he lied. He hates women. That much is becoming clear to me now.

I watched Stefan walk toward the two of them. Vlad appeared happy, unlike I had ever seen him.

I heard Vlad's voice and looked at him as he called out to me.

"Come, Dorin. We are taking a swim."

I nodded to him as I stepped forward. Illona wrapped one arm into Vlad's and one into Stefan's. He looked back at me and grinned. I sighed and followed along until we reached the lake flanking the castle. Private to only our King. I had not visited this spot in so long.

I remembered many a summer that we had swam in these waters. Cool and refreshing. When we were young and carefree, before the evil of the world had begun its march upon our souls. Before we had allowed the enemy to storm our gates and infiltrate our beds.

Before Illona and Stefan had bewitched and bewildered us. Making us weak when we appeared so strong. I felt foolish for believing that we were on the verge of greatness, that we could have it all.

Vlad stopped and stared out at the lake. Illona started to undress, and he grinned. He looked back at me and tilted his head. She stepped out of her elegant dress. Her body perfect, young. Tight and firm. Her skin smooth like silk, pale like a porcelain doll. Mesmerizing.

I found it unnerving that she appeared to look just as she had in my dream, even down the crescent moon shaped birthmark on her inner thigh.

No wonder he found her irresistible, even I found her attractive. I tried to ignore her, but it was almost impossible. Stefan stepped into my view and started to undress. I turned and ignored him. Refusing to give into temptation. Vlad began to take his clothing off. He waved to me to come closer and so I complied.

"Come in and enjoy." He said to me as I glanced at Stefan, naked and running into the water. He splashed as he sank under the waterline and then came up laughing. Illona had already swam out a few yards and was stationary. I looked behind him, and she bobbed above the water and let me see her breasts. She covered them with her petite hands and sank beneath the surface. Vlad continued to undress before me. I stared at him and shook my head, trying to ignore his body and how it made me feel.

"My Lord, if we were to be attacked I could not protect you, any of you."

He leaned in as he took his shirt off and exposed his chest, tight and firm, his abs rolling down his stomach and resting into a perfect V above his pant line. I glanced down and then quickly looked around us. Clearing my throat. There were times that he seemed to enjoy tempting me to ravage him. Because, if we were alone, I would find it nearly impossible to keep from leaning forward and kissing his lips. I desperately wanted to taste his forbidden fruit.

I stared into his eyes. They seemed to be growing blacker in color. The blue slowly being swallowed up whole by a menacing shadow. One I could not place nor deny. I noticed the dark circles still rested beneath them, and his skin had refused to return to its olive tint.

"Do you feel well?" I asked. He glanced behind him. Stefan laughed as he splashed water at Illona and she giggled, returning the favor to him.

He placed a hand on my shoulder and then started to untie my leather straps which held a piece of my armor in place. I couldn't fight him as he continued with his mission to get me in the water.

"No one will attack us, I am Vlad the Impaler, you, my fierce dragon. No enemy would dare attack us here... and yes, I feel fine, except for a bit of restless sleep, why do you ask?"

I looked at his lips and then back into his eyes. A piece of my armor fell to the ground and he began work on my other shoulder.

"You look pale, my Lord, and you seem cold to the touch."

He paused and placed a hand to my face. It sent a wintery chill through me. His hand felt even colder against my flush skin.

"It seems I'm more accustomed to winter now, a casualty of war. The poisons embrace." He glanced at the scar on his shoulder and so did I. It looked faded, healing much faster than any other wound ever had.

"You said *lost sleep*, do you dream?"

He let my other shoulder piece fall into the grass at our feet and grinned at me.

"I dream of great conquest and a noble son born unto the house of Bran."

"And of your Lady, our Queen?"

He glanced back at her and then at me. "No, she is never in my dreams, although I would prefer it. She tortures me, so. I can't tell you how much my love grows stronger for her with each passing day. It swells my heart, as her belly grows." He paused and leaned into my face. "She has bewitched me, as I said before, I am a conquered man."

Those words splintered my heart. I fought back my pain. If only he could feel this way for me.

He reached down and started to untie my leather that laced my side together. Then he undid the other side and grabbed the bottom of the metal plate, lifting it over my head. I let him do all of this without protest. There was no need. I enjoyed his attention because since we had returned, I had received so little of it. My heart was starved, as was my soul.

I nodded to him as he started to take his pants off. He slid them down and stood up, his cock too large to ignore, but I tried my best as I cleared my throat. He laughed and tapped me on the shoulder.

"I order you to enjoy this, my brother."

I sighed and set my sword down on the ground. I stood up as Vlad walked away from me and entered the lake. His perfect ass slowly being consumed by the water beneath him. He suddenly sank under the surface and came back up, shaking his head. His shaggy black hair swung out to the sides. He stopped and waved to me.

"Come." He yelled.

I obey my king.

My Lord.

My only true God now that I had abandoned my faith to the one above me.

I stripped as Illona watched me.

Was she an enemy who had infiltrated the walls of Bran Castle, and that of Vlad's heart? I would not allow her to break him. I would not allow Stefan to break me. I would kill before I would see that happen. I walked into the water and dove in, allowing the murky deep to consume me. Knowing that my allegiance to my King may cost me my life.

SERPENTS SPEAK

THE DAYS THAT FOLLOWED WERE a blur of organized splendor. The hunters gathered as much game as they could for the upcoming feast. The seamstress and her loyal maidens worked diligently on Illona's wedding dress. The guards stood at their post. We doubled every man on watch to be certain as the entire castle was caught up in one thing...the union that would be.

All the while I suffered. Guilt-laden for allowing Stefan to seduce me. Heartbroken for the loss of Vlad's love. Tortured by a memory of lying with him in the garden, with white flowers gently floating down above us. His eyes trained on me. His attention, mine.

None of it real. None of it would ever find fruition.

I needed to shed this weakness and return to my former state. Dorin, now known as Dorin Dracul, of the house of Bran. A loyal companion, protector, and red dragon of our Lord's army. Death defines me now. A death I suffered at my own hand.

I feel empty, alone.

Faithless.

God is but a memory.

Love but a torturous reminder.

This defined me, not whimsical fantasies. Not hopes of love. Not dreams of being his or him being mine. I would wither away if not for the sight of him, so I linger, as does disease and famine.

As plague did in this house so very long ago.

Stealing what family I knew and thrusting Vlad into this position of power.

Robbing me of him.

Robbing me of love.

Guest after guest arrived, many from distant lands. Royals from weaker kingdoms seeking mercy and acceptance. They came to show their support and adoration for Vlad. Some loved him, and some feared him, but as he always said, he did not care which...only that they knew he was their true King.

With Vlad it was not about the power, it was about loyalty. It was his undying need to rule as he only thought that he could. He was fair, brutal in war, but gentle in his rule. Because of this, the people of Romania truly adored him. They would die before they allowed anything to happen to him. As would I. I had bound myself to him forever.

I adjusted my red armor and turned to see Illona at my open door. I stared at her as she stood there in white. She grinned and stepped in, taking a quick look around my room. She glanced at the bed and touched her stomach. A small bump was starting to show. Our future King.

"You look very handsome." She murmured. I spied her small frame behind me. I turned and stood my ground as she looked me over. Her large brown eyes compassionate, but I sensed deception.

"My brother talks of nothing but you, my dear dragon. It seems you have stolen his heart."

I coughed uncontrollably. She didn't move. The words took me by surprise and stuck in my ribs like sharpened daggers.

"I don't know what..."

She held a hand up and spoke to me in a calm tone. "Your secret is safe with me. I would never deny one happiness. Don't you agree?"

I narrowed my eyes. "Agree, my Lady?"

"With standing in the way of happiness, of course. You do know that Vlad is happy with me, don't you?" she paused, and I felt my mouth becoming dry. This was not what I expected. Her candid nature was shining through. I started to feel a bit foolish for doubting what Stefan had said to me.

"I..." she looked me over and grinned, ignoring my need to answer her.

"I never understood the pageantry of a warrior until I saw you and Vlad for the first time in full armor. You both embody it."

"I appreciate your kind words, but shouldn't you be with your seamstress today? Instead, you visit me. There is no need."

She grinned as she touched her stomach again and then looked up at me. "I wanted to thank you."

I tilted my head. "For what?"

"For not saying anything to him. Your loyalty is your true strength." She paused and let a small grin arch her lips.

"Saying what?" I added.

"My brother told me that he mentioned things about me, to you. I appreciate the fact that you have not shared this information with our King."

"I did not believe him."

She laughed. "Oh, why would you doubt what I am when I know what you are, Dorin?"

"And what would that be?"

She grinned at me and waved a hand at the large mirror behind us. I turned and looked into it as it rippled against all logic and a scene lay out before us. One of privacy and privilege. The day that Vlad and I had spent in the garden. A private memory that belonged to me and no other. I shook my head and stepped toward it, reaching out as Vlad leaned in and kissed my lips. We were so young, so innocent. Full of life...before war had hardened us. My heartbeat caught in my throat, my chest rose and fell, my breath felt haggard.

"What sorcery is this?" I asked. She stepped up beside me and touched my hand. She felt ice cold. The warmth had left her body.

"I will never give him to you, do you understand this, red dragon?" Her words came out like the hissing of a snake. I jumped back from her when I turned to see that she looked pale with blackened eyes. Demonic in nature, the complete opposite of how she appeared in life.

My voice cracked. "Are you a demon?"

She took a slow breath and returned to her former self. Pale skin, soft eyes, pinkish lips, and rosy cheeks. I trembled inside.

Knowing she had bewitched him. Knowing that her dark magic had infiltrated every corner of our beloved home.

"If you love him you will accept this as it is, as I accept you as you are. We all hide away our demons, do we not?"

"I would never do anything to hurt him, and that was a mistake on my part, I apologize my Lady. I was overtaken with lust. I'll pay for my sins forever."

"Are you nervous Dorin? Do I make you uneasy? I shouldn't. I am just as you are. I love him as intensely as you do, but we need to understand each other. I may appear different to you, but which one of us is truly the demon? One who can transform? Or one who lies in wait?"

"I understand you," I muttered in defeat. Something about her presence wouldn't allow me to gather my courage. She stepped up and placed a now warm hand to my face. Her eyes never leaving my own.

"Good, because he needs you. I need you. This new empire needs you."

I felt a cold wind, and she was gone. I closed my eyes as a single tear rolled down my cheek.

***

Three days passed and I ate nothing. I barely drank. My thoughts consumed with worry. I had gone from loyal dragon to treacherous snake, not without help from the most conniving of all creatures, that of Illona.

Our secret slowly poisoned me.

My lust for him.

Her ability to shift and cast spells.

He was surrounded in treachery.

She had truly infiltrated this world I lived in, and I did not know how I would survive it. How I would stand at Vlad's side and watch as she ruled not only him but me. She now had all of the power. She had him, this kingdom, and a child who would go on to rule. A creature born of her and I wasn't even certain of what she was now. A demon? Retribution? My fate?

Pathetic that I had allowed it to come to this.

This sorcerous was here to devour us whole. A serpent among men. I could feel the weight of it upon my chest and the longer it festered, the more egregious the wound became.

I was finally summoned to him on the day of the wedding. I stepped into his chambers with dark circles under my eyes and fatigue in my heart. I stood there in my red armor and wanted to tell him the truth so very badly, but I could not. I could not hurt him in this way. He turned and smiled at me and then his expression changed while he studied my face. He walked toward me and placed a hand on my shoulder, gazing into my eyes.

"Are you ill my friend?"

I nodded, just to appease him. "I will have the doctor summoned at once."

I shook my head in defiance. "I am fine. It is nothing that will not pass. I apologize for my appearance, my Lord."

"No need to apologize, my brother. You have not chosen sickness. It seems it is hunting you."

I paused. His words weighed so heavy on my heart. I had chosen this, and it was my fault for allowing her to remain within our walls. I feared what he would think of me if he knew the truth. If he learned of what I had allowed to happen with Stefan. If he was alerted to the fact that his future Queen was a sorcerous. A sorcerous who was pregnant with our future King. And I...I loved him, and Illona knew this. She knew she could destroy me with one wave of her delicate hand.

My eyes lowered as the very thought of it continued to eat me alive. One piece of my now damned soul at a time.

"I wanted to ask a favor of you Dorin, but if you need rest, then by all means, return to your chamber and sleep." My eyes lifted to his own. I could not deny him of anything. "No, I am fine, what do you ask of me?"

He tapped my shoulder a couple of times and then removed his hand. "I would ask that you walk Illona down the aisle for me. I know it is customary that I have my father do this, but seeing that I am alone in this world, I would desire that someone I consider a brother do this for me. Blood or no blood, you have always stood by my side, loyal and unwavering. It would be an honor if you accept my request."

I swallowed hard. I thought about his words and what they meant to him. I knew then as I would always know, that Vlad loved me. I took a slow and steady breath and regained my composure. "Her father will be in attendance my Lord. He should present her to you, not me."

Vlad turned and faced his mirror. He looked stunning. Better than I had ever seen him look before. He had even trimmed his shaggy hair. This I did not expect him to do. He loved it that way and for him to take the time to look less heathen and more respectable meant that he was going into this whole heartedly. He glanced at my reflection in the mirror and grinned.

"I despise him, Dorin, as he despises me. I ate with him last night, along with Illona, and her brother. You should have been there, the pride this man spews. He honestly believes that I am beneath him. That I am lucky to be marrying Illona. It is he who should be grateful. Grateful for our protection. Not that she isn't a great prize because she is."

"Ours," I whispered. Vlad grinned at me and then sighed. He turned and faced me, pulling my head in and resting his forehead against mine. I noticed how cold his skin felt, even colder than it had been by the lake.

"Of course. As I said before, to me, you are a brother...now and forever."

He swayed on his feet, and I placed my hand on his side.

"Are you sick, my Lord?" I asked, and he opened his beautiful eyes and stared into mine. The blue had completely been eaten away by shadow. My heart fluttered in my chest. Even now, I could not control my feelings for him. He grinned at me and moved back only a couple of inches. He stared at my mouth as he spoke to me.

"Her father is a liability. I would ask that you watch him closely. I don't trust him. After the ceremony, I would prefer for him to leave, regardless of what Illona wants."

"Do you fear that they will try to harm you?"

He shook his head and then laughed. "He would be a fool to try, but after this wedding, well...I would prefer if we stay diligent, watchful. Make sure that he is escorted back to his rightful place."

"I would be happy to do this for you."

He smiled. "I will send five of our best with you Dorin. It will be a ten-day ride there and back. Are you certain you can do this, in your state?" he added a small laugh. "You've looked better, my friend."

"I worry more for you. You still lack color, my Lord. It's been this way since you were wounded by that woman. It seems the poison has left you shaken."

He shook me and pulled me in toward him. Our lips so close, his breath hot on my skin. I fought my desire for him. I so desperately wanted to taste his lips. He placed his hands on my face and stared into my eyes.

"Stop worrying about me. Attend to yourself, Dorin. For once. The last thing this kingdom needs is to lose its most valuable weapon. It's greatest asset, our red dragon."

And there it was. The words of truth had escaped his full lips. I am a weapon, as I had always been. I need to hear these words and take them to heart. Bury them deep within my chest and allow them to rekindle my passion. Let my loyalty to this land wipe away my disloyalty to its King.

My king, my lord. My one true love.

I nodded to him. I almost felt as if his mission for me was a blessing.

I would be able to get away from everything. I had no way to fight her. She had secured her place at his side leaving me nothing in return. Was I to accept her offering of her brother to me? Visiting well into the night, sucking my cock, as I dreamed of the man standing before me? This could not be my fate.

I stood outside the large cathedral doors waiting for Illona to arrive. Everyone from far and wide was already crammed into the large hall. All that was left to do was to escort this sorcerous to Vlad and allow her to love him for the rest of his days.

I closed my eyes and clenched my fists as I fought back visions of his naked form in my mind. I still lusted for him, even now. Even with everything that had taken place. I heard footsteps and glanced to my right as Illona approached me, dressed in red from head to toe. Her face was draped in red lace, her wedding dress made of the same. A small string of diamonds rested across her forehead and cascaded down her back. The dress lay off each of her delicate pale shoulders, showing off her protruding collar bones. Her fingers clutched a large bouquet of flowers in red black and white. The colors of Bran, the colors I had always knelt to and honored.

She walked toward me as six maidens flanked her sides. They moved behind her like an obedient flock of birds. She stepped up to me and grinned behind the thin lace. I stared into her eyes as she looked me over.

"You are a proud dragon, and I am honored to have you presenting me to Lord Vlad." I bowed to her as she watched me. The words were absent from my tongue. I had nothing to say to her. She reached down and touched my cheek, causing a humming wave to race along it and down my neck. I instantly felt a little better. Some sort of magic bewitched me. I rose, and her fingers lost contact with my skin.

"I appreciate your obedience, my dragon." She whispered to me.

"I serve Lord Vlad and the house of Bran, including my Lady Illona, soon to be Queen and sovereign mother to our future King." She grinned and touched her stomach. I turned and stood rigid, staring at the two large doors. She laughed quietly and then slid her arm into my own. "Must we always be so formal now, I mean the things we have seen together. Consider me a friend, dear one. Confide in me. I promise to serve you well."

I wanted to fight her, but whatever spell she had placed on me held my emotions at bay and my ability to fight her boiling in my blood.

I clenched my fist. "I serve my King."

"And heir." She said as she touched her stomach. I sighed as the large doors opened and we stood there as everyone in the room turned to look at us. I felt frozen in place until she started to take a step forward and I was forced to follow suit. She walked with pride as did I, passing royal subject after royal. Their eyes raced over the two of us and in all of my days I had never felt so stripped bare. The uncomfortable nature of it stabbed at me as we walked along a path that seemed to take a lifetime.

Illona took her time, slowly taking it all in. She relished it, as I hated every minute of it. I felt like the entire world knew of my treachery now and I could barely look up at the large black cross hanging at the front of the cathedral.

God had truly abandoned me, as I had abandoned him. I had ruined my grace when I spilled my seed into Stefan's hand and his sister's black magic wove itself around Vlad's neck and created an abomination.

A child of this creature that stands beside me.

I almost stumbled, and Illona helped to hold me up. I regained my composure, and we continued until I could finally focus on Vlad, who looked as beautiful as ever.

His expression was one of joy and peace. I had never known him to be at peace before, but it suited him. My heartbeat slowed down the closer we got to him and that of the high priest. I focused on his face. His eyes. Now blackened and foreign to me. The same black that consumed Illona's eyes as she tortured me in my room with memories of him and our forbidden love.

I would fall on my sword if I could only find the strength.

End the suffering, once and for all.

Remove myself from this torturous spell.

Illona whispered something to me and it echoed on the wind. My heartbeat slowed, and all of the worries seemed to slip away. I found peace and tranquility in her voice. She must have known that I was beside myself with guilt and need to confess. She stripped it all away.

We stepped up to the platform, and Illona looked over to me. I turned to her and lifted her lace veil, which was custom. Her lips were exposed first, round and soft, then her small nose, followed by her large and soulful eyes. Regardless of her ability to trick and weave her spells she was stunning, even more so this day. In fact, I had never seen a woman as beautiful as she was. Her beauty radiated in the room, and a small murmur rose up as we turned and I held her hand up. It was also customary for the man presenting the new Queen to her King to show her to the people of the land.

She stared out at the crowd and her grin was genuine.

Her power over us, complete.

They loved her as anyone would. She bewitched those who laid their eyes upon her as she had me. We turned, and Vlad walked down to us. I held her hand out to him and he took it as I let go.

Releasing her. Feeling my heart take leave of me as she stole it by taking him.

DEVIL HIS DUE

HER FATHER LINGERED LIKE A plague in Castle Bran for four weeks after the ceremony. He had claimed he would be returning home, but instead he ate our food, drank our wine, and ravaged as many women as he could have in his bed.

He was a disgusting man, barbaric, but it didn't bother me as it should. Each day Illona would visit me, showing me memories in my mirror, and each day my ability to care waned.

Slowly I was consumed by her spells.

Bewitched, as was Vlad.

As was this entire kingdom.

He rarely spoke to anyone, rarely left his room. At night I could hear him mumbling to himself roaming the halls of Bran. Our world had changed from day to night. Light to darkness.

Illona had cast a deep and disturbing spell over the entire land. Her belly grew, and with it, the creature she had created with Vlad.

Then one night I was summoned to her father's chamber.

"Come, my Lord, please." The guard had said in a desperate huff at my chamber door. His eyes filled with terror and need. I raced along with him through dark corridor and chilled night air.

I arrived to see Illona standing there by her father's bed with a knife in her hand. She turned and dropped it as the blood splattered to the ground. Her face hardened and her eyes filled with tears. I felt pity for her, against all good reason.

She had brought this darkness upon us. This curse to our land. Cast this spell over me which forced me to protect her.

I heard a moaning and spotted Stefan as he started to move on the bed, his naked frame bruised and battered. I ran to him and helped him up, covering him with a white fur. Illona looked on with a blank stare. I glanced down at her naked father, his cock erect and his mouth gaping wide open. She had buried the blade deep in his chest, and the blood pooled around the metal.

"Illona, what have you done?" I whispered in a slight panic.

She looked at me and shook her head, trying to compose herself, but her hands were trembling. I expected her to be stronger, to stand up straight and tell me why she had killed him, but instead she was finding it hard to express her feelings. I looked down at Stefan and shook him.

"What happened here?" He hugged me and sobbed. I turned my face to Illona, who swallowed hard and tears streamed down her cheeks, but she made no noise at all. Her tears were silent. Her voice stolen. She appeared to be in shock. She finally spoke, her voice quiet, as if she was telling a secret long hidden away.

"I heard Stefan cry out, as I had before, only, this time, he called for me. I ran down the hallway and could hear my father yelling at him to stop struggling, and heard the sounds of his fist against skin…Stefan begged for mercy, but with each blow he got quieter and quieter. I could not help myself, I opened the door and watched as father was about too… but I could not let him, I could not. Stephan should not be punished for his desires."

I stood there and held Stefan as my heart sank deep into my chest. She continued.

"My father was a beast, he always has been, but this, he had never done this to Stefan..." she said as she stepped toward us.

"He did this to others?" I asked in horror.

She looked down at her bloodied hands.

"Power is not something you are born with. It is something you acquire. Something you create. Something you take by force." She touched her stomach, and a feeling of dread raced through me. She settled her glossy eyes upon me. "I only needed to become stronger and with this, I have." She placed her hands on her stomach and stretched the material over her skin. I could see movement. My eyes widened in horror.

"What is it?" I asked.

"The future." She whispered to me. "A future where man cannot prey upon the weak. A future where man will pay for his sins."

Stefan kept his face buried in my chest. I held onto him tightly as she stepped up to us and placed a hand on his head. Her voice softened. "Stefan...he was not your father, my brother died in the womb. You were taken from a woman in town. Father refused to allow his legacy to go undone, so he stole you...he took you from your mother and claimed you as his own. I am so sorry. I should have told you. I should have warned you about his perversions. I failed you, and I am so sorry...I truly..." Stefan broke free of me and ran, the bloody fur fell to the ground.

Illona started to chase him, but I stopped her. I glanced at her dead father in the bed. She struggled for a moment, but I held her still until her eyes rose to meet my own. She was so distraught, something I never thought I would see in her. I honestly believed she was nothing more than an opportunist who had taken my home away from me, taken Vlad and everything that I held dear. But, as I held her she sank into my chest and sobbed, releasing her dark past and hidden secrets. Weakened by the truth and sullied by the lies of her past.

I raised my hand and touched her hair. I stroked it, feeling a need to protect growing inside of me. I wasn't sure if it was my sense of duty or the spell she had cast. I felt pity. I realized that she was trying to escape a hell she lived in with her own father. One she had turned to sorcery to escape his evil will.

Desperate, alone. Frightened and beaten down.

She only wanted a better life for her and her brother. Using me, using Vlad…it was her only way to secure her place here. To find a new home, escape his abuse and salvage what she could of a torturous life.

She looked up at me and shook her head. "The child is of royal blood. It is Vlad's heir, but I did not bewitch him to impregnate me, I promise you that. He did this of his own free will. Please forgive me. Please. Please help me, I can't be held accountable for this. They will kill me and along with it, his child. Vlad's legacy. They will also find out about Stefan and you. We are all in grave danger if the truth of his death reaches my homeland. Our guards are as loyal to their King as you are to yours. There will be bloodshed, so many will die." She buried her face in my chest again, and I stood there trying to understand it all and accept her admission and apology.

***

I rode with five guards with their father's body in the carriage. I would do my duty and return the King to his homeland, but he would not arrive as he had left. I told Illona I would handle this and as I thought about everything I decided that it would be best if we claimed that her father fell ill in Bran Castle and then would die on the way home.

Plague claiming him as it had so many others. It seemed a reasonable explanation. One that could pass as truth. In turn, this would protect Illona, Stefan, and prevent a war. A war we could not afford with a weakened King on the throne in Castle Bran.

I would return this wretched beast to his rightful place without destroying his name, and then I planned to return home with a new resolve and the ability to fix what had been wronged. Illona could be saved. I felt this to be true. Perhaps in saving her, I could also salvage what soul I had left inside of me.

I dreamed of a future, pure and clean. Of a King restored to his former self and a Queen, who could nurture the legacy that grew inside of her belly. A future I now seemed tasked with protecting at all cost.

We rode for five days. Without much rest. I pushed harder than I needed too, but the thought of what lie ahead meant more to me than a good night's sleep. It was reckless of me but seemed logical at the time.

We stopped as the horses needed water and the men needed to rest and eat. I slid from my Stallion's saddle and walked to the carriage. It reeked of flowers and incense. We had packed it to hide the stench of his rotting corpse. His body was starting to turn colors. Not that I pitied him. His soul rested in Hell, where it should. Amongst the demons, damned for eternity.

There was a special place reserved for those who took advantage of the weak, raping, and pillaging. It wouldn't shock me to learn that Illona had suffered the same fate at her father's hands. It would certainly explain her bitterness and need to rise above men.

Death was something I had experienced in the battlefield, but I had never watched as it ravaged a body beyond its limits. Truly, it was a frightening reminder of mortality. I covered my nose as my lead guard stepped up and pointed to the ridge. I could spot shadows and then I could hear the horses as they approached. I looked at him and then back to the men as they rushed toward us at a breaking speed.

I stepped forward as a party of ten rode up and stopped, the man in the middle wearing the colors of Illona's homeland. He stared at the carriage draped in red linen and then back to me. He jumped down and tapped his horse. Glancing at me as he approached us. He stopped and drew his sword, raising it and pointing the broad tip of it at the carriage. The guards behind me clutched at their own as he held a hand up and turned it sideways in his hands. He lowered it to the ground and went to one knee before me. I stared down on him.

"Rise," I said as he stood up and his expression remained emotionless.

"I am Anton, head of the guard of the house of Wallachia, protector to its Lord and heirs." I nodded to him and pulled my sword, I held it sideways and lowered it, rising slowly. "I am Dorin, from the house of Bran. Red Dragon and commander of the army for our Lord, Vlad Dracul."

He nodded to me as a murmur rose behind him. I never formally introduced myself, but I knew that my reputation preceded me as a brute force and highly skilled killer. I had slain so many at Vlad's side that my legend was as secure as his own.

I never pondered this. Not on the battlefield or off of it.

"Lord Dorin, I seek my Lord and Master. He was supposed to return..." I looked at the carriage and back to him, quickly interrupting him. "I regret to inform you that your Lord fell ill and died in Castle Bran. I was heading to your homeland to return your King to his rightful place so that you could give him a proper burial."

"What?" he said as he ran to the carriage and jumped into it. I followed him. He coughed as he smelled the stench of his Lord's body rotting away. He pulled back the red linen and cried out as he saw his face, contorted and sunken in. His cries did not remind me of a loyal guard but more of that of a lover. I had my doubts as to Anton's relationship with his King. He jumped out and shook his head as his eyes looked glossy and his guard watched on in horror.

"What sickness struck him down?" I stared at him, hoping I would sound convincing. "It was fever, a terrible fever that ravaged him for days. I wish that I could tell you that he did not suffer, but I am afraid that I cannot."

Anton stumbled from the carriage and then stopped, he reached down and picked up his sword, steadying himself. I hoped that I had sounded convincing. He held his sword, glancing at me and then slid it into his sheath. I relaxed a little bit as he returned to his horse and climbed up. He gripped the reins tightly in his hands.

"I would ask that you relinquish this task, we can take our Lord home and give him a proper burial. There is no need for you and your men to travel any further."

I stepped forward, ready to argue, but he called out to his guard to surround the carriage, and I stepped back as he rode up to me. He looked down on me and his facial expression remained somber. He was visibly shaken.

"Is Lady Illona and Stefan in good health?"

I nodded to him. "Yes, both are."

"Good, send them my blessings."

I nodded to him as he started to ride off, his guard taking the carriage of their fallen Lord with them. I sighed and looked back at my men.

Suddenly a horse came galloping up alongside him, and their party stopped. He turned back and rode toward us. I stood my ground as he approached me.

He paused and his horse shifted from one foot to the other, antsy and irritated, as was his master.

"Drop your sword, Lord Dorin." He said as he unsheathed his sword and gripped it firmly in his black gloved hand. My eyebrow rose. I started to reach for my sword just as I spotted Stefan riding up to the boy who had spoken to Anton.

He stared at me and then turned, kicking into his horse's sides and riding off toward his homeland. I swallowed hard and tried to make sense of it all.

"I apologize, I don't understand what this is about."

Anton rode up next to me and flipped his sword in his hand, lifting the hilt into the air above me.

"Murder of our King."

His hand came down, the hilt of his sword striking me on the side of the head. Everything faded to black.

PAYMENT DUE

I WOKE TO A STENCH THE likes of which I had never experienced before. Rotting flesh and stinking iron filled the air. I coughed and rolled onto my side, feeling the heavy chains attached to each wrist. I sat up and pressed my back against the moisture laden wall. Very little light poured in from overhead, but I could see a small metal grate above me. I leaned to the side, forced to strain so that I could study what it was, only to find myself quickly yelling out as warm liquid hit my face. Men's laughter followed. I wiped my face and grimaced. It was urine.

I shook my head and quickly turned when the sound of the door unlocking rang out in the small room. I pushed my back against the wall and stood tall, stripped of my colors and armor. I stood in my undergarments, filthy from the cells dirt floor. I was no longer Dorin Dracul, I was now a prisoner and at their mercy.

A guard stepped inside and then a shadow followed. I narrowed my eyes, fighting the absence of light, and then he came into focus. It was

Stefan. I rushed toward him, and the guard quickly hit me in the jaw. I fell to the ground with a groan, spitting out blood and dirt. I tried to control my laughter, but it escaped me. The irony amused me as none other had before.

Stefan stood above me and then spoke to the guard.

"Leave us." He said calmly. The guard hesitated. "I said, leave us, now."

He complied without saying a word. I pushed myself up onto my knees, and Stefan looked me over. "Are you okay?"

I laughed and shook my head. I raised my hands and jiggled the chains. "Do I look like I'm fine?" Sarcasm thickly laced my tone. *He couldn't be serious in asking me this, could he?*

"Dorin, this was not my doing. It was hers."

"I looked down and spat again, watching my blood hit the dirt floor. "By *her*. I would assume you mean Lady Illona?"

He shook his head and knelt down to my level. "You have to believe me. I had no idea what message she sent with me. I assumed it was news of her child and the wedding. Reasons as to why she would not return home to bury her father. I did not know they had brought you here until this night. I was not told of any of this."

I leaned toward him. "Then tell them the truth. Tell them that I saved you."

He stood up and paused, biting into his lip. "That may be difficult."

My brow wrinkled. "How can this be difficult? He tried to rape you. Illona killed him, and I agreed to return his body to his homeland as a favor to her."

"I told you that she was treacherous, I warned you."

"Then why come here if you can't help me?"

He rushed me and placed his hand on my face. He leaned in and kissed me. He tasted of bitterness and pure betrayal. He pulled back and sighed. "I could have loved you," he whispered to me.

He stood up and ran out of my cell. I cried out to him as I watched two guards enter the room. One stepped behind me and held my shoulders as the other bludgeoned me with his fist. Each brutal blow knocked the wind out of me. Each hit harder, each vicious strike leaving me to my memories. Flashes of a garden so long ago. With my King. The one who had stolen my heart and sealed my fate.

***

I woke to laughter. I was lying on my side in a great hall. The chains dug into my flesh and left my skin caked with blood. My body ached, and my soul cried out for freedom.

I wanted so desperately to turn Illona over to this mob, but my thoughts wrapped themselves around the child that she carried in her womb. What of its fate? Did it deserve death as she did? Could I damn it to eternal fire along with her? Even if I did claim this to be true and tell all, who would believe me?

No one.

I was a Kingslayer. A death bringer.

No one would believe me if I tried to tell them that their beloved Illona was a sorcerous, a caster of spell. Poisoning me with her serpents tongue.

I lowered my head as someone spit on me and was shoved back. The crowd yelled out obscenities at me. If only they would hand me over to the people, then my death would be swift. Why draw it out for all to see?

Anton entered the great hall and made his way toward the throne. He reached it, and I spotted Stefan sitting on the large golden chair. The jeweled crown upon his head. In his sister's absence, the kingdom would be his to rule now. His alone to control and conquer.

I started to rise, and a guard hit me in the back, taking me to one knee. Stefan raised a hand, and the guard stepped back from me. I coughed, and then laughter escaped my lips, I couldn't help myself. I stared up at him with muddied face and busted lip.

"King Stefan," I said. He didn't reply.

"What did she promise you, the world? Power? Is this why you betray those you claim to love and admire?"

I felt another blow to my back, and I cried out. The pain flowed through me like the wind.

"Dorin Dracul, Lord and master of the dragon army, also known as the red dragon."

I bit my lip and stared down at the stone floor beneath me.

"You have been charged with the highest of treason, the murder of our beloved King, my father, and father to this kingdom."

I didn't say a word, so he stood up and pointed his sword at me.

"Do you deny this?" he asked me.

I lifted my head and smiled at him, defiantly spitting in his direction. A guard jerked me to my feet and struck me in the gut, stealing my ability to catch my breath. I fell to my side, and Stefan returned to his throne.

"As reigning and sovereign King I pass down judgment for our people and that of our slain master." He stopped short, and I closed my eyes.

"Death!" he yelled out in the great hall, and the crowd cheered.

***

I woke up on the floor of my cell after another brutal beating. I had been kept for months. Rotting away. It had left me broken and awaiting death as a release. I deserved this. It was time to end my suffering and allow the world to go on without me. The great red dragon, reduced to nothing at the hands of a sorcerous and her seductive brother. It would be a fitting end to a pathetic existence.

She had stolen everything from me.

My title.

My power.

My King.

What was left for me, but death and hellfire?

A woman entered and knelt down in front of me. She placed a small bowl to my lips. The water felt refreshing, but I choked on it. My body was on fire. The fever raged through me. One I knew all too well. I must have an infection, and without treatment, it could take me before whatever death march they had planned for me.

A beheading, I would assume, which was custom. I had no idea why they had waited, other than the public beatings that happened weekly to entertain the people of this land. I was now a mockery. A joke. A warning to any that opposed their power.

No one came for me. Not Illona, nor my Lord and King. My friend, or as I had believed him to be. It was as if I never mattered to him and it had broken me. Completely shattered my soul. Without him I was nothing. I had no fight left in me. No reason to live.

I felt the water go down my throat, and it burned. It had a bitter aftertaste. I rolled over and continued to cough. The water churned in my stomach. I cried out and thrashed on the floor. The woman stood up and backed away from me, dropping the bowl and its remaining contents on the stone floor as it bubbled and smoked.

Poison. A welcomed end to a long and torturous existence.

I tried to catch my breath and the room spun. My vision blurred, and I could not speak. I grabbed at my stomach. The cramping so severe. Finally, I felt relief. My skin became colder. My heart slowed in my chest. My limbs relaxed. Death was upon me.

"Hello, dear friend," I whispered. My eyes closed for what should have been the last time.

HE HAS RISEN

MY EYES FLUTTERED, MY FINGERS flexed. My legs cramped and then I kicked up my knee only to feel resistance against wood. I reached up and felt it above me. I pushed on it, and a small amount of dirt fell through the crack and into my mouth. I spit it out and the panic started to settle in.

I was buried alive, or so it seemed.

I dug at the wood in a panicked fury, ripping my nails from flesh, ignoring the small tinges of pain that should be worse. Perhaps my adrenaline had kicked in as it had in battle, numbing me to any and all wounds. I couldn't be certain. All I did know is that a death of this nature was not befitting for me. No one deserved this, as evil as they could be.

I continued to fight until the air started to run out. I gasped, slowing as I clawed to break free. I started to lose consciousness and then I heard digging above me. Then a tap to the wood. I called out, desperate to get

their attention. Surely it was a mistake. Surely, this couldn't be my intro-
duction to Hell, could it?

Wood was torn away, and I took a deep breath, it hurt my lungs. I
coughed again, feeling the wetness on my lips. I reached up and touched
it, pulling my fingers back to see blood. I shook my head, and there he
stood, Stefan. I pushed myself up and took a swing at him, only to fall
upon a mound of dirt. He easily stepped out of my way with his hands
raised into the air.

"Dorin, calm down." He said to me. I tried to catch my breath, but
my chest hurt. It felt like I had been kicked by a horse and left to die.

I raised my head and stared at him with such confusion. "Calm
down?"

"Yes." He took a step toward me. "You are free. I have saved you."

I started to laugh, and it forced me to sit down on the edge of the
coffin. My coffin. I glared down at it.

"I was buried right here, left for dead. You left me in that cell for
months, beaten and dying."

He shook his head. "I had no choice. She wouldn't let me do anything
else."

"She who? Illona?"

Stefan sat down next to me, and I could see that he was visibly shaken.

"You have no idea what she has become."

I coughed again and tapped my chest. "I know what she is. She's a
sorcerous."

Stefan turned to face me. "No—she is worse than that. She is undead."

I laughed and then quickly stopped, holding my side. It cramped up
and stopped my breath for a quick second. I stood up and tried to walk
it off.

"Undead, well if that's your word for demon then okay, we shall call
her this."

Stefan stood up and grabbed my hand. I looked down at a small black
book. "No, she is undead. Not living. She is Vampire."

I bit my lip and held the book in my hand. "What?"

He started to pace in front of me. I watched him, turning my head from side to side while my muscles ached. I leaned over and coughed, blood trickled from the corner of my mouth. I spat it out and reached in, pulling out a tooth in horror. I held it up to him.

"What is wrong with me?" I yelled. He stopped and looked me over. He pointed at the book in my hand. "That book holds the secrets to ending her life. It is the only thing between us and total ruin."

I threw it at him, and he held his hands up to shield his face. It dropped to the ground and he quickly picked it up and brushed it off.

He shook the book at me. "I speak the truth. She has been poisoning herself for a long time, little by little, preserving her body. It is the same poison that laced the blade that wounded your King."

I stood up straight and pointed a finger at him. "What did you say?"

"I..." he started to say, and I lunged at him. The entire treacherous plan had become crystal clear. I knocked him to the ground and struck him as hard as I could. He struggled to push me off of him, but not before I hit him twice more. Busting his lip open and bloodying his nose. I rolled off of him as he kicked at me. He caught me in the side, and I cried out, forced to crawl on my knees. The ache in my body was becoming worse by the minute, not better.

I leaned back on my knees while he fingered at his nose. He cried out. "You broke it!"

I pointed at him. "I would do more if I had a blade in my hand."

He stumbled to his feet. "Listen to me. It was her...all her. She sent the poisoned blade to your party. She had your King injured, and she is now lying on that stone slab, in your cathedral, ready to rise again."

I blinked a few times and pushed myself to my feet out of sheer will. I stretched my arms out and my bones cracked. I hissed and rubbed my elbow.

"She's dead?"

"No—haven't you been listening to me? She cannot die."

I took a deep breath and coughed it out along with more blood. "You just said she was lying in the cathedral."

"Yes—yes I did, but she is not dead. She appears dead, but she will wake, as did you."

I swayed on my feet and felt my chest. Suddenly my heartbeat slowed down, I cried out and fell to the ground, writhing in pain. I thrashed about, and Stefan fell to his knees next to me, grabbing hold of my hand. I tried to speak, but words failed me. I felt it shutting down, all of it. Lungs, heart, soul. It slipped away from me and toward a heaven that I would never be a part of. An afterlife that now rejected me. I closed my eyes and ground my teeth, body shuddering and time jumping forward then back again.

I could hear my mother's voice, whispering my name while she held me in her arms.

I could feel the belt against my skin as my father whipped me.

I could smell the heat of battle. Blood and stone. Dust and retribution.

The stench of rotting flesh all around me.

Then my heart took its final lumbering beat. My last memory was that of my Lord, Vlad. Standing before me, smiling in the sunlight. His skin tan with health and vigor. His grip on me firm and reassuring. His eyes were bright with life and hopes of a future.

A future now gone, robbed from him and of me.

I could feel Stefan above me. Speaking to me as if it were an echo on the wind.

"Dorin? Dorin?"

Then I could hear it. Easy as someone speaking my name. A heartbeat, but it wasn't my own. It was faint at first and then pounded in my ears, calling out to me. Its sweet nectar flowing through it, a river of living blood.

Blood. The essence of life.

I let out a demonic cry, releasing the last bits of humanity from my now newly born corpse. An animal now resided where Dorin the red dragon had once lived.

Stefan flinched, and I reached up and grabbed his shirt, pulling him to me. I stared into his eyes, mine now red like fire and brimstone. He trembled, as he should.

"I can hear your heart beating." My eyes lowered and stared at his chest. I could see it glowing with what I desired. My mouth ached and my stomach growled.

Stefan quickly reached into his bag and pulled a fresh kill. A white rabbit. He dangled it in front of my face. I jerked it from his hand and bit into its side, sucking everything I could from the small thing. Once drained, I tossed it aside and stood up. I felt better, stronger. Renewed. My eyes darted from one side of the horizon to the other. I could see so far, feel every living thing around me. The beating hearts caused a reaction in me. I reached up, fingering at my mouth and felt the two elongated teeth. I quickly closed it and shook my head as glared at him.

"What have you done!?" I screamed at him. He held his hands up, and they trembled. I took a step toward him and something peculiar came over me. I felt pity, where none should exist.

Here he was, brother to that which stole all that mattered away from me, and yet I couldn't end him. I couldn't bring myself to tear at his flesh and drain him. He deserved it, yet I couldn't. I closed my mouth and felt my teeth shift, holstering my newly formed weapons.

"Lord, I only did what had to be done. You were dead anyway, and I saved you. I gave you the poison that my sister gave to Vlad and herself. I saved you so that you could save him and the child."

I tilted my head.

"The child."

Stefan stood up. "Yes, remember? Illona is with child. The heir to Bran, the heir Dracul."

I looked up at the sky and stared at the moon, full and red. Blood red. An omen.

"The child should die along with her."

I started to walk toward the two Stallions and Stefan followed me. "Wait, wait!" he yelled out, and I stopped and turned back to look at him.

"The child should not pay for her sins."

I laughed. "The child is the product of her sins, a creature, just as she is, just as Vlad surely is now. It's an abomination. We are an abomination."

"So what is your plan? To ride in and destroy her, the child and your Lord and King?"

I pulled myself onto the back of my horse, and it shifted from foot to foot. Uneasy with me as I was with it.

"Yes."

"And what of you?" he asked me.

"Once I destroy them I will task you with relieving me of this affliction. Now tell me, how do we die?"

Stefan pulled himself onto the back of his horse and clutched the book in his hand. "Sunlight, beheading, or a stake through the heart. One made of blessed wood."

I laughed. "Ironically she lay under her demise."

"My Lord?" Stefan asked me.

"The black cross of Bran blessed by the high priest."

I kicked into the side of my Stallion, and it took off, crying out into the night sky as we sped toward home and salvation.

THE LONG RIDE TO HELL

WE RETURNED HOME TO BANNERS flying. I entered the town to vacant streets. The eerie red flags embossed with the dragon flew in the wind. It appeared to have been abandoned and forgotten. Dark and foreboding.

My heart ached for the city that once stood proudly. For a King who allowed her people to sleep with safety and forced her enemies to cower in fear.

My King, now and forever.

The storm had followed us, and the rain had begun. Dark clouds surrounded the castle like an army approaching. But no army came. No one would dare. It reeked of death and destruction. It was no longer the home that I remembered. It was now a lake of blood and fire. Turned foul, utterly lying in ruin.

I pulled on the reins, and my horse spun in a half circle. I spotted the first body then the next. They lined the road leading to the castle gates.

Each one impaled upon a large stake. Some still in the throes of death. I drew my sword and relieved each one as I passed them by, severing heads from their rotting bodies. They need not suffer as I had. Death should be swift and kind. My death would linger, just like my love had for him, festering in the filth and decay. Lies and deceit.

I can be merciful. I can demonstrate mercy from a soulless shell.

Once proud, but now deconstructed.

I have nothing left to lose, which makes me the most dangerous adversary.

We reached the black gates, and I spotted the bloodstained banner. A fallen crest. A dragon now soaked in blood.

It pained me to see it this way.

It was home, just the same. A place where I had planned my future, one that had now been stripped away from me.

I turned my horse to face my companion in battle. "Understand that here we leave the boy behind and become the man."

Stefan nodded to me. He clutched the small black book to his chest. I glanced at it. "Where did you find this thing?"

"Our high priest. He is a master of fighting the dark arts, or I mean, was. He had died before we left for this place."

"Illona did this?"

He nodded. "I would assume so. Listen, Dorin. I'm..." I stopped him with a wave of my hand.

"No need to apologize to me. Apologize to your maker when you meet him in heaven."

He laughed. "I won't be saved. There is no salvation for me. Not my kind."

I shook my head. "Don't discredit your good deeds. I can't imagine that any God would let you fester in hellfire because you prefer a man in your bed. I think the devil has better souls to devour, like mine."

I rode up to the black gates and called out. No one answered me. My horse turned a few times and I decided to dismount and lower the gate myself. No one remained within the walls with a beating heart. I would have heard them. This also meant that my King lay dead, ready to rise again.

I drew my sword and stared into Stefan's eyes. "I can do this alone, no need for you to see what must be done here."

He followed me as I rode through the gates. I stopped and turned my blade toward him.

"This is not a game."

He stammered when he spoke to me. I felt powerful, and he cowered next to me. "The child isn't responsible for this."

"Why do you plead for its' life? You know it's just as dark as she is. A creature of the night, it will be born into the world and bring destruction along with it."

Just then we both turned as a blood-curdling cry came from the Castle. It was a woman's voice. I raced toward the outer road that wound up the castle's perimeter. I pushed as hard as I could until we reached the top, then I dismounted. Drawing my sword and holding it up. I struck my horse with an open hand on the backside, and it took off, racing away from me. I turned back and rested my steel gaze on what lay out before me. Just beyond the tip of blade stood the black cathedral. The crown jewel of Castle Bran. Again we heard another cry, and we raced toward the two large black doors. I pried them open with little resistance. My new form allowed me to do things I did not think possible. I could feel the strength in my body, unnatural, yet needed for this task at hand.

I stood in the doorway, eyeing the long aisle which lay before us. At the head of it hung the black cross. Beneath it, Illona, on the stone slab. She cried out, and it echoed into the tall ceiling. No angel would come to help her. No God would relieve her of this pain. Only one thing could free her. My cold hard steel to her throat, separating her head from the body, evil from her being.

I started to walk toward her, picking up speed with each animalistic groan that escaped her lips. She was in labor and about to birth something never seen in this world. I could feel it in my bones. It made my cold skin ache and my teeth break through my gums. I spit blood onto the wooden floor, and it sizzled. I didn't allow it to stop me. My new found power was a blessing in this time of need. Only a power that matched her own could halt this sacrilege.

"Illona!" I screamed, and she stopped and turned her head. Hissing at me. I lifted my sword and pointed it at her. Making it clear that my intention was just and her end was near.

"You die this day and that bringer of death along with you."

She let out a deep laugh and then cried out again in terrible pain. I started to run toward her and just as I reached the last pew a sword clashed against my own. Vlad stood before me, with red eyes and blood upon his lips. His skin pale and matching mine. He growled and pushed me back. My feet dug into the wood and caused some of it to splinter under my heel. I found my strength and pushed back against him, almost matching his. I leaned in close, eye to eye.

"Don't do this, my Lord. You know this cannot be."

"You will not harm my child." He yelled. His voice cracked in desperation. He didn't sound like himself at all. She controlled his will now. His strength had been stolen just as Stefan had predicted it would be.

His sword lifted, and it came down hard on mine. I ground my teeth and felt my body pushed toward the ground. I was forced to one knee.

"My Lord!" I pleaded with him, but it was to no avail. He only seemed to be built for one thing. Protection. So ironic, as I was once his protector and closest friend.

"Dorin, the red dragon. Leave this place and never return."

I yelled out, pushing his sword up and off of me. I rolled back and landed on my feet. I gripped my sword with both hands. My teeth now exposed and protruding from my bloodied mouth. He tilted his head at me.

He whispered to me. "Don't make me end your life." He sounded almost like himself. Like the friend that I once served and believed in.

"She can't be. We can't be. We are an abomination, demons, Vlad. Demonic in nature." I yelled. My voice weary and heavily laced with a daunting truth. He lowered his head and for one moment in time I fooled myself into thinking that the end was near. That my words had hit their mark. That he understood that what we are is not as it should be. To live on blood, beyond humanity, beyond death. This couldn't be. It was a curse, not a blessing.

Our curse and it needed to end here. End this night.

He looked up at me and lowered his sword. He walked toward me and let the tip of my blade rest right under his chin. His red eyes settled on mine. So beautiful, even in this deathly state.

"My friend, I have always loved you," he spoke with such grace. The words ripped through me. Gave me pause. Illona screamed and then I heard it, a small cry. New life. A child had been born. An unholy thing. Vlad closed his eyes. The whimpering rolled out like waves, and even I felt a sense of sadness. A sense of responsibility. A need to protect this precious thing that now took its first breath in this godforsaken place.

"A Queen." Illona hissed as she raised the child above her head.

Vlad opened his eyes and growled at me. My moment had passed. He lifted his sword and stabbed me in the side. I stumbled, holding onto it, my eyes narrowing. The shock of his betrayal complete. I screamed and ran my sword through his shoulder. He hissed and placed his hand on the blade. He gripped it with such fierce hatred while blood ran down the side of the blade and dripped onto the floor. I smelled it and my teeth elongated even further. I growled and tried to pull his sword from my flesh.

Then I heard it. The crunch of bone and a blade made its way through the front of his chest. He started to drop to the ground in front of me, and Illona stood behind him, eyes red and wild, blood running down her legs and onto the floor. The child cried out behind her on the stone slab.

"A Queen, he gave me a Queen. He is no longer needed." She hissed with hatred.

My eyes darted to it and back to her. She tilted her head and leaped into the air above me. I rolled to the side and then onto my back. She landed on me, snapping her teeth and scratching at my face. The cuts healed as quickly as she created them with her sharpened nails. It infuriated her. I lifted my foot and kicked her off of me. She flew back and onto the wooden floor. Sliding a few feet, but quickly recovered. I spotted the large black cross hanging high above us.

I scrambled to my feet and rushed toward the child. Stefan ran by the stone slab and scooped up the child into his arms and scurried away. I wanted to pursue him, but Illona grabbed my foot and knocked me to the ground. My forehead hit the wood with a loud crack and left a cut winding from my eyebrow to the top of my hairline. It bled, but as I turned to face her, it closed, healing quickly.

She jumped on top of me and bit into my arm, tearing at my flesh. I screamed. The pain ripped through me. Her poisonous bite felt like fire under my skin. I knocked her off of me, and she spit a chunk of my arm out and onto the floor. She lowered to the ground and crawled to the right when I tried to take a step and then she slithered to the left. She moved like a demon of nightmares. A seductive spider with a deadly stinger.

I spotted Vlad's sword lying on the ground and faked a move to my left, and she followed, then I lunged right and gripped it in my hand, turning over as she fell upon me and the sword quieted her screams. She reached for me, long nailed and bloodied as I held her above me. My blade had impaled her. I grit my teeth and then I saw him. Vlad had pushed himself up and was holding a hand over his bloodied heart. It seeped out over his fingers and dripped onto the floor at his feet.

He made his way to us and grabbed the sword from my hand as I rolled out. I rushed toward the large stone slab and jumped, kicking off of it and reaching toward the sky. I grabbed the bottom of the cross and forced it from its perch. It fell, with me on it, I rolled off as it hit the stone slab and pieces of it splintered off. The loud thunderous roar echoed out in the Cathedral. The cross had fallen, the deed, done.

I ran toward a piece of the blessed cross, grabbing it in my hand as it crackled and hissed. My dead flesh bubbled beneath it. I grit my teeth and Illona broke free of the sword and turned to face me. Suddenly she transformed into the girl she once was. Beautiful and innocent. Bloodied and bruised. She lifted her hand toward me, the tremor in it pulled at what compassion still resided within my blackened heart. I paused.

She grinned. "Dorin, my dragon. Please, please help me." She pleaded with me, but there was only one way that I could set her free, and it ended where it began.

With the spark of life.

She stepped up to me and placed her cold hand on my face. Her temperature now matched my own. I closed my eyes, and she leaned in to kiss me. Just before her lips reached mine, I buried the black wood deep into her chest. Finding her heart and releasing her battered soul to damnation.

She stumbled back from me. She touched it and then let her head fall back. The scream that escaped her lips cracked and blew out every window in the cathedral. Once done she dropped to her side, and her shell started to splinter and crack. Long black lines ran the length of her porcelain skin. Across her lips and racing toward her neck. Then she disintegrated into dust. Black and wretched, never to be light again.

I stumbled back, feeling as if I had watched my own demise. This was my future, let it be quick. Vlad moved and let out a small moan. Sunlight started to break through the horizon. I could see it splintering above us. I looked up, and so did Vlad.

"Let me see one last sunrise, my friend." He muttered.

"It will be the death of us."

"Best a noble death than a cowardly one."

I nodded to him and helped him to his feet. We made our way down the long aisle and toward the open doors. We stumbled out onto the steps as I spotted Stefan riding off with the child in his arms. I took a step toward them, and Vlad stopped me.

"No—let it end here, let this be the last blood shed this day."

I held onto him as he lowered to the stone steps. The sun was climbing behind us, and soon we would be engulfed in its mercy.

Vlad rested on his back and stared up at the sky. He let his eyes move to study my expression.

"I meant what I said to you."

"What is that, my Lord?" I choked out through tear stained eyes.

He laughed and blood bubbled up and escaped his lips. I leaned in and touched his cheek. He placed his hand over mine.

"I have loved you since we met. I apologize for my weakness. I was but a coward to not allow myself to be with you. For that I have regret. I should have shown you love, given you my heart, but in many ways, I did. I was just bound by duty, by the throne. By my name, as cursed as it shall be. I wanted my legacy to be one of honor, and now it will be on the lips of children. The monster, Vlad the Impaler. Blood drinker, killer of his own people. Demon of the night."

I wiped the bloody tears from my cheek, and he grinned at me. He pushed himself up and cupped my face.

"Sweet dragon." His eyes inspected mine and then lowered to my lips. They lingered. The warmth of his love caressing me. Soothing my heart and releasing me of my torment.

"Stay with me, please. Please don't leave me, I love you." I whispered. My lips were trembling, my still heart breaking with each passing moment.

He looked down at the spreading pool of blood on his chest.

My voice shook with desperation. "I can fix this."

He shook his head. "The blade was blessed when I became King." He whispered to me.

He was dying, and there was nothing that I could do but exercise mercy upon him. It broke me, forced me to cry out in such anguish. He gripped the back of my head and drew me to him. Pressing his lips against mine. I tasted the chilled blood on my tongue as he forced it inside my mouth and passionately gave to me what I had longed for all of these years. The kiss could have lasted a lifetime and yet ended too soon. He pulled back and rested his forehead against mine.

"Release me from this death." He whispered. I shielded him, allowing the light to burn my back and blister my skin beneath my clothing. I grit my teeth. My body shook uncontrollably. I locked my eyes onto his. My lips quivered, the pain beyond all measure, but I refused to allow the light to take him away from me.

"I need you, my Lord. Without you I am nothing."

He reached up and gently touched my face, letting his fingers glide across it and onto my lip.

"I will always love you, my dragon. My brother, my love."

He pushed me aside, and the sunlight engulfed him. I screamed as I watched his skin crack and disintegrate before me. His dust slowly rose into the sunlight with small flashes of fiery light. I lay down and accepted my fate. Rolling over onto my back and extending my arms.

Without his love, I was lost.

I parted my lips. "Please forgive me, my Lord, our God in heaven. Please accept me as I am. I ask for your forgiveness."

I closed my eyes and felt the heat. The sun cascaded across my skin, and it started to crack and splinter. The pain something I welcomed, for it meant the end.

A dark shadow fell over me. It blocked out the bright light of freedom. My eyes focused in on black wings. A beautiful face leaned into mine. A man with large eyes, full lips, and smooth skin. He looked angelic, pure. Beautiful and seductive beyond all measure.

"God?" I asked.

The man smiled at me and studied my lips. He reached down and touched them, gently moving his thumb.

"Some call me that, but you can call me Lucifer." He paused. I blinked a couple of times and shook my head.

"No...let me die!" I cried out, and he embraced me in his dark wings.

"Not this day, my dragon. It's a long ride to Hell. Trust me, I know."

My desperate plea reached out to the heavens above and fell upon deaf ears.

***

In the blink of an eye, I found myself standing on the edge of an abyss. The stench of sulfur burned my nostrils. I peered below me and could see the lake of fire, thrashing about in great turmoil. A face would appear on the surface of the fiery sea, then a hand, followed by another.

"Dorin."

I turned to see Lucifer standing behind me.

"Why am I not suffering as they are?"

Lucifer retracted his large black wings, tucking them behind him. Now he appeared more human in nature, although his eyes glowed with evil intent.

"This is your chance at salvation my immortal friend."

I swallowed hard and beat back the feelings of dread. "There is no salvation for a creature such as myself."

He clicked his tongue against his white teeth and quickly grinned at me.

"So tormented. Have you done this your entire life? Denied the possibility of hope?" he asked me.

I sighed. "I deserve none."

Lucifer approached me and placed his fingers under my chin and forced me to meet his fiery gaze.

"You asked to be forgiven as life slipped away from you," he whispered.

"By God," I replied without hesitation.

He chuckled under his breath. "Am I not a suitable replacement? Did I not come to your rescue in your hour of need?"

I scanned my surroundings. "I didn't ask for this. I expected death to claim me as it should...as it..." I stopped. My heart ached at the very thought of him. The memory of my love disintegrating before my eyes.

Lucifer quickly positioned himself behind me. He pressed his warm body against mine. His arms wrapped around me and I tried to move, but couldn't break free.

"Salvation must be earned for a creature such as yourself."

My eyes closed. His hand lowered and pressed against my stomach. Lust quickly followed. I ground my teeth together as my new fangs elongated inside of my mouth. I could taste the blood and it excited me.

"I know that my desire was an abomination in the eyes of our God."

He laughed and nibbled at my ear. I shifted my weight from one foot to the other, and he stopped.

"Foolish boy." He hissed.

He moved in front of me and touched my cheek with the back of his hand.

"Your sexual desires do not dictate your ability to achieve salvation."

My eyes widened. "What?"

He smiled and leaned into my face. He smelled of sweet flowers and a blend of sandalwood.

"The only sin that leads to damnation is the taking of life."

I swallowed hard. "I've taken many."

He stepped back and shook his head. "Oh no, none of that mattered. It was war. All's fair, or so they say." He looked at his fingernails and then back to me. "I'm talking about your own surrender."

I sucked in my breath. "You mean when I begged to be released from this corpse?"

He shrugged his shoulders. "I don't make up the rules, I just enforce them and don't play martyr with me. You asked for death so that you could follow him into oblivion. Nothing more and nothing less."

I let the reality settle in. My eyes lifted.

"So what now?" I asked.

He looked me over. "Now you must make a choice. Stay with me and fight for salvation or jump into the lake of fire."

I closed my eyes, and he whispered into my ear. "Be more, become the dragon. Stay with me and his death will not have been in vain. Save others as you failed to save him. Find love with me."

Love.

The worst of all four-letter words.

Nothing trumps it, but loyalty.

Just as treacherous. Just as devastating.

Both have ruled over me for as long as I can remember.

Love.

I stared down at my hands and spotted the slight tremor.

He always does this to me. Always.

My name is Dorin. I'm a vampire. I'm a slayer of the king of all vampires.

Dracula or as I knew him, Vlad the Impaler.
But before I killed him, I loved him.
More than anything. More than salvation.
For that, I traded my soul...
I lifted my head and gazed at my new Lord.
"Yes, I will do this, but not for me...for him,"
Lucifer smiled. "Welcome home, my Hellhound."

Thank you for taking this journey with me.

Dorin's story continues as he fights with a team of five as a Hellhound. Each Hellhound is a fallen warrior who asks for forgiveness upon their death. Each one collected by Lucifer. He joins a Roman, two Vikings, and one pissed off girl as they battle the rising tide of Hell.

Please follow Rue Volley on Amazon to keep up with the series.

ABOUT THE AUTHOR

Rue Volley is the author of The Devil's Gate Trilogy, Hellhound, The Blood & Light Vampire Series, a witch's tale, and various novella's released both independently and within anthologies.

Rue is an award-winning author, graphic artist, and screenwriter. She is credited with two films.

Hellhound (original script, 2014)

Awakening (contributing screenwriter, 2015)

IMDb: http://www.imdb.com/name/nm7043310/

Miss. Volley began her writing career in 2008 as she penned her freshman effort, The Blood & Light Vampire Series. She self-published the first novel in 2010 and within six months she was courted and signed by Vamptasy Publishing (UK).

Over the course of the next five years, she released over thirty books establishing herself in the publishing world as a prolific writer. She is best known for dark fantasy and mystery erotica. Bringing her wicked (somewhat dark) sense of humor and perfected ability to create engaging characters to her ever-growing fan base.

Rue has a deep love for comic books and film. She gives credit to amazing artists like Garth Ennis, Alan Moore, Frank Miller, Neil Gaiman, and of course, Stan Lee, for her love of the written word.

Rue enjoys walks by the lake, small town living, and spending time with her family. She loves coffee, chocolate, and believes in love, as twisted as it can be.

Rue is represented by Gladys Gonzales Atwell, Publicist, and Hot Ink Press, Publisher as well as Encompass Ink.

Website: http://www.ruevolley.com/

Twitter: https://twitter.com/ruevolley

FB: https://www.facebook.com/RueVolleyAuthor